HUGO WOOLLEY was born in West Sussex
two grown-up children. His mother was an
father a farmer and lawyer. As a dyslexic, he wen
because, in those days, dyslexia had hardly bee
was known as 'word-blindness' and dyslectics
below intelligence. How wrong they were!

Hugo is a caterer by training, ran various bars and restaurants in London before starting his own sandwich shops in the City of London in 1984 with his youngest brother, Oliver. In 1993 he opened designer sausage shops in Kent and Sussex, well before sausages became a fad. Unfortunately, after just over a year of trading, he was badly injured in a car accident and was airlifted to hospital, where Hugo remained for eight months being glued back together. Whilst in hospital he started writing, mainly about his experience during 'my crippledom' – as he called it.

In 2002, when Hugo was mainly recovered, he and Pippa moved to Cornwall to run a B&B. He wrote and self-published various cook books on sandwiches, and then a book of breakfasts and brunch. For the past four years, Hugo has been writing an historical fiction trilogy – the *Charlotte's War* trilogy.

GIRL
ON A
GOLDEN
PILLOW

HUGO WOOLLEY

SilverWood

Published in 2022 by SilverWood Books

SilverWood Books Ltd
14 Small Street, Bristol, BS1 1DE, United Kingdom
www.silverwoodbooks.co.uk

ISBN 978-1-80042-230-8 (paperback)

British Library Cataloguing in Publication Data
A CIP catalogue record for this book is
available from the British Library

Page design and typesetting by SilverWood Books

To my wife, Pippa

Prologue

1925

It was the end of a cold February. The magnificent house of Burg Krupp stood at the top of a low hill, ringed by a collar of naked deciduous trees and overlooking the six-hundred-hectare estate of lush green parkland and large fishing lake in the valley below. The little village of Frose lay beyond the lake, on the outskirts of the city of Aschersleben, in the middle of a new, united Germany.

The boy was in bed, reading a book his wonderful and heroic father had presented to him. It was about the Tenth Magdeburg Hussars, otherwise known as the Green Hussars. His father had just been promoted to major in the glamorous light cavalry regiment. Major Helmut Krupp was a decorated war hero, a dashing, tall cavalry officer with lavish moustaches and a twinkle in his eye. Before he left to support Field Marshal von Hindenburg in the presidential elections, Jost's father gave his son the book about his regiment and its history.

"Thank you, Papa," Jost said in awe. "I shall read it. I will have to know about the regiment before I join, will I not, Papa?"

"Absolutely, boy," his father said, playfully ruffling his son's short brown hair. "I am off now to help the Field Marshal. Look after your mother."

"I will, Papa." Jost looked up at his father. His huge brown cavalry moustache was extended wider by his smile. "I will kill any man or beast who may threaten her."

And so he did. Jost Krupp was twelve when he first killed a man.

*

Jost was a serious, enigmatic child, good-looking with hazel-brown eyes and, already, a strong jaw and straight nose. He hardly ever mixed with children of his own age. He was tutored privately by a rotund woman, Frau Heisler, who he despised inwardly but outwardly he was charming to. This was generally how he would get his own way. He spent a lot of time at his father's barracks in Aschersleben, learning to ride and the art of swordcraft. He would talk about politics with his father's fellow officers. He was never a lonely boy, but he hardly developed any friendships.

Jost had never had the relationship with his mother that most boys enjoyed. She had very little to do with his upbringing. She was constantly entertaining and had no time for her son. Jost was, it seemed, just part of her marriage contract with Helmut – to provide a boy to succeed the estate.

*

The evening of the general election, Jost and his mother, Anna, were left on their own. All the servants were away in Hanover, voting and attending rallies for Field Marshal von Hindenburg. Jost was instructed by his mother to go to bed and read; it was early, she had a headache and wanted to be alone. Though it was only eight o'clock, Jost complied. He did not want to make polite conversation with his mother, and she did not enjoy playing chess or cards.

A few hours after Jost went to his room, as he lay in bed reading his book, he could hear some slight high, breathy cries coming from somewhere downstairs, followed by urgent hushing sounds. The house was substantial and all rooms on both floors were situated around a large hallway. These sounds came from the drawing room immediately below Jost's bedroom. These worrying noises were from a woman … his mother! She must be in distress or being attacked.

Jost put on his dressing gown, tailored to look like a Green Hussar's longcoat, and crept out of his room. He went into his father's dressing room and unsheathed the slightly curved cavalry sword. It was nearly a metre long and was heavier than he imagined.

He stole down the stairs, both hands gripping the hilt of his father's sabre. The cries were getting louder and Jost was most concerned. He ran to the open door of the drawing room. There he saw his mother, her back against the wall. A blonde man in cavalry uniform had his right hand around her neck and his left hand was up under her skirts, thrusting between her legs. Her eyes were shut tight and she grimaced, rhythmic gasps of what sounded like pain coming from her open mouth. Jost was confused. In the wall mirror, Jost could see the man was puce with his exertions and wore an expression of anger, teeth gritted, sweat on his temples.

The man was plainly hurting his mother. "Stop!" Jost yelled and swung the sword at the officer's back as hard as he could.

"No!" his mother shouted. The man arched his back in excruciating pain. A large gash of blood seeped through the cut in his olive-green jacket, seeping rapidly into the gold piping. The gash slanted down from his right shoulder blade to just above his ribs on the left of his body. Jost stepped back, astonished at the damage he had inflicted with just one swipe of the blade. The man whirled around, his hands behind him, trying to press on the wound. Jost noticed the front of his breeches was undone. When the man saw Jost with the bloodied sword, the tip resting on the floor, his face was a mixture of fury and astonishment. He staggered towards Jost and tried to grab the sword. Jost stepped back and quickly raised the blade. It sank deep into the man's chest, between his ribs. Rage changed to surprise and then horror as his eyes half-closed and he fell heavily to the ground. The sword sank gradually up to the hilt guard, the bloody blade slowly protruding from his back.

Jost looked with pleasure at his work, a slight smile of satisfaction on his face. Jost's mother stood, frozen against the wall, her mouth gaping, her head shaking.

"What have you done, Jost?"

"I killed him, Mutti. He was hurting you," Jost said, trying to sound proud. He felt he had done well, but it was so quick.

His mother staggered away from the wall. She stepped over the man's legs which were still moving slightly. She had some underwear around her left ankle. Jost saw and pointed in disgust at the garment. She bent down to the man's face. His eyes were half-closed; there was no breath. She stroked the man's cheek.

"He is dead, Mutti. I know it," Jost said with anger, annoyed that his mother doubted it.

"You have killed him," she said in utter horror. "You have killed Ernst!"

"You knew him, Mutti?" Jost was confused. "How could you know that terrible man?"

His mother stood and flicked the underwear off her shoe, her blonde hair dishevelled, the buttons on the front of her dress undone, revealing a cream silk chemise. She tried to pull the front of her dress together and came over to her son. She looked angry. She took him by the shoulders; he was just a little shorter than she was.

"How could you, Jost? Why did you kill Ernst?" She gazed across at the body and burst into tears. "What am I going to do?"

"I will telephone Papa at the barracks and—"

"No! You will not!" She looked at him strangely and seemed to be annoyed with him when all he had done was his duty.

"Why?" Jost said angrily. "Why shouldn't I? We must tell my father and get the police. That man was trying to hurt you."

"No, he wasn't, darling," she said. "He was ... he was ..."

Jost looked at his mother with suspicion and doubt. He was confused and wanted his father to straighten it out.

"I'm phoning Papa." Jost pulled away from his mother. He had hoped to be a hero for saving his mother's life. Instead, she, for some ridiculous reason, was angry with him.

He strode purposefully towards his father's study. He switched on the desk light and picked up the phone receiver. He depressed the holder twice.

"Number, please," said a nasal female voice.

"Officer's mess, Tenth Hussar's barracks at Aschersleben, please."

"And you are?"

Jost's mother peered round the study door. She looked frightened and worried, her hand held to her mouth. Her blonde hair was tousled over her forehead, not neatly coiffured as normal. Make-up was smeared around her eyes, black tears coasted down her cheeks.

"This is family Krupp, Burg Krupp, number 222," Jost said calmly. He noticed his mother had disappeared from the doorway.

Jost would never see his mother again.

*

After Jost phoned the barracks, his father returned to the house accompanied by two of his fellow officers, all in uniform. His father found Jost waiting for him in his study. He sat the boy at his desk.

"I want you to write down everything that happened here tonight, Jost. Don't leave anything out. Where is your mother?"

"I think she has gone, Papa."

"Gone where, do you know?" he asked his son gently. He could see Jost was in control, unshaken and not at all traumatised.

"No, Father. She asked me to go with her, but I didn't want to."

"Quite right, boy. You did the right thing." He strode to the study door. "Now, write down everything, no matter how trivial or unpleasant. Yes?"

"Yes, sir," said Jost, and started to write.

*

Jost never knew if his father read his account of the evening. Helmut Krupp never mentioned the occasion again, not even when Jost's mother was being tried for murder. The body of "Ernst" was magically taken away and a new Persian rug was placed over the bloodstains. In the early hours of the morning after the event, Jost watched from his bedroom as his father and the two other officers, all in shirtsleeves, started a huge bonfire and burned all Anna's clothes, photographs and books. Anything to do with Jost's mother was eradicated.

At dawn, all the servants were dismissed except Helmut's valet and his old family nanny, now housekeeper. The morning was filled with the back doorbell chiming and new staff appearing around the house to serve Jost's breakfast and start the fires.

*

Three months after she walked out of the house, Anna Krupp was arrested in Berlin, tried, and executed for murder. The whole trial, conducted in Berlin, was kept quiet. The Krupp's lawyers took over every aspect of the trial; they defended Anna, as well as prosecuting her. She had not a hope of being found innocent. The death of Second Lieutenant Ernst Wein of the Green Hussars at the Krupp mansion, Burg Krupp, was never reported. Anna Krupp tried to implicate her son, which lost the sympathy of the court. Instead, it was found that she was an adulteress and was trying to ensure her indiscretion was not made known to her husband. For that reason, the identity of the victim would not be revealed, to protect the victim's family and to not disparage the honour of the regiment.

Jost and Helmut were not in court for the sentencing. Instead, they went fishing on the lake in the extensive grounds of Burg Krupp. Most of the estate was acquired using money inherited by Anna after the death of her parents and the sale of their estate. Both Helmut and Jost seemed unsympathetic to Anna's plight.

"What do you see in your future, Jost?" his father asked as they had lunch at a *Wirtshaus* after their morning's fishing.

"I want to study law and then join the army," Jost disclosed to his father. Helmut beamed with pride and grasped his son by the shoulders, his huge moustache extended by a joyous smile. He was nearly in tears with emotion.

"You will be an excellent politician one day, my boy. With law and the army behind you, you will be chancellor, even president, by the time you are my age." He shook his son by the shoulders and patted him on the back. He turned his son to face the rest of the men in the tavern – mainly Hussar officers – and announced: "My son is going to be President of Germany one day." He raised his glass of wine to Jost's beer stein, and the whole tavern cheered.

Jost grinned modestly and thought, I shall be neither a lawyer nor a politician. I will make huge amounts of money, and when you die, Father, I will do nothing except enjoy myself.

1

Paris, 1925

Sir Sussex Tremayne worked, Ferdi thought, for the Admiralty in London. He must be in his late fifties, probably early sixties. Strange to see him in the Musée Rodin looking totally out of place. He looked typically English: a full white naval beard and white hair streaked with flashes of creamy yellow, a dark-blue overcoat over his large figure – the shape of a rugby player – and a bowler hat in his gloved hand.

Sir Sussex was looking at the sculpture entitled *The Cathedral*: a pair of elegant hands encircling each other, and the subject of Ferdi's sketch. Ferdi realised too late that he had been spotted.

"Ferdinand?" Sir Sussex exclaimed in surprise. The peacefulness of the room was suddenly shattered and Ferdi felt like telling Sir Sussex to be quiet. "Ferdinand, it *is* you." Sir Sussex came over to where Ferdi sat on a grey upholstered bench, with his large hand outstretched. "How is my godson?"

"Very well, thank you, sir." Ferdi stood, irritated at being interrupted from his study.

"My dear old chap! What are you doing here?" Sir Sussex was jovial, like a slightly thinner Father Christmas.

"This is part of my studies, sir. I'm at ENSBA – the École Nationale Supérieure des Beaux-Arts."

"So I gather." Sir Sussex sat down heavily on the bench next to Ferdi and looked at Ferdi's sketch, then at the hand sculpture.

Baron Olivier Ferdinand Saumures of Luxembourg – to give Ferdi's full name – was handsome, athletic, neat and dashing in his fawn wool suit, checked waistcoat, yellow paisley bow tie, crisp white shirt and shiny hazel-brown shoes. His round, clean-shaven face had intelligent brown eyes set wide

13

apart, and his dark brown hair was swept back to a shine with hair oil. Ferdi was a serious, bright young man and hated surprises and nonsensical banter. His godfather was beginning to annoy him, and he just wanted Sir Sussex to go and leave him alone.

"You must be twenty … twenty-one?" Sir Sussex looked at his godson.

"Twenty … just. Last November, sir."

"Splendid. Good show," Sir Sussex said. "How long has it been since we last chatted, Ferdinand?"

"About two years, at Mother's funeral."

"Yes, yes, that must be it. What have you been up to for the last few years? Where have you been living?"

"I stayed at the house in Petworth for a bit, at the Burton Park Place, then went to Berlin for a while to study art. My tutor suggested I should study here in Paris."

"Where are you living now?" Sir Sussex did not seem particularly interested in Ferdi's answers. He kept looking at the statues around the room, now empty of people.

"We have an apartment in Rue de Dragon, in Saint-Germain."

"Who is 'we'?"

"A friend of mine. We met in Berlin."

"Nice chap?" Sir Sussex was now taking an interest.

"Yes, nice enough. He doesn't have much money, so I suggested he stay at my apartment. He's good company."

"What does he do?"

"He's a student as well, an art student, and he also gardens to make a little extra cash."

"Gardens?"

"Yes, he's a gardener. He has one or two clients in Paris. I never see him. He is always out, either studying or gardening."

There followed a long pause, long enough for Ferdi to think it was OK to resume his sketch. Sir Sussex Tremayne sat watching a young couple wander around the gallery. When they left, he said, "Tell me, would you like to work for me?" Ferdi was slightly stunned. He put his sketch on the bench and slowly stood, looking down at the large, elderly gentleman. "I work for the government, you know, hush-hush stuff."

"What kind of work? I'm a student in Paris. I don't really need a job."

"Well, it involves gathering information. Not conventional work, you understand." Sir Sussex stroked his beard in thought. "I work for SIS, which stands for Special Intelligence Service, and I run part of Section Six – the lads call it MI6 … Military Intelligence Six." Sir Sussex sounded a little condescending, Ferdi thought, but he became slightly more interested and sat back down.

Ferdi Saumures had known Sir Sussex Tremayne all his life. His Luxembourger father died when Ferdi was twelve, and he inherited the baronetcy. His mother was English, and Sir Sussex became a near constant companion to his mother, the baroness.

"Sir Sussex, is it a coincidence that you are here?"

"No, Ferdinand, it is not." He paused. Ferdi was amused to see his godfather looking at his own pudgy, sausage-fingered hands, and then at Rodin's sculpted hands. "I have not seen you for a couple of years, not since your mother's death." He looked rather unhappy. Ferdi knew he had always been in love with Ferdi's mother. Sir Sussex then cheered, slapped Ferdi on the back and said, "What do you say to some lunch, dear boy?"

"It's eleven o'clock, sir!" Ferdi was slightly alarmed. He was curious about what his godfather intended for him, but he also wanted to finish his sketch.

"Come on," Sir Sussex insisted. "Got your coat? It's bloody cold outside. We'll go to a little place I know just up the road in Rue de Bourgogne – you'll love it, and it's quiet. I'll tell you all then. A chap is meeting us there."

Ferdi gasped in amazement at the audacity of his godfather's arrangements.

"My God, sir, you really know how to surprise a fellow!"

*

As they came to the door of the restaurant Tomate Bleue, Sir Sussex whispered in his ear.

"Now, I need you to keep everything you hear confidential – to yourself – you understand?" Ferdi nodded slowly, not quite sure what to expect.

As they entered the restaurant, a bald waiter with a long cobalt blue apron greeted Sir Sussex and took hats and coats.

"My other son is here, monsieur?"

"Oui, monsieur, he is in the last booth at the back."

"Thank you." Sir Sussex tapped the waiter on the shoulder as he turned to the cloakroom. "May we just have coffee for now, and may we be left alone for at least thirty minutes? A family meeting." Sir Sussex's French was remarkably good, which surprised Ferdi.

"*Bien sûr*, monsieur."

The small restaurant was completely empty of customers. There was a lot of clanging and shouting from the kitchen, somewhere to the right and rear of the dining room. Sir Sussex walked down past the six tables towards the far end of the restaurant. Each table was separated from the next by a wood panel surmounted by a frosted glass screen.

On the seventh table sat a slight young man, nondescript, ordinary – no individuality – with short mousy hair, dressed in a dark grey suit, blue tie and white shirt. As an artist, Ferdi instantly looked upon ordinary men like this as dreary. The man had, however, a generous smile and introduced himself as Martin Stanley as he stood to greet them.

"Olivier," started Stanley, "may I call you Olivier?"

"Yes, do, but all—"

"Olivier, please sit here." Stanley drew out one of the four chairs at the round table. Sir Sussex sat beside where Stanley stood, plainly happy with Stanley taking control. "Sir Sussex tells me you are British." Stanley leant on the back of the chair nearest to where Ferdi sat.

"Half British, half Luxembourger." Ferdi was shy and unsmiling.

Ferdi began to regret agreeing to this encounter. He looked at Sir Sussex as the old man lit a cigarette.

"Ah, coffee. And palmiers, how delicious!" Sir Sussex said with a broad smile as the bald waiter approached and gave a slight cough. After a minute, the coffee poured and the waiter out of earshot, Stanley resumed.

"Baron, I understand from Sir Sussex that your upbringing was mainly in England. He said you were in the army at school."

"The BNCA, a cadet force – hardly the army," Ferdi said.

"And that you were very good at sport, running, rugger, et cetera."

Ferdi looked at Stanley with a worried frown. He did not reply. He turned to Sir Sussex and was about to say something, when Sir Sussex interrupted.

"Sorry, Ferdinand, dear boy, I think I should have explained a bit more about this" – he indicated towards Martin Stanley – "Stanley here works for me, or rather in my department, in Section Six."

"What do you want from me, Sir Sussex?" Ferdi displayed no emotion.

"A little update, I think the young say, Stanley?" The old man puffed on his cigarette.

"We are in need of some intelligence gathering," Stanley said. Sir Sussex sipped his coffee and crunched on the little palmier biscuit.

"Yes," Sir Sussex carried on, "a man called Adolf Hitler heads a German political party, the National Socialist German Workers' Party – Nazi Party for short – and he is beginning to concern His Majesty's Government."

Ferdi was bemused. He was an intelligent person, more so than most. He had very little time for people who didn't get straight to the point, and this was beginning to annoy him.

"I'm sorry, Sir Sussex, but I'm not sure how I can help you."

"I'll get to the point, then, Ferdinand." Sir Sussex put on some half-moon glasses and picked out a piece of paper from his inside pocket. "You are presently sharing an apartment with an Austrian by the name of Franz-Joseph Deller."

"Yes, sir. But how did ..." Ferdi sat up, now interested.

"Herr Deller is an Austrian subject who has been mostly educated – like you – in England. He is a fellow student of yours at the ENSBA, and he's basically living off your good nature, as far as I gather from what you said to me earlier."

"Yes. He is good fun to be with, good company."

Sir Sussex looked back at his notes. "General Werner Deller and Frau Clara Deller – his parents – both work for this man Hitler and have spent a lot of time helping with the new Nazi Party. We believe Frau Deller is particularly close to Hitler."

"You want me to get Joseph to see what these people are up to via his parents, is that it?" Ferdi was impatient.

"You have grasped the situation well, Ferdinand. I said to you, Stanley, didn't I, that he would be just the fellow?"

"But I don't think Joseph knows what his parents are up to. He never talks about them. I don't think he likes them," Ferdi said.

"Then you'll just have to get him to find out what his parents are up to," Sir Sussex insisted.

There was a pause. Ferdi's interest was conflicted.

"We want you to join MI6," Stanley said, "our department, undergo training and then recruit people like Deller who will be useful should we need more intelligence about these people in Germany."

"What do you mean, undergo training?" Ferdi said. Sir Sussex looked slightly worried.

"Ferdinand, are you a pacifist? Do you have communist ideals?"

"No, sir. I just enjoy my art."

"But what are your other interests? Books, science, sport?" He gestured wildly, searching for an idea. "Women?"

"I do read, and I am interested in politics. And I am certainly not a communist." He looked angrily at Sir Sussex. "Frankly, I would be more worried about Russia, not Hitler or what is going on in Germany. The country is broken, in any case."

"Russia is an ally," Stanley said dismissively, "and not my department's problem" – he looked into Ferdi's eyes – "at the moment."

"What is this training, Sir Sussex?"

"Just a month of training at Box Hill in Surrey. Quite near your home in Petworth."

"What kind of training?" Ferdi was beginning to get agitated.

"Some espionage, intelligence gathering, using a radio transmitter, some physical stuff and small arms training; nothing a bright young lad—"

"And when am I supposed to study my art? Why do I need training in small arms to get information about the Dellers?"

Sir Sussex Tremayne looked a little confused. "Ferdinand, dear boy, I'm sorry but I thought you would enjoy the opportunity to serve your country. Most young men would be excited at the prospect of becoming part of MI6."

"I would be delighted to serve Britain. I am mostly English, after all. It's just I'm not sure I want to do it at this stage in my life. I am confused as to why you need me to do this now."

"Because we want you to recruit Franz-Joseph Deller," Stanley said, "as part of your team."

"What team?"

"Ferdinand" – Sir Sussex sighed – "this is just an initial meeting to see if you would be prepared to help us with some intelligence work." He took out a cigarette from a silver case and offered it to Ferdi, who took it with no thanks. "I can tell you a lot more but, for both your safety and ours, we have to ensure you are the right person. Now, I have known you for most of your life, and I know you as a very intelligent chap."

"Thank you, sir."

"Are you willing to work for us at our department?"

Ferdi looked at Sir Sussex but didn't speak.

"Your role may change, depending on what we need, but at the moment, you are in a good position to gather information about these Nazis, and perhaps Adolf Hitler, with Deller. We have other people doing the same thing, but we don't have many people who are close to the Nazis ... at the head. There are other Nazis we need to know more about." Sir Sussex looked at another piece of paper. "Anton Drexler, who was the leader; Kurt von Schleicher and Helmut Krupp, both Nazi Party members who have the ear of President von Hindenburg; Josef Berchtold, who we think is deputy; Rudolf Hess; Göring... the list goes on and on." Sir Sussex sat back in his chair and looked pensively at Ferdi, evidently hoping for some kind of answer.

"Sir Sussex, Joseph is a little unreliable. His life is his art, drinking and having a good time."

"We just need the information," Stanley said. "You don't even have to say it's for the British secret service."

"We don't need anything now," Sir Sussex interrupted. "We just need to get things in place, organised. And some kind of commitment from you – if you agree, Ferdinand."

2

Both young men shared a large second-floor apartment, leased by Ferdi, in Rue de Dragon in the Saint-Germain region of Paris, a typical narrow cobbled street with cafés, a bakery, a flower shop and a hairdresser.

It was a crisp, bright amber morning, the morning after Ferdi's meeting with Sir Sussex. Though both art students, they were complete opposites in character in most ways. Not only was Ferdi shy, serious, and sensible, but importantly – to Franz-Joseph Deller – he was titled, rich and enjoyed the quiet life. Joseph was relatively poor, and he was gregarious. He had a charm and a twinkle. A thick tuft of untidy black curly hair perched on top of his square head, crowning his skinny, bony frame.

"Ferdi, can I borrow your watch chain?" asked Joseph while buttoning up a black waistcoat that was too big for him.

"Why? And why are you wearing my waistcoat?"

"I'm going for an interview for a gardening job," Joseph said, struggling with his starched collar and stud – an untied black tie was getting in the way.

"Fine, but you can't have the pocket watch."

"That's OK, I just want your waistcoat and chain for show." Joseph went over to a mirror in the tidy sitting room and adjusted his tie. "I'm hoping to get a job with an English lady in Avenue Foch."

"Sounds a bit grand."

"Yes, I should have said I was a baron, like you."

"That would not do. They would wonder what you're up to." Ferdi paused and realised he was wondering what Joseph was up to, too.

Franz-Joseph turned from the mirror with a smile. "They have a wonderful art collection: the Barrett Collection."

"Yes, I've heard about it." Ferdi looked concerned. "What has this collection got to do with the job?"

"This English lady has a very attractive daughter – married, unfortunately – and she recommended me for the job. I asked if I could see the collection and she said I may do … one day."

Ferdi looked sceptically at his friend. "Did she really say that, or have you just imagined it?"

"Anyway, I'd better go," Joseph said, changing the subject. "It's going to take me about thirty minutes to get there if I cycle fast."

"Well, just you be careful," Ferdi said with concern, handing over his fob chain. "Be polite, and don't ask to see the collection!"

*

Joseph enjoyed beautiful things, including women. He loved wine and food and was intent on being a great art collector and having his own gallery. Although Austrian, he spoke English with virtually no accent, having been educated mostly in England like his friend Ferdi.

Joseph and Ferdi met in Berlin at the Academy of Arts. Joseph was not the best of pupils and found he relished the challenge of womanising. However, Joseph was never successful in love or meeting women. He was not handsome; he had lots of charm, but it only seemed to work with people much older than himself. His parents were not prepared to fund what they thought was his hedonistic behaviour. They believed their son spent his time in bars and at parties, hoping he would get lucky with a girl. They believed his studies in art were a waste of his time and their money.

Ferdi, however, was the opposite to Joseph: stylish and reserved. When Ferdi got a place at the *École* Nationale Supérieure des Beaux-Arts, Joseph convinced his parents the ENSBA was for him as well. He said he would be sharing an apartment with his good friend, Baron Olivier Ferdinand Saumures. Joseph's plan was to find a rich wife in Paris, with the help of Ferdi's title and money.

*

You could say Avenue Foch was the spine of the French capital. A long, elegant Napoleonic road bordered by two wide landscaped boulevards providing access to the grand residential homes – it was the epitome of an avenue. Plane trees, pollarded to match each other, lined the avenue like guards stood to attention. At the top stood the imperious Arc de Triomphe, proud and immense at the centre of a dial of straight roads.

The house at Nineteen Avenue Foch was a vast and elegant late-nineteenth-century mansion. Three floors were built from honey-coloured stone, surmounted by a fourth floor with an array of eight oval-topped, white ornate dormer windows, evenly spaced across the large expanse of grey-green tiled roof. A cobbled drive curled around to the front of the grand entrance porch. The house was one of the very few in Avenue Foch that stood in its own grounds. It was built by a distinguished banking family who abandoned the house in the early twentieth century after being made uncomfortable by Paris society about their Jewish faith. They fled to America and started banking in New York instead, very successfully.

Lady Joy Barrett bought the house primarily for her son, Sir Jason Barrett. A man in his thirties, Sir Jason was an important British diplomat, like his late father. Lady Joy also brought up Jason's two younger sisters there: Stella, nearly twenty-eight, and Alice, aged twenty-two.

Sir Jason Barrett's escalation into diplomatic society was rapid, and French culture embraced him and his mother with enthusiasm. Nineteen Avenue Foch was a huge attraction for all the right reasons; it was large, opulent and in the centre of Paris in more ways than just position.

On the fourteenth of June 1919, Bastille Day, the Arc de Triomphe played host to the French and British armies, who marched through the huge main arch to celebrate the end of the Great War. Joy Barrett had just bought Nineteen Avenue Foch and observed the parade from her new house. She watched her pretty young daughters run up and down the columns of marching soldiers, waving their Union Jack flags, daringly blowing kisses to the British soldiers and delightfully shocked and squealing in glee when a soldier winked back at them.

Alice, Lady Joy's youngest daughter, loved Paris. It was a far cry from her previous home in Lewes, Sussex, and her boarding school in nearby Brighton. Stella, her older sister, was a constant companion until she married Jean de Tournet, a rich French steel magnate who she met at one of her father's diplomatic parties in London – the last such party before her father died of a stroke in 1918. Stella was only nineteen when she married. She was petite and pretty, and enjoyed the attention of a tall blonde man with a lush moustache – a rich Frenchman with broad shoulders and thin hips; nothing like the French men she had envisaged. He loved her for her father's influence in France, and her money.

Sir Jason was a rising British diplomat in Paris. His mother jumped at the chance of moving to Paris and buy a house where Jason could entertain, something Lady Joy enjoyed organising more than either her late husband or her son. She decided that if her son was to become the British ambassador, he should have a residence commensurate to his station. Jason kept explaining to his mother that if he did become ambassador, it would more than likely be somewhere else.

Sir Philip Barrett left considerable assets and property, more than enough to buy the beautiful house in Paris. The house was run-down and in need of considerable restoration, which Joy supervised assiduously over five years. She hung huge crystal chandeliers, installed Corinthian columns on either side of the vast entrance halls, and added gilded mouldings and marble floors. She restored the historically important nineteenth-century panels in the *salle de séjour* – the drawing room – along with the white marble Molinari fireplaces and the painted ceiling in the great dining room, created by the French artist Henri Rousseau.

The house became not only a home but also a much-admired residence housing the now famous Barrett Collection of both classic and modern European art. The whole of Paris wanted to be invited to tea or attend one of the soirées chez the Barretts of Avenue Foch.

*

Alice adored her house, and it was to be her house one day; her mother had promised it to her in her will. Jason had a small castle on the banks of Lake Constance; Alston Hall in Wimbledon, just outside London; and an apartment near the embassy in Paris. Stella and her husband had property in Paris, Gothenburg in Sweden, and outside Boston in the United States. Alice had the expectation of this lovely huge house in the centre of Paris. Lady Joy's plan was that Alice would marry and bring up Joy Barrett's grandchildren, keeping her constantly entertained in her later years. Alas, the way Alice was behaving, it seemed grandchildren were a distant hope. Stella, after two miscarriages, was reluctant to get pregnant again.

Alice was a shy, intelligent person and did not venture out much. She was unlike her sister who spent every day at some tea party or at the opera, accompanied by her husband, Jean, or one of her many French acquaintances. Alice was much happier at her desk, writing poetry or reading about flowers, shrubs and gardens. She had plans for her future that did not include socialising, gadding about … or men. She had only one man in mind, one type of man.

Alice had a beautiful face, marred slightly by a large, angular nose. Her eyes were green, framed by sweeping eyelashes. Stella unkindly called them "bovine eyelashes" but both girls knew she was only jealous. Her round face was enhanced by a wide, some might say overgenerous, mouth. When she smiled – which was rare – dimples would appear in her cheeks and her whole face would light up. Her auburn shoulder-length hair was pulled back into a neat bun. Fashion for her was an inconvenience, and she thought how exhausted her sister – and to some extent, her mother – must find it keeping up with the trends.

She was not exactly thin, but curvy, with a small waistline that was usually hidden under shapeless dresses. Her mother would sigh every time she saw her choice of clothes in the morning, wondering why she did not show off her figure, make herself pretty, see some men. It was not as if she was short of money for clothes.

*

The house in Avenue Foch had a large garden behind it of one thousand two hundred square metres, over a third of an acre – a rarity for a house in the centre of Paris. Alice enjoyed walking around it and watching the different seasons pass by, the shrubs grow, the flowers open, the smells and scents of the garden throughout the year. It was so peaceful – you would never think you were in the centre of one of the busiest cities in Europe.

As she strolled through one of the many pathways in the garden one mild February morning, surrounded by the daphne which gave off a heady scent in the early spring, she heard her mother talking to someone on the other side of the border, on the little lawn.

"I am so grateful you can help us, Joseph," said her mother, in English. "It is so difficult to get French gardeners who appreciate an English garden."

"Lady Barrett," said a cultured young male voice, "it is a privilege to find an English garden in the centre of Paris, especially such a lovely one." He stopped abruptly in surprise when Alice appeared from behind the bush. Alice saw a young man in his twenties with a clump of black curly hair and narrow eyes set close into a square head. He was an inch or two taller than Alice; not particularly handsome, but he gave Alice a lovely, wrinkly smile when Lady Joy introduced him to her daughter.

"Joseph, this is my daughter Miss Alice Barrett. Alice, this is Joseph, who is going to do the garden for us. Those dreadful creatures, the Francis brothers, have never done a very good job."

"What a good idea," Alice said, looking at Joseph from head to toe, slowly

24

and quite blatantly. "Are you sure you'll be able to manage this entire garden on your own, Mr Joseph?" She noticed his thin body and sinewy arms inside the sleeves of his shabby grey wool suit. He wore a creased white shirt with a newly starched collar, a thin black tie and a black wool waistcoat with a large gold belcher watch chain – plainly his prize possession, as he kept playing with it.

"Oh, just Joseph, Miss Barrett."

It was an educated, deep voice, not one of a gardener's. Alice was slightly taken by it.

"Have you always been a gardener, Mr Joseph?" She persisted in trying to be formal.

"He is a student, Alice, in Paris. Art, I think you said … um?" Lady Joy had forgotten his name already, her attention taken by the way Alice was looking at this young man.

"Joseph, Mrs Barrett." His eyes widened in alarm at his mistake. "I mean, Lady Barrett."

He was charming, Alice thought. He had a lovely, gentle way about him. "I am studying philosophy and art as well," he carried on, "but I am not getting very much money from my father, so I must supplement my expenses with a bit of work."

"Well, Joseph, you come highly recommended by Madame de Tournet's friends. She is my other daughter, you know."

"Will your husband need to see me?" He appeared comfortable with people of high station and seemed to be at ease with grand society women like Alice's mother.

"My son, Sir Jason, is always very busy with diplomatic things. My husband died in the last war."

"My condolences," Joseph said, slightly bowing his head.

*

Joy always suggested her husband, Sir Philip Barrett, was killed in some military action, rather than dying, as he did, of a massive stroke at his desk in the Foreign Office after a large lunch with the French ambassador, at the end of the war.

Joy Barrett was an elegant woman, used to being admired by people even in her old age. She was slightly larger than she was as a girl, but still felt she was a slim ingénue. Her silver-grey hair was cut and finger waved in the modern style of Jean Harlow and other Hollywood stars. She wore a fawn tweed day skirt with a matching double-breasted short jacket over a light, cream, cashmere sweater. On her head, a small black narrow-brimmed hat set on the side was held in place with a long hatpin. It was a young style, but she never seemed to look like she was trying to look younger than her fifty-two years. With two young and pretty daughters in their twenties in Paris, she did not want them to see their mother as a drab old English woman. The Parisians could be very cruel to women in prominent positions in society who dressed badly, especially English women.

*

There was a slightly uncomfortable silence on the lawn. Joseph was looking around the garden.

"I will leave you with Alice, young man. She's the one you should talk to about gardens. If she were a man, she would be a farmer!" Lady Barrett turned and sailed back into the house leaving an astonished Alice and a delighted Joseph.

"Well!" said Alice, not knowing what to say to the young man. He just stood there, hands in his pockets, looking at Alice with an expectant smile.

"Well," she said again and looked at Joseph. "When are you starting?"

"Now, I think."

"In those clothes?"

"I brought some things with me, just in case."

"Oh … well, I will leave you to our garden. Do you know where everything is?"

"I think so. The garden shed is just there." Joseph pointed to the bottom right corner of the garden where a grey slate roof could be seen above a large rhododendron bush. He started to walk towards it. Alice decided to walk with him.

"Your mother thought all the tools were in there."

"I think they are. I'm not sure what the Francis brothers did for tools. There's a huge lawnmower thing in there. We used to have it in England at our house in Lewes on the south coast." She tried to think of something else to say; she enjoyed talking to Joseph. "The shed used to be where the horses and carriage were housed. You can see where the drive used to be." Alice pointed at a flat length of lawn that was a slightly different shade, which ran down beside the boundary wall.

"Um … I had better get my things off my bike," Joseph said, turning and indicating he should be going the other way.

"Oh, yes." Alice was feeling self-conscious for some reason.

Joseph trotted off to the side of the house and reappeared moments later with a small suitcase and a tool bag.

"My goodness, you have the whole kit and caboodle."

"The what?" Joseph said.

"Kit and caboodle – American, I think, for everything you need." Alice was impressed with Joseph; his slightly shy smile, his narrow, intelligent eyes and his pleasant demeanour showing his competence and keenness. It was such a shame he was not just a little better-looking. However, he had an air of vulnerability she found attractive.

"I'd better get on," he said as he trotted past on his way to the shed. "I can see already that there's some ivy growing up that elm – it needs getting rid of. Bye."

"Adieu," she said, then thought it sounded a little dramatic and wished she had just said "Bye".

"Where is the rest of your family?" Joseph was now walking backwards towards the shed, then he stopped and wandered back towards her.

"I am quite on my own, really," Alice said. "Stella, my older sister – I'm the youngest – is hardly ever in the house. She and her husband live in Avenue Georges Cinq, but she also spends a lot of time in Sweden and America, where her husband, Jean, works. He does something in steel."

"I think I met your sister at one of her friends' house. I was doing their garden."

"My brother," Alice carried on, "who is much older than me, spends a lot of his time at the embassy being terribly diplomatic. I'm not sure what he does but he comes home late or stays at his apartment next to the embassy, and every now and then we have to entertain lots of people here."

"It must be nice to have your mother here, though?"

"It's such a huge house, but we pass each other every now and then." She looked at her wristwatch. "I must go, I mustn't hold you up. Au revoir, Joseph."

Alice walked up the lawn towards the house. As she approached the large windows, she could see Joseph's reflection watching her walk back to the house. Her heart skipped a beat. She tried to walk as elegantly as possible, placing one foot directly in front of the other. She took a last look at Joseph in the reflection of the French windows, opened the door and slipped in. As she turned to close the door, she looked up and saw Joseph suddenly turn around, aware that he was staring. She smiled to herself, delighted she had made such an impression.

"*Chérie?*" Her mother startled her. She was standing at the entrance to the salle de séjour.

"Oui, Mama?"

"Don't get too many ideas about that boy. He's a penniless student with not much of a future."

"Oh, Mama, how could you?" Alice said, trying to sound angry. That did it for Alice. Her mother had inadvertently made her want Joseph. Did Joy do this on purpose? Did she know that if she forbade Alice from consorting with such a person, it would result in the complete opposite?

*

Later that afternoon, while thinking about the new gardener, Joy wondered if she had been foolish to warn her daughter not to have anything to do with the young man. She had seen how Joseph looked at her daughter. He was a nice boy, despite being a student and their gardener. His parents were pretty respectable, apparently; just not rich. Stella had found him working for one of her friends, and they had discovered that Joseph's parents believed, with his artistic background, he should study in Paris and hopefully meet a patron to sponsor his art. He was quite a good painter as well as a very keen gardener and garden designer. He was also studying philosophy and religion with the thought he would enter the church when his art inevitably sent him into penury.

Joy wanted Alice to get out and expand her outlook on life. She was twenty-two and had still not made any friends in Paris. She never went out, not even to the opera or concerts – she would rather go to quiet galleries and museums. She didn't seem to want to meet anybody. Joy did not think it was shyness but possibly laziness.

Lady Joy thought at one time she should move back to their house in Wimbledon and try to launch Alice through the debutante season when she was seventeen. But Alice flatly refused to go back to England and her mother was unable to convince her. Stella had given up attempting to get Alice to socialise. She had tried on countless occasions to get Alice to parties or the opera.

Joy knew Stella and Jason would not approve of this new development which had started in the garden, but that was a worry for another day. For now, Alice had an interest in another human being, a member of the opposite sex, which was wonderful. He seemed well educated but poor – like most students – and he was English, well spoken with a very slight accent, possibly Scottish. Joy could not quite put her finger on it.

3

Throughout February, the strange attraction Alice and Joseph had for each other had become bigger than Joy – or Alice – had expected.

It started the third day Joseph arrived for work in the garden. Alice was up and dressed in a fine knitted Chanel dress that came to just above her knees, a delicate pink with a small belt at the hips. It was a lovely, fashionable dress she borrowed from her sister's huge wardrobe; part of the reason the dress was perhaps a little too short and slightly immodest, Stella being so much shorter.

Alice had combed her long auburn hair to a glossy shine and wore it loose. She had enhanced her eyelashes and even put a little powder on her face which made her lips stand out and her complexion glow. She skipped down the stairs, swept up a cream cashmere shawl and some gloves, and trotted out of the back door onto the lawn. It was still quite cold in the garden.

Joy was at her dressing table when she heard the back-garden door open beneath her bedroom window. She went to see what was going on.

"Marie!" Joy called loudly for Marie Ducheyne, her maid and housekeeper.

"Oui, madame?" Marie bustled into her mistress's bedroom.

"Who is that on the lawn with Mademoiselle Alice?" she asked in French with a distinctive English accent.

"It is the gardener, Joseph, madame. I have just given him a cup of *café*."

"What are they doing?" she said, almost to herself, and ventured to the window, trying not to be seen by either Alice or Joseph. Joy was a little unsure she was doing the right thing, allowing Joseph to be so familiar. Originally, she thought it nice that Alice was so positively flirting with Joseph. But where would it go?

She saw Joseph in the centre of the lawn, smiling his wrinkly smile towards

Alice as she approached him. They were talking, but Joy could not quite hear what was being said. Alice looked very nice in that dress, Joy thought with some pride. When did she get that? And make-up! She could look so pretty if she tried. That boy looked quite nice when he smiled – not exactly handsome, though, Joy observed critically.

Joy watched Alice go up to Joseph, coyly holding a trug in her left hand. She gaily tossed her hair and had a huge smile as she talked to him. They strolled down to the garden shed behind the rhododendron bushes. Lady Joy panicked. She was not sure if she should let this "experiment" carry on. She turned and rushed out of her bedroom onto the large gallery landing, which overlooked a grand hallway lit from above by a huge glass dome high above the Grand Hall.

"Marie, *mon chapeau … vite!*" Joy walked quickly down the stairs.

"Oui, madame, *tout de suite!*"

Marie, a little flustered, found a hat and jacket for her mistress and passed them to her as she headed for the back door. She did not want to go out the French windows as she planned to be unobserved – she was a little unsure what she was going to do or see when she got there. Why am I spying? Joy wondered. I am an open-minded woman, I think. Alice is of age, a sensible girl, unlike her sister.

Joy checked herself as she got to the back door.

"Stupid, stupid, stupid!" she said out loud and turned to see Marie and her husband, Charles, standing beside her with a duster in his hand. He stopped polishing the silver when he heard Madame shout.

"Madame?" Marie looked very concerned.

"Never mind, Marie. Charles, I am sorry," said Joy, with a nervous laugh. "I thought I saw a stranger in the garden, but of course it was the new gardener." She walked back to the hall and through to the equally spacious reception hall, turned left into the dining room and then through to the morning room. God, Marie is going to think I am barmy, Lady Joy thought. She will know I saw the gardener from the window. What was I thinking? She had taken this long route to the morning room so she could think a little more.

*

Lady Joy found, with some concern, her son, Sir Jason Barrett, sitting at the table in the morning room. He was having a little breakfast, his handsome head bent over a newspaper. His back was to the window that overlooked the lawn and Joy wondered if he had seen Alice and Joseph.

"Darling, how nice. I haven't seen you here in the morning for a long time. You are always so busy."

Jason looked up from his newspaper and saluted his mother with his cup of coffee as though it was a beer mug.

"Good morning, Mother. Why were you shouting?"

"Oh, I thought I saw a stranger in the garden, but it was the new gardener. Are you going to Germany this month or next, darling?"

"Next week, I think. Why?"

"Nothing, really, just wondered." Lady Joy suppressed a small smile. Jason regularly visited an actress called Bertha Stein, who lived in a small castle he owned in the town of Friedrichshafen, on the banks of Lake Constance. It was a business arrangement rather than an emotional entanglement. The relationship was informal and mainly sexual, but he had to admit the attraction was also for Bertha's intelligent conversation.

"Any particular young lady yet, darling?"

"No time, Mother." Jason did not look up. This was his standard reply to his mother's constant enquiries about his marital status.

Jason stood just as his mother sat down with a cup of coffee. She could not mask her disappointment that he was going already. He did the middle button of his jacket up to show his lithe figure and went to a display of flowers, selected a white rosebud and snapped off the head. Then he went to one of the floor-to-ceiling mirrors that covered the square pillars on either side of the door to the dining room and slid the rose stem into the buttonhole in his jacket, ensuring the stalk slid into the little loop at the back of the lapel, holding the buttonhole in place.

He rang the bell pull beside the sideboard. Charles emerged into the morning room from the kitchen pantry door.

"Oui, Sir Jason?"

"My car please, Charles. I think my driver is here."

"Oui, monsieur."

Jason gave his mother a peck on the cheek. "Who's the boy with Alice?" he asked casually.

"Oh, he's the new gardener." His mother looked a little alarmed.

"You've not hired another bloody communist like the last one, have you, Mother?"

"No, an English art student. I think he's called Joseph."

"Nice?"

"He seems quite pleasant." She reached over to pick up Jason's newspaper, a three-day-old copy of the *Financial Times*. She smiled at her son, who was watching Alice and Joseph talking on the lawn. He turned away from the window and gave his mother a quick nod.

Joy watched proudly as her son left. She then saw in the mirror that she had not put on any make-up and that she still had her hat on. She had not done any of the things she said she was going to do that morning. Alice and that boy had put things into disarray!

*

"Good morning." Alice strolled up to Joseph, carrying a trug of cut shrubbery. There were hardly any flowers in the garden and all the arrangements in the house were done by Marie and Lady Joy using flowers brought in from the flower market in Place Louis Lépine.

Joseph had his black wool suit on again, his waistcoat, and a huge grey woollen scarf instead of a collar and tie. He doffed his baker-boy cap. "Lovely morning, if a little cold."

His English was near impeccable; he had no aristocratic affectations, but he certainly did not talk like any gardener Alice had ever met. Not quite the clipped diction that Alice had.

"Would you care for a cup of tea?" he asked Alice. She was a little surprised. "In my garden shed," he clarified. She then understood and was delighted.

"Yes, please!"

They wandered down to the large garden shed, which was really more of a barn. The only similarity it had to a garden shed was that it was built of wood. It had tall and wide double doors and a little window to either side. All the wood was painted with dark creosote – the smell being the only other similarity. They stepped through a smaller door set inside the right-hand main door.

Inside there was a long workbench – well over seven metres – running along the left-hand wall, with draws and shelves beneath it. The wall was covered in plaster and painted with whitewash and had two more small windows. Another door at the back of the shed led out to a large greenhouse and the compost heaps.

On the thick wooden floorboards sat a large lawnmower with a one-and-a-half-metre cutting head, an engine that looked like it could drive a Churchill battle tank, and a little cast-iron seat mounted on top of a roller attached to the back of the mower.

"I would love to have a go on that," said Alice as Joseph switched on the electric lights. "Please, can I mow the lawn one day?" She turned and begged Joseph. Joseph laughed and shook his head. Alice was not sure if he was saying no or marvelling at her audacity.

"Here we are. Come into my sitting room." The shed was about six metres wide. In the far corner, on the right, was a former horse's stable, with a half-wall on two sides and a gap where a stable door used to hang. The tops of the half-walls used to have bars, but these had been removed. Within the stable was an old blue and maroon patterned carpet, a desk with some papers on it and an empty rusting metal manger in the corner. A shabby sofa and a comfortable armchair covered with thick blankets were positioned against the long wall at the back of the old stable. Beside the armchair was a gas stove on a low table and a tray of metal mugs, a kettle, and covered tin canisters marked "Sucre", "Café" and "Thé", all looking brand new. Everything was spotless. Who did all the cleaning? Alice wondered. She couldn't remember it looking like this when the Francis brothers were here.

Joseph admitted he had spent the previous day cleaning the area.

"You were here yesterday?" Alice sounded disappointed. She would have loved to have helped – not that she had ever actually cleaned anything in her life.

"I thought I would make it look nice. Cup of tea?" Joseph lit the gas hob. Alice watched his face, his eyes slightly squinting in anticipation at the gas's initial eruption as the stove sprung into life. He had attractive crinkles in the corners of his eyes, and his tongue poked towards the side of his mouth in concentration. Joseph filled the kettle from a tap over a horse trough that served as a sink and put the kettle on the stove. The dark-blue enamel kettle looked new. He went to his bag and produced a bottle of milk.

"Tea!" marvelled Alice. "How very British. The French seem to only drink coffee or chocolate."

Joseph peacefully got on with making the tea. Alice sat in the armchair, looking around the converted stable.

"Where were you born, Joseph?" Alice asked as he handed her a cup of tea. She put up her finger when she had enough milk.

"Vienna."

"Oh! I thought you were English." Alice was intrigued. "Vienna – how romantic." She didn't know why she said "romantic". "So, what is your surname?"

"My name is Franz-Joseph Deller," Joseph said, sitting on the sofa. Alice decided to sit closely beside him.

33

"But your English is so good." She wanted him to smell her scent, feel her elbow on his arm as she raised her mug up to her lips to blow the hot tea. She felt wickedly provocative.

"I was educated at a boarding school in England from an early age and then went to university at Oxford – the Ruskin – for a while."

Alice was speechless. She was looking at this man beside her with new admiration. She wanted to ask the obvious question: why was he gardening? But she also wanted to know how he managed to go through the whole of the Great War in England as an Austrian. Joseph anticipated her question.

"I spent the whole war with my English great-aunt and great-uncle in Surrey. They were called Dent, so I went to school under the name of Dent – Joseph Dent. I was known as Joe."

"But do you feel Austrian or English?"

"I don't know, really. I only spent about ten years of my life in Vienna – I'm twenty-three now." Joseph looked down at the floor, sadly. "I have only spent a few months in Vienna since the end of the war. I have been here nearly a year."

"What did you do when you were back in Vienna – eat lots of cakes?"

"Ha, no. I had to help my parents, actually."

"With what?"

"Oh … they work for a new political party. My father is ex-army."

"Oh, how boring for you," Alice said with a smile. "This is lovely tea. Is there some more?"

"Plenty."

"What else did you do in Vienna, apart from help your parents?" Alice asked, holding up her cup for refilling.

"Well," – Joseph paused – "I went to galleries and rode quite a lot in the Föhrenberge Park, but," – he chuckled – "I fell off my father's horse and cracked my hip."

"Really? Were you in pain?" She edged closer to him, intrigued.

"A bit. I was taken to hospital and they had one of those extraordinary *röntgenogram* machines – I think they are called X-ray machines."

"The thing that can see all the way through you?"

"Yes. They took lots of images of my hip to find the break. It was fascinating to see my bones. It turned out to be a fracture, not a break. It took ages to mend and walking was painful."

"Are you all right now?" Alice looked concerned.

"A hundred per cent now. It was only a crack in my hip. The X-ray eventually found the fracture and I had to stay in a cast of plaster of Paris for a while. But I'm fine now. I don't do any more riding, though!"

They sat for a long time, talking about Vienna, England and gardening, while sipping tea. After an hour, Joseph said, "I'd better actually do some work."

Alice stood. Joseph rose to see her to the door. As he stood up, she gently placed her right hand on his shoulder and lightly kissed him on the left cheek. Joseph was so shocked he fell back down into the sofa. Alice looked down at him with a smile.

"That was a lovely tea. I enjoyed talking to you, Joseph – or is it Franz-Joseph?" She took up her trug and glided out of the old stable enclosure. Joseph stood and watched her over the low stable wall as she walked towards the big double door. She turned and smiled at him again, somehow knowing he would be watching her.

Alice was pleased by the reaction. Joseph had a very hard, muscular shoulder under his black wool jacket, and he smelt of a man; nothing unpleasant, just a musty smell of oil and hay, with a hint of tobacco. He didn't wear hair oil so there was not the acrid sweet smell she hated. He was just the man for her, she decided. Mother would not approve, but by the time she found out about Alice's plan, it would be too late.

As Alice trotted up the lawn to the house, she threw the trug aside and hugged herself with glee. Suddenly aware she could be seen by someone, even by Joseph, she retrieved the trug and the very few cuttings that were in it and went to the back-garden door.

*

Joseph could still smell her scent, the feel of her lips, her breath brushing against his cheek and the tender touch of her hand on his shoulder. He placed his hand on each part of himself she had touched, to try and hold the memory of her kiss. He had goosebumps and he felt he was blushing.

Joseph was quite taken by the attention Alice had shown him. Apart from her slightly large nose, she was very pretty, possibly beautiful. She had a lovely figure – not skinny like most fashionable girls – and her auburn hair was wonderful when it was let totally loose. Alice seemed to be making all the moves towards him, which he was not used to and something he did not think would be the case with an English girl.

4

Two weeks of having tea and intimate chats with Joseph in the stable's sitting room, Alice decided she needed to move the relationship on.

After each meeting, she kissed Joseph on the cheek. She knew it was something Joseph waited for with huge anticipation, as he would lose the thread of the conversation while he stood in expectation of her kiss, sometimes on each cheek – as is traditional in France – or just one long lingering kiss on one cheek. She would ensure he was standing so that she could get close to him. After each kiss, for some reason, Joseph would thank her. Whether it was for the kiss or her company, Alice didn't know.

Alice had gathered from her brother that he, along with their mother, was going to their summer house in Val-André in Brittany for the weekend to open the house up after the winter. They were taking Charles and Marie Ducheyne with them.

"My mother and the whole household are going to Brittany tomorrow for a few days," Alice informed Joseph on Friday morning over their cup of tea. "I know you would like to come into the house and look at the art. Would you like to come tomorrow?"

"That would be wonderful. I would love to see—" Joseph stopped and looked unsure. "Will nobody be in the house?"

"No," said Alice with a nervous giggle, "just me." She looked slightly coquettish. She was teasing him.

"I don't think I can come into the house if you are on your own. It wouldn't be correct."

"Well, I won't tell anyone if you don't." Alice laughed and Joseph smiled his apprehensive approval. "I would love to see the paintings you have. Your father was a great collector, I believe." Joseph looked excited.

"Tomorrow, then. I will collect you from the shed."

"Oh … right. Can't I just knock on the back door?"

"No, I am not totally convinced that all the staff will be out, and it would not do to allow anyone to see you, would it?"

"Wouldn't it?" asked Joseph, looking alarmed.

*

The next day, Saturday, Joseph sat in a wicker chair reading a paper on the small, covered terrace in front of the garden shed. He was smoking a French cigarette and had a mug of tea on the wicker table beside him. He had been waiting since nine o'clock. He tried to compose himself, to look sophisticated, possibly even classy, but it was difficult. His hair was unruly; his clothes, even the nice jacket he borrowed off Ferdi, hung on him like a wet curtain. He was too skinny, he thought. He crossed his legs, first widely, with his ankle resting on the knee, but thought that looked loutish, so he shortened the spread of his legs. He didn't want to cross his legs like Ferdi, who would place one knee over the other, like a woman; he wanted to look masculine.

It was ten thirty on a cold, February morning. The sun was trapped behind impenetrable grey clouds. The garden was beginning to show a little colour. The lawn looked like a striped billiard table after its first official mow, more like a lawn at a Gloucestershire country house than a lawn behind a Parisian town house.

He heard the French windows of the salle de séjour open, and his heart skipped in excitement. The anticipation of not only seeing the Barrett Collection but also being alone with Alice was quite exhilarating.

From his chair he could just see a pair of shapely ankles walking down the lawn. Alice walked on the front part of her shoes so the heels did not spike the lawn. His view of Alice's approach was slightly obscured by a ceanothus bush about to come into bloom with sky-blue flowers.

He watched as the ankles got closer, and just before she rounded the ceanothus he quickly looked at his paper, pretending not to have seen her approach.

"You're here," she said with a giggle. Joseph took a good look at her. She wore a tight fawn waistcoat over a white silk blouse with full sleeves gathered at the wrist, and a heavily pleated charcoal-grey skirt that ballooned out like a bell from her thin waist. Her auburn curls bounced around her shoulders as she walked.

"I've been here an hour," he retorted. Alice laughed again, putting her hand up to her mouth in reply to his reproach, trying to hide her amusement.

"Come on, then." She held out her hand to Joseph as if she was taking a child for a walk. Again, Joseph was unsure about this forwardness. Was this normal behaviour for a lady? He didn't care, if it meant seeing the collection.

Joseph stood and put down his newspaper.

"Lovely suit, Joseph," Alice said. She wasn't smiling now but looking at Joseph up and down appreciatively.

"You look lovely too," he replied. He was only a few centimetres taller than her, just right to be able to look into her beautiful eyes. She looked wonderful.

Her hand was small and warm as she took hold of his rough, paint-stained hand. She semi-dragged him up the lawn to the terrace and in through the French windows.

They came into a long, light room, the salle de séjour – a vast room which Joseph estimated must have been about twenty by ten metres. It had a cream ceiling with gold filigree cornicing and three large chandeliers that hung from ornate gold ceiling roses. Each opulent chandelier had intricate clusters of glass and light, and hung a metre above the Louis Quinze tables below. The room was furnished with large Georgian high-backed sofas and chairs upholstered in rich dark-maroon fabric with intricate yellow-gold patterns weaved through the cloth. There were thick gold rope tassels that adjusted the high sides of the sofas. On the floor was a carpet of dusty dark-blue and yellow-gold Persian patterns.

A huge white marble fireplace stood at the centre of the long, heavily decorated wall. Painted panels showed a fountain of flowers for each season spouting from decorated Greek urns. Surmounting the mantle was a large triptych mirror with a gold frame of ornate flowers and leaves. Matching Sheraton tables with tiny drawers in the centre stood on either side of the fireplace, each adorned with ornaments of unicorns and Staffordshire dogs. Above were two large oil paintings by the same artist, in the same style. The first depicted a farmland scene with a water well and a horse harnessed to a cart that carried hay. The horse was drinking from a bucket and the farmer was talking to a maiden over a garden fence in front of a small, thatched farmhouse. The other painting was of some fishermen on a riverbank, and in the distance a cathedral spire surrounded by a town could be seen. Swans coasted along the river, unaware of the fishermen who were smoking their pipes in the foreground. Both were serene English scenes.

"But these are marvellous," said Joseph. "It must be an English painter. If I did not know better, they could be Constables."

"They are Constables," Alice said with pride.

Joseph stepped back and marvelled at them.

"And there, at the end of the room, is a Caravaggio – a portrait of a lady – a Courtesan."

Joseph whirled around and to his delight saw a small picture, no more than a metre by a half, of a seated girl holding a bunch of delicate white flowers. She looked French or Spanish, dark with a round face, not particularly beautiful but pretty. She wore an embroidered dress with white voluminous linen sleeves, and her narrowed eyes looked to one side with uncertainty. She was well rounded, as was the fashion in the time of Caravaggio.

"And here, our other pride and joy, the Titian."

Joseph was like a boy in a sweet shop for the first time. He rushed the full length of the room to be close to the masterpiece: a vast canvas showing a scene of a woman seated under an old, gnarled olive tree, a baby in her arms. She watched a troupe of mounted soldiers with lances riding off over some wooded hills, a turreted castle standing proud in the middle distance.

Under the painting was a table covered with ornaments and a large ormolu clock. Joseph walked slowly backwards from the scene of a wife and child bidding farewell to her soldier. He immersed himself in the painting, feeling the wind and heat of the day.

"*Wunderbar*," he said. "Oh, but this is too, too wonderful."

"That is the first time I have heard you speak your native language, Joseph."

"I seldom, if ever, speak it," he said, still looking at the painting by Titian.

"You must come through to the morning room. There are some lovely pictures of fruit by a Dutch painter I can't remember the name of. We even have Augustus John's portrait of Colonel T. E. Lawrence."

"It sounds like quite a collection," Joseph said, eager to see the morning room. He was not sure who T. E. Lawrence was, but he had certainly heard of Augustus John.

"It is well known throughout France and England, even Germany." Alice smiled proudly. "I have a Klimt upstairs."

"He was Austrian, of course. Only died a few years ago," Joseph said wistfully, still looking at the Titian and unaware he sounded a little superior.

Alice walked over to two secret doors that looked like all the other panelled walls, to reveal the morning room beyond. The vast windows, like the drawing room they had first entered, looked out onto the garden. There was one more chandelier in the centre of the room.

"Very English trick in fine houses – movable walls," said Alice, throwing her arms out like a circus ringmaster. "It is so we can make this into one big room suitable for balls." She closed the double doors. Joseph marvelled at the art on the end wall.

They then went through a door with mirrored pillars on either side and down a short corridor into the huge dining room. Virtually square, the room was about one hundred and twenty square metres. Large windows overlooked the front of the house and the driveway onto Avenue Foch. The walls, like the salle de séjour, had eighteenth-century panels. Joseph gasped as he looked up at the painted ceiling depicting a forest with wild animals and birds in vivid colours, painted in the post-impressionist naïve style.

"This was all done by the French painter Henri Rousseau. It was here when Mother bought the house but it was terribly neglected." Alice began to sound like a museum guide. To the right, along the wall opposite the windows stood another large, fine Gothic Revival Caen stone fireplace. It had double-columned jambs in a garnet-coloured Serpentine marble which supported a Languedoc marble mantelshelf the colour of chocolate.

In the centre of the room was a long mahogany table surrounded by twenty-four chairs. Apart from three tall, silver, eight-arm candelabras down the middle, the table was uncovered and unlaid. "Here is my mother by Sir William Orpen. Doesn't she look lovely?"

"Lovely, indeed. Orpen is a marvellous English portrait painter. I don't believe I have ever seen a portrait such as this in a private collection." Joseph looked up with admiration at the art, slightly overcome with the magnificence of the paintings. "Who collected these paintings?"

"My father, mainly, and Jason bought one or two paintings, nothing important. My father did a grand tour of Italy and bought most of the stuff you can see here." She turned to the right wall. "And these are all paintings my brother found around France and Germany on his diplomatic travels. Quite a lot of them were given to him for some favour or other, but they were never very good."

"Really," said Joseph slightly dubiously. What kind of favours? he asked himself.

"Come on, Joseph, I want you to see upstairs." Alice grabbed his hand and tore him away from his scrutiny. He would have loved to have spent all day in the dining room.

"Has anyone catalogued the collection?"

"Yes, I think my brother has a list somewhere for the insurance, I suppose."

"But how is it kept secure? I mean, they have all gone to Brittany with just you here, looking after this priceless art."

"Joseph," she said in mock bashfulness, "are you concerned about my welfare? Do you think a gang of thieves will ravage the house … and me?" Alice put her finger on her chin in a gaiety-girl pose, a picture of coy innocence, which made Joseph laugh.

"No! I was concerned that all this stuff is safe, and, of course, that you are safe."

"Don't worry, my hero, there are lots of shutters and the front door has a metal backing plate. I just opened all the shutters so you could see the pictures in daylight. I know you artists."

She dragged him to the end of the room and through the large double doors into the entrance hall.

Directly across the wide marble hall was another set of double doors that led into the large library, which was nearly as large as the dining room.

"I would show you the art in the library, but I haven't done the shutters and they are all Jason's boring stuff. Very dull."

"Is there a portrait of you?" asked Joseph.

"Yes, but when I was twelve, with my sister. It's not very good. I'll show you another day."

They went through into the inner hallway, still hand in hand, and Alice started up the stairs.

"Miss Barrett, I am sure … this is not proper. What would your mother say?"

"She's not here, and it's Alice when we are on our own – like tea in the shed."

"But it is not 'tea in the shed' – this is your house, your very beautiful and very expensive house."

"Come on, Joseph, I just want to show you my room. I have a small August Klimt that my father gave me when I was sixteen, just before he died."

"Let's go then," said Joseph, letting go of her hand and running up the two flights of stairs, two steps at a time, to the gallery landing. He stood at the top and looked down at Alice who was giggling at Joseph's change of mind.

Once she had caught him up, she took his hand again and led him along the long landing. There was a large window at either end. When they reached the last door on the left, Alice stopped and whispered, "That's my sister's room, it's never used now except for guests if we have lots of people staying."

"Why are you whispering? She's not in there, is she?"

"No!" Alice giggled flirtatiously.

She opened the door to her own room opposite her sister's and walked in. Joseph remained on the threshold and craned his head round the door.

"Where's the Klimt?" he whispered.

"Oh, come in," Alice shouted with a laugh. "It's just here, above the fireplace."

Joseph entered the room, which was quite cold as no fire was lit. His eyes were transfixed by the picture on the wall: a small picture of intricate gold and red patterns, with flashes of black and white. Within the patterns was the face of a beautiful girl, asleep, the pattern forming her bed. Her arm rested elegantly on a gold pillow.

"Oh, this is very special."

"I know," said Alice. "It is called *Girl on a Golden Pillow.*" She had moved very close to Joseph, so close that Joseph realised he could smell her scent. He turned to face her, and as he turned, instead of her moving away as he expected, she came even closer and kissed him on the lips, softly, lightly, lasting only a second. Joseph hesitated, not knowing what to do. His desire was to take her in his arms and kiss her back, but he was unsure of the consequences. Thirty seconds had elapsed; both were beginning to get cold, both looking at each other, Alice's lovely eyes looking up into his face, asking him to kiss her.

She took Joseph's face in her hands and kissed him again, softly. Joseph encircled his arms around her and kissed her back. Alice wound her arms around his neck. Their mouths opened in the kiss and their tongues gently nuzzled. Joseph's hands spread over her back, pulling her firmly into him. He could feel her thighs against his and felt her move her pelvis into his groin. Her body was warm, and they forgot the room was cold.

He broke the kiss, concerned she might feel he had gone too far. He hung his head over her shoulder.

"Alice, I—"

Alice found his mouth again and kissed him with even more fervour. There was an intensity now in her kiss, and Joseph, while still unsure of the wisdom of their behaviour, was getting very excited. The smell of her hair, her

42

perfume, her breath, was intoxicating. He could feel her breasts against his chest. His heart was racing, he was light-headed and he felt himself stiffening. He panicked and drew back, embarrassed. What if she felt his excitement?

"Joseph," Alice said hoarsely, "I want you to make love to me."

Joseph was dumfounded. He had very little experience of lovemaking; little experience of women, come to that. Despite all the bluster about his conquests in the past, they had never quite got to this stage. He thought courtship would be a lengthy process of asking permission, marriage and *then* intercourse. Did she mean lovemaking or making love – or both? He was beginning to worry he might do the wrong thing and ruin the moment.

"What do you mean, 'make love'? Alice, I don't know what to say—"

"Don't say anything, Joseph. Take off your jacket and sit with me on the sofa." Alice was talking normally now.

Alice's chilly room was large. The walls were a very pale lilac and the rugs on the floor were cream with thin pale blue and lilac Persian patterns. At one end of the room was a large bed with a bedhead of an intricate fine wicker pattern set in a cream and gold frame. The head of the bed stood over two metres high and took up most of the wall.

At the other end of the room was the unlit fireplace. In front of it, three boudoir chairs were grouped around a low table. To one side of the fireplace was a chaise longue with cushions, which was used for Alice's afternoon rests. The large, well-cushioned sofa was at the foot of the bed.

"Alice, I really cannot—"

"Joseph, I insist," she said seductively.

Joseph walked over to the sofa. Alice came over and sat beside him and looked into his eyes. She had an expression of anticipation. Her round cheeks were slightly flushed, her eyes wide; she looked excited, happy, and smiled at him alluringly. Joseph sat upright on the edge of the sofa. He felt nervous. Alice sat down beside him and swivelled her knees to touch his. She ran her hands up his chest, under his jacket, up over his shoulders. Joseph shrugged off the jacket. Then Alice was unbuttoning his wool waistcoat from the bottom upwards. He watched the top of her head as she worked on the buttons.

"Alice, we must talk—"

"Shhh …" Alice gently shushed him and pushed the waistcoat off his shoulders. He looked up to the ceiling, wondering what he should do. Should he stop her? He felt her now unbuttoning his shirt. He sat there, excited yet full of anxiety. He didn't want to succumb to his desire to carry Alice onto the bed and make love to her. He wasn't sure if he should be helping or protesting. What was she doing?

Alice took his shirt and collar off, putting the stud in his hand. She was pulling the shirt tail out of his trousers when Joseph stood up suddenly. He strode to the window and looked out onto Avenue Foch. His vest was the last bit of defence, and he felt he should keep it on for … for … he did not know what for.

"Alice, I really want to make love to you," he said, looking out the window, not wanting to see her looking at him with disappointment, possibly even anger, "but I don't think it is wise for us to do this. We are so different, you and I, we have totally different lives. I don't know why you want me. I …"

Joseph turned to face her and was stunned to see she was lying completely naked on the bed. She lay on her back, her arms crossed over her breasts, her legs together and her toes pointed. Joseph let out a long, sad sigh. Her smooth pastel skin was flawless, the colour of cream with flushes of pink. She lay rigid on the bed, looking up to the ceiling, her body pale against the dark-blue bedcover.

"Joseph, darling, take your clothes off and lie down beside me."

"It's quite cold, you know. Should we not be under the covers or something?"

"I just want to see you … all of you."

Joseph did as he was told, with no further protest. The remaining clothes were rapidly taken off. He climbed onto the bed and lay down on his back beside her, his hands self-consciously trying to hide his nakedness, his shoulder lightly brushing against hers. He realised he was holding his breath. As he lay down he glanced at the triangle of curly auburn hair at the top of her legs. He felt a flutter of excitement in his chest and exhaled a soft sigh. They lay there together in silence.

Alice turned her head to face him. He was looking at her naked body. She unfurled her arms; her small breasts wobbled as she moved onto her side. She placed her hand on his chest and stroked the small patch of downy hair in the centre. He took in an unsteady breath.

"Joseph, you are magnificent," she purred. Joseph's thin, muscular body tensed as her hand went from his chest down to his stomach. He looked at her face, and then his gaze wandered down to her breasts, her petite breasts and erect nipples. She fell onto her back with a sigh and a wide smile in expectation. She took his hand and placed it on the top of her inner thigh. She parted her legs slightly and slid Joseph's hand up, deliciously, to areas Joseph had never

44

felt on a woman before. He had only fantasised about touching the intimate areas of a beautiful woman. It was like a dream. Her smooth, silky skin thrilled him; his heart was racing. Alice gasped as he stroked her. Her eyes were closed and she had a smile of pure pleasure on her lips. Encouraged by her obvious excitement, he rose up and plunged his lips onto hers and kissed her with eager passion, his hand still between her legs. Alice pushed Joseph onto his back and straddled him, kissing him furiously and moaning. Her body, not skinny, but wonderfully soft, felt so good against Joseph. He wanted to touch and stroke every bit of her. His hands ran up and down her back, tracing the channel that ran down her spine to her smooth, round buttocks.

Alice broke off the kiss and pushed herself up, her hands on his shoulders. Her hair fell across her face which was glowing with excitement, her breasts rounded and beautifully formed. Joseph reached up to cup them in his hands and Alice gave a sigh of pleasure. She smiled and bit her bottom lip, her eyes wide and eager.

She went up on her knees and, without much difficulty, lowered herself onto Joseph. As he entered his full length into her, she cried out, "My God, Joseph!" and fell onto his chest.

He was inside her; she was on top. He didn't know what to do. He felt the softness and warmth of her. He tried to move but she moaned. He didn't know if it was out of pleasure or protest.

She kissed him again and then levered herself back up and sat on him. She arched her back and ran her hands through her hair. Joseph was entranced. He didn't quite understand what was going on. A blush spread between Alice's breasts. Breathing heavily, she began to move her hips. Joseph started to move with her. It felt so fabulous. He wanted to whoop with happiness but thought it would ruin the moment. Joseph reached up to her breasts and then, suddenly, a huge surge, a wonderful feeling in his groin, swept up from between his legs and engulfed his body. He felt light-headed, and then a gigantic rush of pleasure pulsated in waves and his whole body shook. He gasped out loud. He lifted his hips off the bed to go even deeper into her. His head was spinning and a tear trickled down from each eye onto the pillow. He felt the waves of bliss going into Alice.

Alice rotated her hips faster and faster. She seemed unaware Joseph had climaxed.

"Joseph!" she cried with ecstasy. "Joseph!" Then she fell back on top of his chest, laughing as though she was drunk.

Joseph closed his eyes. He could hear Alice panting in his ear, she was warm on his chest. He felt himself slowly slide out of her, his arousal diminished. She lay on top of him for what seemed like hours. Joseph had no idea that women had the same enjoyment as men while having sex. Alice plainly relished the lovemaking.

Without warning, Alice rolled off Joseph, put on a silk dressing gown that was over the bottom of the bed and went to the bedroom door. Just before she went out, she turned to Joseph who was propped up on his elbows. He looked at her quizzically.

"That was lovely, Joseph, we must do it again soon." She spoke as though they had just played a game of cards or been to a party. He lay down again but realised when he felt the cold on his body that he was naked. He got up and quickly dressed. He sat on the sofa, thinking of the exquisite five minutes of pleasure they had just enjoyed. It seemed like two hours, but he realised, after checking the time on his watch in his waistcoat pocket, it was only minutes.

He waited for fifteen minutes and then Alice appeared, dressed, her hair pinned back. She sat down beside him, perched on the edge of the seat, and placed both her hands on his.

"That was wonderful, darling, but I think you'd better go now, just in case."

"Just in case of what?" Joseph asked, confused, wondering how a girl's mind worked after making love. Should there be a long period of "winding down"? He wished he knew more. It was very frustrating not knowing how to behave. For a start, he thought – he had always thought – couples should be married. Was he being too naïve? It was, after all, his coital debut. He felt different, slightly giddy. It seemed, however, this was not Alice's first time. He had a dim recollection that a virgin bled the first time. Or was it the man?

"Well ..." Joseph stood and looked surreptitiously on the bed for any signs of blood. It was clean as far as he could see. "I will go, then ... yes ...well, thank you for ... well ..." He gestured towards the bed and went to the door. "When will I see you again, Alice?" He thought he should ask as it seemed she was turning him out. "Tomorrow? Sunday, after church?"

"No, I will be going to lunch with my sister and her husband. I was meant to be there today, but I said I had some work to do and would be with them later for tea." And then she said as an afterthought, "but I will see you on Monday, as usual ... for tea, won't I?" She sounded a little formal again. She stood and kissed him gently on the cheek. "Now go, I will see you on Monday. I think you are wonderful."

That last remark made Joseph's heart sing. He stepped out of the bedroom and went down the stairs, through the house and out to his bicycle, as though on a cloud, his brain replaying their lovemaking over and over again. It was indeed wonderful, and Alice was a magnificent if not a rather complicated girl.

*

Alice lay on the bed, fully clothed, looking up at the ornate, swirling pattern of the moulded wallpaper. She was conscious she had her shoes on, and she probably should make the bed. She thought about Joseph compared to Luke Jarret, Madame Belle's son. Luke was far more experienced, but not as well endowed. She was so surprised she came to a climax with Joseph. She remembered Madame Belle telling her students it was essential that you either climax or fake a climax. She said the latter was mostly the rule and, surprising and shocking all three of the young ladies in her class, she demonstrated a fake climax … fully clothed.

Alice swung her legs off the bed and looked out the window. To her shock, she saw her brother-in-law, Jean de Tournet, strolling across the front driveway towards the island of shrubs in the middle. It looked like he was only going over to admire a shrub. His motor and driver were parked to one side of the driveway.

"Christ!" Alice said aloud, angrily.

"What happened?" said a voice behind her. Alice swung round in horror and surprise, only to see her sister, Stella, running over to the window to see what Alice had seen.

"Oh, it is only Jean."

Stella looked at her critically. Alice had to struggle to compose herself and tried to hide her guilt.

"Stella, you surprised me!" Alice was now calming down. "What are you doing here? Don't you knock?" She felt caught out and was slightly angry at her sister.

Stella took a short ebony and platinum cigarette holder out of her tiny handbag, slotted in a cigarette and lit it with a silver lighter. She looked around for an ashtray but as her sister did not smoke, Alice had to find one in a drawer in the dressing table.

"What are you doing here? This room is very cold," Stella admonished. "Come to that, you were meant to be at our house, helping me with the Sunday lunch arrangements for tomorrow. We have the chairman of BMW coming." Stella looked around the room as she spoke, a troubled expression on her pretty face. How would Stella know it was cold? Alice thought, given she was wearing a black jacket done up with a single button, a matching thick grey fox-fur collar and hat, black tailored gloves and a tight black skirt that went down to her ankles.

"We were going to Chez Margot for lunch and I—" She froze. "Alice, what is all this?" Stella was pointing at the rumpled, unmade bed. "I am scared you have done something very stupid. That English gardener has just zoomed out of the drive on his bicycle … I do hope he has nothing to do with—"

"Stella, it is none of your business. And how dare you crash into my room and behave like Mama! I am over twenty-one and I know what I am doing." Alice instantly regretted saying she knew what she was doing. Stella looked at Alice with her mouth open, as though she was trying to work out what to say next. She took a long pull on her cigarette and started to walk towards the door, much to Alice's relief, leaving a wake of smoke behind her. But at the last minute she turned back.

"Why is the house all open again, the shutters pulled back?"

"If you must know, I was showing Joseph the collection." Alice was forming an explanation that might be acceptable.

"The gardener?" Stella was incredulous.

"He's an art student, Stella. He's only a gardener to supplement the meagre allowance his father gives him. He is Austrian, actually, from Vienna."

"But Alice, what does this all mean?" Stella pointed at the unmade bed.

"I have just had a rest, actually, a rather fitful rest at that," said Alice with some conviction, although she could see Stella wasn't convinced. She went across to the bedroom door.

"Would you like some lunch?" Stella asked.

"Yes." Alice felt hungry. "I will get some things – or I might as well stay here, save having to shut up all the shutters again."

"But there are no servants. Alice, come and stay with us. I will send a girl to pick up your things and the chauffeur can come and do the shutters at the same time. You really can't stay in the house on your own, it's not right."

"*Salut, tout le monde.* Heard voices." Jean de Tournet's blonde head appeared round the bedroom door. "Got fed up waiting for Stella. What are you two up to? Hello, Alice," de Tournet smarmed. He went up to Alice to give her a kiss on the cheek. "Jean!" hissed Stella. "Not here. This is Alice's bedroom."

"Oh yes, sorry, I will wait for you downstairs." There was a flash of anger in de Tournet's eyes. Alice was not quite sure why being in her bedroom meant he should not give her a familial kiss on the cheek. He gave Alice a little wink.

48

Alice smiled at him briefly. She had never liked her brother-in-law. He was quite handsome but had a lascivious leer when near Alice. His blue eyes twinkled as his hands would surreptitiously end up on her knee or buttock. She wondered if he honestly thought women enjoyed that kind of attention and believed him to be – as he clearly did – a handsome rogue.

"Jean, I will be with you in a minute, darling." As de Tournet went out the room, Stella turned to Alice. "What do you want to do? I am not going to let you stay here alone. I will come back here after I have gone to the hospital."

"Hospital?" Alice was alarmed.

"No, not for me. We are visiting Madame Rogueries for Mama as she is away. She had a problem with her heart. She is seventy-two, so getting on."

Alice looked at her quizzically.

"Oh, you know, Mama's friend, who helped her move ..." She flapped her hands with impatience, the ash on her cigarette dropping off onto the Persian rug. "Anyway, darling, what do you want me to do?" Stella looked at her brooch watch and went back over to the dressing table. She stubbed out her cigarette and put her holder away.

"I'll come and stay with you tonight and come to church with you tomorrow, if I may," Alice said. "You go with Jean to lunch; he's waiting in the motor. I will lock up the house and tell Monsieur René that there is nobody here." Alice spoke of the local gendarme.

"Shall I send a motor? The chauffeur can help you."

"No, I'm fine," Alice said with a reassuring smile.

"I shall see you later today, darling. Do you know," she said, looking at Alice, "you can tell we are sisters. I used to have an outfit just like that. You are looking quite lovely." With that, Stella left.

If Stella still felt concern for her sister, thought Alice, there was really nothing she could do about it.

When she heard the front door close, Alice looked out of the window and watched her sister and brother-in-law get into the large black motor car. The driver tipped his floppy fawn cap at Stella and his master and closed the door behind them. It was a cloudy, cheerless day and rain was on its way.

"Oh, God," Alice said, looking out at Avenue Foch, the leafless trees, the lifeless grass in the boulevards, the odd horse and cart or automobile passing by. "That really is bloody inconvenient." She took the ashtray and went downstairs to start closing the shutters again.

5

Ferdi sat opposite Joseph in their apartment. Joseph was looking up to the ceiling with a huge grin on his face. Ferdi looked at the floor with a worried expression, a slight shake of his head.

"What were you thinking, Joseph?" Ferdi looked at his friend who was still staring at the ceiling in a slight trance.

"It's excellent, isn't it?" Joseph punched the air with both fists. "I may have a rich wife after all. And the paintings, Ferdi." Joseph could barely contain his excitement. "The art, it's fantastic! Constables, a huge Titian, a lovely what looks like a Van Dyke, a Monet …"

"Joseph, what about Miss Barrett? Why did you take it so far? It's very, very dangerous."

"Nothing to do with me, Ferdi." Joseph shrugged his shoulders. "She did it all – the seduction. I just lay back and took it like a man," he said with a laugh. "I tell you what, I doubt she was a virgin!"

"Were you?" Ferdi asked sharply. Joseph's bravado waned slightly.

"Yes, if you must know." Joseph looked slightly embarrassed, then cheered and said, "But look who I lost it to!"

*

Alice was pleased by her performance with Joseph. All she had learnt from Madame Belle at the Hôtel l'Opéra had proved most useful. Madame Belle Jarret was well known for her instruction to new wives in the art of lovemaking. Alice had told Madame Belle that her husband-to-be was a widower and an experienced lover, and she did not want to seem to be an inexperienced girl but a sophisticated woman of the world. Madame Belle not only taught her the theory of making love but also provided her son, Luke Jarret, to show Alice the practical side.

Luke was a blonde, muscular lad who was cultured and charming. He had been plainly schooled well by his mother, as every so often the sophistication changed to animal lust. He was very handsome, with striking blue eyes, and about the same height as Alice. She thought he may even be partly Eastern European or Russian. He was tanned all over, had no bodily hair, including no pubic hair, and he had a very slight, indeterminate accent.

Her experiences with Luke were exhilarating and she returned to Luke as many times as she could without arousing suspicion in her household. Luke was, after all, a kind of male prostitute. Luke and Madame Belle, however, were very expensive.

Alice felt Luke was developing a fascination for her and was beginning to get a little too excited. He was also "seeing" women in the Barretts' social circle, and she had to give up her "tutorials" despite Madame Belle's assurances of discretion.

Alice was impressed by Joseph's performance, too, and thought that, while she could not love a man like him, he was easily led and manipulated. He would do anything for her. More importantly, he was not a peasant or a shop boy – not a "Luke" either, in more ways than one. Joseph was well brought up, possibly intelligent and relatively cultured, if not a little wayward. And he had no money.

Her only minor disappointment was he was not English after all, but German – well, Austrian. This might be the only blot on her plan. He seemed nearly English. If he passed muster with Stella and her husband, then he must be OK. And Mama liked him.

Alice kept her promise to take tea with him on Monday. Her mother and brother were still away but Monsieur and Madame Ducheyne were back to open up the house again, so they couldn't make love in Alice's bedroom. But this didn't stop her.

*

Joseph thought nothing more could surprise him when it came to Alice. He had made the tea but Alice, holding a large woollen blanket, bolted the main shed door from the inside before entering the converted stable and started taking her clothes off. It was still quite cold, even with the little stove on.

They made love on the sofa, Alice taking command again and Joseph unable to resist. Under the large blanket that served to keep them warm, Joseph was scarcely undressed. Alice had taken his jacket off while wildly kissing him on the lips and all around his neck and ears. The sensation of her lips around his ears was intoxicating.

Again, after they'd made love and Joseph lay there, exhausted, Alice rearranged her hair, buttoned up her blouse, put on her skirt and jacket – she was not wearing any panties – said, "That was wonderful, Joseph," and promptly left the shed.

Joseph stayed on the sofa, his trousers and pants around his ankles, his shirt unbuttoned. He cuddled the blanket that still smelt of Alice's perfume, thinking of this second encounter, dazed by the speed of it. He got dressed and started doing his gardening job, his mind whirling. All morning he kept looking up to see if he could catch a glimpse of Alice, but he only saw Marie Ducheyne every now and then, cleaning near the window.

*

The informal lovemaking happened each morning Joseph worked. Instead of drinking tea, they would make love. But then one morning, three weeks after their first encounter, Alice didn't appear. Joseph tried to see if she was in the house. He went to the scullery door and asked Marie about Lady Barrett, how she was, how their journey to Brittany went, and then about Mademoiselle Alice – how was she?

"Oh, she is fine. She has gone to the doctor for a check-up, though, so she will not be here for your tea," Marie said with a knowing, slightly sneering smile. "I don't know why she couldn't wait for the doctor to come here."

Joseph wondered why she was going to see a doctor. He presumed all this lovemaking was OK, that she had selected a time that would not allow her to fall pregnant. Joseph had only a rudimentary knowledge of how babies were made, how a woman became pregnant. He didn't have any older siblings and his parents were hardly around, so he was never given any guidance about how these things worked. He assumed Alice knew exactly what she was doing. In any case, it was not as though he had a choice. He could have simply refused to make love to her, he supposed. But she was so provocative, almost addictive.

Joseph did not see Alice at all that day, and she was not in the house when he next went to Nineteen Avenue Foch to work. He was concerned he had done something terribly wrong the last time they were together, and he kept playing back their last meeting under the thick wool blanket in the converted stable.

*

Nearly two months passed by and Joseph had still not seen Alice. He wrote notes and left them with Marie Ducheyne to deliver. He looked in the windows every time he went past in the hope of getting a glimpse of her, but

52

she was elusive: either not there or avoiding him. The latter thought upset him immensely. What had he done – or not done? What had he said to provoke this total shunning? After all, it was she who instigated the lovemaking, the passionate couplings under the wool blanket. What was going on? He felt a constant panic in his chest and found it hard to sleep.

As he was giving the large lawn its second mow of the season, he was jolted from his thoughts when he saw Sir Jason Barrett standing in the path of the lawnmower. Joseph ground to a sudden stop and cut the engine. He had only seen Sir Jason fleetingly a few times and was given a brief nod when he waved at him. Sir Jason was glowering at him.

"Joseph?"

"Yes, sir?" Joseph dismounted the mower seat on top of the roller.

"*Guten Morgen*," said Sir Jason.

"Good—"

"What is your family name?" Sir Jason asked abruptly. He had a small, polite smile on his lips that did not quite reflect in his eyes.

"Deller, sir."

"And you are Austrian, my sister informs me?" Dread crept over Joseph.

"Sir?"

Sir Jason stood with his hands behind his back. He looked at Joseph from head to toe. When he got to Joseph's shoes, he asked, "What is your father's name? What does he do?" Joseph looked down at his shoes, wondering what prompted the question.

"General Werner Deller." Joseph licked his lips; his knees felt a little weak. "He is currently on the staff of a new political party, the Nazi Party, in Germany." Sir Jason jerked his head up in surprise and looked Joseph straight in the eyes.

"Very well. You are doing a good job, Deller." He turned and walked back to the house. Joseph looked after him, bemused and feeling somewhat elated. He was not, after all, about to lose his genitalia after defiling Sir Jason's sister, as he had thought.

*

On a warm, almost hot, spring evening, Joseph was sitting on his little apartment balcony that jutted out onto the street, Rue de Dragon in Saint-Germain, two storeys up. Joseph sat on a wooden kitchen chair, tipped back, with his feet up on the railings, the setting sun on his face. The road was a long, narrow cobbled street, four-storey terraced houses with dirty dun-coloured walls running the length of both sides. Everything echoed – the cars, horse and carts, people's voices, mothers calling children.

Sitting on his balcony for the first time that year, Joseph read a book on the art of portraiture. Every now and then he would look up to see what was happening on the street: what was being delivered to the little café opposite, dogs fighting in the middle of the road, cats growling at each other on the roof above.

Paris in spring was just wonderful, and sitting on a balcony in Saint-Germain was one of the best places to watch the real life of Paris pass by.

"Hey!" Ferdi shouted up to Joseph from the café below, his voice echoing down the narrow street.

"What?" Joseph yelled back, not looking up from the book he was reading.

"There's a lovely girl here to see you."

Joseph clattered his chair onto all four legs and looked over the balcony railing to see, far below, Alice's face smiling up at him.

"Oh!" he gasped in surprise. "Come on up. Leave Clark Gable down there. He's meant to be getting us some food."

He watched Alice turn to Ferdi and ask for directions. Joseph quickly dived through the window into the apartment's sitting room that doubled as Ferdi's studio and desperately tried to tidy his own mess. The living room walls were covered in Ferdi's rather strange art: large square canvasses with brightly coloured scenes of Paris and charcoal drawings of overweight nude women, and one very good portrait of a blonde man in uniform that was unfinished.

Joseph threw a jacket over his vest; he didn't have time to put on a shirt or a collar, let alone a tie, so he tied a cream cotton scarf around his neck and stuffed it into his high-buttoned jacket.

Joseph heard Alice call out his name, followed by a knock. Joseph opened the door in a state of nervous anticipation and ushered her in.

"Hello. Come in ... come in. Sorry about the mess." He looked around to see there was no mess as Ferdi was a meticulously clean person. It was only Joseph's bedroom that was a mess. He felt embarrassed. "Well, there was a mess. I tossed it all into my room. I was just reading and—"

"Hello, Joseph. I can't stay long. I just wanted to come and apologise for not seeing you for so long."

"Well, I didn't think we could keep that sort of thing going for very long. I mean ..." – Joseph was sounding slightly petulant while puffing up cushions on the chair for her to sit – "Your brother stopped me at my work and asked me about my family yesterday. I nearly—"

"I know, I know. Joseph, I want *you* to sit for a moment ... I don't need to sit down."

"What do you mean, you know?" All the things he was going to say to her when she next appeared went straight out of his head. He had speeches and angry torrents rehearsed and ready to deliver, but they had all been defused by seeing her for the first time for well over a month.

"Joseph, I will not beat about. I am going to have a baby ... our baby." Joseph slowly lowered himself onto the armchair, unaware his book was still lying on the seat.

"But ..." Joseph said disbelievingly. "How do you know? You don't look preg ... as though you are having a baby."

"The doctor has confirmed it. He thinks I am nearly two months," she stated calmly. She looked at Joseph with anticipation.

Joseph went to the open window and looked out at the house opposite. He could see a woman with a tiny child being bathed in a washing-up bowl on a table by the window. She was chatting away at the child who was waving its arms about and splashing. The woman was no older than Alice, pretty, with strands of mousy hair, half loose, half pinned back, laughing as she got wet with the child's splashing.

"Well, we will have to get married," Joseph said, as though it was an inconvenience. He looked at her stomach and back to her eyes, and was surprised to see she had a condescending expression on her glowing face. He sat heavily into the armchair. "Well, don't you?" he shouted angrily. "Think we should get married, I mean?" The veins on his neck stood out and his face was turning red.

"Joseph, don't get angry. This is not like you." She came over and put her hand tenderly on his shoulder. "We don't need to get married. I wanted a child, an intelligent child, preferably a boy." Joseph stood and shrugged off her hand.

"Why on earth ... what is your mother ..." – he held his forehead in his hands – "how are you going to ...?" Joseph sat heavily down in the chair again. "What are you doing?" he asked eventually.

"We are having a baby. You don't need to marry me. I don't want to get married, anyway—"

"But your mother ... and what about me? It's my child as well ... why can't we marry?"

55

"Marry my employee?"

"That's uncalled for." He was hurt.

"Yes, I'm sorry, but—"

"Lady Barrett is my employer, not you. Is it because I am a penniless student with no privileged upbringing?" he said unhappily, clapping his hand to his chest.

"Well, Joseph, that is not strictly true, is it?" Alice said emphatically. Joseph was stunned to silence. "Well ... is it, Joseph?" She leant forward and whispered in his ear. "I think you are an art thief." She giggled. Her scent washed over him, her breath in his ear making the hairs on the back of his neck stand up.

Joseph leapt up. He was at a loss as to what to do or say. He was frightened but also angry. Alice stifled a giggle, which gave him some relief, but her face quickly became serious.

"Joseph, I asked someone to look into your ... history once I knew I was going to have a baby, and I was quite intrigued as to what was revealed. You are indeed Austrian, your parents are sort of wealthy, your father is an accountant who is currently working for a new political party in Germany run by, now let me see ..." Alice took out a small notebook from her handbag, released the catch by pulling out a thin silver pencil and turned a few pages. "Yes, here we are: Karl Harrer, Anton Drexler and Adolf Hitler. I believe they have a different leader every couple of minutes. He works under a military rank of general. You are a part-time art student, as far as my enquiries can make out, and a gardener in two of the grandest houses in Paris. One being mine. Now why is that?" Joseph looked at her coldly for a minute. He was still angry, but restrained.

"So, I am a part-time art student," he said at last. "Apart from my present status, there is no reason why we cannot marry. As you say, my parents are upstanding pillars of Austrian and German society. I do not get on with my parents and I prefer the English and French way of life. I spent a lot of it in the Home Counties of England ... like you!"

Alice softened. "Yes, but ... I don't want to get married. My mother has promised to leave Nineteen Avenue Foch to me."

"But what about your sister? Or Sir Jason – you haven't told him you are having our baby, have you? Is that why he came to see me?"

"No, no, no." Alice put her hand on Joseph's shoulder. "Jason has lots of properties – in Paris and London. He even keeps an actress in a castle in

Friedrichshafen, Germany. But my mother does not know." Her attempts to sound understanding were not working.

"Will I ever see him ... my ... our child?"

"Yes, of course. In fact, I have a huge favour to ask you."

Joseph was taken aback. What was he to make of this? He couldn't work out if he was angry or intrigued. She was looking so pretty sat on the arm of the armchair, looking down at him.

"I need you to help me, Joseph, through my confinement."

Joseph was not entirely sure what the period of confinement was or how he could help.

"You don't want me there at the birth?" he said with a little horror.

"No, no, darling, I just need you to be with me for the last four or five months when I will be looking huge."

"Why can't your mother, the Ducheynes ... or even your sister help?"

"I don't want them, I want you – you are so much more fun. Anyway, I don't want them to know. My mother will know because I want to use her house in Brittany."

"But Alice, you are going to turn up in Paris at the end of the year, or whenever it arrives, with a baby!"

"I know, but I will say that my husband died or is living abroad or something."

"So, you want me to stop art school, give up my gardens, go off with you to Brittany for weeks ..."

"No, darling, about four or five months, all through the summer. The *École des Beaux-Arts* is closed for the holidays anyway." She tried to sound cheery.

Joseph gaped at Alice. "Five months?" he said in a high, hoarse voice. "As some kind of glorified servant?"

"No, a friend, a companion."

"A companion? And then what – return here to Paris, no job, no work ... even more penniless than I am now?"

"We will get you a job. Jean, my brother-in-law, will get you something. You could become an engineer or a designer."

Joseph sighed and put his head in his hands.

"I was going back to Germany next month," he lied. "My parents want help with the Party. It is quite a new party and they have a job for me there."

"Oh – well then, perhaps you could join them a little later," Alice said with a chirpy smile of encouragement. "I would love to have your company. I will pay you."

"That makes me feel better," he said, throwing his hands up. But then he stopped. The money would be useful for travelling, he supposed.

"So, you will come? It will be lovely. It will be summer, and Val-André is a lovely place: beaches, great restaurants, and not far away. We will buy you a summer wardrobe!" She was getting excited. "Joseph – come on, tell me you will come."

"But why did you have me researched?" he protested at last.

"I had to. My brother made me when he saw we were getting on so well."

"Sir Jason?"

"And my sister told him that I had shown you the pictures in the collection, and Jason was furious."

"God, you didn't tell him that I saw the Klimt, did you?"

"No, no, just that you were a keen art student and that you were very impressed with the Caravaggio, the Titian and the others."

Joseph had his head in his hands again. Alice tenderly rubbed his back to remind him he had a question to answer.

"OK," he said, but he was still not sure he was doing the right thing. He felt he was being manipulated by Alice … again.

"That is wonderful, darling. We will set off for Val-André on the first of July. The baby should arrive in November, early December. I must tell Mother our plans."

"Does she know you're having a baby?" Joseph raised his head and looked at Alice with a sense of impending doom. Alice looked slightly sheepish.

"No, she doesn't. Nobody knows, only you."

"Well, don't you think you should tell her? She is going to have to know. You are taking her summer house for the summer and autumn, so surely she will need to know. Apart from that, you are going to appear with a child at the end of the year … her first grandchild! Do Stella or Jason have children?"

"No," Alice said thoughtfully. Joseph looked at Alice with a mixture of disappointment and astonishment. For a person he thought was quite bright, she seemed to be behaving in rather a stupid way. They both stood. He put his hands on her shoulders and looked into her eyes – her lovely eyes. "Alice, I don't think you have thought this through very well."

"I have, Joseph," she said with conviction. "I just needed to know if you would come to Brittany with me before I tell Mama." Joseph looked at her, unsure of anything. Alice was not being reasonable. She was presuming a lot. She clearly had got her own way throughout her life.

"Is Ferdi really a baron?" she asked with a playful smile.

"Yes, he is. A Luxembourger baron." He put his hands on his hips and said crossly, "Why?"

"He is quite handsome, isn't he?" Joseph was astonished and was about to say something, when Alice said, "Oh Joseph, don't get jealous. He's not my type, and" – she looked absently out of the window – "I don't think I'm his type." Alice went up close to Joseph and gave him a small kiss on his lips, stroking his cheek at the same time. He instantly melted and put his hands on her hips.

"Can I see you before we go to Brittany?" he asked.

"It's best not at the house. Now I know where you live, I will come and see you here, if I may."

"When will you come next?" Joseph was aware that he sounded a little pathetic and carried on in a stronger voice. "I mean, will it be this time next week? I had better make sure I am in, and tidy, and that Ferdi is not around."

"This time next week, then." She gave him a long, gentle kiss on the lips. "Thank you, darling. I am sorry about all this. I should have explained my plans to you more." She slipped out the door. Joseph could hear her clopping down the four flights of stairs and then out into the narrow street. He could hear her walking across the cobbles. He sat and waited until the clopping of her shoes was drowned out by traffic, and slumped into his chair.

Since his very first encounter with Alice, she had confused him. He never knew what her thoughts were … about him, that was. Did she love him? She must like him, at least. Joseph wondered how much he loved her. He was in love with her, he admitted to himself, and not in a minor way.

Alice's love for Joseph, he thought, was like an artichoke; she gave away lots of layers of small, delicious morsels but the indigestible choke stood in the way of getting to the heart.

6

"Mama, I have some news," Alice said to her mother when she returned from the doctor that same afternoon. Lady Barrett was at her writing desk in the study, beside the library.

"Darling, can it wait? I must write these letters so I can catch the post."

"No, I am afraid not. It is very important."

Lady Joy set down her pen with a sigh, removed her half-moon glasses, folded her arms and looked at her daughter indulgently from across the desk. Alice knew her mother thought of her still as a little girl ... nothing could be *that* important.

Alice sat and tried to construct in her mind how she was going to tell her mother about her pregnancy. She had planned for this conversation – she had planned for this moment. This was, after all, the first Barrett baby since she was born, twenty-two years previously. Her sister and brother-in-law had not been able to provide a grandchild for Lady Joy. Her brother, Jason, had little time in his life for marriage, let alone children. This would be Joy's first grandchild.

Alice looked up at the portrait of her father, thankful he was dead as he would never have approved of Alice's plan.

"Well?" Joy said impatiently.

"Mama, I am going to have a baby." Alice lowered her gaze to the floor, preferring not to see the shock on her mother's face.

"My God, Alice, what are you saying? ... Are you sure?"

"Yes, Mother. I have known for nearly a month and the doctor has confirmed it."

"I am going to phone Dr Trénant now." She picked up the receiver from the phone on the desk but hung up when she saw Alice was shaking her head, still looking at the floor. "Alice? Will you please look at me and tell me what on earth is going on?"

Alice looked up at her mother, regretting at that moment having decided to tell her about the pregnancy. She should have told her when she started to show a bump, but she was not sure when that would be.

"I did not go to Dr Trénant. I have a different doctor."

"Who is paying for this new doctor, may I ask?"

"I am, of course." Alice was slightly indignant, and then realised all her money came from her mother anyway. "I am sorry, Mama. I suppose it is your money."

"Well, anyway, that is not the point. Who is the father of this child? Do I know him?"

Alice looked at her mother with apprehension. Her mother was asking the questions in the wrong order – she had not planned this question to come so early. Might as well come clean, she thought. It will come out in the end. Perhaps Joseph was right; she had not been at all objective.

"It's Franz-Joseph Deller, Mama."

"Who? I don't think I know him. Will he marry you? He's got to. I will get your brother to sort it out—"

"Mama!" Alice interrupted, trying to decide if this was going to be a disaster or just a fiasco. Alice's plan was to have a child and bring it up with tales of a father killed by someone or something, and the child would eventually inherit Nineteen Avenue Foch when Alice died. The child would grow up in this lovely house, secure and happy. There would be no husband to inherit half or even all of the house, or share with other children. It would all be solely his or hers. "Mother, I do not want to get married. I want a child to inherit this house when I die."

There was silence. Joy sat looking at her daughter, her head shaking, her mouth open as though ready to say something.

"For heaven's sake, it sounds like you got pregnant on purpose."

"I did." Alice looked at her mother, tears welling up in her eyes. Joy threw up her arms in despair. She eyed Alice as though she was mad.

"My only grandchild is going to be an ... illegitimate ... a bastard ... and you have made him a bastard on purpose?" she screamed. Alice had never seen her mother so angry. "Alice, you might as well tell me who this Deller man is. I will have to talk to him."

"Mother, he has nothing to do with it. He just helped me with the plan.

I am sorry if it has upset you so much." Alice was miserable. She really wished she had not told her mother and had waited until the baby arrived. "I just thought that Stella is provided for, Jason has his properties and job, and I have nothing. I don't want to marry. I don't want a man to take over my life, or my inheritance."

Joy looked at her daughter's tears, seemingly unable to take it all in.

"Alice, what would happen if I changed my will to say I will leave this house to you only if you marry?"

Alice looked in horror at her mother.

"Mother, you wouldn't! You can't change a will … can you?"

"Why not? What happens if I change it to read that it shall only go to you and *not* your husband? Alice, I honestly thought you had more intelligence."

"Are you going to do that? Change your will?"

"I don't know, Alice. Where is this man?"

"He will be here on Monday."

"How do you know he will be here on Monday?"

"Because he works on Mondays and Fridays." There was a pause. The expression on Joy Barrett's face went from confusion to realisation, disbelief, and finally desolation. She stood up and walked out of the room, her hand to her mouth, trying to stifle her tears.

*

It took two days before Lady Barrett got up from her bed. Madame Ducheyne was the only person permitted to enter Lady Barrett's bedroom.

Eventually, Alice was summoned to her mother's room. Lady Barrett, sitting at her dressing table, looking ill and ashen, regarded Alice as she came into the room, and indicated, with a trembling downward-pointing forefinger, where she was to stand.

"Alice, I have considered your situation and I have concluded what is going to happen. There will be no argument; this is my final word on the subject. If you are not prepared to agree to these terms, I shall not only change my will in favour of Jason having this house, but I shall also write you out of the will altogether and you'll go out into this world with nothing. Do I make myself clear?"

Alice thought for a long time. She had no idea her mother would make such an ultimatum. Alice had admonished herself for the past two days for not even considering her mother's feelings in "the plan".

"Yes, Mother," Alice said quietly. Lady Barrett was sitting erect on the edge of the chair, her hands neatly clasped in front of her and resting on her lap, holding a lace-edged handkerchief. It was two in the afternoon. A tray of coffee and half a brioche on a small plate had been pushed to one side. She wore no make-up and looked exhausted.

"In July, when you will be beginning to show" – she waved her hand elegantly around Alice's stomach – "you will go to a hotel in Biarritz, where you and your sister will stay until the child is born in, I imagine, around mid-November. I will arrange for transport and a suite at the Hôtel Georges in Biarritz—"

"Mama, I am sorry to interrupt, but I thought I could go to Alston House in Brittany. We need not bother Stella."

"On your own?"

"I would take a friend, and I thought Franz-Joseph Deller should also come."

"The gardener! But Alice, this is preposterous." Joy erupted in anger. "Why do you want to take that man with you? Why don't you go with Stella?"

"Does Stella want to sit with me for five months?"

"I have no idea. But why this man, Alice?"

"Only because he will be a huge help and good company."

"I am sure he will," Joy mocked. "But what about my summer? Am I to stay in Paris whilst you have a lovely time in Brittany?"

"I thought you could go to England and see all your old friends in Lewes."

There was a long pause. Joy looked out of the window. She was breathing heavily and trying not to cry. She had placed a hand on her chest. Alice knew she should keep very quiet.

"Alice," Lady Joy said, still looking out of the window, her voice breaking slightly, "I love you very much."

"As do—" Alice started but Joy put up her hand to quieten her.

"This awful tragedy has exhausted me. I do not have the strength to argue any more and I think I will go to my bed." She turned to look at her daughter with a sad smile. She looked at Alice's tummy, where her grandchild was growing. "Go to Brittany with whomever you like. Stay there for as long as you like, but the child will have to be brought up by Stella and Jean." Alice was about to protest but again Joy put up her hand and her eyes conveyed a warning.

"If Stella does not want the child, I will have to think of something else, get you married off or something, but I will not have this family involved in a scandal. And believe me, this will develop into a monumental scandal – even by French standards!"

"Thank you, Mama," Alice said contritely.

"Who else knows about this … child and its paternal origins?"

"Only you and Joseph," said Alice, "and perhaps Ferdi, Joseph's great friend."

"Who is Ferdi?"

"Baron Ferdinand Saumures. He is from Luxembourg and also is an art student," Alice said with pleasure, noting her mother's expression change very slightly to approval on hearing the title.

"I think I met a Baroness Saumures at Cowdray Park one—" She stopped and looked sadly at Alice. "Well, let us leave it at that. No one else may know, especially the servants. I will tell your sister," Lady Barrett said. "Now leave me. I must write to Stella and ask her to come and see me as soon as possible."

7

[faded text from previous page bleeding through]

Pléneuf-Val-André was on the north Brittany coast, nestling at the eastern end of a long, sweeping sandy bay. The bay curved round to the west, where the houses depleted but for a few large, new residences, built mostly by wealthy Parisians. The western end of the bay rose to high cliffs and a small headland. Perched on its own on this headland stood Alston House.

Alston House was bought by Lady Joy Barrett, Alston being her maiden name and the name of the house she was brought up in in Wimbledon. It was newly built in 1920, primarily for Joy's Easter and summer holidays. She had always enjoyed Val-André; it was quiet, and quite unknown to British tourists. And the bright young things preferred the Mediterranean – Cannes, Antibes – or Biarritz on the south-west coast of France, near Spain. It also had a similar climate to an English summer; it never got scorching hot like it did in the suntanning regions further south.

From the coast you could see a stretch of tiny islands that protected the bay from the rough seas of *La Manche*. The bay offered shallow waters that stayed warm throughout the summer. Elderly holidaymakers, bathing sedately, mingled with children and parents in the safe, shallow and warm turquoise water.

Alice drove herself and Joseph from Paris to Val-André in her new bright yellow Citroën Cloverleaf. It was a lovely July summer's day, so they had the roof down. The smells of hot, dry grass and exhaust fumes blasted into the car, and the noise made it nearly impossible to talk.

As they turned off to Val-André at the town of Lamballe, there was a new smell: a mixture of pine and the sweet and salty metallic scent of the sea and sand. The road, shimmering in the heat, ambled along, getting narrower and narrower. The Citroën struggled as it climbed up the hills and spluttered down the other sides until finally, as the narrow road came to the summit of a hill, the huge expanse of the sea came into view: a long bay with a hook of land to the right, a clutch of houses with red roofs, and a church. The imposing and impressive Hôtel Val-André stood proudly overlooking the sea in the centre of the bay. Out to sea was a group of small islands surrounding a larger one, not big enough for houses but home to a large population of seabirds.

They entered the town and took the road that ran alongside the bay. There were lovely grand houses made of large sandstone bricks mingled with grey and maroon blocks. One or two of these mansions were still under construction. The houses all overlooked the almost white sand of the huge expanse of beach. Small parties of adults and children were gathered on the sand, enjoying the pre-lunch sun. Two large red and white kites swept from side to side in the warm breeze. It was quite hot, and Alice was glad of the wind as they drove.

As they approached the western side of the bay, Alice turned off the coast road and onto a sandy track that went up a steep hill. The road had cobbles on the steep parts for winter traffic, which bounced the little yellow car and made Alice giggle. Joseph was full of anticipation. He could not wait to see the house and all that Alice had promised. He enjoyed watching her drive, relishing the sun and wind, laughing at his jokes and smiling generously at him.

They climbed up further, passing houses built into the hillside, all facing the kilometre-long bay. They came to the top where there were no more houses, just a small wood of pine trees blotting out the views. They stopped at a gate. Joseph leapt out of the car and opened the tall ornate iron double gates, set in a high boundary wall, for Alice to drive through.

Beyond the wall was a gravel drive. At the end of the drive stood a large white double-fronted house with a shallow-pitched grey slate roof and large full-length Georgian-style windows on the ground floor. The house overlooked the bay to the east, with panoramic views of the sea round to the little fishing village of Dahouët to the west.

"Welcome to Alston House," announced Alice as they came to a stop.

"*Gott im Himmel!*" said Joseph. "How high up are we? I can see for miles."

"Oh, I don't know, you're going to have to work that out for yourself. You've got plenty of time."

The drive led to the gravelled parking area in front of the house. Joseph thought it was beautiful. The vast lawn bordering the drive consisted of coarse, tough olive-green grass cut short; not like a typical English lawn of soft, luscious green.

A small, skinny girl of about twenty with thick, dark eyebrows, wearing a simple full-length fawn cotton dress and a white apron, scuttled out of the front door.

"Mademoiselle Alice!" She curtsied and went to the back of the car and looked around for a while. "*Où sont les bagages?*" she said in a piping voice with an accent Joseph had not heard before. She was used to the suitcases being on a rack on the back of the Barrett's Bentley. Joseph went to the back of the car and opened the boot, pulled out the suitcases and started into the house.

"Non, non, monsieur, I shall do this," she said in her strange Gallic accent.

"This is Claudine, Joseph. She is, well, everything. She will look after us, mostly. She lives in a little village called Dahouët, just down there" – she pointed towards the west side of the headland – "and she gets help from her sister, Claudette, and her father—"

"Don't tell me," said Joseph. "Claude!"

"Well …. yes!" Alice giggled. They both tried to stifle their laughter until Claudine was inside the house.

"Let me show you the house," said Alice as she started to walk along the white and grey gravelled driveway towards the front porch. "I've always loved the crunching sound of thick gravel on a driveway," Alice said. She seemed happy and skipped along like a twelve-year-old. She must be in love, Joseph thought ruefully. He adored the way she looked so content.

"I didn't know you'd been here already, Alice. I thought this was your first visit."

"Why do you think I was so hard to find in April, darling?" Alice smiled self-consciously and glanced back at Joseph as she skipped through the large double front doors.

Alice looked as though she was getting fatter – not pregnant, but portlier. She was now wearing looser clothes, and Joseph noticed as she pranced through the front door that her slim body was gaining more curves, which Joseph found most pleasing.

They entered a wide, square hall with a sideboard adorned with a large vase of pink peonies.

"Ah, my favourite flowers," said Joseph.

"Mine too," said Alice with a small element of surprise. The hallway was bright and airy. A soft, warm breeze wafted through the house and there was a pleasant smell of flowers, sea and pine in the air.

An archway led through to a corridor, and further along, a glass door opened into a dining room.

"I'm going to get into some clean clothes, Joseph. Why don't you explore, have a drink and make yourself at home? Claudine will get anything you need if you ring the bell." Alice pointed in the direction of the dining room.

Joseph strolled through the dining room and looked out of the wide-open French windows. The views were breathtaking. The green of the coarse grass lawn contrasted with the strip of emerald-blue sea beyond and the vivid blue sky at the horizon. As he wandered out of the double glass doors onto the terrace, he could see the sandy bay which stretched out and the main town at the end of the bay. The midday sun was beating down on the sand, causing it to look almost white. The house was built on a headland fifty, maybe sixty metres above the bay, towering majestically like a medieval castle over the houses below. The panoramic views were spectacular, and Joseph felt elated. He would paint, he decided, and sit for hours looking at the view, and stroke Alice's brow, fondle her and pamper her as she went through her pregnancy.

The sun terrace ran all around the house and stopped on the western side where a garage had been recently built.

"There is a generator thing in the garage." Alice had come out to join him. She now wore a flowing deep blue silk trouser suit, the trousers resembling a long skirt. The jacket was the same deep blue silk with a large white and yellow flower print, and the silk tousled in the mild breeze. On her head she wore a headscarf of the same material, tied at the nape of her neck. Alice looked elegant, sophisticated and modern, and Joseph was delighted by what he saw. She held a glass of rosé in each hand and offered one to Joseph, which he gratefully accepted.

"Why a generator?" he asked.

"Apparently, the electricity supply has only just reached us in the last year or so and it is prone to getting cut off in the winter, so most of the houses out here have these generators. It makes a terrible din! We only get electricity at night in the summer, for some reason, but that doesn't matter – what would we need electricity for during the day other than the wireless?" She strode across the lawn to look at the view of the bay. Joseph watched her as he sipped the wine. It was cool and crisp. There must be a refrigerator somewhere, he thought, looking at the glass of wine. That would need electricity.

Alice got to the wooden fence that edged the cliff. She looked down at the bay and Val-André beyond. A set of narrow, steep steps zigzagged down the cliff face to the sand below. A reassuring metal handrail on either side followed the steps down.

"Golly, those are steep," Alice said to Joseph as he wandered over to join her.

"A nice way to get to the beach. It must get covered at high tide, though." Joseph started down the steps. "Quite narrow ... we could go down hand in hand if you like, if you feel unsafe." Joseph held out his hand. Alice smiled at him but said nothing and started to wander back to the house. Joseph looked at the steps and decided he would explore later. He ambled back to the house and joined Alice on the terrace.

"Come upstairs with me," Alice said, putting her wine down on the terrace table, a slab of grey slate balanced on two large oblong blocks of granite.

"Isn't that how all this started?" Joseph said, both hands gesturing towards her belly. Alice looked at her bump and started to giggle. But he was not making a joke. When she saw his expression was serious, she froze and looked worried.

"No, I mean, come and see the rest of the house. Your trunk has already arrived and is in your bedroom." He noted how she emphasised *your* bedroom so there were no misunderstandings.

Joseph wanted to sleep with Alice again, but as she was adamant they would not marry, he wondered if this meant no coitus. He longed to make love to her. But due to his ignorance about life, he thought a man could not make love while a woman was pregnant.

The bedrooms, all six of them, each had their own small bathroom, something Joseph had never seen before, or even heard of. Not even in the smartest hotels did each bedroom have its own bathroom. All but two rooms had wonderful views – the rooms that overlooked the front drive had views of the high wall and the pine trees inland. However, these two rooms had beautifully painted murals of the bay covering the entire wall as though the walls were made of glass and you could see the view.

Joseph sat at the dressing table in his assigned room that looked out to the ocean. He was mesmerised by the beauty of the sea. His room was large with a low ceiling, the walls white with a hint of blue making the room bright, cool and airy, the large windows flooding the room with light. The paintings were boring English watercolours of the Sussex countryside.

There was a knock at the door.

"*Entrez*," he said warily. Claudine appeared with his suitcase. Joseph leapt up to help her – it was obviously very heavy.

"Non, non, monsieur, *je vais bien*." She struggled over to the ottoman at the end of the bed and heaved the rather tatty leather case onto it. She gave a little curtsey and raced out the door.

Joseph looked at the case, then at the trunk underneath the window. He had no idea what was in it. Alice had insisted on buying him a wardrobe of clothes. She had taken some measurements while they were still in Paris and, along with Monsieur Ducheyne, bought him a selection of new outfits to suit the beach, walking and the odd evening meal. Joseph was not at all happy about this. He felt like some kind of gigolo, a kept man, even a servant ... and this was his livery!

Joseph changed into some of his more familiar clothes and went down to lunch in the sunroom. On the table were cheese and bread, dressed lettuce and some grapes, and more rosé.

"Alice?" He looked at her over the table, trying to gather the words he wanted to say. "I don't think this is going to work."

"What is not going to work?" Alice was alarmed. "It's going to be just as we imagined – a long holiday, two friends together having a lovely time."

"Us ... together ... here, being chaperoned by Claudette?"

"Claudine," she corrected.

"Claudine." He sighed and carried on. "Anyway, I don't think it's possible for me to stay. It's an extraordinary situation. I have no idea what people will say..."

"What people, Joseph?" Alice looked concerned. "We are stuck up here on top of a cliff. The nearest neighbour is a Swiss banker and his wife." She leant closer to Joseph, a conspiratorial hand to the side of her mouth. "So he says, but she is more than likely his mistress. And they are a hundred metres away, the other side of a high wall and a wood. There is no one we know for many kilometres. We'll have a lovely holiday."

"What are we going to do all this time? I mean, you are going to get bigger and bigger. I'll be bored out of my skull—"

"Joseph, darling, you must look after me. I need someone to talk to. I cannot talk to Claudine, now, can I? I thought you would love this. You can paint, go on long walks, listen to music. We can go to Kérouf's for dinner now and then; he's a wonderful chef!"

"It's not that. It's us, Alice, you and I – well, mainly me with you – together ... but not together."

"Joseph, I thought we discussed this on the way down."

"I was more concerned about your driving, actually, and the noise meant we could hardly have a real discussion."

"I thought I drove rather well," said Alice, pretending to be hurt.

"It was good driving." Joseph was beginning to concede; a little smile came over his face, his misgivings beginning to thaw.

"Joseph, just give it a while. Stella is coming down in November, when the baby will hopefully be born, to take over from you."

"Stella? Why have you told her?"

"I had to, and Mama—"

"And your mother? Christ, Alice, it's getting worse. Do they know I am the father?"

"No, of course they don't know who the father is. I don't think they have a clue, either."

There was a lull in the conversation. Both were deep in thought. Joseph was still unsure about the situation. Why had she not told her family about him being the father?

"But your brother has been looking into my background, you said."

"Did I?" Alice didn't sound surprised enough, and Joseph felt angry at her deceitfulness.

"Yes, you said, when you came to my apartment ages ago, that Sir Jason was looking into my parents. He was worried about the collection. Or was it because you told him I was the father?"

"Oh, that. He wanted to know more about you because I had *showed* you the collection."

"Why did that worry him?"

"Because he always worries about who sees the collection. It is just his way," Alice said airily.

"Well, I think it is a little intrusive. I don't like to think that my parents have been brought into this."

Alice and Joseph finished their lunch in silence. Joseph said he was going to wander down the cliff steps and walk across the sandy bay to the town. Alice said she would rest.

"Whilst you are in the town, buy a crab or a lobster from the fishmonger – he's a super fishmonger. We will have it for supper. Claudine is a wonderful cook."

"How will I find the fishmonger?"

"All the shops are in one row. You can get everything there. There is a nice little bar at the end of the row of shops. You should try a Calvados."

*

Joseph set off. He put on a large straw hat he found in the downstairs cloakroom, picked up a shopping bag and made his way down the meandering steps, down the cliff to the sandy beach. The six flights of steps were not too steep, so it wouldn't be too tiring on the way back up, and there was a good handrail to help heave himself up.

The bottom few steps were carved out of the outcrop of rock and led onto powder-like sand. The tide line seemed to finish just where the steps terminated, so Joseph presumed the steps were always accessible.

He walked up the beach, over an area of large pebbles and onto a wide tarmacked promenade that stretched for about a kilometre, all along the bay to the main town of Val-André. It was very hot, the sun making his exposed skin tingle. He thought he should put some oil on to prevent sunburn.

*

Joseph bought a large live spider crab which the fishmonger assured him was a rare delicacy. He then found the little bar at the end of the row of shops. The entrance to the bar didn't have any tables and chairs outside, unusually, which did not make it very enticing for Joseph. He liked to sit and watch people go by, but then again there were not many people about on the high street.

"Would you care for a drink, monsieur?" A waiter hurried out of the bar when he saw Joseph hovering.

"There are no tables outside," Joseph pointed out.

"Through here, monsieur."

The waiter took Joseph through the long room, past dark walls covered with posters advertising drinks, and empty round metal tables and white wicker chairs. The long bar was bustling and waiters scurried about with trays of drinks and coffee. The waiter led him out onto a wide terrace half-covered by a white and yellow striped awning, overlooking the beach and the sea. In among lots of very busy tables stood a tiny round table with a single empty chair. Some people were in beach clothes, some in light day clothes, drinking, chatting and watching others on the beach or the promenade.

This was what Joseph wanted. He ordered a Calvados, a black coffee and a cigar. He put the canvas bag with the spider crab down on the table. The live crab started moving around in protest at being cooped up and started to crawl out of the bag. The waiter, seeing the crab's bid for freedom, offered to take the bag and put it somewhere out of the way, and promised not to let Monsieur go home without it.

Joseph sat back in the wicker chair, smoked his cigar and sipped his Calvados. There was a slight south-westerly breeze which could not be more ideal in the hot sun. He watched people enjoying themselves, on the beach, in the sea or just sauntering along the promenade, not going anywhere in particular. He observed the hustle and bustle of the waiters, their seamless efficiency, silver trays held high, sashaying between the tables like rumba dancers, ensuring customers had everything they desired. Bowls of winkles were being served and Joseph ordered a bowl for himself. He spent a pleasant thirty minutes prising out the tiny black curls of meat with a pin and spitting out the little shell-caps. They tasted of the sea and summer holidays … it was bliss.

Perhaps it wasn't going to be too bad after all, thought Joseph. He could escape to this bar if he got bored or fed up, and watch everyone enjoying themselves. He might even meet a girl or a lonely rich widow! Alice wanted him as some kind of lapdog, a companion, like those strange spinsters who kept rich old widows' company. He was certainly not going to be one of those – he wasn't a spinster, anyway.

Joseph sat in the sun in the busy bar for two hours, drinking coffee and Calvados. He consumed another bowl of winkles and smoked a cigar. He eventually staggered to his feet, paid the waiter and left a large tip, and started back to the house.

"Monsieur!" The waiter chased after him with the canvas bag containing the spider crab. Joseph saluted him. He was a little drunk, and very content.

*

The days settled into a routine for the rest of the summer. After lunch, Joseph would go into town and play boules with anybody who would play a few sets with him. He would then have coffee and Calvados at the bar with whoever was there at the time. Friendships were short-lived; holidays were usually a family affair, and nobody had time to drink and chat all afternoon. The weather was glorious and hot for nearly six weeks. He would stroll back at about seven o'clock in the evening, in various stages of drunkenness depending on who he met up with at the bar.

On Sunday, he would stay at the house with Alice. She insisted he should be nearby for at least one day. The bars were closed in any case. He would read or paint.

As time went on, Joseph tried to avoid talking to Alice, for she was getting more and more uncomfortable with the pregnancy and would rather sit in the shade reading or lying down with a flannel over her forehead, with Claudine or Claudette running back and forth with cold drinks. If the girls were not available, Joseph ended up running around for her.

"Alice, what happened to our lovely holiday?" Joseph asked as he brought her a glass of water and a magazine as she lay out on a steamer chair. "'We will go to the restaurant,' you said, 'go on lovely walks.' You haven't moved from the house since we got here."

"Well, you go off each day to—"

"You could come too!"

"I can't do those steps." Alice sounded petulant.

"We could drive to the town, Alice. I don't want to be stuck here all the time."

"I am sorry, Joseph, but I would rather stay here. It's lovely here. Look at that view and … well …"

Joseph stood and glared at her. She was not being at all reasonable. He would have liked her to be more loving. She looked guiltily up at him. "I will come with you to the beach next week, I promise."

Joseph was not sure that he wanted her to join him at the bar. She would probably complain about the uncomfortable seats or that it was too crowded. What happened to the girl in the shed back in Paris? Why couldn't she be like her and not this selfish, self-centred girl who treated him like some kind of skivvy?

*

Joseph's daily routine was marginally changed when he met a girl called Caroline, an English girl who was a nanny to two young French girls. She was very pretty, with bobbed sandy hair, white eyebrows and large grey-green eyes set wide in a heart-shaped face, which exaggerated her cherubic lips.

Her body, in the short wool jersey swimsuit with the fashionable deep V-neck, intrigued Joseph. It was shapely, voluptuous, and her skin was milk-white with the odd freckle and tinges of rose red where the sun had caught some unoiled skin.

Every day, late morning, she would swim with the sisters with her mistress looking on. The girls' mother could not be more than twenty, and her husband – who accompanied them once – was twice his wife's age; a balding man who sat on a beach chair and leered at the nanny as she swam with the little girls in the shallows of the sea, just below where Joseph sat at the bar.

Joseph decided to take a swimming costume and paddle in the sea at about the same time as the nanny and her charges came down to the beach. He ensured he was close enough to be able to talk to the nanny if the opportunity arose – which it did, the second day he paddled. One of the little girls pitched a ball wildly and it went out to sea, to be carried even further by the slightly gusty offshore wind.

"Let me get it," Joseph said gallantly and whisked off his white shirt, kicked off his espadrilles and swam out to get the small red ball bobbing on the waves.

"No, no, monsieur, we have many other balls," the nanny protested in French with a heavy English accent.

Too late; the ball was retrieved. The nanny was most grateful.

"Everything all right, Caroline?" The mother, on seeing the nanny talking to a stranger, rushed up to the water's edge to ensure there was nothing "going on".

"My apologies, madame," Joseph called to the mother rather than the nanny, "but I could not see your daughters be without a ball to play with. My name is Joseph Deller. I have Alston House at the top there." Joseph pointed to the magnificent house perched on top of the headland.

"You are very kind, Monsieur Deller." She smiled briefly and turned to walk back to her beach chair, secure in the knowledge that Deller was more than likely a gentleman.

"Thank you, monsieur," the nanny said, smiling. "What do we say to Monsieur Deller, girls?"

"Thank you, Monsieur Deller," the sisters chorused and went on to play with the ball.

"What are their names?" Joseph asked, walking closely to the nanny as she followed the children.

"Madeleine and Cerise," said the nanny, "and my name is Appleby, Caroline Appleby."

"You are lucky to have such nice children, Caroline."

"Oh, they are not mine. They belong to Monsieur and Madame de Gere. We are on holiday and I just look after the girls."

"Well then," Joseph said excitedly, "when you are free next, come for a drink at the little bar up there."

"I couldn't possibly, sir. But thank you." She giggled, somewhat flushed, and gave a shy smile which was very becoming. Deller was intrigued.

"Come on. Just a drink at the bar, up there, this evening?"

Caroline was silent for an awkward thirty seconds. She looked at Joseph, then in the direction of the bar, then back at Joseph. "I will have to get back to the family by eight this evening."

Joseph's heart thumped in excitement. "Six o'clock at the bar, then?"

"Lovely. See you then."

She went off with the little girls, looked back and gave a little wave, and then quickly looked up the beach to make sure her employer did not see her indiscretion.

After the encounter with Caroline, he went back to the bar and stayed there for the rest of the afternoon. He waited for Caroline to arrive at six.

At six on the dot, Caroline appeared at Joseph's table. Joseph nearly did not recognise her. He had been watching the approaching pretty girl in a light cotton floral dress and a broad-brimmed straw hat, not realising it was Caroline. He regretted having too many beers and not enough coffees at the bar; he was feeling quite tired.

"You are here, Caroline," Joseph said delightedly. He rose from his chair and wobbled a bit. Caroline's smile changed to concern. Joseph quickly said, "Had a bit of an afternoon snooze. Just woke up."

"I see."

Joseph came around the table and pulled out a chair for her. He watched her cross her long legs and went back to his seat. A waiter appeared at their side.

"What would you like to drink, my dear?" Joseph asked.

Caroline thought for a moment. "May I have a glass of rosé? I have only just discovered rosé."

"*Une carafe de rosé*, Sami, *s'il vous plaît*."

"*Bien sûr*, monsieur Joseph."

"They know you quite well here, 'monsieur Joseph'," Caroline said with a smile. "Have you been coming to Val-André for many years?"

"No, this is my first time." Quickly realising his mistake, he added, "this year." Caroline kept looking at him in a slightly sceptical way. "How long have you been coming to Val-André with the family?" He offered Caroline a cigarette from a tatty packet of Gitanes.

"No, thanks," she said with a little shake of her head. "This is the first time I've been to France. It's so lovely." She looked out towards the bay and the calm sea. "I am trying to improve my French, so we should really be talking in it." She looked back at Joseph. "You speak French very well. Or do you speak English very well?"

"I am Austrian. I hope I speak French and English well."

"My word." She was impressed, which pleased Joseph. He wondered how far he could go with this girl as he watched her looking out towards the sea and then at Alston House.

"That looks a lovely house, your house. Have you had it for long?"

"No, not really." Joseph settled back in his chair, trying to look sophisticated. He enjoyed impressing Caroline. She was pretty, innocent – an English rose – and a good candidate for a conquest.

The waiter arrived and quickly and efficiently poured the pink wine into two glasses. He bowed slightly at Joseph and offered a slight wink as Joseph met his eyes.

"Do you live with anyone else there?" Caroline asked.

She is fishing, thought Joseph, wondering if I am married. He paused for a moment as he considered what would be the best lie to offer.

"Only the servants. Why?"

"I would love to go up there, see the view from the lawn."

Joseph sat up. He realised this was not going to end the way he had hoped. "I'm sorry, I would love to show you but we … I am having work done on the house. It is not really habitable."

Caroline giggled. "You don't really live there, do you?"

"Well, of course I do. Why would I lie about that?"

"Oh, I don't know. To impress me, maybe?" She took a sip of wine, still looking at Joseph over the rim. She enjoyed teasing him, he realised. Joseph laughed.

"Where are you and the family staying, Caroline?"

"At the Hôtel Val-André. It's very nice, lovely French food."

"Do you like French food?"

"It can be a little rich and garlicky sometimes. They use odd ingredients like olive oil and a lot of funny-looking fish." She leant forward and put her hand under her chin. "I had flowers in my salad last night, yellow nasturtiums, I think." She took a sip of her wine. "What do you think?" she asked, her pretty eyes wide, waiting for Joseph to comment. Joseph leant forward towards her, an elbow on the table, a glass of rosé in his hand. He saluted Caroline with his glass and swallowed half the contents. He gazed into her eyes.

"We must do this every evening, Caroline," he said dreamily.

"I would love to." Joseph sat up with an expression of glee on his face. "But we return to Paris tomorrow."

Joseph was so disappointed. He looked around for a waiter. "Sami!" he shouted. The waiter scurried over.

"Oui, monsieur Joseph?"

"Where can we go dancing around here?" Joseph asked.

"Rennes, monsieur. Le Club de L'Ours Rouge. *Fabuleux.*"

"I can't go dancing, Joseph, I must get back." He was bitterly disappointed. "I'm sorry. But this was a lovely drink. Thank you."

"Rennes is not far away," Joseph protested as Caroline stood. She offered her hand for him to shake. He grabbed it and kissed it. Caroline blushed and giggled nervously.

"Thank you, Joseph, for the drink." She picked up her handbag, thanked the waiter, and left the table. Joseph and Sami both watched as she wandered off along the promenade towards the hotel. She suddenly turned, waved and blew a kiss, and then carried on towards Hôtel Val-André.

"*Très jeune et jolie*, monsieur."

"Yes, Sami, very young and pretty. Possibly too young and … anyway …" Joseph sighed and drank the rest of the wine. How he would have liked to have made love to Caroline. She was, excitingly, not as innocent as he first perceived her.

*

Joseph finally staggered back to the steep steps up to Alston House as the evening sun was beginning to set to the west. He had to stop more than once on his way up.

As he got to the top, he saw the bulbous form of Alice with one hand in the small of her back and the other draped over her pregnant dome.

"You missed supper, or should I say, you forgot."

"Oh … I am very sorry. That is quite a climb!"

"You do it every day, Joseph," she chided, and then announced, "Your friend, Ferdi Saumures, is here. He has been here all day, painting, and he has brought some letters."

Alice turned on her heels and walked away briskly. Too late, Joseph called after her.

"Ferdi? Here? Why on earth has Ferdi turned up here? And what letters?"

8

Baron Ferdi Saumures strolled out of the sitting room onto the lawn and wandered over to Joseph, who was on his way back to the house. Ferdi, tall, dark and handsome, looked like a *matinée* idol; his hands casually in the pockets of his loose cream linen trousers, black espadrilles on his feet, a white linen shirt open at the neck, and a sky-blue cashmere jumper loosely tied by the sleeves about his shoulders, dangling over his back like a little cape.

"Ferdi, this is a great surprise," Joseph said breathlessly. He tried to look hospitable, but he was wondering why Ferdi was here, so his welcome was slightly stiff.

"You're out of shape, my dear Joseph." Ferdi had a smug grin on his face, a cigarette in a short ivory holder between his teeth. "I have some letters for you that arrived at the apartment and they looked important. As I fancied a little holiday, and knowing you were here—"

"How did you know we were here?"

"Alice gave me the address and an open invitation."

"Did she now? I thought this was meant to be a great secret. Where are these letters?"

"The letters are inside on the hall table. I'm sorry if this is an inconvenient time for me to arrive. You don't have a phone and I had difficulty in getting a telegram to you, for some reason."

Joseph slightly regretted the less than enthusiastic greeting he had given his friend. If he was picked up on it later, Joseph would put it down to his climb up from the beach.

"Oh Ferdi, it's lovely to see you. You're the first visitor we've had in nearly two months. Come in, have a drink."

"I've had a couple already and some lovely turbot. We didn't wait for you."

They walked onto the terrace. The evening was setting in and still warm, a light breeze and a tomato-red sun sinking slowly towards the horizon. Alice was sitting beside the table on the terrace on a teak steamer chair, cushions stuffed all around her, reading a magazine and taking in the last of the sun. She and Ferdi must have eaten at the terrace table as the remains of the turbot and salad were still there.

"Joseph, darling, have some supper." She spoke to him as though they were a married couple. "Claudine will want to clear soon."

"I'm just going to get the letters Ferdi has brought down from Paris ... *darling*." Joseph said.

The letters were all from Germany and marked with the national socialist emblem on the top left-hand corner: a spreadeagle on a round laurel wreath with a swastika in the centre.

"They are from my parents. They are in this new political movement called the National Socialist Party, which has just got a new leader, Adolf Hitler. Look, they have made me a member of the Nazi Party and sent me a membership badge!"

"How nice," Alice said lazily and not really listening.

"They want me to go back to Germany to help them."

Alice sat up and looked angrily at Joseph.

"When are you going?"

"I don't know – we will have to discuss it. But not right now." Joseph gestured towards Ferdi who was looking in the other direction, his attention clearly elsewhere.

"So, Ferdi, how is the painting going?" Joseph asked, trying to veer away from the subject of his impending departure.

"Very well. I will have to do you. I have sketched Alice. Look." Ferdi produced a large pad of thick white sheets of drawing paper and turned over a few sheets of landscapes to reveal an impressive portrait of Alice in delicate pastels.

"You must have been here ages," Joseph marvelled.

"This took a couple of hours. But I must have one of you, Joseph."

"Oh, OK. Now?"

"Tomorrow morning, Ferdi," Alice chimed in, her voice sounding tense. "I just need to talk to Joseph, if you don't mind, about his plans. Joseph, will you come with me, please?"

She pulled herself up with the help of the edge of the heavy garden table, causing the cushions to fall onto the terrace. She strode off to the edge of the lawn and looked over the fence out to sea and the descending sun. Joseph followed meekly behind.

"Can you wait for the baby, at least, Joseph, or until Stella arrives?" She sounded a little more pleasant. "I'm sorry. Being heavily pregnant can get one very crotchety."

"'Crotchety'? What is 'crotchety'? Something to do with music?"

"I forget you are German."

"Austrian," he corrected tersely.

"Austrian … It just means a little irritable. I think it is 'grincheux' in French. Anyway, will you wait until the baby comes? Surely you want to see it when it is born; it is yours, after all."

"Probably …" Joseph was about to say something hurtful but saw Alice's expression fall and changed his mind. "He is, but he will not be in name. I will not be bringing him up; you won't marry me. I am just some kind of … prostitute!"

Alice laughed. He was about to really lose his temper.

"I'm sorry, darling," she said as she gently caressed his upper arm. "I'm not being reasonable. We had discussed this … you had agreed. I need this baby so that I can leave the Paris house – a property I own – to someone and not to my husband."

Joseph hung his head. He was still slightly drunk from the afternoon's debauchery at the bar. "Yes, yes, yes, all right," he conceded. He wanted to argue but the drink had sapped all his energy.

"All right, what?"

"All right, I will stay to see him born."

"He may be a 'she'."

"He'd bloody well better be a boy, after all this trouble." He drew away from her and took her face into his hands, at which she seemed somewhat surprised. "But, *darling*," he whispered, "you are going to have to understand me better. I am not your husband, so I do not want to be treated like one. I want to be treated like your lover – like you used to treat me." He kissed her and then withdrew, sensing she would have liked to have carried on. She stepped back slightly, looking both pleased and concerned. Joseph gazed into her eyes, satisfied he had moved something – very slightly – deep inside her emotions.

He strode back over the lawn to the house, and went to the outside table to help himself to some tomato and shallot salad. He slid a tranche of cold turbot off the bone onto his plate, ladled lots of béarnaise sauce over the top and broke off a bit of baguette. He sat down in the steamer chair and attacked the meal with a fork.

"We should put nasturtium flowers on the salad," Joseph said, slightly to himself. His mind returned to his encounter with Caroline. He really wished he had met her earlier. They could have had a bit of a fling.

Ferdi sat beside Joseph on a deckchair.

"So, Ferdi," Joseph said in between mouthfuls, "how is Paris?"

"Great, thanks. I've been made a curator of a new gallery in the l'Opéra district. It's called Galerie Bayser, owned by Pierre and Rose Bayser."

"Really?" Joseph said, disinterested. "I'm very happy for you. Any women in your life? You have always been popular with that strange accent and being a rich baron."

"No, no ladies in my life. Just my art."

"Ferdi, come and watch the sunset," Alice said as she walked back slowly from the edge of the lawn. "It can be absolutely wonderful. I want to hear more of your news." She took his hand and then looked at Joseph. "Would you like to come too, Joseph?" She said this as a loving partner: kindly, gently, without sarcasm.

Joseph stopped eating just as a chunk of bread was about to enter his mouth; he noted the pleasant tone. "In a minute, Alice," he said quietly. "I'll just finish this and call Claudine."

"Lovely," she said with a glint in her eye and a slight smile, something Joseph had not really seen since their first meetings in the garden shed. His heart skipped a little.

Joseph watched Ferdi and Alice stroll hand in hand slowly across the lawn, chatting. He was not sure why he hadn't ever considered Ferdi a threat. Perhaps he was not Alice's sort, somehow.

*

Joseph opened the letter from his father. It was two months old.

Sehr geehrter Franz-Joseph,

By the time you receive this letter we will be in Berlin, helping our new Führer, Adolf Hitler, with his campaign for the Nazi Party. We would like to use your undoubted talents with languages to help us with the foreign affairs.

Your English will be especially useful. We, the Party, also have a project for you to help with, selecting paintings for official buildings. We know you have a good artistic knowledge.

I appreciate we have not seen eye to eye about certain aspects of our politics, and the possible annexation of Austria, but this new party has many ideas to get us out of this particularly desperate financial depression. You will enjoy the huge amount of young people joining the Party and the extraordinary support we have for Herr Hitler, who has only just been released from prison after serving nine months for his political beliefs.

Herr Hitler's rallying speeches are wonderful and should be heard more often. He explains the "big lie" that has been told to Germans all these years. You will understand our enthusiasm for this new German Reich, and how we must root out these old, indifferent leaders and the lying Jews.

I trust this letter finds you. We would like to see you as soon as you can. We will be with your aunt and uncle in Berlin, at Bülowplatz.

Yours affectionately, your father,
Werner Deller

Joseph looked at the letter in astonishment. He flipped it over to see if there was anything else on the back. It was blank. He never thought he would get such a letter from his father. His shoulders dropped. He looked up, as though in prayer.

Oh God, must I go and see them? Joseph thought. He hated the Germans; they were so serious. Why did they have this thing about the Jews? They were an asset, he'd always thought. He would never have got the money to get to Paris if it was not for the local pawnbroker, who was a Jew.

Joseph folded the letter and thought about his dysfunctional Austrian parents. They had never been close to their son, their only child. They only wanted him to help with their English. But, then again, if all went wrong here with Alice, he would always have a place to go. He could become a soldier or something. He even had thoughts of being a clergyman in the army. He needed to stay close to Alice, though, but that seemed to be going wrong.

Joseph rubbed his temples. He had a headache from thinking about too many things at the same time.

*

"Ferdi?" Joseph sat down beside his old flatmate, out on the veranda in the evening heat. Alice had gone to bed. "What do you think of the Nazis in Germany?"

"Why do you ask, Joseph? You are Austrian; what do *you* think?" Ferdi sat up and eyed Joseph seriously.

Joseph looked slightly surprised. "Well, my parents want me to help them with the Party and I am curious about what they are up to. They are looking after the leader, Adolf Hitler. A fellow Austrian, apparently. They may have a job for me."

"As it happens, I may be able to help you." Ferdi drew closer to Joseph. The sun was nearly completely down. Light filtered from the dining room onto the terrace.

"In what way?" Joseph looked at Ferdi with some uncertainty.

Ferdi cast his eyes down to the stone slabs of the terrace for a few moments, thinking of what to say and trying to work out how much he should tell Joseph about Sir Sussex Tremayne's offer.

"Joseph, if you join your parents, and the Nazi Party, do you think that is what you would like to do?"

Joseph seemed a little surprised. "I really don't know. These Nazis, as far as I can see, want to rule Germany *and* Austria. They want to get rid of Jews, communists … although I suppose getting rid of communists is no bad thing. And they seem to be taking over quite rapidly, as far as I read in the papers. I have not really taken an interest lately – not since I have been holed up here, with Alice."

Ferdi thought some more. "What did your father's letter say?" He knew exactly what was in the letter, as he had steamed it open before bringing it down here for Joseph.

"Well …" Joseph looked again at Ferdi with some suspicion, but his interest seemed piqued. He took a large mouthful of brandy and carried on. "They want me to join the Party to help with various projects. I don't quite know what it will entail, but it's a job."

"What would you say if you found you did not agree with their politics … if it is not to your taste?"

"Ferdi, why are you asking these strange questions?"

There was a pause. The men looked at one another, each frowning in concentration.

"Joseph, a friend of mine in the British government wants to get someone on the inside of the Nazi Party."

"Like my parents?"

"Precisely. But I wondered how you would feel about sending me the odd report about what you have heard?"

"What?!" Joseph jinked back from Ferdi as though avoiding a punch. "You mean like a spy?"

"Well …" Ferdi hesitated. What should he say? Joseph was drunk, and Ferdi thought that if Joseph reacted badly, he could always deny he had said anything and, the following morning, make out he was talking about something else. "A kind of spy, I suppose."

"But who am I spying for? I didn't know Luxembourg had a secret service."

"For the British government. What do you think?"

Joseph drained the glass of brandy and stared up at the night sky. He wobbled a bit, then quickly looked down and pressed his fore and middle fingers against his temple, his eyes firmly closed.

"Are you OK, Joseph?"

"Bit of a headache from the wine, I think." He sat down again and looked seriously at Ferdi. He then spluttered a loud laugh, "Me – a spy!" He chortled. Ferdi, appalled by Joseph's reaction, desperately waved at him to keep quiet. He looked up at Alice's bedroom window. Still spluttering in amusement, Joseph put his forefinger to his lips. Ferdi wondered if he should have tried this at a better time, when Joseph was fully sober.

"Joseph, I will talk to you tomorrow about this, when you are less … weary."

Joseph tried to look serious. "Good idea. I have to go to bed anyway … lots to do tomorrow. Could you close up, Ferdi?" Joseph wandered back into the house. Ferdi wondered what the "lots to do" would be.

Now Ferdi was worried Joseph was going to talk to Alice about being a spy. He would have to get to him in the morning before he saw Alice. But by then, Ferdi thought, Joseph may have completely forgotten about it.

9

Joseph stirred the next morning at around ten thirty with his sheets tangled in his legs. He angrily kicked the sheets away and then regretted his exertions. His head felt like it had a cannonball inside it, and each time he moved, the ball would thump against the inside of his skull. He remembered the French had a phrase for what he felt, *une gueule de bois* – a wooden mouth. His mouth was dry and his tongue was like sandpaper. He saw that there was still some brandy in the balloon glass on the bedside table, which he drank down, hoping for some reduction in the cannonball's rolling. He had got quite used to the morning after the night before; however, this was a bad one.

He was wearing just his pants, vest and one sock. He got up and put on a white robe. He thumped on the floor with his foot, went to the door, held his hands to the side of his head and shouted.

"Claudine, *café, s'il vous plaît!*"

He fell back onto his bed and lay still until his headache went away.

There was a knock on the door. Joseph sat up, waited for the ball in his head to settle, drew the robe across his chest and legs, and croaked, *"Entrez."*

To his surprise, Ferdi appeared with a tray of coffee and a little bottle of aspirin. "Ferdi! Where did you appear from? Oh yes," – Joseph remembered – "you arrived yesterday. Thanks for the coffee."

Ferdi placed the tray on the side table, shoving an empty brandy glass to one side. He poured a coffee for Joseph and himself and sat at the dressing table, looking out towards the morning scene. There was a light cover of white cloud, turning the sea into a light grey, as opposed to a lovely dark blue. The sun was struggling to come out, but it was still quite warm.

"I just wondered, Joseph, if you had any thoughts about what I said to you last night?" Joseph looked over the top of his coffee cup as he took a large, welcoming mouthful. His brow furrowed. "About your parents?" Ferdi prompted.

Joseph, still confused, swung his legs over the side of the bed and poured another coffee, and took a couple of pills from the bottle. "My parents?" he said, trying to jog some kind of memory. "I got a letter from my father and it said—" He jerked his head up in remembrance, looked at Ferdi and said, in a hushed voice, "Did I dream it, or did you want me to be a spy?"

"You did not dream it, Joseph, and it is not so much being a spy, but just getting us ... me ... information about this man, Hitler."

"Ah ... yes." Joseph looked blankly at Ferdi, still trying to remember what had been said last night. "What will I have to do?"

"Well ... you will need to join the Nazi Party and help your parents and send any relevant information back to me."

"What kind of information? I don't think I am going to be much use. I don't know this man, Hitler."

"But your parents do. They work very closely with him."

"Do they?" Joseph was astonished. "How do you know that?"

"I just do. Listen, Joseph, I need to get some kind of commitment from you. I thought I would draw your portrait after lunch whilst Alice has her rest and talk to you more about it. Is that OK?"

"What day is it?"

"Sunday," Ferdi said curiously.

"That will be fine. Good idea."

"I will leave you to get up." With that, Ferdi left the room.

*

Lunch was long and amicable. It was nice to have Ferdi there, thought Alice. It made Sunday lunch so much more enjoyable and formal. They had lunch in the dining room as the sun had still refused to emerge from behind the thin white cloud.

Claudine had produced a magnificent rolled ballotine of chicken and mushrooms, with a lettuce and tomato salad and a Far Breton prune cake – something Claudine made constantly for Joseph and Alice. Alice loved Far Breton. It was the taste of Val-André and finished off the lunch deliciously. Everybody felt very happy and peaceful, especially Alice. She had been worried about Joseph. She loved his company – when he was with her, that was; something that became rarer as the pregnancy went on. Since Ferdi arrived,

Joseph seemed slightly more gregarious and more attentive to her. She, in turn, rewarded him with kisses, stroking him when he came close. He seemed to have less to drink when she gave him her attention, which she wished she had discovered earlier in her confinement.

*

When Alice went to bed for her rest, kissing Ferdi on the cheek and Joseph on the lips, Joseph and Ferdi sat opposite each other in the sitting room, with cups of coffee and a small glass of sweet Bénédictine liqueur. Ferdi had a large pad of sketching paper and was drawing an outline of Joseph on the thick cream-coloured paper.

"What do you think of my proposal? It would mean leaving here as soon as the baby has been born."

"But it will be a job, and I need a job."

"I don't know if we can pay you anything. I suppose we could, but not a lot. I will have to ask someone about that."

"I think I need to go now, Ferdi."

Ferdi looked up from the sketch pad, worried.

"Why?"

"I feel Alice is tricking me. I am falling in love with her again."

"You are not going to desert her?"

"She doesn't really want me, Ferdi. She just needed me as some kind of … nursemaid."

"What do you mean?" Ferdi sat back in the armchair and continued to sketch Joseph as they talked.

"She just wanted me to impregnate her so she would have a pet baby!" Joseph spoke loudly, hoping she would hear him in her bedroom above.

"I'm sure that's not the case. She likes you very much, Joseph."

"Does she?" Joseph looked up at the ceiling, above which Alice slept. "How much will she like me when the child is born, I wonder? Especially when I tell her it's not …"

"Not what?"

"Never mind." Joseph looked up at the ceiling sadly.

"If you do choose to leave Alice, please come and see me before you make any plans."

"What, come to you in Paris, you mean?"

"Here is my card for the gallery where I work now."

"You have a job for me at the gallery? I don't want to be a—"

"No, not at the gallery; in Germany. But you must stay here for the next two months, until November at least, for Alice."

Joseph thought for a long time. He sat still and Ferdi carried on with his sketch. Joseph then whispered: "A spy, eh?"

"Keep that to yourself, Joseph. Strictly between you and me," Ferdi said firmly.

"What are you going to do with Alice's sketch, and the sketch you are doing now of me?"

"I will take them back to Paris and turn them into oils. Why?"

"I would love a sketch of Alice, that's all. I deserve that at least, don't you think?"

*

October started out wet and windy. It was just like an English autumn. Alice was huge – like a beached whale, as she described herself. Ferdi had returned to Paris in mid-September after staying for nearly three weeks. He was great company and both Joseph and Alice enjoyed having him around. Joseph spent a lot more time with Alice at the house and only went to the bar a few times, with Ferdi.

But when Ferdi went back to Paris to open his new gallery, Joseph and Alice grew apart again. Alice was constantly complaining about the baby and how big she was. Any loving attention from Alice disappeared a few days after Ferdi left, and arguments about Joseph leaving continued. Consequently, Joseph spent a lot of time in the bar, drinking and playing cards with the few remaining tourists or Sami the barman.

Joseph was in the bar when a breathless Claude, the gardener, arrived and told him to phone Alice's sister in Paris and get hold of the doctor.

"But the baby is not due for another month," Joseph said, a little dismissively.

"It's arriving now, monsieur, and madame wants her sister immediately!" Claude scowled and went back to the house.

Joseph leapt up from his seat in the bar. The hasty movement made his head swim, but he went as fast as he could to the hotel and phoned Paris. He got Sir Jason Barrett on one of his rare visits to his mother. He said he would convey to Stella that Alice needed her. Joseph was unaware if Jason knew about the imminent arrival of a niece or nephew.

10

Charlotte Joy Barrett was born the day Stella arrived at Alston House. She was born at six forty-five in the evening, on the fifth of October, nearly a whole month early. Joseph and Claude were pacing up and down the front hall at the bottom of the stairs when they heard the cry of a newborn baby. Claude shook Joseph by the hand and Joseph mounted the stairs, three at a time, and knocked timidly on Alice's door when he heard silence.

"*Entrez*," said Stella. "Oh, it's you, Joseph. Alice has a daughter, you will be pleased to know." She spoke to Joseph as though he was some kind of domestic, but Joseph didn't care. He dodged past Stella and went straight over to Alice who was looking exhausted. A nurse was brushing her hair and she looked lovingly at a swaddled baby in her arms, unaware of Joseph's presence. A doctor was putting away his instruments.

"Hello," he said quietly.

Alice looked up and, in a voice close to tears, said, "She is called Charlotte." She looked deeply into Joseph's eyes. "She is the most beautiful thing I have ever seen."

Before Joseph had a chance to reply, Stella rushed everybody out the room. "Please allow Alice to rest now." Joseph was reluctant but did what he was asked. He decided to go to the bar and wet the baby's head.

*

It was five days before Joseph saw his daughter again. Alice kept her in her room, nursed her, fed her and gazed at her with awe. Each time Joseph asked to see Alice or the baby, Stella would give an excuse of her sleeping, being tired or just not wanting company. Finally, Joseph stormed into Alice's room.

"Why can I not see my daughter?"

"Because she is not your daughter. Remember our bargain?"

"So, you have finished with me, have you?" Joseph whispered angrily.

He was about to launch into a tirade when Charlotte awoke and cried loudly. Joseph went over to the cot and picked the baby up. Alice looked at him, clearly irritated, but allowed him to embrace her daughter just this once.

"Joseph, you said you wanted to leave and go back to Germany. Why don't you?"

"Because I want to see this child grow up a bit," he said, smiling at a now quieter Charlotte cooing in his arms. Alice got out of her bed and put on a robe and slippers. She took Charlotte from him, put her in the cot and shoved him out the door.

"You must go now, Joseph. I am worried about Charlotte."

"Go where? Why are you being like this? Do I mean absolutely nothing to you?"

"Go!" she shouted, angry tears forming. "Just go!"

"I will – to the bar. I'll be back later." He stormed off down the stairs and went to the safe in the small study. He opened it and took out all the cash he could find, about two thousand francs. He was going to have a huge party in the town. He put on a coat and went out into the early evening. The wind was strong and clouds scudded over the slate grey sky. White waves danced across the sea, and every now and then a wave crashed against the cliffs on the island out to sea and sent up massive spires of angry white water. Rain was on its way. Joseph walked towards the head of the steps down to the bay. He was being buffeted by the strong winds and was worried he would be blown over the cliff if he was not careful.

He heard Alice behind him, shrieking his name. He turned to see her standing at the edge of the terrace, beckoning him to come back. He was fed up with being pushed around by these Barrett women and he flapped his hand back at her, telling her to go away and leave him alone. He started down the steps. The wind was very powerful and he was grateful for the railings.

Just as he got to the first turn on the steep cliff steps, he looked up and saw Alice coming down the steps in her slippers behind him, her face distorted in rage. She was calling out to him but the wind was too loud for him to hear what she was saying. She drew up close to him.

"Only last week you said you were going to Germany, to your parents or something," she yelled over the wind, her anger evident. The wind was now mixed with rain, and her hair was becoming wet and straggly, sticking to her face like brown seaweed. She looked like a crone, a witch.

"Well, I've changed my mind. I want to see Charlotte grow up a little."

"Joseph, you promised to see me through the birth and then leave."

"Why should I? What is wrong with you? I have a perfect right to see my daughter grow—"

"That's just it, Joseph. I explained to you, over and over again; I don't want you to have *that right* and I thought you understood that. Why can't you just be a friend, and allow Charlotte and me our lives?"

"Have you not loved me at all?" Joseph screamed against the wind. "Why did you want me to be here?"

"Because I needed company and I hoped you would understand about my need for this child."

"Well, I think it is a bit unfair, actually. And anyway, the child …" His words were whipped away by a huge gust of wind.

"What did you say?" Alice shrieked.

Joseph went up to her and shouted in her ear. He could smell the scent of the baby on her clothes.

"Charlotte cannot be mine – I am infertile." Her expression was a mix of horror and confusion. "My doctor had told me when I was younger" Joseph stood back, enjoying the reaction to his revelation. Her face had lost all its beauty; her complexion was washed out and grey in the poor light, and the shadows under her eyes made her look a little scary. She was totally bemused by what he had said. Then, the realisation turned into devastation.

"How do you know? You bastard!"

"No, I think you will find Charlotte is the—"

To Joseph's horror, Alice raised her hand in which she held a large stone. She swung it at him, striking his cheekbone. Joseph slammed into the wall of the cliff. Stars swam in front of his eyes. He staggered and held onto the railing. He was astonished. This was more than he had expected. He was about to say something else to her when he saw she was about to strike him again with her left fist. He ducked and her arm swiped over the top of his head. He swung a punch at Alice's face. He had had enough. His fist missed her and crashed into the rocky cliff. Pain shot up his arm. She screamed at him and swung the stone at Joseph again. He saw it coming and ducked. The momentum of her missed attack, along with a gust of wind veering off the cliff wall, made her lose her balance. The back of her thigh hit the metal stair railing. She slipped. Joseph saw her feet fly up and he tried to catch her ankles, but she was gone. She fell fifteen metres. He heard her scream – until it came to an abrupt halt when her head hit the stair railings below, sending her body into a spin. She continued to fall headfirst, finally crashing onto the dark grey rocks below. Her head turned sharply, her neck snapped, her face now blank, white, and expressionless.

Joseph looked down to the rocks below. She lay on her chest, her legs at impossible angles and her head tilted, face to one side, contorted by her broken neck and jawbone, her wet auburn hair splayed out like an octopus over the rock. He wondered if there was any chance she would survive the fall, until he saw blood pouring out of the back of her head, over the rock and onto the sand below. He froze, his hands pressed firmly over his mouth. He had killed Alice. The Barretts and the de Tournets would never believe it to be an accident.

He thought he heard shouts from the garden above. It was now getting quite dark. He panicked. He raced down the steps to Alice's body and dragged it from the rock to the edge of the incoming tide, close to the base of the cliff. If anybody looked over the edge from the headland, they would only see a large patch of blood. Joseph hoped the darkening skies and the approaching tide would hide all the evidence. He wedged the body under a rock so that she would not float out to sea. He then walked away, taking a quick look back to make sure he had covered his tracks. When he saw Alice's lifeless grey face, his stomach squeezed into a knot. He felt terribly sick. This was a woman he was in love with, fervently but unrequitedly. This was the last time he would see her, her beautiful face now distorted; an image that he would carry in his mind for ever.

"Christ," he shouted out loud. "What have I done?" He fell to his knees, looking at Alice's body, her eyes still open, her broken jaw twisting her mouth as though she was grimacing. He burst into uncontrollable sobs. The knot in his stomach had lessened but a huge lump formed in his chest. This was a woman he wanted to be with for the rest of his life. He would have convinced her eventually, made her love him. But now, he realised, this would never happen.

He stood, feeling a huge weight on his shoulders, and started to walk up to the top of the beach, towards the path which hugged the cliff, so as not to be seen from above. He reached the pathway into town, the one he took most days to the bar. He walked in a kind of stagger, head down and arms hanging limply at his side, his left cheekbone stinging as the rain hit it, but he did not care. It was Alice who had caused the injury.

As he came to the town, he found a bench on the promenade. He sat and looked at the wild sea and the empty beach. The sand was grey; it had lost its creamy white of summer. He looked back at the cliff steps to see if he could still see Alice's body, but it was a long way off and getting darker as the storm worsened. The wind howled mournfully. No one was about, so he sat on the bench with his head back, watching the ominous dark grey clouds, the rain gently pattering on his face. He had killed his love, his reason to live. He might not ever see her child or get to know her.

Joseph had always been a religious man, but he felt that God had deserted him. God had seen Joseph, possibly, as a dishonest man. Well, he had been dishonest, a little, but he was in love. Joseph stood up from the bench and clasped his hands together, closed his eyes, cast his face to the clouds and shouted into the gusty wind: "God, forgive me! God, please forgive my dishonesty. God, receive my Alice into your loving arms."

At that moment, the rain cascaded down in a huge torrent onto his body. His clothes were instantly sopping, the raindrops whipping onto his cheeks in the wind. He felt cleansed, released.

He had over two thousand francs in his coat pocket – enough to buy a car or a first-class ticket to Paris and a few new clothes. His plan had been to have a huge party at the bar to celebrate the arrival of Alice's daughter. However, it could also be enough to escape, find another life, and try and forget.

11

The Bayser Gallery was a combination of two terraced houses between which an arch led into a picturesque courtyard, built in 1674 for the Marquis de Louvois. The windows on either side of the arch exhibited a masterpiece in each. The narrow street of Rue St Anne, between the Louvre and the Opéra, was silent when Joseph arrived. He had spent two nights in a small hotel in Saint-Germain, plucking up the courage to meet Ferdi. He had tried to find Ferdi at his old apartment in Rue de Dragon, only to be told that he had moved.

"Come in, Joseph, come in," Ferdi said. "Why are you here? Have you left Alice?"

"Alice is dead."

Ferdi stepped back and sat down heavily in a chair in the corner of the gallery reception, astonished.

"I killed her."

Ferdi looked aghast. He stood and took Joseph by the arm, drew him to a set of stairs and went up to a long landing, at the end of which was an office with frosted glass panels. He bundled Joseph into the office and sat him on a leather sofa. "What on earth happened, Joseph?"

"It was an accident. She fell down the steps to the bay. It was very windy and …"

"What about the baby?"

"She was born a couple of weeks after you left." Joseph felt weak. "They think I killed her, Ferdi, but it was an accident."

Ferdi paced the office floor. "An accident, you say. So, you did not *actually* kill her?"

"No, I couldn't! It was a terrible—"

"Only you just said to me in the gallery that you *had* killed her."

Joseph looked at Ferdi with confusion.

"I think I meant that I was responsible. What shall I do, Ferdi?"

"I don't know, Joseph, but you cannot stay in France."

"No," Joseph said. "I'd better go to Austria. Or to my parents and become a Nazi."

Ferdi continued to pace up and down. Joseph just watched him, hoping he was going to magically sort the situation out. But how could he? He wasn't a lawyer or an important politician. Joseph became downcast; misery swept back over him.

"I need a drink, Ferdi." Ferdi took no notice. Joseph sighed. "I wish I could see Charlotte grow up."

"Is she called Charlotte, your daughter?"

"Yes," Joseph said. "She is so tiny, and she will have no parents to raise her."

"Who is going to look after her?"

"Her grandmother, or her aunt, Stella, I imagine." There was a long pause. "She hit me with a stone, Ferdi," Joseph whispered, looking at his friend.

"Why, what had you done to cause her to hit you with a stone?" Ferdi looked concerned.

"I don't really know. I was on my way to the bar—"

"But you should have been with her and Charlotte."

"She didn't want me there. She wanted me to go away."

"Well, I suppose she was worried about your drinking. You have been drinking quite a lot."

"I suppose. But she drove me to it, Ferdi. I loved her, you know." Joseph bowed his head and let out a deep, tragic sigh. "What is to become of Charlotte?"

"She'll be fine." Ferdi patted Joseph on the shoulder. "I will make enquiries for you and send you news, to Germany."

"Would you, Ferdi? That would be kind." Joseph thought for a moment. "I'm going to Germany? Why am I going to Germany?" He looked up at his friend, hoping for inspiration about his future. "Will I have to become a Nazi, Ferdi? My father has made me a member anyway – look, he sent a badge." Joseph produced a small round buttonhole badge with a swastika on it.

"You don't have to become a real Nazi." Ferdi pointed at Joseph, an enthusiastic smile on his face. "Except, if you did, it would help me with the information I need."

"Of course." Joseph brightened slightly. "I could be a spy."

"Joseph, all you need to do is write to me with what you think is important. Try to become a member of Hitler's close circle, with your parents."

"I could become a soldier. Girls love a uniform. My father is a general, you know, in the army." Then Joseph remembered. "A man called Himmler has formed a kind of guard for Hitler, called the *Schutzstaffel*. I will try to join that with my father's help." Joseph stood and suddenly felt very tired. "Can I stay here, Ferdi? I don't like being on my own, in a hotel."

"Yes, you may," Ferdi said kindly. "I'll find you that drink." He seemed relieved that Joseph was going to help him in his mission to gather information about the Nazis. "I'll come and see you in Berlin. I have to go there at least three times in the next few months. We could celebrate Christmas together. I love Christmas in Germany."

Joseph's eyes welled up. He felt he did not deserve to be treated so kindly.

*

Joseph arrived at his uncle and aunt's house in Bülowplatz, Berlin, a week after Alice's death. He decided to surprise his parents and not warn them of his arrival. He rang the bell and his uncle Peter opened the door. He was stooped and had aged considerably. A large grey moustache grew over his chubby jowls, and his hair, curly and thick, was almost white. He had a large paunch. He looked at Joseph over the tops of his metal-rimmed glasses.

"What do you want?" he asked abruptly.

Joseph couldn't remember the last time he had met his uncle. "It is me, Uncle Peter. Franz-Joseph Deller."

Uncle Peter looked at him with confusion. "What are you doing here? My brother is in Munich with Clara."

"What is he doing there? I thought he and my mother were staying here."

"They were, but he is helping" – Peter waved his hand back and forth, trying to remember – "set up something with that man, Adolf Hitler. They could be anywhere. Stay there. I will get his last address." Uncle Peter closed the door.

Joseph stood as instructed on the porch step, feeling an element of alarm. What was he going to do? It was four in the afternoon; it had taken him nearly a day and a half to get to his uncle and aunt's house. Joseph put his hands in his pockets to keep warm. He felt the Nazi membership badge in his pocket. He pulled it out and fixed it to his left lapel in the hope it might be helpful to be seen to be a Nazi member.

A few uncomfortable minutes passed. Joseph's uncle had not returned.

After five minutes he was ready to knock on the door. He was getting cold and it felt like it was about to rain. The door suddenly opened and a small woman of about fifty stood looking at Joseph with a wide smile.

"Franz-Joseph, I am your aunt Hertha. Come in!" she said, beckoning him in. Joseph picked up his suitcase and walked into a narrow, dark hallway. "Your uncle is not at his best at the moment. He suffers from …" She stopped and looked embarrassed. "He is not well. It's all this politics and the high taxes …" She stopped again. "Put your case there and hang up your coat here." She pointed at the hallstand and once Joseph had hung up his coat, she grabbed his hand and took him through to a kitchen at the end of the hall.

"Come and sit," she said kindly. "I will make coffee. Peter is trying to find out where your parents are, I think."

"Thank you, Aunt Hertha." Joseph spoke for the first time. He could not remember when he had last seen his aunt. She looked so kind. She had a gentle, generous smile, and her white-grey hair was drawn into a tight bun at the back of her head. Joseph remembered her having bright red hair.

The portly figure of Uncle Peter came into the kitchen. He was looking at a sheet of paper. When he saw Joseph, he stopped abruptly. "Oh. You have come in." He sounded disappointed.

"Of course he has come in, Peter. He's our nephew, for heaven's sake!" Aunt Hertha said impatiently. Uncle Peter ignored her.

"Basically, your parents are with Hitler," said Peter. "He is in Munich at the moment, but apparently he will be back here in Berlin quite soon – and so, I suppose, will your parents."

"But are they not living here?" Joseph asked, in some distress.

"No."

"Peter!" Hertha scolded, and gave him a small smack on his shoulder. "I am sorry, Franz-Joseph. Werner and Clara have a small basement apartment next door. You can stay there, but I must give you some food." Peter shrugged and sat down at the table.

"Sit down, boy. Coffee, Hertha!" Uncle Peter demanded.

*

After an awkward and quiet five minutes spent drinking coffee, Joseph was shown his parents' small apartment in the basement of the adjoining house. The apartment was small, dark and smelt of damp. Joseph was rather surprised the lights worked. Despite having brought him to the apartment, his uncle was now muttering whether he should allow Joseph to go inside. Peter stood at the front door, looking at the bits of paper and correspondence on the doormat.

"When were my parents last here, Uncle?"

"No idea," Peter said, still looking at the doormat. "They were here in February, I think."

"But that was nine months ago! I got a letter from them last month, saying they were with you."

"They were. They moved into here in September."

"But Uncle, you just said—"

"I do not have time to chat." Clearly irritated, he turned and moved stiffly up the steps to the pavement, holding onto the railing. "Your aunt will expect you in an hour for supper," he said, not looking back.

Silly old fool, Joseph thought. Peter was only five years older than his father and yet looked at least twice that. He behaved like a seventy-year-old man, not a man in his late fifties.

He walked around the apartment. Off the main hallway was a sitting room to the right and a study to the left. The hall carpet was of an indeterminate dull colour. Further along was a dark storeroom with no window, a bathroom opposite and then the lavatory. At the end of the hallway was a large bedroom to the left and a bright kitchen to the right. A back door led out to some steps up to an overgrown garden.

Joseph lit the gas heater in the study. He had decided he would sleep in there on the large sofa. He did not want to sleep in his parents' room. He also lit the gas fire in the sitting room. The kitchen had a gas hob and oven, with a kettle on top. An old copper water heater took quite a few attempts to light. On each attempt Joseph thought he would be blown up. The store cupboards were virtually empty.

He shaved, removing a day and a half's stubble – no wonder his uncle had treated him with suspicion. He put on a clean shirt and a jumper and then his jacket. He went into the sitting room to see if it had warmed up a bit. On the mantlepiece was a small photo of his mother and father, but none of him. A black and white portrait photograph of a man with a small black moustache and thin black hair swept across his forehead hung above the mantlepiece. It had been signed Adolf Hitler. There were books on the shelves either side of the chimney breast.

The sitting room was sparsely furnished. What furniture there was looked new and hardly used: two easy chairs, a small sofa, a low table and a cupboard containing, Joseph was delighted to discover, a half-full bottle of schnapps. He poured himself a large glass and drank it down quickly, like he was drinking water, and poured another.

The front door opened, and there was his aunt Hertha.

"You found a drink then, Joseph? I thought you would be too young for schnapps," she said, eyeing the glass in Joseph's hand.

"I am twenty-three, Aunt." He had hoped his aunt would be a bit more understanding.

"Come next door and I will give you some good *Sauerbraten* and *Kartoffelklöße*. You must be starved of good Austrian food, all that time in England and France."

Joseph remembered the rather unpleasant sour meat hotpot and indigestible potato dumplings but managed to smile his appreciation.

They had beer with the hotpot, which helped Joseph swallow the stew. His uncle would eat his supper in his study as he had work to do.

"What does Uncle Peter do for work, Aunt?"

"Not much now. He writes for a political magazine every now and then, mainly about the economy. That is why he is so ..." Once more, she did not finish the sentence. "But ever since your cousin died in the war, he has not done any of his banking work."

"He was a banker?"

"He ran part of the Reichsbank for many years, but it ..." She drifted off again and went to the sideboard where she produced a stack of apple pancakes from under a cloth, with a bowl of whipped cream. "Eat as many as you like, Franz-Joseph. Peter is fat enough. And you are far too thin, like your ..." She giggled. Joseph ate with relish.

After a cup of thick hot chocolate, Joseph said he would like to go to bed as he was very tired.

"Of course, Franz-Joseph, you must be exhausted," his aunt said, reaching up and stroking his cheek like a mother would. She clearly missed her own round and dumpy son, Cousin Harold. He was just twenty-two when he died, the same age as Joseph, so that was probably why his aunt enjoyed having him there. "Take a bag of coffee for the morning, and the rest of the pancakes," she said.

"Thank you, Aunt Hertha. I will pop in tomorrow before I go to find my parents."

"Do you know where they will be?"

"Uncle Peter seems to think they will be arriving with Herr Hitler at the

Reichskanzlei at midday. They should be with him."

"I hope so, dear." She looked up at her nephew, sadness in her eyes. "It must be … Oh well, never mind." She tenderly stroked his arm.

"Thank you, Aunt Hertha. Goodnight. Say thank you and goodnight to Uncle Peter for me."

*

Clara Deller was a particular favourite of Adolf Hitler's. She was blonde and pretty and had a curvaceous body. She was, however, eight years older than Hitler, but you would never think so. She was sometimes reminded of her age, unkindly, by her husband. Werner Deller was aware of Hitler's slight infatuation with his wife but declined to object; in fact, he encouraged Clara to flirt as much as she pleased with the leader. Werner was convinced that once Hitler was granted German citizenship – which Clara and Werner had already been granted – he would become the most powerful man in Germany.

Clara wisely portrayed herself as being somewhat stupid, which Hitler enjoyed. When Hitler returned from Munich to Berlin he became infatuated with the young daughter of his housekeeper, and Clara was then out of favour. The day that Joseph appeared at the Reich Chancellery she realised she was only a minor cog in Hitler's entourage. Her status was diminished. She had got used to being close to his side for the past eighteen months.

Joseph spent a lot of time getting into the chancellery with his Austrian passport and papers. However, his Nazi membership papers and badge, sponsored by his father, General Deller, helped him get into the inner sanctum of the *Reichskanzlei*. He was guided up to a room full of people drinking coffee. A large meeting table had been set out with a dozen seats. He recognised his father talking to an ugly large man with a head like a bulldog, his face scarred and his nose broken. The ugly man eyed Joseph suspiciously as he stepped up to his father.

"Good morning, sir." He tapped his father on the shoulder. Werner turned and seemed to hardly recognise him, dressed as he was in a charcoal-grey suit, white shirt and a dark-blue tie.

"Franz-Joseph?" He looked at his son with undisguised disappointment. "You have arrived, then. It is about time. Where have you been?" Werner was in full SS general uniform. He was the opposite of his older brother, Peter. He was tall, slim, handsome and had a full head of black wavy hair with a slight dusting of grey above his ears. Unlike most officers in Himmler's SS, he preferred not to sport the Saxon hairstyle of shaving the hair above the ears. He was clean-shaven and had high cheekbones with slightly sunken cheeks, and a dead-straight nose.

"Where is my mother, sir?" Joseph thought he would see if he got a better reception from her.

"She is talking to Hess over by the window. You will have to go when Herr Hitler comes in for the meeting."

"I see," Joseph said. "Can I go and see her, or are they busy?"

"Go over. Herr Hitler is not here yet," the general said, a little more kindly. As Joseph turned away from his father, he heard the other man say, "Your boy, Deller?"

"Yes, my only son, Röhm. I think he is after a job."

Joseph was disappointed by his father's indifference. He had not seen his son for at least two years. After the friendly letter he received, he thought he might have become more amenable.

"Franz-Joseph, you have arrived!" His mother stroked her son's arm with affection. The man she was talking to was dark, handsome and had thick eyebrows that met at the bridge of his nose. "Franz-Joseph Deller, Rudolf," she said proudly. "My son."

"Your servant, sir," Joseph said with a small bow of his head and a click of his heels.

"Franz-Joseph, this is Herr Hess, one of the most important people in the Party."

"Thank you, Clara," Hess said with a slight smile. "Are you to join us, Deller?"

"In the Party, sir?"

"Yes, in the Party. We need young men like you."

"He is already a member of the Party, Rudolf." Clara tapped the badge with its swastika emblem pinned to Joseph's lapel. "He speaks English and French terribly well. We have asked him to help us in any way he can." Clara looked at her son.

"What do you do?" Hess asked, looking him up and down.

"I am an artist. I studied art here in Berlin and in Paris. I have just returned."

"Have you a girl, Franz-Joseph?" his mother asked. Joseph felt his heart quicken; he didn't know what to say. He decided to lie.

"I nearly got married, Mother, but she died."

His mother looked suitably sad. "Oh, I am sorry, darling boy. Was she French?"

"Yes, she had a huge house in Avenue—"

"Will you forgive me, Clara," Hess interrupted. "I must find the Führer. Do you know where he is?"

"I believe he should be here soon," Clara said, then stepped in closer to Hess with a charming, possibly flirtatious smile that surprised Joseph. "Rudolf, would you see if Heinrich needs my boy in his new guard?" Hess looked a little dubious at Joseph's skinny frame.

"I will see what I can do, Clara. Please forgive me."

As Hess left, Joseph clicked his heels and bowed his head again.

"What guard, Mother?"

"I will tell you later. We must mingle more. As soon as Herr Hitler is here, we will have to leave. This is his full cabinet, Joseph, very senior men amongst them" – she looked over to her husband – "your father being one of them." She turned to her son. "Where have you been staying, Franz-Joseph?"

"In your house, or is it an apartment?" he said pointedly. His parents had a lovely house in Vienna, where he was born. He was disappointed that they now seemed to live in a comparative hovel.

"I know, it is nothing like the house in Vienna, but it is our home now."

As she was speaking, the conversation in the room went quiet.

"Gentlemen," a small, thin man with large ears called loudly from the entrance.

"That is Joseph Goebbels. He is very nice, charming. He's—" Clara hissed at Joseph but was interrupted by Goebbels.

"Our leader has just arrived. Could all but the Cabinet and Herr Röhm please leave now." The small young man then walked up to Joseph's father. He had a slight limp. He shook Werner Deller's hand and said something that made Werner laugh.

"We'd better go now," Clara said. "Come and say goodbye to your father."

"I don't think he likes me being here, Mother."

"What rubbish." She dragged Joseph across the room. "Werner, here is your son. We are off to the apartment."

"Herr Hitler wants me at the meeting," Werner said, looking uncomfortable.

"Is this your son, Clara?" asked Goebbels, pushing past Joseph's father. He looked at Joseph and smiled, his hands on his hips. They looked the same age. Joseph clicked his heels and bowed slightly.

"Franz-Joseph Deller, sir." He introduced himself when he saw his father looked annoyed by the intrusion.

"The artist?" Goebbels said, stunning both Franz-Joseph and his father. Clara just stood and looked at her son with an air of pride.

"Y-yes, sir!" Joseph stuttered.

"We must talk one day. I've heard a lot about you from your mother. But we have a meeting now." He turned to Clara. "Clara, bring your son to my office tomorrow, would you?"

"Yes, of—"

"You must go now, Clara," her husband interrupted.

12

Concord, or "Concud", as the locals liked to pronounce it, was one of America's most historic towns. It boasted some of the oldest houses in the United States as well as being one of the more affluent areas of the country. The American rebels fought against the British in the eighteenth century and forced a retreating British army down Battle Road and into the sea at Boston. The de Tournets lived in one of the very few red-brick, Georgian-style houses in Concord. The other houses were mainly oak-framed, weather-boarded buildings with a central chimney. The de Tournets' house, misleadingly called Gable Cottage – cottage being an understatement – included about two acres of woodland. In the fall, the leaves turned into a multitude of browns, russet and gold, a common sight in the deciduous forests that carpeted New England.

Life in Concord was busy with parties given by Aunt Stella for her charity events and Jean de Tournet's business contacts and friends. Aunt Stella and Uncle Jean would disappear for a week or two on holiday or on business trips every other month.

The first five years of Charlotte's life were dull. Her stepfather travelled for his steel business between Boston and Gothenburg in Sweden. Charlotte's stepmother was in charge of the local social life and therefore busy with charities and social events. Because she was English, wealthy and married to a charming, handsome Frenchman, the Massachusetts elite elevated Stella's social standing to the very top.

When Charlotte was just five, she went to a small, select private school in Concord. The classes were strictly segregated between boys and girls. There was just her and Elenore Scholz, and sometimes a girl called Clarissa Jax who lived next door to Charlotte, in the class. Their teacher was Mr Scupham, a quiet, small man who squinted through rimless glasses. He had a slight hunchback that meant each time he spoke to an adult, he had to bend his knees to look up. He loved small children as it was easy to see their faces without stretching his neck.

Mr Scupham was liked by the children he taught. He never lost his temper and he knew how to get the best out of every child. He especially enjoyed teaching Charlotte with her agile intelligence and quick grasp of mathematical problems. His wife, who was tiny and rotund, would be in the class with Mr Scupham, knitting and tending to any requirements that little girls might need. She was kind, and if a girl had a problem, it was Mrs Scupham who they would go to.

Charlotte was hardly, if ever, included in any of the social whirl in Concord with her step-parents. She would be left in their house with her Swedish nanny, who Stella preferred to call a governess, Christina Jorgensen. Every now and then, she would be asked to play with Clarissa, who was the same age as her. She was a sickly, red-headed girl who treated Charlotte like a doll. All she wanted to do was to mother Charlotte and play "house". Charlotte wanted to run outside, swim or play ball with Marty Rushton's basketball hoop. The Rushtons were also neighbours and Mr Rushton took a particular interest in Jean de Tournet's steel business.

*

"Clarissa is so boring, Christina," Charlotte complained at the end of the summer of her ninth year. "She never wants to go out, just stay inside and play with dolls."

"I'm sorry, Charlotte, but your parents—"

"Step-parents, Christina," Charlotte corrected.

"Well … they do not want you playing with boys."

"Why not? Clarissa, Elenore Scholz and I are the only girls around here and the rest are boys. I like Marty Rushton over the road."

"Well … you have to be careful of boys." Christina looked awkwardly at Charlotte.

"Is it you and Bo who don't want me to play with boys?" Charlotte put her fists on her hips and shouted. "Bo!"

"We do not make the rules, Charlotte," Christina said angrily, "and you do not shout for Bo like that. He is not your servant. He is my husband." Christina looked like she was going to cry, which was the last thing Charlotte wanted to happen. She hated upsetting Christina.

106

"What have you said to Christina, Charlotte?" Bo came into the kitchen. Charlotte stood with her hands on her hips, while Christina looked angry and distressed. "What have you said?" Bo repeated, wiping the oil off his hands from repairing a lawnmower.

"I am sorry, Bo." Charlotte was contrite; she may have overstepped the mark. "I lost my temper and I shouldn't have. Sorry, Christina."

Bo looked at his wife, and then at Charlotte, then shrugged his shoulders and went back to his lawnmower out in the shed. Charlotte was prone to losing her temper and, just as quickly, suppressing it. Christina always insisted that Charlotte's red hair was the reason for her ready temper, despite it being golden blonde. It was full and lustrous. It swept down her back and was kept off her face by an Alice band but still always got in the way. All Charlotte wanted to do was to cut it all off.

"Well, you will be pleased to hear that Marty will be here tomorrow with his parents for supper," Christina said. "Now, go and brush your hair and wash your hands before lunch."

*

On Sunday, Charlotte and Marty Rushton were exploring the wood at the back of the de Tournets' house. Wild turkeys roamed the woods, along with cottontail rabbits, squirrels and white-tailed deer. Charlotte and Marty loved to hunt and track these animals but never managed to find any deer or wild turkeys. Paths led into three little spaces, each with a small folly and a little wooden chalet-style shed with a slate roof and ornate facia – magical places for children to play in.

As Charlotte and Marty approached the chalet furthest from the house, they could hear an argument. Jean de Tournet was shouting at someone.

"Listen, Marty, they are talking French," Charlotte said.

"That's your stepfather. That's why they are talking French."

"Yes. What are they saying?" Charlotte asked the studious-looking boy. He was freckled and pale with blonde hair.

"I don't speak much French! Why don't you speak French? Your stepfather is French."

"My governess is Swedish, and I don't speak Swedish either. But I am learning French."

"Well, who is Mr de Tournet shouting at?" Marty asked.

"I can't see. We will have to go to the side window of the shed."

"But they might see us."

"So?" Charlotte said angrily. "Let's go. Keep in the treeline."

To Marty's surprise and some discomfort, Charlotte grabbed the cuff of his jacket and pulled him down to a crouching position. "I don't think this is wise," hissed Marty. He may have been right, thought Charlotte, as she was in a bright yellow summer dress, and he in a white linen jacket and blue summer shorts. Charlotte shuffled along the treeline, pulling Marty with her and ducking between the trees. As they came to the chalet, they could see the window was open; no wonder they could hear the argument. Charlotte dropped Marty's cuff and crept up to the window. If she stood on tiptoe, she would be able to see in.

She saw her uncle standing with his back to her, pointing at someone leaning on a wooden support. Tall and slim with greying hair, he looked a bit older than Uncle Jean. Both men smoked large cigars. The man suddenly pushed himself away from the wooden pillar and said quietly, in English:

"Just remember who you are talking to, de Tournet!" He turned to pick up an attaché case from the floor and Charlotte could see his face. "It is not up to you to invite people or introduce them without going through me first!"

Charlotte had seen the man before, she was sure of it, but could not remember where.

A hand grabbed her ankle and she squeaked. She swung round to see Marty with his finger to his mouth, shushing her. They both darted back into the wood before the stranger poked his head out of the window and said, "Probably some animal."

*

That Sunday evening, Charlotte was dressed for a party. She was to meet a relative, according to Christina. She wondered if it was going to be the other man she had seen in the chalet.

It was, except he was not French, he was English, and, to her astonishment, her other uncle, Sir Jason Barrett.

He arrived at the front door as though he had only just got to Concord. He was now dressed in evening clothes. Jean de Tournet sported a white tuxedo and a dark-red rose buttonhole. Stella looked petite and winsome in a stunning, shimmering long silver dress with a huge silk bow tied at her lower back, like a bustle.

"Charlotte, darling, do you remember your uncle Jason?" asked Aunt Stella.

Charlotte went up to her uncle who stood severely before her; no smile of welcome or any indication that he was willing to meet his niece.

"How do you do, Uncle," Charlotte said prettily and gave a small curtsey. "I don't think I remember you."

"No," Jason said coolly, "I doubt you will remember anything that happened in France. You are looking very pretty, Charlotte."

"Thank you, sir."

"Your grandmother sends her best wishes, and" – he turned to Jean de Tournet – "wants to know when she may see her granddaughter again."

"I will arrange something soon," said Stella before her husband could answer. "It must be five years since I have seen Mama. We write a lot, but Jean is so—"

"As it happens, we will be in Paris quite soon, Jason. I have to go to Sweden, so we will travel together to Paris and—"

"Can Bo and Christina come too, Uncle Jean?" asked Charlotte. "They would love to go to Sweden with you."

"No," Jean de Tournet said emphatically. Charlotte opened her mouth to say something else, but before she could speak, de Tournet said, "That will be all, Charlotte."

"Mr and Mrs Rushton and Marty," announced the de Tournets' butler.

"Charlotte, go and play. Take Marty with you," de Tournet said.

"Is *this* the man?" Jason hissed at de Tournet.

"Yes, they live across the way and befriended us," de Tournet whispered back as Stella welcomed her American guests. "This is who I was talking about in the shed." De Tournet gave a wry smile. "He's something to do with the American intelligence service." Sir Jason swung round to look at de Tournet.

"You kept that bloody quiet. Is this not something you should have said earlier?" Jason was incensed.

"Possibly," de Tournet said, turning to see Mrs Rushton approaching with Stella. He put on a fake smile and greeted Mrs Rushton, taking her hand and kissing it lightly. Sadie Rushton giggled.

"And this is my older brother, Sir Jason Barrett," said Stella, seeming a little worried. Her brother was looking angry and not disguising it very well.

"How do you do," he said, his expression lightening as he shook hands with Mrs Rushton.

"Oh!" She trilled, a blush forming on her pretty, round cheeks. "Are you a real earl?"

"Hardly, madame, I am just a meagre baronet." Jason tried to sound humble but he still managed to come over as superior. Stella frowned at him.

"Duck!" Sadie shouted for her husband, who was talking to Charlotte and his son, Marty. "Donald," she called again in a sing-song way. "Come and meet Sir Jason Barrett. He's a real live baron!" Jason cast his eyes skyward.

Donald Rushton walked over to Barrett and de Tournet. He was a tall man with swept-back grey hair, thin but with a paunch that was visible under his grey suit jacket. He was not in evening clothes.

"I'm sorry, de Tournet, I had no idea we were going to be so formal." He took Barrett's hand and shook it vigorously. "Very pleased to meet you, Sir Jason."

"Please, call me Jason."

"I have just been talking to your delightful young daughter."

"No, no, nothing to do with me. She is my niece, my sister's child."

Donald turned to de Tournet. "I am sorry. She's your daughter, Mr de Tournet?"

"No, monsieur, she is our stepdaughter. Her mother, Jason's sister, was murd—"

"She died when Charlotte was only a week old," Stella interjected before her husband could say any more.

There was a silence until the butler arrived with glasses full of champagne and offered a glass to Sadie Rushton. "How delicious. Is this from France?" she said excitedly.

"Of course, madame," Jean de Tournet replied with a charming smile.

"Duck, look," Sadie said to her husband in hushed tones, "real champagne from Paris, France."

"No, my dear, from Épernay, north of Paris," said Mr Rushton. He did not seem to be embarrassed by his wife's enthusiastic and uninformed gaffs. Jason assumed he was quite used to them and preferred to ignore them.

"Duck?" Jason looked at Mrs Rushton, clearly irritated. "Why Duck?"

"Oh yes, sorry," she giggled. "It's what I call my husband. You know … Donald Duck?"

Jason and Jean looked at each other, wondering if either knew what she was talking about. "Haven't you seen Walt Disney's Donald Duck cartoons, Baron?" she asked.

"No, I have not come across a duck called Donald," Jason said, getting impatient.

"No, I don't think we have heard of this duck film," Stella said slightly nervously, taking her glass of champagne from the tray. "Can we have a toast?"

She raised her glass. "To Jason. Welcome to America." They all raised their glasses and saluted each other.

"Tell me, Jason, do you think there will be a war?" Donald Rushton asked during a lull in the conversation.

"I believe there will, Donald. The Germans are becoming very powerful, and together, we, Great Britain and Germany, should put down this communist scourge in Russia and, dare I say, other parts of Europe." Jason looked at Jean de Tournet who nodded sagely.

Donald Rushton looked confused, "Surely you mean between the Germans and the Polish, possibly even the French? That man, Hitler, who now runs Germany, is out for extending his country."

"Now, now, you two," said Stella. "I think we should go through to dinner." She wagged her finger. "No more politics." She turned to address the butler. "Could you find Miss Charlotte and Marty? It's time for dinner."

"Yes, madame." The little butler scurried off.

"A word, please, Sir Jason," said Donald Rushton. "In private, before we go in."

"Certainly," Jason said cautiously.

"I understand you are aware of an organisation called WASP, War Against Socialist Parties?"

Jason took a step back.

"What do you know about this organisation, Donald?"

"Well, I know Jean de Tournet has something to do with this … group."

"I see," Jason said slowly. "I am afraid you will have to give me more to go on, Donald." He looked sternly at Rushton. "I will ask de Tournet, if you would like, if he knows about—"

"Let's leave it for now. Being his brother-in-law puts you a little close to this." Rushton turned to walk out of the room.

"Why do you need to know about de Tournet?" Jason was losing his temper. "Has he committed a crime? Who are you to ask these questions?"

Donald took a wallet out of his jacket inside pocket. He flipped it open to reveal an ID card showing that he represented the United States Secret Service.

"Has he committed a crime, Rushton?" Jason asked again

"No, Sir Jason. It is just that we need to know."

"How do you know he is a member of this organisation? And why are you asking me?"

"He told us he was a member. He was boasting about WASP to William H. Moran, at a dinner last year."

"Who on earth is William H. Moran?" Jason was looking uncharacteristically nervous.

"He is my boss – head of the USSS. He also holds views about communists, as does most of America."

The door to the drawing room burst open and Sadie peered around the door. "Duck, darling, you are holding up dinner."

"And why have you come to me with this? Why not ask de Tournet?" Jason said.

"Because he said you are head of WASP."

Jason's face turned to thunder.

*

At dinner, Sadie Rushton quizzed Jason about his title, wondering if her son married Charlotte, would he have a title, to the total embarrassment of everyone at the table. Marty could not conceal his delight at the prospect of marrying Charlotte. She was, after all, the prettiest girl he had ever seen, even more beautiful than Hedy Lamarr or Carole Lombard. Her hair was a lustrous deep gold, tied into ponytails. She was tall, a little taller than he was, and each time she smiled at him, he could feel a lump turn over in his stomach.

*

Jason said hardly a thing throughout dinner, other than the odd curt monosyllabic answer, fending off Sadie's tenacious grilling about him and his family.

After dinner, Stella announced:

"Mrs Rushton, perhaps we should leave the gentlemen and Marty to cigars and port?"

"Not for Marty, Mrs de Tournet." Sadie looked horrified.

"Then perhaps, Marty, you could escort us ladies to the drawing room?"

"Delighted, Mrs de Tournet," said Marty with undisguised relief. The men all stood as the ladies and Marty left the dining room.

Sir Jason helped himself to a decanter of port from the sideboard and placed it in front of Jean de Tournet as though it was his house, which annoyed de Tournet.

"De Tournet, Mr Rushton has just informed me that you and I are part of WASP." Sir Jason sat back down opposite. Bewildered, de Tournet looked from Rushton to Sir Jason and back again, his mouth open to protest but unable.

"How would he know this?" De Tournet stood up from the table, glaring at Rushton.

"Apparently you told a gentleman called Moran whilst in your cups at a dinner."

"In my what?"

"Cups – drunk … *saoul*." Sir Jason pinched his nose and twisted it, mimicking the French gesture for being drunk. "He asked *me* about WASP. Rushton here is part of the United States Secret Service, are you not, Mr Rushton?"

De Tournet looked worried and started stroking his moustache and chin in apprehension.

"Gentlemen." Rushton stood and went over to the decanter of port that still sat, stoppered, in front of Jean de Tournet. He poured a glass for himself, filled de Tournet's glass and passed the decanter to Sir Jason. "I have no wish to alarm you. Moran and I are the only people concerned with joining the 'organisation', if that is the expression – offer our services, if you will."

"Let me get this right, Rushton. You and Mr Moran, the head of the United States Secret Service, want to join an organisation that may or may not exist?"

"Sir Jason" – Rushton took a sip of his port – "since the Great Depression in 1929, communism has reared its ugly head in our country. The CPUSA and Socialists of America have grown in membership, and we need the support of Great Britain and Germany to stamp out this scourge. I am told that you, Sir Jason, with de Tournet here, are quite senior in the WASP organisation."

"Senior?" de Tournet exclaimed. "Barrett runs the whole—"

"Be quiet, de Tournet!" Sir Jason ignored de Tournet's protestations and carried on. "I am, as de Tournet indiscreetly divulged, a small part of the organisation. I can put you forward to the head of WASP at our next meeting. This is not how this works, however. I believe we approach people after a lot of research."

"I am sorry, Sir Jason, I was not aware of this."

"Nevertheless, as you are working for a national intelligence agency, we would be cautious of disclosing our existence to anyone, let alone providing the names of the officers within that organisation. We are a highly influential group, considering the secrecy that surrounds us. But de Tournet did mention he had researched you, but not Mr Moran" – he looked at his brother-in-law – "as far as I know. Are you aware of our current role, Rushton?"

"Well …" Rushton looked nervously at de Tournet and then Sir Jason. "I imagine, to somehow remove the communist government in Russia and quench the emergence of communism in China."

"Basically correct."

"But I have no idea how you plan to accomplish these goals."

"That will become more apparent if you are successful in joining WASP."

"Are you able to help with this application, Sir Jason?" Rushton looked worried.

"As I say, both de Tournet and I are just minor parts of WASP. I represent Great Britain, and de Tournet, France. I am not sure if the US have anyone already involved."

"I see. Do you know about the aims of WASP?"

Sir Jason was hesitant. He looked sternly at de Tournet and took a deep breath.

"Our aim, Mr Rushton, is to put political pressure on all like-minded governments – Great Britain, Spain, Italy; perhaps Germany if the Nazi Party comes to power – to band together with, we hope, the USA, to take on the Soviets and the Communist Party of China, with the help of Japan, and crush communism."

"My God! What kind of support have you?" Rushton was impressed.

"That is something we will discuss at the next meeting." Sir Jason pondered. "But support and finances are not what we lack; it is soldiers. An army is what we are next looking for. This may come from two fronts: the Germans and the Americans. However, I have said too much already, and I trust this conversation will be treated in the strictest of confidences."

"We are, Moran and I," Rushton said calmly, "part of the secret service and are well used to keeping confidences, Sir Jason."

"Then after I sanction this with the heads of WASP, we will invite you to the next meeting when the board sits in September. De Tournet will be there as your sponsor – he will propose your application to be part of WASP. I imagine you will be asked what political and possibly military influences you can bring to bear to stamp out communism." Sir Jason turned to de Tournet. "I will leave it to you to inform Rushton and Moran of the conditions of the organisation."

Jean de Tournet was still red with rage. He took his glass of port and drained it all in one gulp. He clearly knew he was in the wrong for this informal introduction.

"Who else was in earshot of your indiscretion at this dinner, de Tournet?"

"It was just Moran and I at one end of the dining table, Jason," de Tournet said in quivering restraint, trying to govern his temper. "No one else was able to hear us."

"Mr Rushton, how did Mr Moran know of WASP's existence in the first place and that de Tournet was a member?"

"I believe you are both close friends of Lord Rathmore, Sir Jason." Rushton sounded cocky, as though he had just won a point.

"He is indeed an acquaintance of mine. His newspapers help with getting our message across to the British public."

"And part of the WASP organisation?" Rushton asked.

"I cannot comment on other members of the board, I regret."

There was silence. The decanter was passed round the table again. "Let us join the ladies," Jason said. "I trust I need not remind you, sir, not to repeat any part of this meeting to anyone else."

"You can be assured, Sir Jason," Rushton said.

Jean de Tournet stormed on ahead, out of the dining room.

To bring such distinguished and like-minded gentlemen to the WASP organisation was a clever move on de Tournet's part, Jason had to confess. He thought the scolding he gave de Tournet in the summerhouse, when de Tournet confessed that he had recruited two members to WASP, may have been a little unfortunate. He would placate de Tournet and calm his temper after the Rushtons had gone.

13

Joseph sat in the Kaiser Friedrich Museum, a rather special building sat on an island in the middle of Berlin, overlooking the River Spree. Ferdi and Joseph used to frequent and study there while art students in Berlin. Ferdi had suggested this would be the best venue to meet. Nearly ten years had passed since they had last seen each other – that awful time when Alice had died.

Joseph saw Ferdi strolling through the gallery next door. He was dressed impeccably, as usual, in a pinstripe suit. Joseph looked at himself in a picture glass. He was wearing his SS captain's uniform and felt rather proud at how sophisticated he looked in his black jacket and breaches and shiny black boots to his knees. He stood with his hand on his hip, his chin raised, an expression of importance on his face, and waited for Ferdi to notice him.

"Joseph!" Ferdi exclaimed as they met. His voice echoed around the empty gallery. "I hardly recognised you."

"Hello, Ferdi." Joseph put out his hand for Ferdi to shake. "Lovely to see you again. It's been so long and—"

"Well, let us not dwell too much on the past." Ferdi sat on a bench. Joseph sat beside him. "We need to talk about your reports." Joseph felt a little guilty.

"Yes, I know they have been few. But I find it difficult to get anything you may find valuable. I still haven't met Hitler, even with him being close to my parents."

"You have done some good work, Joseph. Don't worry. But that is not why I am here. You will be transferred to Hitler's headquarters soon."

"Will I?"

"Yes. This is where you will be very helpful with information."

"How do you know these things? I mean, you are not even German."

"I just do. I want you to go to a club, Das Katzenclubhaus, here in Berlin." Joseph felt excited about the prospect of going to a Berlin club. "What do you want me to do there? Dance all night?"

"No." Ferdi was firm. "I want you to make contact, if he is there, with an SS officer, Ulrich Fuhrman. He is one of my men. You will meet a girl there called Theodora. She works with Fuhrman. If he is not there, try and organise a meeting."

"What do I do when I contact him?" Joseph asked.

"Just ask him to contact me at my new Alsace address. Here is my card." Ferdi handed over a card of a gallery in Metz.

"Where is Metz, Ferdi?"

Ferdi looked at Joseph, annoyed. "Please, just give him this card. This is where I will be in future."

"Is this where I will send my reports?"

"No, keep sending them to the Berlin address."

There was a pause. Ferdi looked at the large pictures on the walls of the gallery. Joseph kept looking at Ferdi's card.

"But why don't you go to this club and …?"

"It is better that I am not seen there, that is all."

Joseph looked dubious. "Should I be seen at this club? Is it dangerous?"

"No. You are an SS officer, Joseph." Ferdi stood. "I'm not."

"What if I cannot find Fuhrman?"

"Give the card to Theodora to pass on. Don't mention my name to her. Just refer to me as 'Baron'."

*

Jost Krupp enjoyed the company of the women in Das Katzenclubhaus, one of the smarter clubs in Berlin frequented by officers of the SS.

Jost Krupp had grown into a handsome man and spent a lot of his leisure hours at the club. He never joined the cavalry like his father. He joined the SS and worked his way up from *Unterscharführer*, a junior squad leader, to lieutenant in a very short time, after he had finished studying law in Berlin. He never qualified as a lawyer; he preferred to be among like-minded Nazis rather than law school students who seemed to be nothing but liberal Social Democratic Party members and communists.

"May I introduce you to Captain Franz-Joseph Deller, Lieutenant Krupp?" said the tall, elegant dark-haired woman at the Katzenclubhaus bar. Jost Krupp was in a large, well-stuffed leather armchair, one of his legs dangling over the arm, reading a magazine. It was early afternoon and Krupp had escaped his barracks out of tedium and wanted some peace and quiet without the aimless chatter of soldiers with nothing to do.

"Good afternoon, Herr Krupp. I believe our fathers are good friends," said the captain. Krupp quickly went to get up to salute his superior officer. "Stay, stay, Krupp. No need for formalities here," Deller said. He pointed at the empty *Pilstulpe* beer glass on the low table in front of Krupp. "Drink?"

"Yes, thank you, sir. Another Krombacher," Krupp said, with little appreciation. He sat up straight and did up the top button of his tunic. He looked at the captain, similarly dressed in a black SS uniform – a skinny man, around ten years older than Krupp, with a crop of unattractive curly hair on top of his head and a broad smile. As he sat in the chair next to Krupp's, he emitted an annoying tuneless hum. An attempt to lighten the mood, Krupp supposed.

"You know my father, Captain?" Krupp asked.

"I don't – my father does. My father is General Werner Deller," said Deller, snapping his fingers at a waitress dressed in a short black skirt with fluffed layers of lace petticoats, a little white apron and a small black pillbox hat sporting a *KCH* motif set jauntily to one side of her blonde hair. "Two beers … like before," he said, waving at Krupp's empty glass, "and a schnapps."

Both men watched the girl's legs as she elegantly dipped down to pick up Krupp's empty glass and place it on her tray. She smiled widely, casting her eyes down coyly, seemingly enjoying the men's attention, especially from the handsome young lieutenant.

"Yes, the major general and my father have been through quite a lot getting the Party strong," Deller bragged.

Krupp was mildly impressed by who the captain's father was. But he had also heard about Deller's mother, Clara, a very attractive woman who had basically slept around the Party, getting her son promoted rapidly. "Are you here on business, sir?" he asked.

"Well, I am in charge of art and culture, and I have come to Berlin to see some opera and talk about art … German art. I have been in Munich for quite a long time."

"Oh," said Krupp, disinterested. "What are you going to see?"

"Don't know yet. I have just arrived in Berlin. The lovely Theodora said you may be the best person to show me some sights."

Krupp sat up and looked at Deller with unconcealed annoyance.

"Theodora!" Krupp shouted. The club still had very few people in it, being early for any kind of revelry. The dark-haired lady who had first introduced Deller to Krupp glided across from the back of the bar.

"Yes, Jost?" She wore a dark grey dress with long sleeves and a white collar. It was short, just covering her knees, and had a thin black belt around her tiny waist. She held a cigarette in a silver holder high in her right hand.

"The captain here says that I would be the person to show him the sights of Berlin."

"No, I told Captain Deller that you could show him the sights of Das Katzenclubhaus, that is all."

"Ah yes, that was it, Krupp. Sorry."

Krupp grunted and went back to reading his magazine.

*

The beers arrived with a small glass of schnapps for Joseph. The girl dipped to put the beers on the table. He whisked the schnapps off the tray and swallowed the contents. "May I have another one of those, my dear?" he said, smiling at the girl, who without expression took the glass and left. "Where are you from, Theodora?"

"Turkey, Captain, but I have been here most of my life."

"And what do you do here?" Joseph asked.

"I am one of the hostesses for Madame," she said proudly. She had a heavy accent and a wonderfully low voice. She sat down on the chair beside him and crossed her legs, put an elbow on her knee and rested her chin on her hand. "And what do you do, Captain?" She looked deep into his eyes, a smile on her generous, deep-red lips. This excited Joseph. He had seldom had such attention from a beautiful woman before, except from Alice.

"I am in arts and culture for the Führer."

"Are you?" said Theodora, flicking away the tumbling waves of silky shoulder-length black hair.

"Would you like a drink, my dear?" Joseph asked, enthralled.

"Champagne, please," she said, leaning closer to him, her eyes widening in excitement.

"Really?" Joseph felt a little unsure.

"Tell me more about German art and culture, Captain," she said gushingly. He was hooked. Champagne was ordered, and Krupp made his excuses and left.

Once Joseph had seen Krupp leave, he leant closer to Theodora and said, in a low voice, "I was wondering if you know an SS officer called Ulrich Fuhrman?"

Theodora sat back in surprise.

"No, I don't think I do. We get so many officers here. How do you know … Ulrich Fuhrman?"

"He's a friend. The baron said he would be here." Joseph was feeling slightly nervous – or was it excitement? He could not work out which. Theodora looked thoughtful.

"I could ask one of the girls this evening if you like?"

"No, no, don't worry." The champagne arrived. Joseph wanted to grab the bottle and drain the lot. He felt uncomfortable. Theodora was looking at him with suspicion but then quickly reverted to being a hostess.

"You were going to tell me about art and culture, Captain."

Joseph was trying to enjoy the attentions of the Turkish beauty, but he was thinking he had made a mistake. Was Theodora the name Ferdi said? He took a large gulp of champagne.

"I think I'd better go. I will be back …"

Theodora stood, a forced smile on her face. She put out her hand. "Come with me."

Joseph slowly rose to his feet.

"Bring the wine, Captain."

Joseph picked up the champagne bucket. Theodora started towards some stairs, looking back at Joseph seductively. Joseph was in turmoil about what to do. He wondered what was going on as he followed Theodora up the wide staircase. Theodora virtually had to drag Joseph into the bedroom. "Come on, Captain," she cooed.

As the door closed behind them, Theodora suddenly changed character. She pushed Joseph up against the door. A hook rammed hard into Joseph's back.

"Ow! What are you doing, Theodora?"

"Who are you, Captain? And how do you know Fuhrman?"

"I told you, he is a friend."

"What does he look like?" Theodora flashed back, still with a hand pushing on his chest.

"I don't know!" Joseph said loudly, trying to sound angry and not pathetic.

"Then he is not a friend of yours."

"Well – a friend of a … why are you being so aggressive? I thought we were going to —"

"Well, we are not." Theodora took her hand away and strolled to a sofa at the other end of the room. To Joseph's horror, he noticed she had a flick knife in her other hand. "Who sent you, Captain?"

"I told you, the baron. Were you going to use that knife on me?"

"I will ask for the last time: why do you want to see Ulrich?"

"Or what, may I ask?" Stupid question, Joseph thought as Theodora flicked the knife at him. Joseph reached into his trouser pocket and took out Ferdi's card. "Could you please give Fuhrman this card? It has the baron's new contact details. I am going to go now if you don't mind."

"Fine," Theodora said, suddenly back in hostess mode. She sauntered across and took the card. The knife had magically disappeared. "Thirty-five hundred Reichsmarks."

"What?" Joseph was staggered.

"Thirty-five hundred Reichsmarks – for the champagne and Lieutenant Krupp's drinks," Theodora said lightly.

*

Jost Krupp's father, Helmut, was an adviser to President von Hindenburg and was part of the group who wanted the president to recommend the dynamic and talented politician, Adolf Hitler, as chancellor. He became a staunch Hitler ally and with Hindenburg's son, Oskar von Hindenburg, by his side, they assisted Adolf Hitler to rid the government of most of Hitler's opponents, including one of the original members of Hitler's Nazi Party, Gregor Strasser. Heinrich Himmler's SS had discovered that Ernst Röhm was planning to take over the army and, with Strasser, rule Germany. Strasser and Röhm were planning, with the former chancellor Kurt von Schleicher, to take over the Hitler cabinet.

On 30 June 1934, Jost Krupp, under orders from his father and dressed in a trench coat and trilby hat, went to the home of General von Schleicher and rang the bell. The door was answered by Frau von Schleicher. Krupp raised his hat, and beaming, asked, "Is the general at home, Frau von Schleicher?"

"Yes," she said, smiling widely. "One moment, I will get him. Please come in."

Krupp thanked the lady and stepped into the house. He looked around the hallway and into the adjacent rooms as Frau von Schleicher went to get her husband. There were no servants around. The general emerged from his office, frowning.

"Are you General von Schleicher, sir?" Jost asked charmingly.

"Yes, I am, but I am on the phone. What do you want?"

Krupp snapped to attention, reached inside his coat and drew out a Luger pistol. He shot the general in the head. Then, when Frau von Schleicher stooped down, screaming, to help her dead husband, Krupp shot her in the back of the head. He quickly went out the door and sauntered onto the empty street as though he was just passing by.

*

Lieutenant Krupp, now in uniform, led a group of young SS troopers to a beer hall in Munich, inside which, Krupp was told, Strasser was plotting with Ernst Röhm – the head of the *SA* Storm Troopers, or Brownshirts – to turn the army against Hitler.

"Herr Strasser" – Jost was the first into the beer hall meeting room – "and Herr Röhm." Röhm's stocky figure rose from the chair aggressively; the chair slid back with a jarring noise.

"Who the hell are you? Get out!" Röhm's scarred face was florid and he had an intimidating scowl.

"I am *SS-Obersturmführer* Jost Krupp, Herr Röhm." As Jost spoke, the small meeting room began to fill with SS troopers, all armed with MP40 submachine guns aimed at the five men around the table, much to their alarm. "You are all under arrest for espionage."

"Under whose orders, Lieutenant?" asked Strasser, still sitting, looking as though he knew the answer.

"Our leader and Führer, Adolf Hitler," Jost Krupp said.

"We will see about this." Röhm pushed his way past the nearest soldier and stomped towards him. Jost unholstered his Luger pistol, drew back the action and shot a round into the floor just in front of Röhm's boots. Röhm stopped abruptly. He was shocked and confused.

"My men will hear that and will be in to—"

"Four have joined us in the SS. The others have been arrested," Jost said loudly for all to hear. "Take these prisoners to the Brown House" – Jost waved his pistol at the other men at the meeting – "and we will deal with them after I have interrogated Herr Strasser and Herr Röhm." He turned to the sergeant. "Sergeant, remain with me. We will take these two to the Führer."

*

Strasser and Röhm were taken to the basement of the SS headquarters, Das Braune Haus, a windowless room with stark, whitewashed walls, a low ceiling and a drain in the centre of the mahogany tiled floor. Both men were tied onto chairs.

122

"You were both found to be plotting against our Führer," Jost Krupp said with icy calm. "Along with General Kurt von Schleicher, you are guilty of treason."

"Where is von Schleicher? He has something to do with this," shouted Röhm. "I would never trust that—"

"General von Schleicher was shot dead this morning. That is why he was not at your meeting."

"Who shot him?"

"I did, Herr Röhm. And I regret to say his wife, who got in the way, was also shot dead," Krupp replied. The men gasped and looked at each other apprehensively.

"Who the hell do you think you are?" shouted Strasser. "Do you know who I am?"

"Yes, sir," Jost said. "You are Gregor Strasser and you have been arrested by orders of the Führer." Krupp came smartly to attention and clicked his heels.

"But ..." Strasser started, when two heavily armed SS troopers entered the basement room, followed by the slightly stooped figure of Adolf Hitler. He was accompanied by Rudolf Hess, who stopped at the entrance.

Ernst Röhm was quiet until he saw Hitler – the man he was hoping to overthrow before placing Strasser on Hitler's throne, with von Schleicher as deputy.

"Adolf ... my Führer, what is this? This man claims he has shot von Schleicher. What is to happen to us?" Röhm pleaded.

Strasser simply stared at the small, dark man in a parchment-coloured riding coat and brown trilby hat. Hitler's face was white, his eyes wide with fury.

"Goodbye, Strasser," he said. "Goodbye, Röhm. You are a disgrace to Germany. We could not hide your ... disgusting habits any more." Both of Hitler's fists were shaking at his side. He turned to Krupp, who clicked his heels again. "You know what to do, Lieutenant?"

"Yes, my Führer," Krupp answered in a stern, strong voice.

Hitler glowered at each man, turned quickly and marched out with all the guards following, leaving Jost and two of his men behind to do his bidding.

"Cover their heads," Jost commanded. Each of the accused men had a white canvas bag placed over their head.

"I don't want a bag over my head," shouted Röhm. "I would prefer to look my assassin in the eye."

"The bags are there to reduce the mess. I don't care about your feelings; you are traitors," Krupp said. Strasser gasped under his hood.

Jost Krupp unholstered his Luger pistol and, without ceremony or warning, went behind Strasser and fired a round into the back of his head. He then came to Röhm. His head was turned to one side. Jost raised his pistol to where he estimated Röhm's ear to be under the canvas bag.

"Turn to the front!"

Röhm did as he was told. Krupp stood back and fired the final round of his Luger, without any emotion or feeling, into the back of Röhm's head. The front of the canvas bag was instantly covered with blood and the bullet exited through a small hole.

"Clear up this mess," he ordered the SS soldiers, holstering his pistol and removing his gloves and throwing them into an office bin beside the door. "I will send in a burial party to get rid of the bodies." Jost strolled out the door with a smile of satisfaction. He had proved his value to the Führer. He was sure recognition for his loyalty would be forthcoming.

14

It was such a cheerful February morning, crisp, cold and still full of freshness; a very slight hint of spring approaching if you were that kind of optimist. Paris could not look more enticing. There were no tourists milling about in Rue Auguste Vacquerie at that time of the morning – just people going to work, emerging from their homes muffled against the cold with hats and scarves. The naked trees cast spidery shadows over the pavements, the sun bathing the city in bright morning amber.

Not a traditional morning for a funeral, no miserable rain or hooded clouds. The hearse, a vast Renault Mona with swathed black-curtained windows, drew up at the entrance to St Georges Church – an Anglican church which stood inconspicuously in the narrow road. The coffin of Lady Joy Barrett was carried solemnly by four expert pall bearers, from the hearse, through the church doors to the coffin stools that stood in the centre of the chancel before the altar. There was a small wreath on the coffin lid.

Behind the hearse walked a woman and a young girl, elegant and shrouded in large, veiled hats. Stella and Charlotte de Tournet were followed by the tall figure of Jean de Tournet. Charlotte could not remember her grandmother; she was not even a year old when she went to live with her aunt and uncle in Concord, Massachusetts.

They made a very handsome family. There were not many people in the church; apart from Lady Joy Barrett's servants and lawyer, there were only a few of her friends, an old French diplomat or two, and a representative of the British embassy. Considering how highly she was regarded and her influence in Paris social and political circles, it was surprising how poorly the attendance was for her funeral. Those who were in the church were impressed by these glamorous American people sitting beside the coffin. Stella and Charlotte, however, were English – even though Charlotte spoke English with a soft North American accent.

Charlotte raised her veil, revealing a pretty face with long eyelashes that bordered her large violet-blue eyes. Once she grew through her teens, it was plain she would turn into an exquisite beauty.

"Charlotte, put your veil over your face. You are in a church, in mourning for your grandmother," Stella hissed in English.

"It keeps going into my mouth and it tickles my nose."

"Charlotte!" Jean whispered angrily from the side of his mouth as they sat on the chairs beside the coffin. They were facing the coffin at right angles to the congregation.

Charlotte reluctantly pulled the veil back over her face. As she adjusted the veil away from her nose, she noticed she was being observed by a man with dark curly hair and sunglasses. Beside him was another man who was young and handsome. He had a bearing of nobility about him as he sat erect in his chair, holding a silver-topped walking stick. They sat near the back of the church. The man with curly hair seemed transfixed by Charlotte; she felt his gaze even with him wearing sunglasses. His lips were smiling slightly. He could not see she was looking back at him as the veil covered her eyes. Charlotte tried to appear as though she was regarding the coffin. She stole a glance every now and then out of the corner of her eye to see if he was still looking at her.

"Oh! My God, look!" Stella's voice hissed. She was breathing heavily and surreptitiously pointing at the man in dark glasses.

"What is it?" Jean de Tournet hissed back. He looked in the direction Stella was pointing.

The man stood up slowly and edged out of the stall, leaving the other man, and walked out of the church. Charlotte watched him with interest. Her aunt and uncle carried on hissing loudly at each other about something Charlotte could not hear, but the man had gone. The handsome man just sat sadly, leafing through his prayer book or looking at the architecture of the church.

*

Charlotte was nine at the time of her grandmother's funeral. She was unsure what to think about the attention she got from the sunglasses man in the church. Boys of her own age always wanted to get to know her. She was a beautiful girl and every time a boy came too close, Stella or her nanny, Christina, would close in and pull her away.

Bo and Christina were not at the funeral; they had gone back to Sweden after four years of not seeing their home country. They were to join Charlotte at Nineteen Avenue Foch, two days after the funeral.

The final member of the family entered the church ten minutes after the de Tournets. Sir Jason Barrett wandered in, looking distinguished with his thin, dark, slicked-back hair. He wore a black-tailed jacket, striped trousers, and a black stock with a pearl stock pin penetrating the stiff white shirt and high collar. He gave the impression that the funeral was a huge inconvenience rather than seeming upset about the death of his mother.

He joined the de Tournets, occupying the last vacant chair beside the coffin, and nodded solemnly at Stella. He didn't acknowledge either de Tournet or Charlotte.

The funeral was conducted with sombre respect. Joy insisted on being cremated as she wanted to make sure she was dead. She was convinced dying was a kind of coma and she wanted to ensure she would not wake in a coffin. Her husband, who died during the Great War, was buried in Sussex, England, and Joy wanted her ashes to be placed on top of her husband's coffin.

The cremation was a simple ceremony. None of the servants from the church went, just Jason, Jean and Stella de Tournet, Charlotte, and the family lawyer, Monsieur Russe. Then they went back to Lady Joy's house in Avenue Foch where Monsieur and Madame Ducheyne were waiting.

"Ducheyne?" Jason Barrett stood at the fireplace in the salle de séjour, looking every bit the master of the house. "Champagne, please, for everybody to salute Lady Joy," he announced with uncharacteristic bravado.

"Monsieur Ducheyne, may I have a Naranjina?" asked Charlotte sweetly, in heavily accented French.

"Oui, mademoiselle," Monsieur Ducheyne said, smiling and pretending to bow.

"Jason, we need to talk about *that man* who was at the church," Stella announced.

"Oh, it was not *him*, Stella," Jason said in a derisory way, as a brother would to a younger sister.

"Did you see the young man sat beside him who stayed? Do you know who he was? I don't think he was a friend of Mama's."

"It could not be him, he would not dare, *chérie*," de Tournet tried to assure her. "No idea who the other man was. Must be something to do with the embassy."

"Who are we talking about?" piped up Charlotte. "That man in dark glasses who kept looking at me and smiling?"

"No, darling, just someone Granny knew, or we thought we knew," Stella said.

"Monsieur Russe will read the will after we have drunk to Mama's memory." Jason changed the subject. "Charlotte, you can go into your room if you would like," Jason said, in a way that was a command rather than a suggestion.

Charlotte opened her mouth to complain, but Monsieur Russe interrupted.

"I would prefer it if Mademoiselle Charlotte remained, actually." He positioned himself in the centre of the gathering. All eyes turned on him in mild surprise. He suddenly looked uncomfortable and coughed nervously. "There is a part of the will that relates to Charlotte. She needs to hear it."

"What part?" demanded Jean de Tournet.

"You will find out when I read the will, monsieur." Monsieur Russe tried not to sound impertinent but failed. De Tournet glared at him.

Jason defused the situation by saying, "I think we should get the will read now, in that case, as Charlotte will have to rest after today's excitement." Jason plainly had no idea what children did in the afternoon. He had had little to do with children; he did not like them and when his sisters were children, he was away at school, university or working.

"Very well, if you would like, Sir Jason." At that point, the champagne arrived so Jason agreed to pour out the glasses before the will was read.

"The Ducheynes should also be present," said Monsieur Russe. Again, all heads turned to the lawyer, who rummaged in his dispatch case to hide his embarrassment.

"Very well. You'd better get Marie, Ducheyne. Meanwhile, can I ask you all to stand and salute a very much missed mother and grandmother, so … to Joy." They all raised their champagne saucers and Charlotte raised her glass of orange-flavoured sparkling water.

The Ducheynes returned to the room and stood meekly by the door. Marie gave Stella a little bob when their eyes met.

Monsieur Russe sat down on a central upright chair and opened a large document with ornate writing on the cover: Last Will and Testament of Lady Joy Eleanor Barrett. He cleared his throat and looked up. Everybody else was still standing and looking intently at him. He gestured for everyone to sit, but Jason and Jean de Tournet remained standing.

"This is the last will and testament of Joy Eleanor Barrett, dated the sixth of July, 1925. There are no codicils or later amendments, unless you have found some, Sir Jason?"

Jason shook his head. His thorough search of his mother's paperwork revealed she left virtually everything to do with her investments, properties and legal matters to her bank manager and Monsieur Russe. How she could leave everything to be run by these Frenchmen astonished Jason. But then he had never offered to help his mother with her affairs; he just presumed the family accountants in Ludgate Hill in the City of London would have continued to handle everything since his father's death. He blamed himself for not taking matters more in hand.

"Then I will assume this is her last will." Monsieur Russe adjusted his pince-nez and resumed reading. "I won't read all the usual legal substance – I will just get on with the main part.

"*To Monsieur Charles and Madame Marie Ducheyne, 10,000 francs on their retirement as long as it is at least a year after my death.*'"

Marie Ducheyne squeaked and then put her hand to her mouth when everybody turned to look at her.

"Thank you, monsieur," Charles said to Monsieur Russe and then turned and bowed to Jason. "Your mother was a very generous employer, Sir Jason. I am very much obliged. We had planned to retire next year."

"I bet you had," snorted Jean de Tournet.

"To carry on," Russe said with a little cough to get everyone's attention, "there are some minor bequests to a charity for women in 'trouble'; nothing major." He paused for dramatic effect.

"I now come to the property and the bulk of the estate," the lawyer continued. "'*I leave Nineteen Avenue Foch to my daughter Alice, to include the Barrett Collection and my husband's library.*'"

"What does that mean?" shouted Jean de Tournet.

Jason turned to his brother-in-law and said, with controlled anger, "Sir, this is my mother's will to her family, which, I regret, does not include you specifically. It will, however, be your wife who now takes the house and the collection, but—"

"No, I am afraid it does not," Russe interrupted. "Under the instructions of Alice Barrett's will, it is passed on to Charlotte." Russe held up another sheet of paper in evidence. "She presumed she would die at an old age and placed no instruction that it should be held in trust or realised at a certain age. I hasten to add, I did not draw up this will; my partner Mr Strider of London did."

Jason spun round and looked at Russe in astonishment, his face pale. He then looked at the paintings on the wall – something he was convinced would be left to him. His father would have left his art to his son, thought Jason, not some bloody child. Jason composed himself to some degree but inside he was in near panic.

De Tournet turned on Russe and was about to launch into a tirade when Jason put up his hand.

"De Tournet, that was my sister's will. Charlotte inherits this house, the collection and the library. And that is an end to it," Jason said condescendingly. "However, Charlotte" – Jason turned towards Charlotte quickly, unnerving her a little – "there is a proviso in my father's will to your grandmother that the collection may *never* be broken up and *never* sold." He spoke to her as an adult, not a nine-year-old.

Russe looked at Sir Jason curiously. "Sir Jason, I do not believe there was such a proviso. I can show you—"

"Thank you, monsieur, I will take this up later."

Russe bowed his head slightly in concession. He resumed with the instructions of the will.

"Monsieur de Tournet," Russe said meekly, "unless Charlotte instructs me otherwise, it is my duty to administer her estate until she is of age. You are her legal guardians, but it has been specifically stated that Alice Barrett wanted Charlotte's estate to be managed by us, not by her husband … future husband … or by Sir Jason." He held up the document, Alice's will, for a second time.

Again, Jason was astonished by this statement. Did neither his mother nor his sister trust him? The brat could have the house, the books, but *not* the collection. He again tried to hide his frustration, and he could see the others in the room were all looking at the blustering Jean de Tournet.

De Tournet threw up his hands in surrender. Stella was quiet all this time and watched her husband with gradual irritation. He plainly looked forward to getting his hands on this estate.

"Does that mean this is my house now?" said Charlotte to the lawyer.

"Yes, mademoiselle, it is your house, as are the contents, the collections and the books in the library," Russe said to her officially. "Except, that is, for some items that have otherwise been bequeathed." He carried on with the reading. "'*To my daughter Stella, all my jewellery except my Queen Anne pearls that I leave to the Anne of Cleves Museum in Lewes, East Sussex. Also, the choice of a strand of pearls for my daughter Alice.'"* Russe looked over his pince-nez at Charlotte. "You will now have that choice, Mademoiselle Charlotte. *'The property Alston House in Val-André, Brittany, to my daughter Stella de Tournet, née Barrett, and Alston Hall in Wimbledon to my son Jason Barrett for disposal as he sees fit, and the remainder of my estate to be divided equally between my three children and their heirs.'"*

Russe paused and took off his pince-nez. He scrunched his eyes shut, then opened them again and looked at his audience who were rapt with attention and expectancy.

"This, Sir Jason, is the important bit of the testament: *'divided equally between my three children and their heirs'*. This means that Charlotte has equal dividend of the remainder of the estate. She is a minor and therefore will not have access to her portion without consent from her trustees, her trustees being Gautier, Russe et Strider Droit Privé International."

"What about the costs of her upbringing, her schooling, her ... God forbid, her dowry?" Jean de Tournet protested.

"For God's sake, Jean!" Stella cried out to her husband. "I don't think this is the time."

"We are her guardians, we are bringing her up for her mother, so now she has her mother's money, surely her mother should pay for her expenses?"

"Jean!" Stella went over to Charlotte and put a comforting arm around her shoulders, although Charlotte was not remotely upset.

"That, monsieur, is a legitimate request for funds. Not only are there funds available for her education, her portion of the estate is totally adequate to pay for all future education ... and her education to date, come to that."

"Right," said Stella, her small, pretty face red with anger, "that is enough about who is going to pay what for Charlotte. My mother has died. Let's remember her."

"Aunt Stella, can I stay here, in my house, and go to school in Paris? I don't want to go back to America."

Stella looked at her niece with shock. "Darling, you must go back to America. You have school, your friends, Bo and Christina, and your—"

"She should stay here, Stella," said de Tournet gently. "We will discuss this later; I'm sure we don't want to hold up Monsieur Russe. Is there anything else?"

Stella looked at her husband in surprise.

Russe stood and turned to face Jason.

"That is the bulk of the will. I can go through the small bequests with you at another time, Sir Jason," Russe said. "However, I wish to stress that we have had specific instructions from the will of Mademoiselle Alice Barrett regarding her child. Her will was drawn up by me, two weeks before her death." He turned to Stella with his back to de Tournet. "Alice Barrett had obviously not anticipated dying so early and her requests were in the assumption that her daughter would be well past her twenty-first year. Her will states that you, Madame de Tournet, are to be her guardian until she is twenty-one, and therefore entitled to access to a portion of the estate." He swung quickly around and looked at Jean de Tournet, taking him by surprise. "I regret, Monsieur de Tournet, the will excludes you from any" – Russe paused, cautious of saying a word or phrase that would offend or inflame de Tournet's mood – "financial benefit from Charlotte's portion of the estate. I trust I have made that clear."

"As glass, monsieur." De Tournet looked at Jason and then back at Russe. "So the thousands of francs and dollars already spent by me, or should I say us, does not count for anything," he shouted. Stella sighed. "I want to see a copy of Alice Barrett's will. I am not sure I believe what you say, monsieur."

"That is enough, de Tournet." Sir Jason butted in. "I will send you a copy of both wills in due course. Good day, Russe."

"Good day, madame, messieurs, Mademoiselle Charlotte." Russe shook Jason's hand and left, flushed with anger. Stella and Charlotte went with Russe to see him out.

Jason, still standing at the fireplace, was deep in thought, mainly about the collection. It consisted of around fifteen extremely valuable paintings and some treasured classics worth quite a lot of money.

"You kept very quiet throughout all this," de Tournet said to Jason, collapsing into a large high-backed sofa.

"Unlike you, de Tournet."

"Listen, Barrett, I have taken on Charlotte, taken her to America, educated her for the past six years, been responsible for—"

"De Tournet, listen to yourself. Stella took on the child, she brought her up. It has cost you money, yes, but you have considerable resources. It is not as if you need this money of Charlotte's." Jason was stern but not angry. "You may be interested to know that Alice left that idiot who killed her a sizeable bequest, which I contested and won."

"Really?" De Tournet looked quizzically at Jason. "I wonder why? How would she know if *he* would still be going when she died? Bloody woman."

Jason had been a diplomat too long to complicate matters with a man like his brother-in-law. Like most wealthy men, de Tournet hated parting with his money on anything other than for things that would enrich him further or he would enjoy paying for, such as nights at the Moulin Rouge in Paris, the Coconut Grove in Boston or the casinos of Monaco with his friends.

*

Jean de Tournet turned and went out the door. He put on his hat and coat.

"Is everything all right, *chéri*?" Stella said gently as she returned from seeing Russe out. She was aware her husband's temper was about to erupt into a full-blown volcano. "Are we going home now?"

"Yes, just me. I have to do some work. You stay here and sort out Charlotte," he said, his temper not in evidence, which surprised Stella. "If Charlotte wants to stay in Paris, she should. Get her out of my hair for a while. She could go to the Académie Lubec. It's a fine school; my cousin went there, and she is now married to an English Lord."

Stella was astonished. She had not expected this turnaround. Her husband plainly wanted to either be rid of any responsibility for Charlotte – he had little anyway – or he wanted to move back to Paris. They still had a house in Avenue George Cinq, which Jean's wayward male friends used for illicit visits to Paris.

Stella felt a tug on her sleeve. Charlotte was getting her attention.

"Aunt, will you stay with me in Paris?" Charlotte was never allowed to refer to her aunt as "mother". Her uncle told her that her mother was killed by falling down some steps on a stormy night in Brittany.

"We both will. Uncle Jean may be away for long periods, but I will be here with Bo and Christina. This will be your house when you grow up and it will be lovely to keep it nice for your husband and children."

"Who will be my husband?" Charlotte's eyes shone; she was excited by this development.

"We don't know that yet. We will find a nice gentleman for you who will be handsome, kind and important." Stella was equally excited to return to Paris. She hated the house in America, the endless snow in winter and house always cold. Paris offered stability, history, art and above all, good taste. Concord was full of social climbers and she had to always be on her guard in case she made a societal blunder. Her status – so far – in the New England social network was high, but she felt that any minute they could discover her husband's indiscretions and she would be marked a pariah among the Concord elite. Boston offered quite a lot of culture, but their house was twenty miles away, an hour at least in a car, and Jean hated going into town with his wife to the theatre or a concert. Her husband's social life in Boston, however, was becoming notorious.

*

Charlotte and Stella went back into the drawing room to join Jason. Charlotte saw her uncle looking into the fire with an expression of deep thought.

"Uncle Jason," – Charlotte went over to him and looked into the fire to see what he was staring at – "do you live here?"

Jason looked up suddenly at his niece. Charlotte stepped back in surprise at his swift movement. Jason looked at her in fury but a nudge from Stella caused his expression to mellow. "No, I live near the embassy. No one lives here now your grandmother has died."

"So you don't mind if we live here?" Charlotte asked bluntly.

"No, you should, with your uncle and aunt. Charlotte" – Jason stood imperiously at the fireplace – "I would like to talk to your aunt quietly about your grandmother's will and what we are going to do with it. Perhaps you would like to go to your mother's room and read or play? Madame Ducheyne will come and find you for tea." Charlotte obeyed her uncle and ran upstairs.

Her mother's room was lovely: spacious, with pale walls that had a hint of lilac, and a huge bed with a large cream wicker bedhead. The bed was wonderful for bouncing up and down on and making a tent for illicit reading at night. Above the fireplace was a picture that belonged to her mother and now Charlotte. It was a small picture of intricate patterns in shades of gold and thin red lines and circles. There, in among the design, was the face of a beautiful girl, asleep, with her arm on a golden pillow.

Charlotte took off her shoes and lay down on her bed, her arm draped over the pillow like the girl in the picture, and promptly fell asleep.

15

September 1939

Adlerhorst was the headquarters of Hitler's High Command. Franz-Joseph Deller proudly walked along the wide corridors of power, sporting a new SS lieutenant colonel uniform. Thanks to his manipulative mother, Clara, on the higher levels of Hitler's closest advisers, he went through the ranks with frightening speed. He held the rank of major for only a month.

He saw Albert Speer coming in the other direction. With him, deep in conversation, was a man Joseph vaguely recognised but could not remember how. Both men were in dark business suits. As the two men drew closer, their conversation stopped abruptly. Joseph came smartly to attention and saluted with his arm outstretched. "Heil Hitler!"

"Ah, Colonel Deller, Heil Hitler. May I introduce you to Sir Jason Barrett," Speer said.

Joseph felt weak. Sir Jason looked at him with raised eyebrows. He had aged badly since Joseph last saw him in 1935, in a Paris church with Ferdi, at Lady Joy's funeral. He was now almost completely grey. His skin was sallow, but his eyes were sharp as he came up close to Joseph, forcing him to back up against the wall.

"You are the one who killed my sister!" Jason's hands were clasped behind his back, anger all over his face.

Speer was confused. "Do you know Colonel Deller, Sir Jason?"

There was a long pause. Sir Jason's eyes, still on Joseph's startled face, softened.

"He was our gardener." Jason then broke into fake laughter. Joseph looked from Speer to Sir Jason and then back again, a worried expression across his face.

"I knew he was in Paris in the nineteen twenties," said Speer. "He was a student of art. His father is Hitler's adjutant and one of his military advisers, General Werner Deller."

Joseph breathed a sigh of relief.

"May I have a quick private word with him?" Jason asked charmingly.

"Yes of course, but we are due to meet the Führer in ten minutes and we must not be late."

*

Still confused, Speer went into his office and sat down at his desk. He picked up the phone and dialled a single number. When Rudolf Hess answered, Speer said, "Hess, what do we know about Jason Barrett? He seems to know that idiot Deller ... Clara's son."

"He is head of an organisation called WASP, an organisation that fights against socialism and communism; part of Lord Rathmore's lot in England."

"I see," Speer said. "Why is the Führer so interested in him?"

"Well, apart from anything else, he and WASP organised to fly Franco from the Canary Islands – where he was, in his words, 'banished' – back for a secret meeting in a Spanish forest before the Spanish Civil War. He did a lot to put Franco and the Nationalists on the Spanish throne, as it were. He is going to help us immensely."

"Is he British secret service?"

"No. He is a diplomat in Paris. He has many fingers in many pies ... political influence. Why are you worried? He has been vetted."

"Not by me, he hasn't. We are about to meet with the Führer, Herman, Goebbels and yourself to discuss France and the Axis alliance with the Soviets."

"What about the Axis alliance?"

"WASP are against the Reich's involvement with the Soviets, he tells me. He has influence in the US and Britain."

Hess sighed on the other end of the line. "He knows nothing of our war plans, Speer. However, he is helping us with the invasion of the Low Countries and France. He was a huge help to the Spanish Nationalists."

There was a tap on the office door. Speer's secretary came in, followed by Jason.

"We will be with you in five minutes, Hess." He replaced the handset and looked up at Jason. "Everything all right with Deller?"

"Yes, fine, Herr Speer. I was just surprised to see him here, of all places."

"What was that about him killing your sister?" Speer was concerned.

"Bad taste, really. She committed suicide after he spurned her. That was all. She was an overemotional girl." Jason wore a false smile of assurance. Speer was relieved but then wondered what woman would kill herself over Deller? "Will Deller be joining the meeting?"

"Good God, no," Speer said, getting up from his desk. "He is just something to do with culture and propaganda. He is Goebbels's problem. Now, we must not be late for the Führer."

*

Two days after his impromptu meeting with Jason Barrett, Joseph was out of uniform and wearing sunglasses. It was mid-September; summer had rolled into autumn with a hot, lovely day. He spent a pleasurable few hours watching girls in thin cotton dresses as he sat at a bar overlooking a small lake in the Nördlicher Park in Bad Nauheim. He had been wandering around the park on his way to the post office. He was taking as long as he needed to ensure he was not being followed, and he was nervous about posting his illicit communication. So, he was doing what any young officer would do on a hot Friday – relaxing and watching the girls go by. He was plucking up courage to post an encoded letter to Ferdi Saumures at an address in Berlin.

He finished his drink and was about to walk to the post office when a man in his thirties sat down uninvited at his table. He was good-looking, squat, his hair short and the sides shaved to well above his ears – the fashion for the Gestapo.

"Can I help you, sir?" Joseph said with some authority.

"I thought I would join you, Major Deller."

"How do you know my name?" Dread seeped into Joseph's chest. He had to cough to clear his throat.

"I am sorry," he said, raising his summer fedora. "Ernst Kaltenbrunner, Gestapo." Joseph's heart turned over. He felt himself go pale and hoped it was not noticeable. This was the most powerful Gestapo man at Adlerhorst – apart from his boss, *Reichstatthalter* Hermann Göring. He was a general at the age of thirty-six.

Joseph pulled himself together.

"I am sorry, sir. By all means join me. Can I offer you a beer?"

Kaltenbrunner nodded assent with a strained smile. Joseph stood to summon a waiter, then sat and looked at the man opposite, his slightly pointed features and a couple of what looked like fencing scars on his left cheek and jaw. He was also enjoying watching the girls in cotton dresses sitting at a nearby table.

"I should say, though, General, I am now a lieutenant colonel," Joseph said with undisguised pride.

"Really?" Kaltenbrunner said, clearly disinterested.

"What, apart from this lovely day, brings you to this bar, sir?" Joseph asked nervously.

"We have been following you, Major Deller, and—"

"Following *me*? Why on earth …?"

"We follow everybody who leaves Adlerhorst without permission."

"*You* were following *me*?" Deller said incredulously. Why would the head of the Gestapo be following him?

"No – my men have been following you." Kaltenbrunner smiled, like a python. "I was called." A chill ran down Deller's spine. The letter in his pocket now felt very heavy. "We really wanted to see if you were going to meet up with the Englishman, Sir Jason Barrett."

"Really? Is he still in Germany?" Deller was suitably surprised.

"We have momentarily lost him. When he left Adlerhorst he was put onto the train from here, Bad Nauheim, to Zurich, but he never arrived at the Swiss border. We think he remained here. You apparently had a meeting with him just before he left for the station."

Joseph looked at the young general, trying to process what Kaltenbrunner was implying. His eyes widened as a thought occurred to him.

"Have you checked if he has gone to his castle in Friedrichshafen? He has a woman there, I believe, on the banks of the lake." Joseph sat up and looked angrily at the young general. "Why do you think he was going to meet up with me? I killed his sister – by mistake, I hasten to add – he hates me." Joseph heard himself wining and tried to control his emotions.

"I was told that Sir Jason wanted to talk to you in private."

"Yes, he threatened me … a bit … about his sister." This was not what Sir Jason had done, but Joseph prided himself in some good acting.

"Ah, I see," Kaltenbrunner said, looking directly at Joseph and slightly unsettling him. "What is Barrett like?"

"I hardly know him. All I know is he is a senior British diplomat, the *chargé d'affaires* in Paris. I don't know his politics or why he is here." A waiter brought the tall, frothy beer steins to Joseph's table.

"Are you part of WASP? I gather he is head of this … group." Kaltenbrunner leant back casually, saluting with his beer and offering a charming wink to the girls at the next table. Joseph was confused.

"No, I am not a member of WASP. I have no idea what it is. I am, however, a senior member of the Nazi Party." He indicated the membership badge on his lapel. He felt courageous.

"Just remember, Deller, we are now at war. We cannot trust anyone, especially someone from Great Britain."

"Absolutely, sir. I was, however, surprised to see Barrett at headquarters, considering our war status," Joseph said with bravado.

"Me too, Deller." Kaltenbrunner drained the whole half-litre stein of beer. He smacked and wiped his lips, smiled at Joseph and put out his hand to be shaken. "That was a lovely beer, thank you, Major … sorry, Colonel Deller. We will check Barrett's castle in Friedrichshafen. Nice chat." He got up. Joseph did the same, slightly startled by the man's swift change of character. Joseph was aware of two men at a nearby table and a man at another all standing at the same time when Kaltenbrunner waved at them. "I will leave you to your restful afternoon," he said to Joseph, and off he went.

Joseph sank back onto his chair. He took a surreptitious look at the letter in the inside pocket of his blazer and drained his beer. He summoned a waiter and ordered a brandy and another beer. He decided he would have to post the letter another time.

Berlin, October 1939
Baron,

I am writing this to you in haste. I hope it gets to you in time.

I really don't know where to begin. It's been quite a difficult few months.

I am a colonel now! Mother worked her spell and I am an SS lieutenant colonel. Can you believe it? However, I did not count on us going to war!

On the very first day of being this exalted rank, I was working in Hitler's headquarters in Adlerhorst with my father, when who should I bump into but Sir Jason Barrett. I thought he had tracked me down about Alice, but he was here to see the "Great Chiefs", as I call them. He took me aside and cornered me in a corridor. He wanted to meet me after his meeting with Hitler. Christ knows why he was having a meeting with the Führer – we were meant to be at war with the British! It was September.

We met in the car park just before he was taken to the station. We sat on a garden bench as though we were old friends. I can tell you I thought he was going to take out a gun at any second and shoot me. Instead, he asked me to join an organisation called WASP – War Against Socialist Parties. He said he would write to me with my duties. I got the impression I had no choice, or he would tell one and all that I killed his sister. Which I didn't, of course.

I don't know what to do, Baron. I don't know what he wants me to do about this WASP thing, but he has told me in no uncertain terms that I must not tell anyone of my joining this organisation.

At the time of writing, I still haven't received any instructions from Sir Jason. Now we are at war, I think I am about to get posted to somewhere. I just hope it is not somewhere like Poland. My mother keeps telling me that she has ensured I remain in Berlin, but I don't believe she has any say in things nowadays, and my father certainly wants me to go and fight.

I nearly got caught by the Gestapo with this letter. I burned the original and managed to sneak this out with the general headquarters post.

Christ, I'm in a mess again, old friend. Haven't seen you for a few years now. I hope all I have sent you is useful. I'm not sure how much more I can send. I truly hope you are safely back in Luxembourg. However, I am told that, like Austria, Luxembourg will be annexed to Germany soon.

God bless you and keep you.
FJD

16

Sir Jason Barrett was in London when he got the news that the Germans had made considerable ground through Northern France and into Paris itself, and his superiors forbade him to return to Paris. He was in London to arrange the possible evacuation of the Paris embassy and the consulates around Northern France, but the Germans had overrun the evacuation plans.

Because of his intimate knowledge of French politics, Jason was asked into the British secret service as a liaison between the directors and operations, led by Sir Sussex Tremayne.

*

Charlotte was in Paris studying at the Académie Lubec, a school for young ladies. Her step-parents were at Alston House in Val-André on a short holiday when they heard the shocking news of the invasion of Paris.

"Paris has been attacked by the Germans, Jean," Stella screeched, clattering into the study where Jean was reading peacefully. She had been listening to the wireless.

"Really? How awful," de Tournet said impassively, still reading a day-old newspaper.

"Jean!" Stella stamped her foot. "Charlotte … she is still in Paris."

"I will call Jorgensen," – de Tournet sighed – "when we get into town. He will pick her up. Don't worry, for heaven's sake."

"But we must go back, Jean. There are Bo and Christina to—"

"We are not going back to Paris." De Tournet looked up from his paper. "Charlotte and the Jorgensens will have to get themselves down to Biarritz."

"Then I will go back to Paris myself." She went out the door. De Tournet slowly folded his paper. He was not going to win this argument with Stella.

Stella could not get anybody to take her to Paris, no matter how much money she offered. There was hardly any fuel and they only had enough to drive a short distance, according to her husband. Stella was worried about Charlotte. Jean de Tournet did not seem to be at all concerned about his business contacts, or that his Paris office would have been abandoned.

However, de Tournet managed to get hold of Bo Jorgensen in Paris. De Tournet was on the only working phone in the area, at the front desk of the Hôtel Val-André.

"Jorgensen?" Jean de Tournet bellowed into the hotel phone; the line was terrible. "It's Herr de Tournet here." De Tournet spoke in Swedish.

"*Ja*, Herr de Tournet. I was worried about you. The Germans are—"

"I know, that is why I am calling. We can't get back to Paris. We have booked a suite in Biarritz and I want you to bring Fröken Charlotte down to meet us there at the usual hotel as soon as possible. No time to pack anything."

"But Fröken Charlotte is at her school!"

Jean de Tournet sighed impatiently.

"Go immediately to the school and … hello … hello?" The line was dead. "Your call has been cut off, sir," said the operator. "It sounds like the line has been completely cut."

"What's happened?" Stella asked, preparing to hear bad news.

"I think the lines to Paris have been cut."

"By the Germans?" demanded Stella, holding her hand to her mouth, her eyes shimmering in tears.

"I don't know!" Jean shouted.

"What are *you* so upset about, Jean? You don't even like Charlotte."

"She is my stepdaughter, Stella. Of course I like her."

"What is going to happen when the Germans get into Paris? We must get her to safety. She is technically British, after all."

"No, she is not. I made her a French citizen when we took her to America."

"You did what?" Stella was furious. She was about to continue the conversation when the concierge of the Hôtel Val-André interrupted.

"I have a Mr Bo on the phone."

Stella raced to the desk and grabbed the receiver.

"Bo? I want you to collect Charlotte *now* and drive her south with Christina and meet us in Biarritz – we will travel into Spain from there. Lock up the house."

"Yes, madame," a crackly voice said the other end of the phone. The line went dead.

"Bo? Bo!" she shouted hysterically. She dropped the receiver and started to sob. Her husband looked on, angry and frustrated, ready to put on a sympathetic expression should Stella look in his direction.

All Jean de Tournet wanted was to get to Spain. He had business connections there and it was a neutral country. He could duck in and out of France, Italy, or across to America if there was a way, and carry on with his steel trade. The war was making him richer and richer. Charlotte was going to make it difficult, holding everything up just because she did not want to go back to America when war was declared. He didn't much care what happened to Charlotte in any case. If the Germans killed her, he would have a valuable property in Paris and a collection of wonderful art.

Jean and Stella drove back to Alston House. It had many memories for Stella, not least because it was where she rescued Charlotte from her murderous father. It was the last time she and Alice were happy together as sisters, before Alice fell to her death on the cliff steps. Stella was convinced Franz-Joseph Deller, the gardener, pushed her down the steps after a row and killed her. Joseph disappeared straight afterwards and the police had a warrant for his arrest.

"What shall we do, Jean?"

"We will go to Biarritz and wait for the Jorgensens and Charlotte to arrive. I can go into Spain and do my business whilst you wait."

"How do we get there? There is no fuel anywhere around here."

"We can see about a train from Rennes to Biarritz and I will have a car there to go into Spain."

"What do you mean, a car into Spain?" she said angrily. "You cannot abandon me now, not until Charlotte is safe."

"Stella, I have to keep the business going or we won't have any money after the war."

"But what about Charlotte? Will she be OK?" Stella was beginning to crumble again. Jean had to stifle a sigh and could only cast his eyes up to the heavens when Stella was not looking.

"Chérie, I am sorry about Charlotte. Once we are in the Hôtel Georges in Biarritz, we will have another go at Paris. It is a little more civilised there. We will pack and hopefully I will have enough petrol to get to Rennes or find some on the way."

Stella conceded and started to pack. The servants, Claudette and Claudine, and their father, Claude, were given instructions to close the house up. Stella was not convinced the Germans would ever get as far as Brittany, but seeing as they had managed to get to Paris so quickly, one never knew.

Jean de Tournet was pleased to get out of this small little town on the edge of nowhere, with no petrol, no telephones that worked and hardly any electricity. All he wanted to do was head off to the comfort of the Hôtel Georges and leave Stella there, or better still, take her back with him to America so he could get on with selling steel.

17

The staff and students of Académie Lubec had been evacuated two weeks previously. All, that is, but the headmistress and five students who had not been able to leave for one reason or another. Three of the girls had not heard from their Jewish parents for most of the year and they were preparing to be taken by the American embassy for evacuation. As to the two other students, one French–Russian, the other being Charlotte, both had lost contact with their guardians.

Charlotte was sitting in a small room with the four remaining classmates, discussing the probabilities of Paris being occupied and what was going to happen. There was a knock on the door as it was opened.

"Mademoiselle de Tournet?" Madame Pippinous, the principle, popped her head around the door.

"Yes, Madame Pippinous?" Charlotte stood respectfully.

"Ah – there you are. You are to go straight back home. You are being taken back to *Angleterre*."

"Why?" asked Charlotte.

"Well, I imagine it may be something to do with the war, mademoiselle," she said, annoyed at being questioned. "Now, get along with you. A car is waiting outside to take you back home."

Charlotte said goodbye to her friends, who were in shock at the sudden departure of their English friend. She was hardly English; she spoke French with only the very slightest of American accents. However, she did not look French. Charlotte was tall and slim with long, elegant arms and legs. She was self-conscious about her height and stooped a little – she hated standing out. She was constantly told to stand straight by her tutors which accentuated her breasts, which were quite developed for a fifteen-year-old and the envy of her peers.

Charlotte had grown into a beautiful young woman over the past five years. Her aunt thought a Paris education and then a finishing school in Switzerland or England would give Charlotte the best chances in life.

Charlotte put on a beret to hide most of her hair which was tied back into a long, glossy ponytail. She put her cloak over the prescribed shapeless black and royal-blue school dress, even though it was a hot, sunny June day outside. Paris was the centre of haute couture, and this was what the girls of the prestigious Académie Lubec had to wear? Not that it upset Charlotte too much. She wasn't bothered about her looks, and she wasn't concerned whether men or boys gave her a second glance. She knew that if she tried she could look pretty, but she couldn't be bothered. She didn't seek the attentions of the opposite sex. She was fifteen, and there was plenty of time for that.

Bo was standing beside the black Renault, a large square vehicle that served as the de Tournet's runaround despite being twice the size of most cars in Paris.

"Hi, Bo," Charlotte said. "What's the fuss? Why am I going to England?"

"Miss Charlotte, the Germans are on the outskirts of Paris; they are walking in. The bloody French army are in pieces and the British have disappeared ... I don't really know where ... but your father ... stepfather," Bo corrected himself, "wants us to go down to Biarritz, but I am not sure I have the fuel. We must hurry. It has taken nearly two hours to get here. So many people are trying to leave Paris. Christina is packing some things and we will pick her up on the way out."

All through this flustered speech, Bo was hustling Charlotte into the back seat of the car. Charlotte kept trying to interrupt with a "But ...". He looked uncharacteristically agitated.

"What about my trunk, my clothes and things, Bo?" Charlotte boarded at the school even though it was only a few kilometres from her home. Both she and her aunt preferred it that way.

"Christina is packing your things at the house. We must go. There has already been fighting in the streets."

"Good gracious," Charlotte exclaimed, slightly excited. What an adventure – and what a fun journey it would be down to Biarritz.

Bo got into the driver's seat, started the motor and headed north to Avenue Foch. Charlotte fired questions at Bo about what was going on. The streets were nearly completely void of traffic now, which was most disquieting for Bo. As they went up an empty Avenue Raymond Poincaré towards Avenue Foch, he suddenly slowed and stopped.

"Why have you stopped, Bo?"

"Look up ahead. There are soldiers – lots of them. Roll up your window."

"French? English?"

"I don't know. We will go up very slowly and see."

Bo edged the Renault up to the junction. Nineteen Avenue Foch, home, and where Christina waited, was on the other side – the north side – of the wide, open avenue. Avenue Foch was made up of three roads: a central main road and two residential roads providing access to the houses on either side, separated by two wide grass boulevards with trees running down the middle. The Renault would have to drive across using the crossroads. When Bo had set off two hours before, all the roads going towards the River Seine were completely packed. They were now ghostly quiet, not another car in sight.

"What about the house? What about the collection and the library, Bo?"

"Christina is locking it up. She has closed all the rooms and locked them, and she has covered all the furniture. Don't worry, it's very secure ..." Bo's last words drifted away as they came up to the main central road in the avenue. No soldiers could be seen coming down the road, only some walking in line some distance away.

Bo gunned the engine and crossed the first boulevard, then the main road, then the second boulevard. As he approached the third and last road, the road Nineteen Avenue Foch was on, he could see, motoring south towards them, a large open-topped grey half-track – an enormous armoured vehicle with tank tracks at the back and big chunky wheels at the front to steer. On its side panel was a large black and white cross, and on each front fender flew a square flag with a scarlet field and a swastika in a central white circle.

The vehicle had spotted the Renault. It swung over the grass boulevard that separated the roads, leaving a wake of soil and turf, and thundered straight towards Bo and Charlotte.

Charlotte squealed in surprise as Bo braked heavily. He turned and looked at Charlotte in panic.

"Charlotte, listen to me. This is terribly important. From now on, you are my daughter, Freya. Do you understand? Freya, Freya Jorgensen."

"But why, Bo?" Charlotte said with alarm. She should have been on the verge of tears, but she was not. She was holding her nerve.

147

"Because that will make you Swedish – a neutral. And you must speak nothing else but French from now on."

"I speak a little German," Charlotte said as she watched the huge German vehicle pull up in front of them and loom over the bonnet of the Renault.

Charlotte could hear a lot of hobnailed boots running up to the car. A gloved fist on the end of a grey-sleeved arm with a white shirt cuff knocked on the window. Bo rolled the window down. The car was now surrounded by uniformed bodies. All Charlotte could see were seven belted green-grey jackets, each with a pair of arms pointing a rifle at her and Bo. She looked out the window at the tall, uniformed man with a forage cap set on the side of his head.

"Who are you, monsieur?" he asked in heavily accented French.

"I am Bo Jorgensen, and this is my daughter, Freya Jorgensen." Bo pointed to Charlotte.

The German officer turned to look at her. She had wound down her window in the back of the car and offered up a smile.

"Are you French?"

"No, we are Swedish. We are servants to a household in Paris," Bo said.

"Papers!"

"Ah …" Bo hesitated. "Our papers are at home. I was on my way to pick up—"

"Where do you work? What is the address?"

"It is just the other side of Paris. Nanterre."

"We require the car. No civilians may have a car during this occupation of Paris."

"You have occupied Paris?" Bo said in genuine surprise.

"Paris fell to us an hour ago. You will see the might of the German army roll down to the Arc de Triomphe in two hours' time."

"Sir, we have to get back to Nanterre to pick up my wife." Bo carried on as calmly as possible. "We must get back to Sweden, or at least to the Swedish Embassy. We need our car to transport our luggage."

"I will have to take this up with my superior. You will drive me to the headquarters. Now!" The German officer barked some orders to the soldiers.

"Bo – or should I call you Papa?" Charlotte giggled. "Why are you telling him we live in Nanterre?"

"Because we do not want him to know where we really live."

"But he will see us drive into the house – it's just over there."

"Listen, I'm trying to think fast. It's not easy. I had no idea the Boche

148

would be here. Paris taken so quickly? It's horrifying. Christina will be terrified!"

Charlotte was quite excited by it all. She watched the soldiers climb back into the huge vehicle in front of the Renault. The officer was swaggering about. He looked back at Bo and Charlotte every now and then. The German half-track vehicle was still parked firmly in front of them, so they could not drive off without the officer.

"Charlotte … Freya, let me do the talking, please. It is very important that—" Before Bo could tell her what was important, the German officer opened the passenger door. He had removed his pistol from its holster and was holding it in his right hand as he got in. Bo was watching it intently. Though Bo was a trained soldier, he had never seen combat or had a loaded weapon pointed at him.

The officer rolled down his window and waved the truck back with his gun, then brought his arm in and lay the gun on his lap.

"Nineteen Avenue Foch, monsieur," the army officer said, indicating the direction with the point of his pistol. Bo blanched and turned to look at Charlotte.

"Did you say 'nineteen', monsieur?" Charlotte asked innocently. "But that's my house!" She said it without thinking and instantly realised what she had done. The officer swung round and looked suspiciously at Charlotte. She smiled nervously, as sweetly as she could, and said, "I mean that is where we work. Why are you taking us to our house and how did you know?"

"Monsieur, what is this?" said the officer, raising his gun from his lap.

"My daughter is correct. It is where we work, for Monsieur and Madame de Tournet."

"Well, let's go there and we will sort this out there with my superiors."

They set off. Within two minutes, through completely empty avenues, they drove into the oval drive of Nineteen Avenue Foch. The whole driveway was jammed with large grey trucks. Troops of soldiers stripped down to their vests were scurrying about and taking boxes into the house. Officers with clipboards stood around barking orders.

"But this is appalling," said Charlotte. Bo flashed her a warning with his eyes. "What are Monsieur and Madame de Tournet going to say?"

They all got out. The officer clicked his fingers at Bo with his hand outstretched for the keys of the car. He then holstered his pistol and indicated for Bo and Charlotte to go into the house. They went through the front door, avoiding soldiers carrying boxes who all stopped dead in their tracks when they saw Charlotte – until their superiors marshalled them on with their work and then gawped themselves.

The German officer went up to a trestle table desk that was placed where the front hall table used to be. The sergeant sitting at the table stood to attention, stuck his arm out and clicked his heels. Bo looked around in astonishment. He had only left the house two and a half hours earlier, and all was quite normal. Where were Christina and the staff?

18

A speedy conversation in clipped German ensued. The sergeant sat and started rapidly writing down details of the officer's report. A bespectacled SS captain wandered over to the officer, interested in what he had overheard. The army officer stood to attention when the SS captain appeared at his side. He looked nervously at the black uniform of the SS and gave a Nazi salute.

"Bo!" A shrill voice rang out in the hall. Bo turned to see Christina running towards them. He walked quickly over to her and, uncharacteristically for him, embraced his wife in a loving hug. As he did so he hissed in her ear in Swedish.

"Do not mention Charlotte by name. I have said she is our daughter, Freya, and we are all neutral Swedish citizens."

"What do you mean, our daughter?" Christina released herself from the hug and wiped the tears from her eyes.

"She is French – technically British. They will intern her."

"But we are Swedish. They won't intern us."

"Charlotte has a French passport and French papers. I am going to have to lie about her papers."

Christina took in a sobbing breath with her hands to her mouth.

"Who is this woman?" the SS officer asked in a clipped, abrupt way. He wore thick round tortoiseshell spectacles that he pushed back up his nose.

"She is my wife, monsieur, and mother to Freya." Christina nodded in confirmation and went over to Charlotte and pulled her in close.

Bo said something to Charlotte in Swedish and Charlotte answered. "*Det är bra* – that is fine." She had no idea what Bo had said; her very limited Swedish only included a few of the usual phrases. Christina looked at Charlotte in astonishment. Charlotte saw a mix of confusion and surprise on Christina's round, florid face and quickly kissed her "mother" on the cheek.

"You may only speak in French or German here," the SS officer said.

The sergeant, who was speaking on a field telephone, covered the mouthpiece and said something to the SS captain. The army officer who brought Bo and Charlotte in had disappeared.

"*Kommen Sie mit mir!*" the SS captain said sharply. The captain was about the same height as Charlotte. Apart from his black uniform, he seemed unthreatening. They all followed him at a brisk march to the library, avoiding soldiers laying down telephone wires. The officer knocked on the double doors of the library. A barely audible "*Herein!*" could be heard the other side of the heavy panelled white door. They went in. The library had all the furniture you would expect in an English library, but the deep mahogany leather chairs and sofas and pie crust coffee tables were now all pushed to the sides of the room. Bo, Christina and Charlotte gasped at the changes that had been made in the huge library. Charlotte's grandfather's desk was in the middle of the room, surrounded by cabinets and boxes of files. Wires came down from the ceiling and were connected to two telephones and a desk light.

Sitting behind the desk was an elderly *Wehrmacht* colonel. He was looking down at papers on his desk. He wore a blue-grey jacket with a high collar. A cross-shaped medal from the Great War dangled from the top button, a strip of colourful ribbons ran over his left breast pocket and a gold spreadeagle riding a swastika sat above his right breast pocket. There were oblong scarlet collar boards inlaid with an ornate gold pattern. His gold shoulder boards glistened in the sunlight streaming into the library through the immense Georgian windows. Little shards of bouncing light speckled and danced across the desk from the large chandelier that hung above. The room was humid; no windows were open and the heat from the hot June day was trapped.

The SS officer came smartly to attention and saluted with his arm stiffly thrust out in front of him.

"*SS-Hauptsturmführer* Hans Wil, Herr Oberst." He then announced the visitors in rapid, loud German to his superior officer. The colonel raised his head. He had a thin layer of close-cropped grey hair, and sweat glistened from his scalp. He answered the salute with a small wave of his hand and a grunt, and looked at the three Swedish people through hooded, watery eyes. A cigarette burned in the crook of his fore- and middle fingers, the sun picking out the curl of blue-white smoke. He looked at the girl and frowned.

"Where are Monsieur and Madame de Tournet?" he asked in guttural French without any form of greeting. "And where is" – he looked down at a list – "Lady Joy Barrett, the owner of this establishment?"

Bo stood forward. "The de Tournets, *mon colonel*, are in America with their daughter, and Lady Joy Barrett is dead these past five years." Bo stood stiffly to attention, his military training forbidding him to slouch before a superior officer.

"And Charlotte de Tournet?" he said, still looking at Charlotte with a frown.

"The daughter – we think, in America, *mon colonel*."

"I see. And you are the chauffeur?" The colonel's voice was high and crackled at the end of each question, as though he was very tired.

"Yes, *mon colonel*."

"And the woman is the housekeeper?" He pointed at Christina.

"Yes, *mon colonel*."

"And you are both Swedish?"

"And our daughter, Freya, *mon colonel*."

"There is nothing here about a daughter." He tapped a piece of paper in front of him. "Papers?" He held out his hand, clearly irritated that he, a regular army colonel, was having to behave like some kind of border guard.

Bo approached the desk. He heard a sharp "tut-tut" from the officer beside him and his hand indicated for Bo to step back again.

"We have not got them here, *mon colonel*. They are in our master's house in Biarritz, where we are meant to be now."

"I see," the colonel said as he leant back in his chair, plainly not convinced. "How do I know you are Swedish? You may be French trying to get out of the country. You may be Jewish. Are you Jewish or do you have Jewish relatives?"

Bo and Christina looked at each other with confusion.

"Monsieur." Charlotte stepped forward, bobbed a sweet curtsey and put on a charming smile. For many years now, Charlotte had found that with a little smile and a small dose of humility mixed with some charm, she could get virtually anything she wanted from people – especially from men. "I left my papers behind in Biarritz. I forgot to tell Papa that I picked his and Mama's papers up but forgot mine. The papers are in our quarters downstairs."

"Go and get them, child," said the colonel, seemingly unmoved by Charlotte's pretty speech. "You will have to remain here until your daughter's papers can be found."

"They are in Biarritz," Bo protested.

"No, I think you are lying about this," the colonel said quickly back at Bo with no discernible emotion.

Bo and Christina were taken by surprise and Christina even let out a little whimper. "Why would we lie about such things, *mon colonel?*"

The colonel looked straight at Bo with his hooded, frightening grey eyes. Bo was about to protest again but the colonel said quietly, "You will continue to work in this house, but under the employ of the German army, the SS and the Gestapo. Your daughter will be ... *Wie sagt man verlagert auf französisch?*" He turned to Captain Wil and asked what "relocated" was in French.

"*Relocalisé – ich denke*, Herr Oberst."

"She will be relocated to work if you do not fully cooperate. Is that understood?" The colonel stood up and came around from behind his desk. He was surprisingly short.

"Well, of course, we would be delighted to—" Bo started.

"That is fine. It is too hot in here." He flapped his hand in front of his face. "You are dismissed. Captain Wil here will inform you of the conditions. We will inform the Swedish Embassy of your presence once we get all your papers." He said all this as he strode off to the door to the front hallway and waved his hand towards Bo and Christina, indicating to the captain to get rid of them. Captain Wil snapped to attention and ushered Bo and Christina out.

"Where are all the other staff, Captain?" Bo asked tentatively.

"They have also been relocated," was all the SS captain would say.

Charlotte returned to the front hall with the passports.

"Thank you. I will take those," said Captain Wil, snatching them from Charlotte. She was about to protest when Bo caught her arm and squeezed it enough for her to wince, reminding her to be quiet.

"Do you live in this house?"

"Eh – they are on the lower ground floor, Captain. This way."

"So, what was it you were saying about Nanterre?"

Bo looked at the captain. The officer who picked them up must have said something. "That is where our private quarters are, Captain." Captain Wil looked up at Bo through his thick round spectacles and raised a sceptical eyebrow.

"Show me your quarters."

Bo led the way through the front hall to a second and much larger hall lit by a large glass dome far above. They came to a door covered with brown baize cloth, under the main staircase which rose to a gallery landing that overlooked the hall. They went through the door to a small corridor. To the right were stairs that led down to the lower ground floor. Straight ahead were the large kitchens that seemed to have already been taken over by German army caterers. There was chaotic shouting in German and lots of clanging and banging. Captain Wil looked briefly into the kitchen. All the soldiers instantly went quiet and stood to attention. The captain instructed them to carry on.

Christina was looking distraught and on the verge of tears. Charlotte was looking a little pale and worried.

Charlotte seldom went down to that part of the house. She had occasionally visited Christina when she was ironing, to talk to her or to help clean silver or whatever Christina was cleaning at the time. They talked about troubles at school, friends' problems, lessons, the terrible food at the Académie Lubec or the uncomfortable beds. Charlotte could never talk to her aunt about these things.

"What is down there?" Captain Wil looked apprehensive.

"It is quite extensive. There are the staff quarters, sir." Bo said, inviting Wil to go down the stairs first. Wil did not move.

"Just staff quarters? Do I need to see them?"

"There is also the laundry, the staff pantry, the wine cellar, the meat locker ..."

"Don't forget the ironing room, the stock room, the staff kitchen, or the silver vault. These are the keys." Christina proffered a bunch of keys.

Captain Will plucked the keys from Christina's hand. "I will take those," he said sharply.

"Also the butler's pantry and quarters, where we live at the moment." Bo looked at Captain Wil, still gesturing for Wil to descend the stairs first.

"Very well," he said. "But I don't have much time. Make it quick."

They descended the stairs to a long, naturally lit corridor. Bo took the captain into a side room with a glass-panelled door and walls with interior windows. Daylight came from the raised windows that opened to the front of the house, set high up, level with the driveway.

"This is the staff pantry, where the staff congregate and eat." Bo said.

"Very good," said the captain. "You women stay here. You, show me the rest of this area quickly."

"Yes, captain. Follow me."

As soon as Bo and Wil left the staff pantry, Charlotte removed her cloak, threw it over a chair and whipped off her beret. She was getting very hot.

Christina hissed: "Mademoiselle Charlotte, what is going on?" She picked up Charlotte's cloak, brushed it down and hung it on a hook. "I was down here, packing. The doorbell went – I could hear it from the pantry, going on and on, and that man, in his uniform, his gun in his hand, just strolled in! It was awful." Christina sat on a chair and wiped her brow.

"Listen, Christina." Charlotte drew up a chair beside her nanny, put her arm around her rounded shoulders and talked to her quietly. She was in obvious distress. "You are going to have to think from now on. I am Freya, your daughter. If they know I am Charlotte, they will shoot me." Charlotte thought if she overdramatised the situation, it would sink into Christina's mind. Her ploy worked – Christina let out a little cry. "We must get rid of any photos of me, for a start. Are there any upstairs, on the piano?"

Christina was quiet for a moment.

"No, I think Sir Jason just has ones of him and various important people. There is a picture of you as a baby somewhere, and there is the portrait of you and the de Tournets in the library, but you were only five and your hair is lighter." She started stroking Charlotte's hair and then looked around.

"That doesn't matter; it won't look like me now, will it?" Charlotte realised she was losing patience with Christina. She decided she would have to be kinder or Christina would go to pieces.

Bo and Captain Wil returned.

"And where does your daughter sleep?" Captain Wil said on seeing Charlotte as they entered the staff pantry.

"I am sleeping in Charlotte's room at the moment, whilst she is in America," Charlotte said. "She lets me, you see." Charlotte was not about to give up her lovely room to sleep in a horrid cellar, which she thought must be cold in the winter and very dull with poor lighting.

The captain pushed his glasses back up the bridge of his nose and looked at her with interest. He was about to say something when Bo interjected.

"You'd better move your things back to your room, *chérie*. I think the Captain needs the rooms."

Charlotte looked furiously at Bo. She thought very hard for a minute.

"I will go up, if I may, and Christina and I can move my things. Bo" – Charlotte took in a breath with her mistake, but quickly saved it – "my father … can show you my room and everything else later, monsieur."

"That would be helpful." The captain snapped his heels and saluted Charlotte, a hint of a smile on his face.

Charlotte grabbed Christina's hand and they trotted up the stairs to the ground floor and into the large open hallway that was still busy with soldiers moving in, and then up the main stairs to Charlotte's room. Once they were inside, Charlotte locked the door and leant against it and blew out a breath of air. She was baking.

Christina sat on the bed and patted her flushed cheeks with a handkerchief. It was much hotter upstairs. The sun was in its zenith outside, casting heat over the gardens below. The grass in Avenue Foch was turning quite yellow and looking parched.

Charlotte looked around the bedroom. She had not been in her room since she went back to school after Easter. She never came back during term if her uncle was in residence, even though the school was only five kilometres away.

"So where is Freya's room?"

"Freya?" Christina looked at Charlotte confused and then realised. "Well … I don't know. It will have to be one of the attic rooms. There is only one room on the lower ground floor and that is ours."

"Right. Will Bo think of taking the captain up there, to the attic rooms?"

"I should think so. There is no other place he can go unless he thinks Freya sleeps in the butler's office."

"Is that likely?"

"Well, no, there is no bed there."

Charlotte sighed, wondering why she loved Christina.

Charlotte had very little time for stupid people. She often chided herself for this; it was not their fault they were stupid, but she still found it difficult to like them. And yet she was very fond of Christina. She was kind and generous with her love towards Charlotte and, to some extent, towards Bo.

"Let's get packed up, and I'll go upstairs and find a room in the attic." Charlotte was plainly not used to being a servant. "Remember, Christina," Charlotte said as sweetly as she could, "I am your doting daughter, Freya, from now on, OK?" She sounded very American when she said OK.

Charlotte unlocked the door and went up the servants' stairs, leaving Christina to find the suitcases in the top of the large wardrobe cupboard to the left of the fireplace. Charlotte returned, went to the fireplace and took down her mother's painting of the sleeping girl on the golden pillow. She wrapped it in a blanket from the bed and peeked out the door to check if there was anybody in the corridor. The stairs to the attic rooms were nearly opposite her room. She heard Bo coming up the stairs and she raced up the attic stairs.

She had hardly ever been up in the attic rooms. She hoped there was one that was half-decent. There were seven rooms, three on either side of the corridor and a large room at the end, and a lavatory and a bathroom at the other end. By the looks of it, the large room had not been used since her grandmother died. One room at the other end seemed to be occupied, which concerned Charlotte. She selected the best of the habitable rooms, one that was on the garden side of the house. There was a narrow, metal-framed bed with a flat, slightly stained mattress folded in half on the springs of the bed. There was a little pot-cupboard beside the bed, a simple wardrobe behind the door, a pine chest of drawers with a large dressing mirror, a bentwood chair and a fawn steamer trunk covered in shipping labels.

Charlotte checked to see if there was a lock on the door. There was. The room was once white but now had yellowing edges and corners. The sun shone brightly through the single window. The roof sloped on either side, making half the room impossible to stand upright in – if you were as tall as Charlotte. She opened the window to let in some cool air, but it was just as hot outside as inside.

She unfurled the mattress and sat on it heavily. She rested her head in her hands, elbows on her knees, humming and tapping her toes to the beat of her favourite tune, "Limehouse Blues".

She suddenly realised Christina would be struggling up the stairs with the suitcases.

"Freya!" she heard her call. Charlotte jumped up and went to the top of the stairs just in time to help Christina with the final two steps. "Freya, you are going to have to help more now we are in the 'new situation'." Christina raised her eyebrows.

"Yes of course, Christi … Mama. I am sorry. I was a little distracted. I have chosen this room. It's a bit small."

"Are there curtains?"

"I didn't see. There is a trunk there."

"I think that belonged to the Ducheynes. They lived in this room when your grandmother was here. Let me pass with these cases." She kicked her shoes off and placed them on a shelf beside the stairs. She looked at Charlotte's feet. "Take your shoes off."

"Why?"

"Staff may not wear shoes on this floor. It is to stop any noise going to the floors below."

Christina had a suitcase in each hand and a handbag jammed under her arm. She also carried a photo of Charlotte's mother, Alice, as a young woman.

"You can say this is you … you know, 'Charlotte', not Freya."

"Very good idea. Thanks, Mama." They giggled. Christina had calmed down and was more herself. Charlotte was surprised that her nanny had become so distraught whereas she found it all a great adventure. Until, that is, she found she would have to move out of her room into the hot little attic room. As she was unpacking her suitcases, she realised Christina, quite rightly, had only packed Charlotte's plainest clothes.

"I suppose I can't wear Charlotte's nice clothes?"

"No, my dear. I don't think that would be wise."

"We must give this room a clean before we make the bed, Mama. Where will I find some cleaning stuff?"

"I'll show you."

*

Charlotte and Christina cleaned the bedroom. The commotion downstairs seemed to be getting less and less as the day went on. Both Christina and Charlotte went through the day without lunch and were getting a bit hungry. Bo had not been seen since they had left him in the basement parlour with Captain Wil.

Each time Charlotte went downstairs, there seemed to be a German soldier there waiting, offering to help. She had captivated most of the young men in the house already. After sorting out the bedroom, they thought they would brave going down into the servants' quarters to see if they could find Bo and even get something to eat. Every shirt-sleeved soldier they passed would stop and give a little bow to Charlotte and offer her their most charming smile. Charlotte would giggle; Christina would hurry her along and frown at them.

In the servants' parlour, Bo and two German officers were sitting at the dining table with bottles of beer. There were a few long lists and lots of cigarette butts in the ashtray. They had plainly been organising.

The men all stood when Christina and Charlotte entered.

"Ah, Christina, Freya, we have been sorting out the running of the house."

"Have you, my dear?" Christina said, folding her arms, a look of condescension on her face. "And without my help? I find that hard to believe. What do you men know about running this house – or any house, for that matter?" Charlotte began to snigger with her hand to her mouth. Christina and

Bo started arguing in Swedish, something Charlotte had never witnessed. The German officers were not listening. Charlotte was aware the men were looking at her. They started chuckling when they saw her giggling.

Charlotte had decided everybody needed some tea – it was the English in her – so she searched the parlour for some. Bo and Christina had reverted to French. Charlotte found a tea caddy, a kettle and a gas ring in the little kitchen nearby, cups and saucers in the dresser, and some honey. A coffee pot served as a teapot. Christina put a tin of biscuits on the table.

The officers did not speak much French, apart from Captain Wil who was fluent. Christina did not speak German but Bo did. The situation had turned into an international debate about how to run the house. For the first time in her life, Charlotte found she was serving Bo and Christina, and the officers, tea and biscuits.

After an hour, and more lists, the Germans left and went upstairs. Bo sat the ladies down and looked seriously at them.

"The house is being prepared for the SS and the Gestapo," he said in a low voice.

"Oh?" said Charlotte.

"What does that mean?" Christina asked.

"They are the secret police and they have taken over lots of buildings in Avenue Foch, apparently. This is where they are going to entertain their guests, and soon they are going to arrive."

"Who is going to arrive?" Charlotte demanded.

"I don't know, but we are to stay down here until midnight."

"What?" gasped Christina. "That's preposterous."

"We can go up to the kitchens to get something to eat, but only one of us. SS guards will be everywhere. Those lieutenants were here to sort out the kitchen and serving staff. They are all up there now having a briefing with the new waiters."

Bo sat down. He looked tired and old. There was to be a very important guest arriving at nine o'clock along with his staff – he did not know who. Four of these guests were staying at the house. He told the women about the brigade of serving staff, chefs and other servants that were coming to join them. Christina and Charlotte were to help with the washing up and clearing away at midnight.

"I was beginning to enjoy this adventure, but I don't think I am now," said Charlotte.

"We have to be very careful, Char" – Bo bit his tongue – "Freya … Freya, I'm sorry. We are going to have to be careful as these guards will kill us if we sneeze the wrong way, according to the German officers." Christina looked like she was about to burst into tears.

"Where are they going to get the food? There is nothing in the house except scraps."

"They are bringing in tons of food," Bo said.

"Even with the shortages, I don't see how they are going to manage."

"Don't worry yourself, Christina, my love, please." Bo was becoming exasperated. "It is not our concern."

"This is all very worrying. How long will these Germans be here for?"

"I am not sure how long they will need us here, my love," said Bo. "We don't seem to feature in their plans to run the house."

"What do you mean, Papa?" Charlotte asked.

"Well, they seem to have taken over entirely. I don't think they want us to stay here."

"Do you know this?" Charlotte asked, concerned.

"No, I just get the impression."

"*Men vi* är *svenskar*, Bo. But we are Swedish," Christina said miserably.

"*Detta måste vi göra* för *vår dotter*, Christina. We must do this for our daughter." Charlotte was angry rather than disappointed. It was five o'clock. She was still in her school dress and feeling sweaty and dirty.

"Freya, you will need to smarten up a little, put your hair back again. You can't go upstairs, I'm afraid. Use our bathroom."

"What are we going to do tomorrow, do we think?" Charlotte asked. "Will we have to stay here? Because I would rather stay here and look after the house than go to Biarritz." Bo and Christina looked horrified.

"We have got to get you out of here, Freya," Bo said fervently. "We must get you to your step-parents."

"I don't want to go to my uncle and aunt. I want to stay here." Charlotte looked at Bo and Christina's expression of complete confusion. "They are not nice people – well, Uncle Jean isn't."

"But Charlotte, it is not safe here," Christina hissed.

"We cannot protect you here," Bo interjected.

"I think I would like to disappear. Just say Charlotte de Tournet was killed."

Christina gasped. Bo shook his head in despair.

A clatter of feet could be heard coming down the steps from the main kitchens and the servants' entrance.

"Now what's happening?" Bo said with fatigue in his voice. There were men in white jackets with high collars and women in grey overalls and grey turbans, all with the Nazi emblem above their left breast pockets. There must have been ten of these people, all making themselves at home.

"*Guten Tag*," each of them said somewhat warily as they saw the towering figure of Bo. They chatted animatedly as they walked down the link corridors, looking into each of the rooms as they went past.

A shout of command came out of nowhere. They all stopped and looked in the direction of the officer barking instructions. It was one of the SS lieutenants who Bo had been talking to earlier on in the parlour.

The men and women all stood smartly to attention. There was a deathly silence. Charlotte could hear a pair of heavy boots descending the stairs from the kitchen. She hurriedly tied her hair back and brushed down her school dress. She anticipated that someone important was approaching. She peaked out of the parlour door and looked up the corridor to see who it was. Christina tugged at her skirts to caution her from doing anything foolish.

The officer wore a black uniform trimmed with silver piping, a black leather cross belt with a pistol holster, shiny black boots that went up to the knees, and black breaches. The scarlet armband with its swastika stood out vividly against the black jacket. His hat, which he wore straight and pulled down over his eyebrows, bore a silver skull below the Nazi spreadeagle.

As he inspected each of the servants, he was introduced to them by one of the lieutenants, and they gave the Nazi salute and shouted, "Heil Hitler!" The man arrived at the servants' parlour. Charlotte stood back and the man swaggered in. He took off his hat. Charlotte found him quite comical to look at with his severe haircut, the dark hair shaved to well above the ears, leaving a tuft of short, curly black hair on top. He seemed quite charming, but the uniform conveyed something sinister. He wasn't handsome, but he had a charisma that made up for it, thought Charlotte.

He smiled charmingly, placed his hat under his left arm and stood to attention. With a click of his heels to Christina, as the senior lady in the room, he took her hand and bowed. Bo was next in line, and the man once again clicked his heels and gave a little bow of the head. He turned to Charlotte, clicked his heels and froze. He eyed her long and hard, his mouth open as though lost for words. He quickly regained his composure and saluted her, then stood back and, still looking at Charlotte, swayed slightly. He looked around for a chair and found one at the little parlour table. His face was ashen.

"Are you all right, Colonel?" Bo asked in German.

"I am sorry," the colonel said. "I have had a very long day. Very warm." He wiped his brow with a handkerchief and then visibly brightened. "Let us all have a drink!"

"Would you care for some tea, Colonel?" Charlotte asked.

"Thank you, that would be very nice," he said after a slight pause, plainly hoping for something stronger. He looked at Charlotte. "What is your name, child?"

"Freya Jorgensen," Charlotte said. Confusion fell across his thin face.

"May we have your name, sir?" Bo enquired.

"I am sorry." He stood, clicked his heels again and said, "*SS-Obersturmbannführer* Franz-Joseph Deller, monsieur."

Bo looked at the colonel quizzically. "I think I have heard your name before in—"

Deller interrupted, rather too loudly.

"No idea why you would know my name, sir. It's unlikely you would know me."

19

After Bo had hurriedly introduced his timid wife, Christina, and their daughter, Freya, Charlotte smiled sweetly and bobbed a curtsey to SS Lieutenant Colonel Deller.

"Forgive my impertinence; your daughter is enchanting, Herr Jorgensen." Deller looked at Charlotte for a long time. She stood still, feeling a little self-conscious. Deller turned to Bo.

"Herr Jorgensen, I believe your daughter is going to help us."

"Yes, Colonel, we ... all of us will do anything to help." Bo indicated the whole family to make himself clear. "We are, however, Swedish neutrals and hoped to be able to apply for repatriation."

"I am sure Colonel von Hass has that in hand," Deller said, "but in the meantime you can help me with some things I need doing around the house. Is that clear?" He had slightly lost his charm.

"Yes, of course, sir," Bo said.

"Very well." Deller turned to look at Charlotte and smiled. "We are expecting a very important person tonight, mademoiselle. I would like you to help with the arrival of this person, take hats, et cetera. Are these the only clothes you have?" He swirled his hands at Charlotte's school clothes with undisguised disapproval of her dull dress, white socks and flat black shoes.

"No, I have nicer clothes upstairs."

"We were told we would not be permitted to go above stairs until midnight, sir," Bo interjected as humbly as possible.

"I am the senior officer here, Herr Jorgensen. Do you have anything, Freya, if I may call you Freya, you could wear for the evening ... not for gardening?"

Charlotte answered sweetly and looked as innocent as she could.

"Yes, I have some upstairs in my room." She remembered who she was, and hastily added, "Or I could use some of Miss Charlotte's clothes." Pretending to be Freya was beginning to become challenging. She would have to make sure she didn't make any mistakes.

"Ah, yes." The SS officer suddenly looked stern. "Miss Charlotte." His voice was almost a whisper. He strode to the doorway without looking back. "See what you can find. Nice but plain. He likes plain, but he also likes pretty. I expect you at the front door lobby at eight o'clock sharp."

Deller went back up the stairs to the main part of the house. Everyone in the servants' parlour could hear Deller barking out orders as he went.

Charlotte turned to see if Bo and Christina noticed how the officer changed when he first saw her.

"What was that about? Who do you suppose *he* is?" Charlotte asked.

"I don't know, Charlotte. You must be careful," Bo whispered as he rushed over to her.

"Freya!" Christina hissed.

"Yes, well" – Bo rolled his eyes – "Freya, you must be careful of that one. He obviously likes you and I think he wants to show you off. Just remember you are a Swedish subject. Under the *Convention de Genève* —"

"I'll be careful, Papa. I have a nice black evening dress that I was meant to have worn to the last day at school in July – it's very grown up."

"He looked a little drunk to me," Christina said quietly, looking worried. "Oh, God … and he smelt so strongly of cologne." Christina seemed to be getting anxious again and was wringing her hands together. "And where have I heard that name?"

The German servants were now coming into the parlour and looking at the three Swedish people disapprovingly. One of the women came up to Charlotte and said, "*Geh sofort die Treppe hinauf!*" Charlotte shrugged her shoulders but knew enough German to know she was telling her to go upstairs. She was not going to let on that she spoke German, even if it was only a little.

The harridan-like, dumpy German woman who smelt of cleaning fluid wore a black SS army jacket that did not fit her large bosom. Her ensemble included a straight black skirt and heavy shoes, and she wore a little black forage cap with SS written on the front, set on one side of her short brown hair. The German woman was astonishingly unattractive, Charlotte thought.

"*Vorwärts!*" she shouted, pointing towards the stairs.

"I think she wants you to go up and change," Bo said. "Be careful, Freya," he warned. Charlotte blew her new parents a kiss and started out the door. The SS lady seemed to be following her.

Charlotte went up the servants' stairs, past the busy kitchens. There was a considerable amount of work going on in there. Not since her uncle, Sir Jason Barrett, gave a War Party two years ago with over fifty guests was there such industry in the kitchens.

She went through the brown baize door and into the cavernous back hall. She stopped in horror to see, draped from the upper landing down to the tops of the doors below, a huge scarlet flag with a large black swastika in a white circle. The Nazi flag covered a large oil painting of the Piazza San Marco in Venice. She turned to look through the high archway opposite the flag. To the right of the library door a large portrait of Hitler had replaced a picture of her grandmother.

"*Steig auf, schnell.*" The harridan shouted again. Charlotte went up the stairs. There were hardly any people about. As she climbed the stairs, she looked through the arch again to see four large soldiers in black uniforms with white piping. Their faces were stern; only their thin, severe lips could be seen outside the shadow of their shiny black helmets. Charlotte did not need the SS woman to tell her to hurry up the stairs.

Charlotte got changed in her former room while the harridan stood outside. She thought about what was happening; her house being invaded by strange Germans, the officers all charming but with an element of menace about them. She was excited by it all. Who was coming to Nineteen Avenue Foch tonight?

Franz-Joseph Deller, she thought to herself. Who is he? He was very sure of himself. Was he in charge? Or the old colonel in the library? Captain Wil seemed nice, with his funny round tortoiseshell spectacles that he kept pushing back up his nose.

An hour later, Charlotte walked down the stairs after getting washed and changed. She had put her hair back with silver and mother-of-pearl combs that had belonged to her mother. Her hair shone like molten gold against the jet-black rayon taffeta dress she wore with its black and velvety floral rose design, wide ruched shoulder straps, a boned bodice and a very full lined skirt which she thought might make her a little hot. She put on her high-heeled shoes over stockinged feet. She put on a little make-up just to accentuate, not to attract attention, as her stepmother used to tell her.

Every inch of her journey along the gallery landing and down the stairs was being watched in delight by three men: Lieutenant Colonel Franz-Joseph Deller and two SS guardsmen. She did not see them at first as she was concentrating on walking down the stairs in high heels. She had hardly ever worn them before. When she saw them she smiled sweetly, slightly self-consciously, as she descended.

"Do you like my new dress?" she asked Deller.

"Mademoiselle, I am stunned by what I see. A perfect vision. You will be the toast of the house when our guests arrive," Deller said, showing signs of the early stages of drunkenness. Charlotte blushed and smiled delightedly, which made her even more captivating. With a flap of his hand, Deller told the guardsmen to go about their duties. They reluctantly went back to the entrance hall.

"What would you like me to do, monsieur?"

"I would like you to welcome our special guests with a smile and take their hats and gloves." Deller placed Charlotte next to a round table in the centre of the main hall, which had replaced the trestle table that was there when they arrived seven hours earlier. A large vase of light-cream and scarlet roses stood in the centre of the table.

Deller strode off towards the library. He was joined by Captain Wil who stopped and saluted Deller. They chatted amicably and then both turned to look at Charlotte. When she saw them looking at her, she gave them a nervous smile and a little curtsey.

The front double doors were open, letting in a soft warm breeze mostly obstructed by four large, black-uniformed guards who blocked the door outside. They stood, motionless, jackboots apart, with their white gloved hands clasped behind their backs, facing out towards the driveway. They must have been sweltering in the heat.

Charlotte was quite proud to think these important people were coming to visit *her* house. She smiled to herself. They would never guess that she was the owner of this magnificent mansion.

She noticed a few changes had been made to the house. Most of the artwork on the walls had been swapped for portraits of Adolf Hitler or boring landscapes with castles, what she imagined must have been German schlosses. She wandered into the dining room and found it laid up for a party of sixteen. Two men in crisp white high-collared jackets were polishing cutlery. They both stopped what they were doing when Charlotte entered, and looked at each other with expressions of curiosity. Again, Charlotte noticed that all the paintings had been changed.

She quickly went back to her post. Apart from her, the harridan and the two guardsmen, the hall was empty of people. It was quiet. There was no noise from outside, no Paris traffic on the usually very busy Avenue Foch. It was still light, and hot.

Charlotte had time to think now. Why was she not frightened? It was an adventure, that was why, and she was young and vital and ready for any escapade. Look at Christina; she was very scared – it got a little tiresome – and Bo ... what about Bo, the ex-Swedish army officer? He was steady, but he looked constantly worried and every sentence he uttered was measured and slightly obsequious, something Charlotte had never seen from Bo. He was completely different. It was quick-thinking to say she was his daughter, but that meant he and Christina would have to stay here, which, Charlotte thought, was a little unfair on them. In addition, what would happen if a German turned up who spoke Swedish? Charlotte would have a lot of explaining to do.

*

As Charlotte was considering her position, Bo and Christina, under orders from Lieutenant Colonel Franz-Joseph Deller, were being ushered out of the house by armed soldiers to a lorry with a canvas-covered trailer. They were quickly shoved into the back where there were a dozen other people. They were told they were going to the Swedish Embassy and their daughter would follow soon.

"What is going on here?" asked Bo as they drove off with a lurch. He asked a couple he recognised who were servants from next door.

"I don't know. We were told we are being taken to our embassy, but I don't think we have an embassy any more," said a man with a thick accent. "We are Polish, you see" – he then indicated to the rest of the people in the lorry – "and these people are all Jewish."

*

Charlotte was looking around the lobby when the Nazi SS officer Deller appeared from the library.

"What is going on in the library?" Charlotte asked in a hoarse whisper. Deller strode over to her, frowning. Charlotte heard a tut of derision from the harridan on the other side of the table.

"Nothing that—" He stopped and looked at Charlotte quizzically. "Why do you ask, Freya?"

"I'm just curious," she said with an innocent look she had mastered over the years that usually extinguished any uncomfortable situations.

"Just a lot of organising for tonight. You must be on your best behaviour, Freya," Deller said.

"Are you in charge, *Obersturmbannführer* Deller?" She stumbled through Deller's title.

"No, Freya, a mere small cog. And I am an SS Colonel, so just call me Colonel."

"What do you do here, Colonel?"

"I am in charge of art and culture," he said proudly. "I am taking stock of the pictures here." He waved his hands over the walls where the replaced paintings hung.

"But where are all the old pictures?"

Again, Deller frowned at her.

"Safe," he said and changed the subject. "Have you eaten?"

"No, and I am starving. I have had nothing since leaving school this morning."

"Go to the kitchen and ask for Igor Mühle. He speaks French and he will give you something to eat."

"Could you come too? I am a little afraid, believe it or not."

"Very well then, come on."

Charlotte was a huge success in the male-dominated kitchen. All the chefs wanted to serve her something or have her taste a dish they were cooking. Deller ended up taking control of the situation and getting some sandwiches and putting her into the morning room, where breakfast was normally served but which was now full of cabinets covered with German emblems.

She was told by Deller she must be at the front door by eight. She was grateful for her sandwich. When she had finished it, she felt very tired.

Suddenly the door flew open. The harridan stood there with her hands on her hips.

"*Komm jetzt mit mir zur Haustür!*" She pointed in the direction of the front of the house. Charlotte stood up, brushed down her dress and walked steadily towards the front door.

The reception hall was a hive of activity. Men in uniform were lined up on either side of the door. Colonel Günther von Hass paced up and down the two rows of uniforms, inspecting the troops. Deller was there, looking at Charlotte with concern and then relief when he saw her at her post by the table. Colonel von Hass was the only officer in the German army's grey mess uniform of the *Wehrmacht*; the rest were all in the black uniforms of the SS.

The colonel told Wil something and the captain scampered over to Charlotte.

"Do you know what you are doing?"

"Taking hats and gloves and laying them on this table?"

"Do you speak any German?"

"Only a tiny bit, I'm afraid," Charlotte lied. She had a German friend at school, a lovely blonde girl. They were great friends and taught each other their home language: Charlotte, English, and Katia, German. Her Jewish parents had whisked her away to America six months ago.

"Then don't say anything, just smile and curtsey. She will help you." He pointed to the sour-faced harridan who was standing on the other side of the table.

"Yes, monsieur."

Captain Wil looked Charlotte up and down, pushing his glasses back up his nose.

"Very pretty, mademoiselle, very" – he tried to find a different word but failed – "pretty." Charlotte gave Wil a bob curtsey and smiled with a slight blush. Wil went over to the harridan and gave her instructions. Every now and then, the harridan would give Charlotte a disapproving look.

Colonel von Hass shouted at Wil, who scampered back to his position, adjusted his uniform, his belt, and stood stiffly to attention. Charlotte could hear a car with a large, powerful motor draw up outside. She felt an air of anticipation. Even the ugly woman sergeant stood, eyes wide and mouth slightly open in expectation. There were lots of barked orders outside and troops coming to attention. The colonel stood at the front door. He stood to attention and clicked his heels, threw out his right arm with the Nazi salute and boomed, "Heil Hitler".

He turned to allow the party of guests to enter and started to introduce his officers. The first person to step into the house was the unmistakable slight frame and myopic, reptilian features of Heinrich Himmler.

20

Himmler wore a fashionable white linen uniform with four pleated patch pockets, a jacket with scalloped flaps, and a white decorated belt, black tie and white shirt. His collar tabs were those of *Reichsführer*, silver twisted wire shoulder boards with silver oak leaves, and he wore a Blood Order and the Honour Chevron for the Old Guard "V" badge on his right sleeve, which conveyed his immense power. A red armband with the Nazi swastika circled his left upper arm sleeve and swathes of silver lanyards hung over his right shoulder. He held a white encrusted staff of his exalted office.

"Willkommen auf Neunzehn Avenue Foch, Herr *Reichsführer*." Colonel von Hass stammered a welcome to one of the most powerful men in Germany. The Reichsführer acknowledged his greeting with a slight nod in his direction but no smile, no recognition of the simpering colonel. He strode to the table in the hallway, towards the delightful young lady standing there.

Himmler was used to seeing apprehension, sometimes fright, on people's faces, similar to the silly old Wehrmacht colonel stammering beside him. Or like the ugly SS female sergeant standing on the other side of the table, who clicked her heels very loudly and shouted her salute far too stridently and with a slight shake. But this girl was calm and enchanting.

"Und wie heißt du, junges Mädchen?" He asked Charlotte her name. Charlotte said nothing but just bobbed a curtsey and smiled delightfully as she took his hat, baton and gloves and placed them gently on the hall table. She had no idea who this man was, or how powerful, but she gathered by the fawning around him that he must be important.

"Sie ist ein französisches Mädchen, die hier arbeitet, Herr *Reichsführer*." Almost apologetically, Von Hass explained that she was French and worked here, and then guided Himmler round the table, through the galleried hall and into the salle de séjour – the drawing room.

*

The salle de séjour was full of light from the large windows all down one side of the room, overlooking the expansive garden. All the furniture and *décor* had been left by the de Tournets.

"This is a fine room, von Hass." Himmler looked around approvingly. "How did you find this house?"

"Deller and one of his contacts knew the house, Herr *Reichsführer*."

"Magnificent." Himmler strode over to the huge white marble fireplace that stood at the centre of the long, heavily decorated wall. He tapped the solid mantlepiece and nodded in appreciation. "I think I would feel quite at home in a house like this." He turned to his audience and laughed at his own joke, dutifully followed by the bystanders forcing fake laughter to please their *Reichsführer*.

He went over to the wall beside the fireplace and lightly stroked one of the painted panels depicting a fountain of flowers for each season, spouting from an ornate Greek urn. He stood back and looked at himself in the large triptych mirror surmounting the mantle, which had a gold frame of intricate flowers and leaves. He nodded with approval at the two large oil paintings of dark grey seascapes featuring large German warships of the Great War, either side of the fireplace.

*

Charlotte took the hats and gloves of around eight more officers. She sneaked a glance at the harridan on the other side of the table, only to see her glaring at her. Charlotte was taken aback a little. Why was this rather unpleasant woman glaring at her? She was doing all the work, it seemed, not the sour-faced crone.

Charlotte looked around the front hall, now a little quieter. Behind her she could see, on either side of the giant Nazi flag, large modern paintings depicting soldiers in vests, running, and blonde women holding babies, waving to troops marching off to war.

There was a gentle cough and Charlotte looked back to see a young man, no more than twenty-five, with thin straight brown hair. He was tall and slim with broad shoulders. He had a wide smile, a strong jawline and a noble chin. Charlotte thought he was the most beautiful man she had ever met – if a man could be beautiful, that is. Long eyelashes enhanced his large hazel-brown eyes that creased at the edges.

172

Charlotte took in a breath when she saw him. Her heart fluttered slightly, like a startled bird. He leant in towards her and said in a light, low voice, *"Es tut mir leid, Sie zu erschrecken, hübsche Dame."*

She flushed, desperately trying to look away from his gaze, trying to control her rapid breathing. She had little experience of charming, handsome young men.

"I am sorry, I do not speak much German," she said meekly, a shadow of a shy smile on her lips and a look of fascination and excitement in her eyes.

"You are French?" he asked in surprise.

"No – Swedish, monsieur."

"Oh ... I'm sorry, I don't know any Swedish." He leant on the table, even closer to Charlotte, and gazed into her eyes. "You are a remarkable beauty, mademoiselle, a work of art." Charlotte moved slightly away from him and smiled.

"Who are you?" she asked, holding her hand bashfully up to her lips.

"My name is *Obersturmführer* Jost Krupp."

21

"I am here with my friend Theodora. She is …" Krupp looked around behind him to see the guards had stopped a tall, dark lady at the door of the mansion and were questioning her.

"*Die Dame ist mit mir. Steht beiseite, und lasst sie sofort durch*! That lady is with me. Stand aside and let her through immediately!" He stormed over to the guards. They seemed indifferent to the man's rank and stood mildly to attention.

Charlotte was impressed by his walk, his back, his movement. His short black mess-dress jacket was well cut to show off his figure – she was excited by his tight trousers and muscular rump. Swathes of light silver equerry lanyards flopped about over his right shoulder.

He apologised to the lady and plainly managed to charm her as he had charmed Charlotte. They came towards her. The lieutenant was about to say something to her when the harridan snapped her heels and saluted with a shout of "Heil Hitler!" Krupp stopped abruptly in surprise and saluted her back with a mild "Heil Hitler".

"I see why you forgot about me, Jost," said the dark lady in a heavy accent that Charlotte could not place.

"My dear, may I present you to Mademoiselle" – he turned to Charlotte, his hand hovering over her shoulder – "I am afraid I don't know your name."

"Ch … sorry … Freya, monsieur, Freya Jorgensen."

"Mademoiselle Jorgensen, this is the Empress Theodora."

"Your Majesty." Charlotte's eyes widened and she offered Theodora a deep curtsey. Theodora giggled and said in a low voice, "I am not really an empress, Freya. But I am Turkish and there was a famous Turkish Empress called Theodora, and that is why this awful lieutenant of the SS here is teasing you."

She looked Charlotte up and down as she took off her royal-blue silk jacket, with the assistance of Jost Krupp, to reveal her bare, statuesque shoulders. She had flawless skin, the colour of creamy coffee, and her long black hair tumbled over one shoulder down to the top of her left breast. The black crêpe dress was held up by two very thin straps, the material only just covering her breasts. She wore a small silver skull, a *Totenkopf,* pinned to her dress, and, surprisingly, an inexpensive-looking silver crucifix with an overlong shaft on a delicate silver chain. Large diamond drop earrings hung from her earlobes, and a diamond ring adorned her right forefinger. Her lips were full and perfectly shaped, enhanced with bright red lipstick, and she had the bone structure of a goddess. The long, black dress was beautifully tailored, shaped to every contour of her body. She was around twenty-five years old, in her prime.

Charlotte watched as they went through to the salle de séjour, Theodora's arm elegantly draped over Lieutenant Krupp's strong arm. As they walked she moved like liquid across the floor; he, smooth and controlled, lead from the hips like a tango dancer.

Charlotte was still holding Theodora's jacket and could smell her heady, rich perfume. She envied her elegance, her sophistication. Before they went through the door, Jost Krupp turned to take another look at Charlotte and when he saw her looking on, he gave a little wave.

Charlotte was jogged back to her senses when the harridan strode over, snatched the little tailored jacket from her and stomped over to the other side of the hall, like a child getting her toy back, and placed the jacket neatly onto the settle just outside the library door. She stomped back and pointed to Charlotte to go upstairs to her room. Charlotte thought differently. She headed to the servants' door to see if Bo and Christina were there. Charlotte could hear the rapid steps of the harridan coming up behind her. She upped her speed and went through the baize door under the stairs. She was surprised by the speed at which the harridan must have gone; she had grabbed Charlotte's arm just as she opened the brown baize door.

Charlotte tried to pull away but the grip tightened, and she felt herself being whipped around to face the SS woman sergeant. Without warning, the harridan unleashed a hard slap with her free left hand and then let go of Charlotte's arm and gave an even harder slap with the back of her right hand.

Charlotte squealed. She crossed her arms to protect her face. The harridan looked around to see if anybody had heard and quickly pushed her back through the baize door, through to the top of the servants' stairs, hissing at her to be quiet and calling her a French slut.

"*Nimm das, französische Schlampe!*"

Charlotte had never been hit by a woman before. She had known very little violence in her short life. This was a huge shock. As the door swung shut behind them, the awful woman took Charlotte by the throat, drew her down to level with her face and whispered German oaths in Charlotte's ear. She was immensely strong, much shorter than Charlotte and three times the girth.

Charlotte collected herself. She was furious with herself when she felt tears running down her face. To stop this onslaught, she put up her hands and shouted over the woman's tirade. "*Lassen Sie mich! Ich gehe nach oben.*" She would go upstairs if the woman let her be.

The harridan removed her hand from Charlotte's throat in surprise.

"*So sprechen Sie Deutsch, wenn du es brauchst?*" she said with a sly smile. The door of the kitchen swung open and a chef shouted at the woman to clear off.

The harridan grabbed Charlotte's forearm and told her again to go upstairs to her room. Charlotte appealed to her to see Bo and Christina, but the hag would not allow it. Charlotte ran out through the baize door and up the stairs. She could hear laughter coming from the drawing room as she ran, her hand held against her right cheek, now hot and stinging. She thought at one point it was bleeding, but it was the tears running over her smarting face.

Once inside her room in the attic, she switched on the light. She opened the window to allow some cool air to run over her burning cheeks. She could still hear the people below; a little piano music tinkled up from the large drawing room – the windows must have been wide open to keep the guests cool.

She kicked the old trunk in the corner of her room with anger and frustration. How dare that bloody woman slap her. She was furious that she hadn't defended herself better. She saw she had forgotten to take off her shoes and put them on the shelf by the stairs.

She slowly got undressed down to her bra and petticoat, put on a silk robe and walked down to the bathroom to wash her face. To her horror, she saw the awful harridan come out of the bathroom. The woman took one look at Charlotte and smiled – a smirk of satisfaction – seeing Charlotte's pretty face disfigured by the bruised and bright red cheek. Charlotte controlled her anger.

She strode past the woman, went into the bathroom and slammed the door.

God, did that mean the harridan was going to stay the night up here too? Charlotte's heart sank. She would talk to Bo in the morning. She ran the tap and filled the basin with cold water and, holding her hair back, held her face in it, which helped a bit. There was no towel so she wiped as much water off as she could with her hands.

Back in her room, her wet face enjoying the breeze coming through the window, Charlotte sat on her bed, the light on. It was only about half-past-eight in the evening, still warm. She took off her robe and lay on top of the bedcover. She had her mother's painting, *Girl on a Golden Pillow*, resting on the chest of drawers opposite, and she gazed at the lovely girl in her golden bed, asleep. Charlotte gave a deep, quavering sigh.

The day had started as an adventure; Paris had been taken over by the Germans. She was worried she had not seen Bo and Christina since she was bustled upstairs by the German colonel, Franz-Joseph Deller.

Deller, like Lieutenant Krupp, had shown a lot of interest in Charlotte. Until now, she had not understood the reasons why Bo had insisted they were her parents. She realised that he was frightened – not for himself or Christina, but for her. She had not fully grasped the actual danger she was in. She rubbed her right cheek again. She had also not understood that Bo and Christina could be in danger, even being Swedish. Bo had lied to the Germans about where they lived, and about Charlotte.

Here she was, in an attic servant's room that had not been slept in for at least five years, with an awful megalomaniac of a woman just down the hall, who obviously enjoyed beating her. Charlotte had absolutely no idea what was to become of her. She was going to have to escape, but she did not want to leave her home. Regardless, she would have to find Bo and Christina first.

There was a faint knock at the door. She sat up in alarm, fearful it was the harridan come to taunt her.

"Freya?" a kind low voice said on the other side of the door. "This is Madame Theodora. May I come in?"

"Oh yes, madame, please come in." Charlotte was relieved. She swung her legs over the side of the bed, put on her silk robe and neatened herself up as quickly as she could.

Theodora came in slowly. "Oh – you were in bed. I am sorry."

"No, no – don't worry, I did not know what to do so I put myself to bed. I am not allowed downstairs, for some reason."

"Aren't you? That's why I could not find you. We are about to go into dinner and the *Reichsführer* wondered if you would like to join us." Theodora stopped and looked at Charlotte critically. "What happened to your lovely face?"

Charlotte's mind rushed to find an explanation. "Oh, I fell … up the stairs." She did not want to say the harridan had done it. It seemed cowardly. "I fell up the stairs in those shoes." She pointed at the high-heeled black shoes stored under the chest of drawers. "I am not used to them and bashed my cheek on the stairs."

"Oh, you poor thing. I have just the thing to cover that up." Theodora opened her small black handbag and brought out a small silver powder compact. Theodora opened it and took out a little ostrich-down powder puff and dabbed Charlotte's swollen cheek. Charlotte smelt the scent Theodora was wearing and observed the way she sat on the edge of the bed, her legs crossed, the graceful arm administering powder to Charlotte's face. Everything about this woman was elegant, beautiful and stylish. Charlotte longed to be like her.

"Thank you, madame."

"Call me Theodora, please."

"You are kind to do this, Theodora. I don't think I can join you for dinner. I would be far too nervous. Why would they want me to?"

"There are not enough women for the gentlemen to talk to."

"How many women are there?"

"Only me," said Theodora with a smile.

"But I hardly speak any German, and I have no experience in these sorts of things." This was a lie. Charlotte had been among guests at dinner parties all her life, whether it was with her uncle Jason or her guardian, Jean de Tournet, and she spoke quite good German. "In any case, my face is bruised."

"Have a look in the glass and see how pretty you are."

Charlotte looked in the mirror and indeed her bruise had gone. She looked a lot better.

"With a little make-up to enhance those eyes and lovely lips, you will be fine. Please come," Theodora implored. "I will keep an eye out for you."

"All right, then … thank you. Will you stay and take me down so that the guards don't stop me?"

"Yes, of course, but don't be long." Theodora watched Charlotte as she went over to the wardrobe. "How old are you, Freya?" She asked with an element of suspicion.

"Eighteen, nineteen in October." She lied.

"At school?"

"Sort of. I go to a finishing school."

"How do your parents afford that?"

Charlotte remembered who she was meant to be.

"Monsieur and Madame de Tournet pay, which is very kind of them. I go with their daughter, Charlotte." Charlotte hoped she had rescued the situation. She had her own questions too. "Are you married to that officer you came in with, Theodora?"

"No!" Theodora chuckled. "He escorted me to the evening. We are with very important guests and my job is to entertain these important guests."

"Your job?"

"Yes, my job. I am what you might call a 'courtesan'."

"A what?" said Charlotte, putting on her dress.

"A courtesan – a lady who entertains gentlemen."

"Oh, I see," said Charlotte, not entirely sure that she did.

Theodora watched Charlotte struggle with her stockings. "Don't bother with those. You have a lovely long dress to hide your legs. It's too hot anyway."

"Where do you come from?" Charlotte asked.

"Constantinople – now called Istanbul – in Turkey, but I have spent most of my life in Germany, ever since the last war."

"So you really are a Turkish Empress?"

"No, just Theodora. Let me help you with your pretty dress."

"It belongs to my friend, Charlotte. It is nowhere near as pretty as your dress."

"Thank you." She turned and looked at Charlotte's mother's painting. "That is a lovely painting. Shouldn't it be hanging on the wall rather than propped up on the chest of drawers?"

"I am waiting for Bo to put up a nail."

Theodora's expression turned to concern. "But this looks like a Klimt!" Theodora picked it up and looked at it quizzically. She looked at Charlotte in surprise and with a slight expression of worry. "It *is* a Klimt, or a very good copy of one. Is this yours?"

"My mother left it … or rather my aunt …. my friend … Charlotte's mother gave it to her when she was a little girl. It's called *Girl on a Golden Pillow*."

"Right," Theodora said unconvincingly. "Well, make sure it is hung up nicely. Don't let Franz-Joseph Deller see it or he will pack it off to Germany."

Charlotte looked at Theodora in alarm.

"What do you mean?"

"Oh, never mind. Come on, you look fine. We don't want to keep them waiting, even if it is a woman's prerogative."

"Who is the *Reichsführer*, Theodora?"

"He is the most powerful man in Germany, apart from Hitler himself. Surely you have heard of Herr Himmler?"

Charlotte shook her head guiltily.

"Well, just remember at all times, he can chop off anybody's head at whim."

Charlotte was excited again. It was like when she had dinner with the Prince of Wales and his American woman, a dinner given by her uncle, Sir Jason Barrett, after he had visited Hitler in Germany.

*

"*Darf ich Ihnen Freya vorstellen, Exzellenz.*" Theodora introduced Heinrich Himmler to Freya in the drawing room. Charlotte dipped a short bob curtsey.

"Delighted." Himmler clicked his heels and offered a slight bow as he held Charlotte's hand. He gazed at her bust for slightly too long, making Charlotte a little uncomfortable.

"Shall we eat now?" the *Reichsführer* announced in German, and the men all agreed. Himmler jutted out his elbow to Charlotte and escorted her to the hallway and then into the dining room, Captain Wil showing the way with Theodora. There waiting were eight men in white jackets and gloves, all with a serving napkin slung over their arm. A chair was brought out at the head of the long table for Himmler and one for Charlotte to his right. To his left sat the handsome young officer, Jost Krupp. He smiled at Charlotte and waited for Theodora to sit next to him.

When everybody was seated, Colonel von Hass stood at the other end of the long dining table and indicated to the waiters to fill the glasses. After they were quickly filled with a deep-red wine, he snapped his heels and said loudly, in clipped German, "*Meine Herren, das Reichsführer – heil!*" He raised his glass, clicked his heels again and drank as the other men stood and followed his example. Himmler remained seated and waved his hand royally at von Hass. His expression was stern; he plainly did not like obsequious grovelling, especially from an old army soldier like von Hass.

The table all sat again, ten men and two ladies. Von Hass nodded at the head waiter to start the dinner.

"How long have you got that old fool here?" Himmler hissed at Captain Wil, who sat on Charlotte's right.

"Until General von Ardle arrives next week, Herr *Reichsführer.*"

"Then I will deal with him before I go. My dear," he said to Theodora, "I do not speak French. Can you tell this young lady" – he turned to look at Charlotte – "how exceptionally beautiful she is?"

Theodora told Charlotte of the *Reichsführer*'s admiration. Charlotte was already blushing, however, and offered Himmler a shy and captivating smile and thanked him in stilted German.

The food arrived, a chilled cucumber and mint soup. Charlotte was ravenous. She had to remind herself not to guzzle the soup and to try to remember her manners. She looked up after her third delicious mouthful to see the gorgeous hazel-brown eyes of Lieutenant Krupp looking at her from across the table. She quickly cast her eyes down, smiling widely in embarrassment. Himmler was talking intently to Captain Wil about the house, and although she spoke German, it was being spoken so rapidly she could only pick up the odd sentence. As far as she could gather, the conversation was mostly about "rounding up the Jews". She was not entirely sure why they would be doing this but thought nothing of it.

"Mademoiselle, the *Reichsführer* asked if you know any Jews in the area," said Jost Krupp. Charlotte didn't think she did and asked why. "Oh, it is just something we need to know, for our records, you see." Charlotte looked at Krupp and then Himmler with curiosity. She was about to ask a question and glanced at Theodora, who briefly shook her head in warning.

"No, Excellency, I don't think I know any Jews."

She was experienced at not making silly observations or comments at these sorts of occasions after once commenting on the size of de Gaulle's nose in her piping, young voice just as the conversation subsided at a dinner party. It had been held in the same dining room, given by her uncle Jason for Colonel de Gaulle and other French officials. Marshal Pétain, who had been made French Ambassador to Spain, was the guest of honour. The repercussions lasted most of the week and only marginally subsided when Charlotte was told to apologise to the colonel, which she did in her own charming and captivating way.

Charlotte enjoyed the rest of the dinner – a wonderful little fillet of sole with a cream sauce and sweet white grapes, followed by roast veal with a dark red wine reduction, and to finish, a sweet apricot tart and cream. She had hardly seen any of these ingredients for at least two years.

She barely talked to her host, other than to say how delicious everything was and how much she enjoyed the wine, which she had only a few sips of for fear of getting drunk and exposing her identity. She particularly liked the Schloss Johannisberg Riesling from the Rhine area of Germany. Lieutenant Krupp told her about the beautiful countryside around the region of Schloss Johannisberg, very close to where he was born and brought up.

Charlotte was now full of food. As she drank her coffee – real coffee – she looked at the rest of the company around the table. The men were all thin, apart from Colonel von Hass, and very striking in their black uniforms adorned with various medals and crosses. As she came to Franz-Joseph Deller, she remembered the strange thing that Theodora had said to her in her little bedroom about her painting. She then noticed all the paintings on the dining room walls had changed. They were all German landscapes, including one large wartime landscape depicting German soldiers in the last war's uniform, with spiked helmets, rising from the trenches among grenade and mortar blasts. All her paintings, the Sisley landscapes *Early Snow at Louveciennes* and *Avenue of Chestnut Trees*, and the large Berthe Morisot painting of a grain field, had been moved.

"What's the matter, Freya?" asked Theodora.

"They have changed all the pictures … the art, the lovely paintings that were in here."

"They wanted all their pictures instead. I will ask Franz-Joseph later. Why are you so worried about the paintings, anyway?"

"They are the Barrett Collection. They are priceless. Where are they?"

"What is going on?" Himmler asked in German.

"Nothing, *Exzellenz*, Freya was admiring the new pictures that hang on the walls. If you gentlemen would excuse us ladies …" She rose from her chair, and all but Himmler and the old colonel stood too. "We will leave you to your cigars and politics. Freya?"

Theodora raised her eyebrows at Charlotte and gestured towards Himmler as a prompt for her to acknowledge him before departing.

Charlotte stood. A waiter pulled her chair back and she turned to Herr Himmler. He had a kind of repulsive smile on his face. She could not work out if it was a genuine attempt at a civil smile or an expression he used to intimidate people. His eyes were expressionless, like a lizard about to strike at its prey, and wandered from her bust to her face and back again.

She curtsied with her head up and thanked him in German with a heavy

French accent. She tried to look him in the eyes but it was impossible to sustain for any length of time. He was so hard to read. He muttered something back to her and dismissed her with a little flick of the hand. She rose from the curtsey and slowly walked out beside Theodora. Himmler and the rest of the men at the table watched the women leave.

*

As they left the dining room, Theodora turned back to look at the table of completely silent men. She gently turned Charlotte as well, who gave them a parting smile. As soon as the door was closed, there was a roar and lots of loud chatter and laughter. Theodora giggled. "You were a huge success, my dear."

She took Charlotte's arm and they wandered upstairs.

"Theodora, what has happened to all the paintings?"

"Why are you so worried, Freya? They are not your paintings. They will be in the cellar or somewhere. They are not valuable, are they?" Theodora suddenly stopped at the top of the stairs on the gallery landing. She looked at the vast Nazi flag on the high wall that went all the way up to the glass-domed skylight and at all the other pictures. The portraits down the side of the staircase had not been moved.

"They are not valuable, are they, Freya?" she repeated with a little more intensity.

"These aren't" – Charlotte pointed at the little paintings on the stairs – "but the ones in the dining room are part of the Barrett Collection. They are priceless, Theodora. There are books in the library that are also priceless. And in the salle de séjour, where you had drinks this evening, there is a Caravaggio, *Portrait of a Courtesan*, which is one of the most valuable paintings in the world. I hope it is still there, or at least safe."

"Don't worry, Freya, I am sure it is still there." Theodora looked at Charlotte with curiosity. "Why has it upset you so?" She took Charlotte's hand and walked up the stairs. "I will see you to your room, just so you don't get bothered by that harridan woman."

"Where are you staying, Theodora?"

"Here," she said simply. "I'm not sure where. I will have to ask the sergeant, who seems to be in charge."

"Oh, I wish I could join my parents downstairs."

"Why don't you?" Theodora was surprised.

"I don't know. Every time I tried, I got stopped by the harridan or someone else."

"Well, don't worry, you will see them tomorrow. Get a good night's sleep."

Charlotte and Theodora climbed the last flight of stairs up to the servants' quarters on the top floor. At the top of the stairs stood the harridan, waiting in her severe black skirt and white shirt with the sleeves rolled up. Her legs were the shape and thickness of those on a billiard table.

Theodora said a pleasant goodnight to her. She handed Theodora her jacket that had been left on the settle in the hall, then wagged her forefinger to follow her down the hall. They both followed the woman past Charlotte's allotted room to the room next door where luggage had been stacked in the middle of the floor.

"*Dies ist mein Zimmer?*" Theodora asked if this was her room.

"*Ja,* madame." The harridan turned on her heels, strode to the room at the end of the corridor and slammed the door. The heavy clunk of a bolt being slid across quickly followed.

"When did she have time to put a bolt on her door?" Charlotte questioned with an amused smile.

"As if some man will steal into her bed!" Theodora said, and they both howled with laughter.

"Goodnight, Freya, it was lovely to meet you." Theodora genuinely meant it. She felt a sisterly affection for this lovely young girl and felt she was somehow vulnerable, yet so confident. The incident of falling up the stairs, Theodora knew, was a cover-up for something else, but she did not know what. She saw Charlotte as an intelligent, self-assured young lady but with a short temper, it seemed.

"Goodnight, Theodora, I've enjoyed meeting you as well. I don't think I have met a Turkish person before. Are they all as beautiful as you? And why are they giving you a servant's room and not one of the proper rooms?"

"Because, Freya, I am basically a servant. Goodnight." She blew Charlotte a kiss and slipped into her room before Charlotte could ask any more questions.

22

"What do you mean, relocated?" Charlotte seethed at Captain Wil when she found out Bo and Christina had been taken away.

It was lovely and cool in the servants' parlour on the lower ground floor. It was an early, fresh morning when Charlotte rose from a fitful sleep. She sneaked down the stairs to the lower ground staff quarters, where she found Captain Wil, yawning and drinking coffee. He must have been up all night; he had a dark shadow of whiskers on his cheeks and chin.

"Mademoiselle, your parents have been taken to another house to work until their papers and your papers are verified as being Swedish. Now, I cannot tell you any more." Wil was being annoyingly officious. "You are to report to Madame Theodora for instruction about your duties here in this house."

"My duties?" Charlotte screeched, her cheekbone, where she had been struck the night before, becoming painful. "Are you telling me my duties are to help run the household now my mother and father have gone?"

"Your duties, mademoiselle, are to do as you are told, or you will be shipped out of this house to a work camp in Germany. Do I make myself clear?" With that, Captain Wil strode off.

Charlotte was shocked, angry and worried about Bo and Christina. She stormed out of the parlour and bumped into a young waiter who had served them the night before.

"Mademoiselle, you must be careful. You will put your life, and your parents' lives, in danger."

"What rubbish!" She looked at the young man, his straight mousy hair sprouting out from a crown on the top of his head and short-cropped up to the tops of his ears. He had a scrunched-up, gnome-like face.

"Mademoiselle, I implore you to be careful. I work with these people." He looked around to make sure nobody could hear him. "They are animals with people, especially non-Aryan Germans."

"Aren't you a …. what is it … a German?"

"No, I am from Strasbourg."

"You're French? How did you get to be an SS soldier if you are French?"

"I am German, I have German parents, but I was born and brought up in Strasbourg."

"Well, that is not the point … come in here." Charlotte, losing her patience, pulled the young man into the empty parlour and closed the glass door. She was still seething with anger. "Do you know anything about my parents?"

"No, I'm afraid not. I didn't see them yesterday; I arrived late."

"Oh, I see." She mellowed. "What do you mean – be careful?"

"Do you know about the SS and the Gestapo?"

"No, not really. I was not interested in the war or the Germans until my house got taken over yesterday." The boy was shocked. He sat at the table with his back to the high window so he could not be seen if anybody came down the central corridor.

"These people are the very worst to get on the wrong side of. You're not Jewish, are you?" he said in alarm.

"No," Charlotte cried. "Do I look Jewish? What is this preoccupation with the Jews?"

The boy looked incredulously at Charlotte.

"Well, don't worry about that." The young waiter stood, shaking his head slightly in disbelief. "As I say, the SS are the strong arm for the secret police, the Gestapo. They have taken over most of the houses in this road. This house is where they are going to entertain the … how do you say – *Großkopferten?*"

"Bigwigs?" Charlotte ventured. "But they are not going to kill me if I kick up a fuss."

"Mademoiselle," the boy said solemnly, "they have killed so many people just for getting in their way or not obeying orders. And they will kill you if you get in their way or anger them" – he clicked his fingers – "just like that. I have seen it too many times."

Charlotte looked at the boy, stunned. It explained the SS woman sergeant's behaviour, and why Theodora quickly interceded last night at the dinner.

"With the *Reichsführer* here, they are all on edge, and they will do you

186

harm or ship you off if you do not do everything they ask of you. And I mean *everything!*" With that he opened the door and looked right and left. "My name is Helmut, by the way. May I call you Freya?"

"Yes," Charlotte almost whispered. She was taken aback by his audacity and frankness. "How did you know I was called Freya?"

"All the boys know who you are, Freya." He disappeared up the corridor, an embarrassed flush in his cheeks. Charlotte looked after him, her mouth wide open in disbelief.

This could explain why Bo and Christina had been transferred. Bo must have kicked up a fuss about her. Oh God, how was she going to find Bo and Christina now? They would be on their way to the Swedish Embassy.

*

"There you are." Theodora appeared at the parlour door thirty minutes later. She was in her dressing gown, a wonderful, shimmering gown printed with peacock feathers. "Do you know it is nearly half past seven in the morning? It's far too early for a Turkish working girl."

"Yes, I love the morning," Charlotte said, still looking worried.

"Where can I get some tea, or a chocolate, or even coffee?"

"I don't know, I'm afraid. In the breakfast room, I suppose," Charlotte said quietly, and not very helpfully.

Theodora looked at her new friend. Charlotte was sad and sat at the table with a hand under her chin. She was dressed in her school uniform again. Theodora sat down beside her and put her arm around her shoulders.

"Are you all right, darling? You are not hung-over?" she asked.

"No, I am not all right, Theodora. My parents have been moved – 'relocated' was what Captain Wil said."

Charlotte told Theodora about what Helmut had said, remembering that for all she knew, Theodora might be an ardent admirer of the SS. She did not mention Helmut's name; she had to be careful not to say who told her about these people ... these Nazis.

"Darling ..." Theodora shifted her chair even closer to Charlotte and leant in towards her ear. "If you get on the bad side of any of these men, they will kill you or have you killed. If they ask you for any information they know you have knowledge of, they will do anything to get it from you, and it will not be at all pleasant. Your beauty and charm will not save you. However, stay on the right side of them, be charming, smile, pander to their every whim, and they will lavish lots of luxury and treat you like a lady."

Theodora bowed her head in thought. She put her hand on her chest and said gravely, "The only way you and I will survive this war is to cooperate with these men, stroke their inflated egos, laugh at their wretched jokes and their morbid sense of humour. I am not strong enough or brave enough to escape. I had a friend" – she stopped, sighed and swallowed – "a dear friend who tried to escape the clutches of the SS. She died whilst trying to escape back to Poland. She killed the Gestapo woman who looked after us. Karolina begged me to go with her. I couldn't …" Theodora quickly composed herself. "Anyway, Freya, my darling—" She drew back from Charlotte in alarm. "What in God's name are you wearing?"

"My school uniform. I thought I needed to dress plainly."

"School? At eighteen? I thought you were at finishing school."

"Yes, a finishing school with Charlotte de Tournet. Her parents pay for me—"

"A finishing school? In Paris? They should have a little more refinement, wouldn't you say? Christ, it looks awful … oh, Freya …"

Charlotte felt a little hurt and, seeing this, Theodora backtracked. "I'm sorry, but we need to dress you so you look like the beautiful woman you are, and not a teenage schoolgirl."

Charlotte had forgotten she had lied about her age and rather enjoyed being three years older.

"Where are your papers? We will go out and see if we can find you some clothes. We are in Paris, after all."

"This is the whole problem, and why I am …" She paused and sighed. "I don't have any papers; they are at the de Tournets' house in Biarritz."

"Oh … how very odd. How have you been going about Paris, then?" Theodora looked at Charlotte with suspicion. Charlotte tried not to panic. Her lies and the situation she was in had suddenly become rather complicated. She had no way of proving who she was. She could not prove that she was Freya, as the only people who knew her as Freya had been relocated to God knows where. Her French pass, hidden in the trunk in her room, proved her to be Charlotte de Tournet, a French citizen of fifteen years old, so that was no help. Charlotte flushed in embarrassment. "I am afraid I have no papers. They are all lost."

"What about the finishing school? Where did you go?"

"They must have closed when the Germans arrived yesterday."

"But you must have something, somewhere, to say who you are?" Theodora was becoming angry. Charlotte shrugged her shoulders. "I'm afraid

I haven't." Charlotte considered pretending to be stupid and start sobbing, but she didn't think she was that good an actress – it never seemed to work with Christina.

"Then we'd better get you sorted out with some papers. Come upstairs with me and we will get some decent clothes on, and when the rest of the household gets up, we will go and see Lieutenant Krupp or Officer Wil. He seems to be in charge of the house. If we are nice to him and use all of our charms" – Theodora looked blatantly at Charlotte's figure as she spoke – "we will see what he can do."

Charlotte was relieved. For a moment, she'd thought she had lost an ally.

"I had forgotten," Theodora carried on as she got up from the table, "that you are young and on your own, probably for the first time." She turned and put a hand on Charlotte's shoulder. "Us girls must stick together, darling. You are a brave thing. Not many girls of only eighteen would come into a strange environment, stand up to Wil and the horrible Nazi woman sergeant, and entertain *Reichsführer* Himmler, only a day after leaving her friends at finishing school. I am proud of you." Theodora patted Charlotte's shoulder like a general bestowing an award to a foot soldier for her bravery.

"I must find my parents somehow," Charlotte said.

"One thing at a time, darling."

Charlotte took Theodora to the backstairs up to the baize door only to find they were blocked by a row of guards. They tried to push through. An SS guard, his helmet jammed nearly over his eyes, towered over them and pushed the women back through the door.

Through the little window in the baize door was a wall of black uniforms. Charlotte could see the guards were lining the hallway. She heard footsteps descending the stairs above her head. It was eerily quiet. As they got to the bottom of the stairs, in one arranged movement the guards came smartly to attention and gave the Nazi salute.

Heinrich Himmler saluted the guards with a slight upward wave of his baton of office and, accompanied by two officers, marched towards the door. Luggage came down the stairs, followed by morning onlookers in dressing gowns. The guards stood down and marched to the front door to stand guard.

So, he was gone. The second most powerful man in Germany, apparently, and Charlotte had dined with him. Something to tell the grandchildren, she thought.

23

"Jost, darling, we have a crisis," Theodora cried as she walked into the morning room hand in hand with Charlotte. It was now nearly nine o'clock. Lieutenant Jost Krupp gulped his coffee and quickly stood up in deference to the ladies entering the room. He put on an expression of mock concern. He had plainly heard this kind of announcement from Theodora before.

Charlotte was dressed in one of her "borrowed" light cotton voile dresses selected by Theodora – a calf-length misty-yellow dress, short-sleeved, with a thick cotton belt of the same colour around her small waist.

"Empress," he said, "I am at your disposal, but can we please have breakfast? I have a lot to do as Colonel von Hass has been removed by the *Reichsführer* and there is nobody except me and Captain Wil to run this house. Colonel Deller is next to useless but is the ranking—"

"Of course, darling." Theodora drew Charlotte forward. "Isn't Freya looking pretty?"

"Yes, indeed she is," Krupp said in genuine admiration as he looked at Charlotte.

Charlotte offered a wonderful smile and a blush to Jost Krupp. She was mesmerised by his eyes, bright and hazel brown, like a Labrador dog, with long, sweeping dark eyelashes that a woman would kill for. The creases at the corners of his eyes when he smiled, along with the long dimples accentuating his strong, square chin, made him a very handsome man. In fact, he was the most striking man Charlotte had ever met, and she had met quite a few handsome and successful men. His German accent as he spoke French was mild, unlike Theodora, whose accent was very pronounced.

Charlotte's heart fluttered in excitement when he got close to her and drew out a chair next to him. She felt her cheeks flush again as she turned to thank him. Thank God for Theodora's powder – she hoped the blush would not be so noticeable.

"Why are you not with the *Reichsführer*, Jost? I thought you were his equerry," Theodora asked.

"He has relinquished me." Krupp looked excited. "He wants me to remain in Paris for a while." Charlotte was thrilled and tried to conceal her delight. "Can I get you ladies some coffee? Some brioche?"

"Do you think there may be some chocolate?" asked Charlotte.

"Watch this." Krupp picked up a little handbell and rang it. The service door beside the bookcase opened and Helmut, the gnome-like waiter, appeared.

"*Wie kann ich zu Diensten sein, Leutnant?*" He clicked his heels and asked if he could be of service, in a rather weary way.

"*Heiße Schokolade für die Damen. Schnell.*" Krupp demanded hot chocolate for his guests. The waiter clicked his heels again and disappeared back through the door.

"You know there is a bell pull just beside the sideboard there," Charlotte pointed out.

"So there is." Krupp looked to see a slightly concealed brass and white porcelain bell-pull handle. "What can I get you, princess?" he asked Charlotte, who giggled slightly, her face lighting up with the attentions of this handsome young German officer. "I shall get you some brioche," he said before she could answer.

"Can I have some brioche too?" Theodora looked a little left out of Krupp's attentions. She stood at the other side of the dining table, a slight, mocking smile at the corners of her eyes. Krupp immediately raced around the table and sat with her.

Helmut the waiter burst through the door, expertly balancing a tray on the tips of his fingers, with two cups and saucers, a tall silver coffee jug and a separate jug of steaming hot milk. He placed a large cup and saucer in front of each lady, filled the cups with hot chocolate and then a dash of hot milk. The women and Krupp sat in silence and watched the small waiter scamper around the table. He placed the hot milk in the middle of the table. He wafted out of the room as swiftly as he came in, fast and efficient. Charlotte noticed that all the cutlery, crockery and table furniture was badged with the Nazi emblem. They were not using any of the house crockery or cutlery.

They were on their own in the morning room. The large full-length

French windows were all open to let in a little cool morning air. The sun was quite high in the sky and beating down on the garden. There was no noise from outside, no birds or sound of traffic.

"Jost, darling, we need some papers for Freya," Theodora said, spreading strawberry jam onto her brioche. Just then the door opened and Lieutenant Colonel Franz-Joseph Deller entered the morning room with two other SS officers, laughing. Captain Wil was one of them. Krupp stood up and clicked his heels respectfully to Deller.

Deller was delighted to see Charlotte and went over to her without acknowledging anybody else in the room.

"Mademoiselle, we are glad you were able to stay with us."

"Thank you, monsieur."

"And how lovely you look on this hot, sunny morning. It is quite refreshing after months of fighting a war."

"I am grateful, monsieur," Charlotte said. "I love the garden at this time of year."

"So do I," agreed Deller, looking out of the window at the large garden and mature shrubs.

"I have a question I would like to ask you, if it is convenient, Colonel," Charlotte said. She looked guiltily at Theodora who had a particularly anxious expression on her face.

"Have you, mademoiselle?"

"Well two questions, really."

"Fire away," Deller said jovially.

"Do you know where my parents have gone?" Deller's smile vanished for a couple of seconds.

"They have been sent to the Swedish Embassy for assessment, but they said you would be happy here for a bit." Charlotte was happy Bo and Christina were safe. "And the other question, my dear?"

"Tell me, monsieur, what has happened to all the paintings that were up in the dining room and the drawing room?" This clearly took Deller by surprise.

"Why do you want to know, my dear?" He looked slightly taken aback.

"Oh ..." Charlotte collected herself, smiled and put on her most charming of expressions, coy and demure. "It was just that I wanted to show Theodora the painting of Lady Joy Barrett and the wonderful Sisley landscapes."

"How do you know about Sisley? Are you not a servant here?" He looked surprised.

"My parents are housekeeper and chauffeur here. I am not, as it were, working here as a servant. I was a companion for Charlotte and—"

"Charlotte?" Deller stood up, confusion on his face. Everybody else stopped talking. Theodora stood and looked with concern at Charlotte. Had she said something wrong? Had she gone too far?

"I thought Charlotte lived in Boston in America with her aunt and uncle?"

"She does, but she goes … used to go to school here in Paris," Charlotte said quickly, still confused as to how this man knew so much about her.

"Where is she now?" He sat down, looking perplexed.

"In America or Spain, I think. My parents and I were going to meet them all in Biarritz, but the house was taken over unexpectedly."

"Right." He looked at Charlotte with interest. "How old are you, Freya?"

"She is nearly nineteen, Colonel," Theodora interrupted. Deller glared at her.

"In October, I am nineteen," she said, defusing any friction.

There was an uneasy silence. Nobody spoke or ate anything or drank their chocolate. They all just waited for Colonel Deller to say something.

"I knew the family quite well." Deller said this airily to all the people in the room, clearly hoping it would impress. It changed the mood in the room instantly. He wandered over to the sideboard, took a plate and helped himself to some slices of ham and cheese. Then he went over to a bell pull beside the sideboard and rang for service.

Charlotte was astonished. This man was beginning to worry her. When he had sat down beside her again, she looked into his grey eyes and asked, "How do you know the family, Colonel?"

Deller looked bashful. "I was the gardener here when I was an art student in Paris. I knew the Barretts, especially Charlotte."

Charlotte was intrigued. She had never seen this man before. He certainly never came to the house when she was here. He must be showing off. "And yes, the portrait in the dining room of Lady Joy as a young lady is lovely," he said to Theodora.

"But where is it, Colonel?" Charlotte asked with as much humility as possible.

"My lovely girl, you must call me Franz-Joseph. You are too pretty to sound as though you are in the army."

"Lady Joy's portrait?" she asked again, as lightly as possible. His face turned grave but soon melted when Charlotte smiled, beseeching him for an answer.

"We had to put all the Barrett Collection in storage to protect it whilst the German army are here. As the house belongs to the enemy, we do not have to ask permission to use it, but we have to respect the owner's things, furniture, paintings etc. We Germans are not plundering barbarians." He seemed to be talking like a politician to everybody in the room, but mostly to Charlotte. "Freya, I trust that answers your question." Deller said like a frazzled schoolteacher. "Now have your breakfast. I must go to work. Krupp, I want you to look after these ladies, give them everything they need. We have important guests tonight."

"How long do you intend keeping us here, Franz-Joseph?" Charlotte asked. "I am a Swedish citizen but have no papers."

"Krupp will see to that. You will have to have temporary papers for the moment. But you can't leave the house for quite a while. It is not safe outside the gates. There is still some fighting."

"Thank you, Franz-Joseph," Charlotte said in a husky voice. She rested her hand on Deller's arm. "You must be careful as well. We would hate to see you, or any of your gentlemen, get hurt."

*

"Well done, Freya, you are a natural manipulator of men," said Theodora as they walked up the stairs to their rooms.

"Oh, I don't know about that." Charlotte looked at Theodora, who seemed shocked. Charlotte did not think she had used any manipulation. "I hope you will help me perfect the art of 'getting what I want' from these men."

"Of course, darling, I will do my best," Theodora answered cautiously, draping an elegant arm around Charlotte's shoulders. "But be warned: these are all, and I mean all, including dear Jost, very dangerous men. The minute they find out they have been duped, they will bite back hard, very quickly and without thought of the consequences. Let us go into Charlotte's bedroom and talk seriously."

As they got to the top of the stairs, a woman in grey overalls, an apron and a headscarf emerged from Charlotte's old room. She had just finished cleaning it. Charlotte and Theodora went inside. Theodora closed the door and sat on the chaise longue in the window bay. Charlotte sat on the ottoman at the end of the bed.

"Who is Jost Krupp?" Charlotte asked as soon as they were settled. Theodora looked at Charlotte curiously and waited a couple of moments before replying.

"He professes to be a poet. He has told me he is the official poet for the SS.

He also looks after the top people in the SS and ensures they are entertained. He is very ambitious and dangerous." Theodora became serious. "Freya, he is also the son of one of the most powerful men in the Party, and is trusted by everybody all the way up to Hitler. He did not get the Blood Order for just being handsome."

"What did he get the Blood Order for? And why is it called the Blood Order? Sounds horrid."

"I am not sure what he got it for. He would have been part of the executions of Hitler's enemies, I presume. It is something you must not ask about."

"Why?"

"I don't think you will like the answer. That is why I've never asked. It was probably something dreadful – I don't know."

"Oh," said Charlotte simply. "He seems very nice and terribly handsome."

"He is handsome, but if you sleep with him, it will more than likely be for exercise, not love."

Charlotte became flustered.

"Sleep with him? I am not going to sleep with him." She felt embarrassed and like the schoolgirl she really was. Theodora sat up and looked with concern and surprise at her sudden modesty.

"Freya, have you slept with a man? Has a man had sex with you?"

"No, I haven't slept with a man. I'm not married." She added, more quietly, "I have had hardly any experience with lovemaking – if any." There was a long pause. Theodora stood and opened all the windows; it was very hot in the room.

"Freya, now please answer me truthfully. How old are you?"

Charlotte thought for a while. She decided to take a chance.

"Theodora … I am forteen, fifteen in October."

"*Bok*!" Theodora swore in Turkish. "And a virgin, I suppose," she added in a slightly derogatory way. She strode towards the fireplace and turned to look at Charlotte with a frown on her face that made Charlotte uneasy.

"Actually no," said Charlotte sadly. "My stepfather raped me when I was twelve and has had" – she searched for the words – "sex with me whenever he could for the past three years." Tears shimmered along the rims of her eyes.

"Oh, my dear." Theodora ran over to Charlotte and threw her arms around her. This was not only the first time she had told anybody about Jean de Tournet's disgusting visits to her in the night, when Aunt Stella had made her husband sleep in another room, but also the first time she had ever cried about it in self-pity.

24

"Freya, I am sorry, I had no idea." Theodora rose from beside Charlotte and wandered over to the window. The sun was well up, burning down on a deserted Avenue Foch.

"Freya, do you know what I do?"

"You entertain the German officers."

"Yes, but do you know how I entertain these men?"

"Keep them amused, talk to them at dinner, help them—"

"Yes, I do – but that is only part of what I do. Sometimes I have to sleep with them. I pander to their basic instincts. I flatter them, I flirt and lie in their bed naked with them. For that I am paid, with dresses, jewellery and my life."

"Your life, Theodora?"

"As long as I am of use to them and amuse them, they ensure that I am not sent to a prison camp. My mother had an uncle who married a Jew. My mother was from France and emigrated to Turkey and married my father. My grandfather was an important Turkish politician, I believe."

"I don't understand. Why will the Germans send you to a camp, just because you have a great-uncle whose wife is Jewish?"

"Freya, where have you been all your fourteen years? Have you not heard of the subjugation of the Jews by Hitler and the Nazis? The disintegration of the German Social Democratic Party?"

"No," Charlotte said meekly. "I was in America until five years ago – I didn't hear much at school about politics here." Theodora dropped down onto the ottoman beside Charlotte again, an expression somewhere between disbelief and disappointment on her face.

"How does a daughter of servants end up in America *and* go to finishing school in Paris?" Theodora was getting angry. Charlotte looked hard into Theodora's dark brown eyes, trying to see if she could trust this Turkish woman who worked as a prostitute for the people who had taken over her house. "And come to that," Theodora continued, "how can a daughter of servants be cultured enough to cope with sitting at a table of powerful men and have the … how do you say – breeding – to know what cutlery to use and how to behave in such illustrious company? How would a servants' girl know how to address an empress?" she said, remembering the first time they met, a small smile forming in her eyes.

Charlotte turned her head, looked at the floor and gave a deep sigh. "Because I am the daughter of Alice Barrett, who died when I was born. Her sister, my aunt Stella, and my uncle brought me up in Boston, in America. This house was left to me by my grandmother." Charlotte paused and took a deep breath. "I am Charlotte de Tournet, and this is my house."

"But your … those people who were your parents …?"

"Christina is my governess and Bo is our chauffeur. They thought to conceal my identity by saying I am Swedish."

"Are *they* Swedish?"

"Yes. They are, I imagine, quite safe, in the Swedish Embassy. However, I am still a little concerned about them."

"Freya – I'd better keep calling you Freya." Charlotte smiled in delight. Theodora was a person to be trusted and this proved it. She put her arms around Theodora's neck and gave her a kiss on the cheek. "Freya!" Theodora said with some urgency and unravelled Charlotte's arms from around her neck. "We are going to have to think what we are going to do. You know Captain Wil wants you to become a courtesan, like me?"

"Oh, that *is* exciting."

"You do know that it means being with these men, 'entertaining' them … possibly even *sleeping* with them?" Theodora looked terribly worried as she warned Charlotte.

"Charlotte the harlot," Charlotte whispered in English gleefully, looking at the bed behind her. Theodora shushed Charlotte. She wouldn't have known what Charlotte said, speaking hardly any English herself.

"I am going to somehow get you out of here." Theodora started pacing the room.

Charlotte looked around. "You know this was my mother's room? Now it is my room. That painting upstairs? Well …"

"This is your house?" Theodora said.

"Yes, my grandmother left it to me."

"You probably know all the places to hide, secret corridors ..."

"There aren't any secret corridors," Charlotte said sadly. "Theodora, why not train me to do what you do? You will get into terrible trouble if we escape."

"I'm not escaping," Theodora said emphatically, "you are! You cannot do this – be a whore. You would have been too young at eighteen. Now I find you are fifteen ..."

"Yes, I can."

"Freya," Theodora said sternly, "you cannot have a clue what this entails. This is not lovemaking as you have probably read about at school."

"It cannot be any worse than my uncle hammering at me." Charlotte felt angry. Theodora viewed Charlotte in despair.

"Listen, darling, it's not very nice, what I do. I do it to stay alive. If you escape, I will only get a telling off."

"Theodora, I want to stay here with you. I don't want to go to my aunt and uncle. I want this opportunity to" – she thought for a moment – "to disappear. My other uncle in England does not like me; my stepmother, Aunt Stella, is going a little mad; my stepfather is a beast and a rapist. Bo and Christina are the only people who liked me in the family, and they have more than likely been deported back to Sweden. All my friends have disappeared or have gone to the safer parts of Europe; two of them were German! This is my house, and even full of strangers it is still my home." Charlotte let out a huge sigh after her speech.

She had never really talked to anybody like this. She was always a little reserved with her school friends, even Christina, to whom she was closest. Christina, and to some extent Bo, were the closest Charlotte had to loving parents. However, she could hardly confess to them about the awful behaviour of her uncle, Jean de Tournet – their employer.

This was where her independence, her determination and, to some extent, her courage came from. She was not reliant on anybody else. Now it had all changed. After knowing Theodora for just two days, she felt she had known this beautiful, dark, elegant and kind woman all her life. The sister she had never had.

*

Theodora looked at Charlotte, her mind in turmoil. She enjoyed Charlotte's loveliness, the smile that put joy in Theodora's heart. She also admired her stubbornness, her determination and, above all, her courageousness. She felt a strong filial instinct towards her, something she had never had for a person. She had become extremely fond of Charlotte in a very short period of time. She also had a secret that she felt she could impart to Charlotte, but only if necessary, and not before she had made plans to get her out of the house.

Suddenly the door to the bedroom burst open and Colonel Franz-Joseph Deller strutted in, not noticing Charlotte and Theodora sitting together on the ottoman. He grinned as he surveyed the room. He stopped in surprise at seeing the women, his eyes slightly lazy, his body swaying faintly.

"Oh! Ladies" – he bowed dramatically – "I am sorry for the intrusion. I was made to understand I had this room to stay in tonight." He slurred his words. He must have been drinking already.

"Colonel, we were just trying to find some clothes for Freya to wear. This was Charlotte de Tournet's room and there are lots of clothes left behind that will fit Freya beautifully."

"Yes, it's a lovely room, I have always loved it." He strode over to the fireplace and looked at the blank space above the mantle. "Where is the painting that was here?"

"I have no idea. Freya, did you see a picture there?" Theodora looked at Charlotte, her eyebrows arched in a comical way.

"I can't ever remember a painting there," said Charlotte smoothly. She slowly walked over to Deller's side and put up a hand to the space where the Klimt used to hang.

"Shame," he said.

Theodora watched as Deller stared at Charlotte who was standing beside him, her face turned up towards the space where the painting was, the sunlight from the window lighting up her features. He couldn't take his eyes off her. He looked smitten, then confused. Charlotte had seen his expression change too.

"Colonel, are you all right?" she asked, her smile turning to concern. It took at least thirty long seconds for Deller to compose himself.

"Are you sure we have never met, Miss Jorgensen … Freya?" Deller said shakily.

"I am sure, monsieur le Colonel, unless you have been to America or here in Paris lately."

"No, I have not been to Paris for many years, almost ten." Joseph lied.

"Well, I have never been to Germany, so we can't have met." She smiled again at him and quickly turned on her toes.

199

Deller stood by the fireplace, his eyes closed, a hand on the mantle as though he needed to hold himself steady for a minute. Both women stood beside the ottoman, waiting for him to say something.

"Would you like us to leave you?" Theodora asked quietly when the silence got a little awkward.

"No, no, I should leave you to find some clothes." He could not bring himself to look at Charlotte. "Good day, ladies, I will see you at dinner. I must go to work. I will sort out the bedroom situation with Captain Wil."

He left the room as though in a hurry to get out.

*

Charlotte speculated about Deller and tried to define what she thought of him. She felt she had met him before, but it was a very slight feeling. She could not imagine why she would have seen him, or how he knew about the Klimt painting, *Girl on a Golden Pillow*. She wondered why he was drunk, or nearly drunk, at eleven o'clock in the morning. She had heard about alcoholics and thought they were meant to be quiet, morose or lonely people. Colonel Deller didn't seem to be any of these.

"Well, my dear, you have put a spell on him."

"Who do you suppose he is?" Charlotte said. "He seems to know Charlotte ... well, he says he does. He knew where the bell pull was to summon the kitchen ... he even knows about my Klimt. And he says he was the gardener!"

"He must have had dealings with whoever lived here, Freya." There was a pause. Charlotte was still looking at the door Deller had just exited.

"Theodora, do you know much about Colonel Deller?"

"No, not really. He speaks very good French and English and is a curator of art or something – I am not sure. He came to the club in Germany a few times. He met Jost there."

"Why did you come to Paris?"

"I was recruited, if you can call it that, from my club in Berlin."

"Your club?" Charlotte imagined Theodora elegantly strolling through a crowd of white linen tables full of customers sipping champagne and cocktails, flirting with the rich gentlemen.

"No, not *my* club. It was called Das Katzenclubhaus, in Berlin, on Köpenicker Strasse, near the Köllnischer Park. We were quite close to the general headquarters for the SS and they liked to entertain there or just watch the shows, gamble at the tables and enjoy themselves. It was owned by Frau

200

Schoepke, a vile woman who enjoyed nothing but to bully us foreigners – even though she was something Slavic herself."

"You worked there as what, a waitress?" Charlotte was a little incredulous.

"I started off as a waitress, yes. I was about your age. But as my German got better, I was gradually given more and more responsibility and I ended up running it for Frau Schoepke." She stopped abruptly. "Freya," she implored, "don't get any romantic ideas about this place I worked in. It was nothing more than a high-class brothel. The officers and 'gentlemen' of Berlin would come and be entertained by us girls. We had beautiful clothes, but we had to get them paid for by the men we entertained. We had to make sure we never had a dissatisfied man, or we would be fired."

"Where did you live?"

"In a very run-down house across the filthy courtyard at the back of the club. I hated it. So as soon as Lieutenant Krupp asked me to come with him here, I jumped at the chance."

"Was Lieutenant Krupp at your club often?"

"He was part of the *Sturmabteilung* set."

"What were they?"

"Fanatical young Nazis, I suppose you could call them. They were a little wild but terribly sweet to us girls. These young men all had very important fathers, they all had titles – 'von' something or 'Baron' such-and-such." She paused and lowered her head. "But they could turn on you in an instant – no matter how pretty, or how—"

"But what about the girls at the club? Won't they miss you?"

"Two of them should have come with me but I think they have been taken somewhere else. I am not sure where they are."

"Are they as lovely as you, Theodora?"

"In their own way" – she turned and looked at Charlotte – "but none of them are anywhere near as beautiful as you." Charlotte reddened.

"Thank you," she said modestly. She thought for a while about being a courtesan.

"Theodora, how do I become a prostitute?"

"You are not going to be one, Freya! You are going to leave this place as soon as I can organise it. I have contacts in Paris that could help."

"I thought you had never been to Paris?"

"That's correct, but these are contacts made in Germany. Unfortunately, I have no idea where they are in Paris. Anyway, we must get you away to safety."

"But if that is going to be difficult or dangerous for you, I would rather become a courtesan, like you."

"We shall see." Theodora paused. "I am a prostitute," she said quietly, "because of my circumstances. My father killed himself when his building firm went bankrupt in 1930. I was about sixteen, and he left no money for us. My French mother went to work with Frau Schoepke at Das Katzenclubhaus, and when she became ill and too old to interest men, she got me to take over."

"What a life," Charlotte marvelled. "Why didn't you run away?"

"My mother's illness – it was the only way I could pay for the doctor."

"But you are so elegant, sophisticated ... I mean, you could be from a rich family." Charlotte realised she sounded slightly superior. "I mean ..."

"We were rich – until my father lost it all gambling at Das Katzenclubhaus and other places. His business was ruined. That is why we ended up there. I was privately educated until I was fifteen – your age." Charlotte was aware of their similarities. She tried to understand who Theodora was.

"How do you stop getting pregnant, if these men are ... are ...?" Charlotte asked, her knowledge about pregnancy being sketchy but quite advanced for a young, unmarried woman. After her uncle raped her, she had read a lot about sexual behaviour, secretively, in the Paris Library. Theodora looked slightly shocked by this personal question.

"I wear a ring inside me."

"Inside you? You mean ..." She gestured towards Theodora's abdomen.

"Yes, an Ota Ring. But you must never tell anybody. It is terribly illegal."

"Illegal? No, of course, I won't tell anyone. But why didn't I get pregnant when that bastard raped me?"

"He must have withdrawn before ... or you were just lucky, or just too young, I suppose."

"Yes, I think he ... I don't want to think about it." Charlotte shivered in disgust.

"Anyway, nobody will be going to bed you here, I'll make sure of that. You will just be entertaining them, chatting to them, enchanting them with that lovely smile, and pandering to their egos. And these men have large egos."

There was a knock at the door.

"*Hereinkommen*," Theodora shouted.

The door opened and the harridan entered. She did not have the usual scowl on her face or balled fists on her hips. Charlotte unconsciously rubbed the side of her face which was still slightly red from where the woman had struck her.

"My name is *SS-Unterscharführer* Hildegard Becker," she said in loud German, standing to attention, eyes looking straight ahead. Her normally sullen demeanour had slightly improved with the semblance of a smile. Her forehead and ruddy cheeks on her squashed-up, square face had a sheen of sweat.

"What is it you want, Sergeant?" Theodora asked in German. "I don't know what has come over the woman," Theodora whispered to Charlotte in French. "I think Colonel Deller has got to her."

"I have orders to help you move clothes and any furniture to your quarters, *gnädige* Frau."

"Oh!" Theodora was surprised and looked around for something for her to take up to her room. "Well, can you return in fifteen minutes? We are not quite ready."

"*Jawohl, gnädige* Frau." The sergeant clicked her heels, strode out the door and closed it behind her very quietly.

The two women looked at each other and began to giggle, then, realising she might hear them, stifled the chuckles with their hands.

"Well, what do you think of that?" Charlotte said. "She must be terribly hot in that uniform. Let's get her to take up something heavy." Charlotte looked about the room. "What about the bed?" They both rolled about with laughter.

"Freya" – Theodora became serious, quenching any levity – "if you are not going to allow me to send you to somewhere of safety, then I want you to be able to protect yourself." Her hands went to the back of her neck and she unclasped a necklace. It was the one Charlotte had noticed before – a thin silver chain with a large cross. It was not a very pretty crucifix and it had always surprised Charlotte that this chic woman would wear such a cumbersome object.

"This has been my protector for many years."

"I didn't see you as particularly religious," Charlotte said, holding the cross. It was surprisingly heavy, with a short tubular crosspiece and a very long shaft, also tubular. It was fashioned to look like a tree or a twig. The bottom end of the shaft came to a slight point.

"I am not at all religious. I have no religion. Now look." Theodora turned the cross over. On the top and at the cross of the long shaft were small silver spheres.

"Press the top button hard with your nail – your thumbnail," she instructed Charlotte. As Charlotte pressed the little silver button, a thin blue steel blade over ten centimetres long shot out the base of the cross. The button clicked.

"Christ!" Charlotte was amazed. She touched the tip and it stung her. It was so sharp it produced a tiny drop of blood. Charlotte put her finger in her mouth and looked at Theodora with astonishment and intrigue.

"What is it for? Is it a weapon?"

"If you ever find yourself in a position of extreme danger with a man, all you do is charm him, get up close to him, place the end of the cross near the centre of his chest and just to his left, and press the top button. The blade will shoot straight into his heart. To retract the blade, find some glass or metal, and …" Theodora pressed the bottom button and pressed the blade back up into the shaft.

"See? Nobody will know for ages how he died. They will think it was a heart attack. When you withdraw the blade, wipe any blood off the wound so it does not show. And if you can't get to his chest, shove it down his ear – the blade will go straight into his brain."

Charlotte gasped; she was astonished. But then she looked at the cross with reserve. "But Theodora, will I ever use it? It's incredible. And what about you? You need it."

"You'll do it, Freya." Theodora put an arm around Charlotte's shoulders. "I think you may have a bit of a temper, am I right?"

"Christina says I have a temper. She says it is my red hair." Theodora looked at Charlotte's lovely gold hair. "If that is red hair," she said, stroking her own raven-coloured hair, "this is grey."

"Christina, being Swedish, thinks blonde is nearly white. This, according to her, is red!" Charlotte looked at the cross sadly. "I could not kill anybody, Theodora."

"Then just poke it anywhere you choose and it will give them a terrible sting," Theodora said with a short laugh. "They will think a bee has stung them."

With some trepidation Charlotte took the cross, held it at arm's length and pressed the top button. The little blade shot out with such force. She retracted the blade again as Theodora had taught her, then sat and looked at this dangerous weapon.

Could this really kill a man? She gave Theodora a hug and put the chain over her head. She pulled her hair out from beneath the chain and shook it loose. The cross lay comfortably and reassuringly on her chest.

25

Charlotte and Theodora proved to be a huge success at Nineteen Avenue Foch, or La Palais, as it was renamed. A steady array of senior SS officers and the Gestapo, and even some *Wehrmacht* officers, spent enjoyable times there being entertained by the household. Now and then, a German cabaret would be brought in from Berlin; they would perform in the large library on a makeshift stage. La Palais was like an elite club. Only certain people were told about the house in Avenue Foch, and only certain officers and very important people were invited to stay there.

The house was run by a combination of people. It was headed by SS General Konrad von Ardle, a tall, plump, middle-aged man. He was completely bald with a small black moustache that looked like a thick eyebrow on his upper lip. He wore a monocle which could make him look a little comical; his right eye was perpetually surprised, while his left eye gave the impression he was about to nod off. He took an immediate shine to Charlotte.

He was ruthless, with a temper the household – except Charlotte and Theodora – were constantly subjected to. He had been known to strike miscreants down with his riding crop or anything else that came to hand, but this was rare. If he needed calming down, or a difficult favour was to be asked, Charlotte was always given the chore of placating him or requesting the favour, which often seemed to work.

Captain Wil took charge of the day-to-day management of the house and the numerous guards, and he took care of the "entertainment". There was a host of chefs and waiting staff, all under the command of the head butler, Detlev, and his wife, Bertha. They lived in Bo and Christina's quarters. Both were fierce and very precise, with no apparent sense of humour. They were almost identical: painfully thin, with short white-blonde hair – Detlev's being a tiny tuft on top of his head, the sides severely shaved. Charlotte and Theodora, along with most of the household, hated them. Charlotte slightly resented the fact that they replaced, to some degree, Bo and Christina, who would have made a far better job. However, Bo, Charlotte conceded, would not make a very good butler.

Helmut, the little German waiter from Strasbourg, was still racing around all the hours God gave, never seeming to sleep or have a day off. He kept Charlotte and Theodora up to date with the household tittle-tattle.

As the hot summer of 1940 came to a close, the autumn swept in with a vengeance, bringing cold winds. La Palais was constantly busy. Theodora and Charlotte were joined by Gabriella and Elfriede. Both women were tall, elegant and shapely. Both, however, did not possess the style or sophistication of Charlotte or Theodora, so consequently lasted only two weeks at the end of the summer. They quarrelled with each other, with Theodora, and finally – and possibly why they were packed off back to Berlin – with General von Ardle.

Charlotte had learnt well from Theodora. She watched how Theodora moved, sat, talked to men and gesticulated. She learnt how to do every action with elegance and poise. She imitated Theodora's actions and quickly became a master of grace and refinement herself, with slow, purposeful movements.

Charlotte had started to wear her hair in the style of a new Hollywood star, Veronica Lake: long, loose and lustrous. A large swathe of her gold and shiny hair tumbled over her shoulder, and a side parting enabled her hair to fall over part of her face. The result was that every time she looked up, her head would be coquettishly to one side, and as she tilted her head to greet someone, she would draw her hair to one side with an elegant hand and offer them her delightful smile. It often stunned men and sometimes women alike.

*

The fifth of October 1940 was Charlotte's nineteenth – technically, her fifteenth – birthday. General von Ardle insisted she celebrate with a trip to the Paris opera house, the Palais Garnier, to see *The Magic Flute*. This would be the first time Charlotte was allowed out of the confines of the house and its immediate area since she arrived five months previously. She and Theodora had walked up and down Avenue Foch but were always escorted by a guard or two. Sometimes they wandered up Avenue de Malakoff to a little café, but a guard would stay with them. Once, a Gestapo man escorted them and would not leave them alone, and insisted on talking at them in a boorish way.

The birthday saw a little more leniency in allowing Theodora and Charlotte out, unescorted. The general drew up new papers for Charlotte. The danger then was with Parisian women. They despised any collaboration between the Germans and French women, so Theodora and Charlotte had to speak German when they were out in Paris, which was not so dangerous. However, they were still looked at by the Paris inhabitants as though they wanted to spit at them.

*

November arrived and with it, autumn proper. Charlotte had no money, and the shops and cafés only took German Reichsmarks, so she asked Captain Wil if she could have some money to buy some clothes. They were in the drawing room.

"What kind of clothes?" he asked. "You have all the clothes that girl left behind."

"Well, Captain Wil, for a start, the girl was fifteen – I am nineteen, and" – she looked around modestly, making sure no one was listening – "I need underclothes, nice ones, for a grown-up woman, not an adolescent girl."

"Ah …" Captain Wil looked a little embarrassed. He regarded Charlotte up and down, pushed his spectacles back up his nose and looked in the direction of the general's office. Wil was not handsome; his round, chinless face was dominated by round tortoiseshell glasses on a sharp nose. But he had a charming smile – when he chose to use it. "You'd better come with me. He may be a little more amenable with you around."

Wil strode into the study. A young SS soldier sat at the desk in the outer office. On seeing Captain Wil, he sprung to attention and clicked his heels.

"Where is the sergeant?" asked Wil.

"Gone on an errand for the general, sir."

"I would like a word with the general."

"Yes, sir, he is in. Shall I ring him? He has got someone—"

"No, I will go straight in."

"Yes, sir. But he has got a person …" the young soldier said in some alarm, but Wil took no notice of him.

Wil knocked on the study door. The general shouted to enter. Wil went in. Charlotte held back a bit, slightly regretting the whole thing. Wil beckoned her in to go in first as he held the door open.

"What is it?" the general barked, and then saw Charlotte. He rose from his desk when Charlotte entered.

"Captain Wil, Freya, how lovely to see you so early in the morning." It was ten o'clock.

Charlotte's grandmother's study was a large but cosy room lined with wood panelling like an English billiard room. The general sat behind Charlotte's grandfather's desk, now back in its usual place. A large window flooded the study with light and backlit the general.

"We were just talking about you, Freya." The general adjusted his monocle. Charlotte was aware of another person standing up from a large leather chair in the corner of the study, behind Wil. Charlotte saw a man in his late thirties, thin, dark, and shorter than her, with a long, hairy neck and a prominent Adam's apple. He had a dark shadow of a poorly shaven chin, dark eyes with red eyelids that looked sore, and a cigarette dangled from his thin lips. He wore an old brown suit, crumpled and dirty. His black tie was pulled down and the top button of his once-white shirt undone. He was the kind of man one would take an instant dislike to, thought Charlotte. He was a caricature of a film villain.

"Captain Wil," the general said nervously, "may I introduce you to *Kriminalkommissar* Karl Hueber of the Gestapo." The general gave a nervous laugh.

"That's right, Captain, head of the Paris division," Hueber said, smoke from his cigarette puffing out as he spoke. "Miss Jorgensen?" He walked over to Charlotte and took her hand in his and stepped back as if admiring a picture. "You are indeed … lovely." His breath smelt as he spoke in a high-pitched tenor voice. Charlotte pulled her hand away from this awful little man. Everything she hated about a person was there before her: smelly, presumptuous and disturbing. He did not seem to notice Charlotte's obvious repulsion. Charlotte turned away abruptly from the little man.

"Excuse me, please, Herr Hueber," she said softly but firmly and went to the general's desk.

She was about to make her request when the general said, "*Kriminalkommissar* Hueber wanted to have a word with you, Miss Jorgensen."

Charlotte turned back to look at Hueber and smiled slightly at him.

"You wanted to talk to me? Why me?"

"We think you will know of the whereabouts of Charlotte de Tournet."

Charlotte felt the blood drain from her face. She sensed a little nausea rise from her stomach. Her expression held a slight smile; her eyes, however, conveyed concern.

"I'm afraid not, Monsieur Hueber," Charlotte said at last. "As far as I know, Charlotte de Tournet is in America."

"We have received a request from the British embassy in Spain to find the whereabouts of Charlotte de Tournet, from a Madame Stella de Tournet. Charlotte de Tournet has not been heard of since she was collected from her school in June." Hueber strolled back to the chair in the corner of the room and gently lowered himself down, pulling each trouser leg up slightly as he did so, and then crossed his legs, revealing white skin and hairy ankles above his short grey socks. He put his elbows on the arms of his chair and clasped his hands together. He stared at Charlotte. After removing his cigarette from the corner of his mouth, he pursed his lips in an expectant fashion and waited for a comment.

Charlotte eyed the other two men who were looking at her with concern. Wil was confused, his mouth a little open; the general, anxious, looking from Charlotte to Hueber and back.

"I suggest you are in contact with Fräulein de Tournet," Hueber said, now in German.

"I am not. How can I? ... I have no idea how you came to think that," Charlotte said steadily.

"Your parents told me." Hueber stood up again very quickly and came up close to Charlotte, took her by the shoulders and turned her around so the light from the window shone in her face. Charlotte's shock turned to anger.

"What do you mean?" she shouted.

"Herr Hueber ... please," the general said in alarm at Charlotte's treatment. Hueber swung round and looked daggers at the general. General von Ardle quickly sat down in his chair and wiped his forehead. He looked as though he was desperately trying to control his temper. He removed his monocle and polished it and returned it to his right eye.

"Where are my parents?" Charlotte said, slightly less aggressively. "I thought they would be back in Sweden."

"You have not answered my question, Fräulein Jorgensen," said Hueber, the cigarette in the corner of his mouth wagging as he spoke, ash, smoke and bad breath wafting over Charlotte's face.

"I am sorry, but I have no idea why my parents would say that. They know where she is. From last we heard, in America." She pulled herself away from Hueber's grasp. "How am I meant to be in contact with her? I have not been out of sight of anyone here since June!"

Hueber seized her by her arm.

"You are under arrest. You will be taken to Eighty-Four and I will ask you again, when I am sure you will be more forthcoming." Charlotte gasped and tried to release her arm.

"Hueber, that is enough!" shouted the general, standing again, his temper lost, the monocle in his eye looking as though it would break in two. "Release Miss Jorgensen immediately. This is my office. As far as I gather from this … 'interrogation', Miss Jorgensen has answered your question. Remember she is a Swedish citizen."

"Is she, General?" He rounded on the general, his dark eyes drilling into him. "Have we seen her papers? No. She may be a British spy or a French freedom fighter. We have important people coming to this house. She may be sending information to this de Tournet girl and—"

"I thought Charlotte de Tournet was twelve or thirteen – a schoolgirl," said Captain Wil.

Hueber looked slowly over towards Wil. He scowled at him, then glared at the general.

"Very well, I will leave it at that – if you take full responsibility, von Ardle—"

"*General* von Ardle, if you don't mind," the general corrected, sensing Hueber was on the back foot. "Yes, I can safely say I can take full responsibility for Fräulein Jorgensen. I shall bid you good morning. Heil Hitler!" The general put up his hand in a mild salute. Hueber stood to attention, clicked his heels and gave the Nazi salute, turned quickly on his heels and stormed out of the study.

"What a nasty little man! I cannot do with these common, jumped-up …" The general noticed Captain Wil was still looking at Charlotte. "Are you all right, Freya?" the general asked kindly, back in French. Charlotte was thinking. She was very close to tears.

"My German is not that good," she said. "What do you think he meant about what my parents said, and what is 'eighty-four'?" They heard the outer office door slam as Hueber stormed out. The general brought round an upright chair to the front of the desk for Charlotte to sit on, and then slumped down at his desk and offered the chair in the corner to Captain Wil.

"Freya, what do you know about the household here?" the general asked.

"General, I am the daughter of Bo and Christina Jorgensen and I was the companion to Charlotte de Tournet."

"We know this, Freya," interjected Captain Wil, "but we have no proof of this. There are no records, photos or even papers to say as much."

"And this is a very sensitive establishment," the general continued. "Any hint of a person who is not totally trustworthy will come under suspicion."

"I am sorry there is not much proof. All my papers are in Biarritz. Send me back to Sweden if you think I am a risk. I was two the last time I was in Sweden, so I have no idea what to do. I think you must trust me. Ask Theodora how trustworthy I am."

"Well, we have asked Theodora." The general sat back in his chair. "You have been a huge help here with Theodora, your German is coming on, you are very popular – not surprisingly—"

"But I am not going to be much help here in the future with my present non-existent wardrobe. I have to dip into Theodora's wardrobe all the time. And I need other things."

"Where are all your clothes?" asked Captain Wil.

This was a question Charlotte had not prepared for. She had thought of virtually every other scenario for her new identity, except for *that* question. She went on the offensive and asked a question to a question. "What is 'eighty-four', and where do you suppose my parents are, Captain Wil?"

Captain Wil and the general looked at each other. The general replied, "Eighty-Four Avenue Foch is the headquarters for the Gestapo. They" – he cast his eyes up as if looking for inspiration – "interview people there."

"What kind of people?" Charlotte asked bluntly.

"Freya, you do not understand the seriousness of your position here, do you?" The general was getting a little distressed.

"I am sorry, General von Ardle, I am just concerned for my parents – understandably. Were my parents 'interviewed' at this place, and are they still there?"

"I have no idea where your parents are and, like you, presume they have been … err … repatriated. Am I correct, Captain Wil?"

"Yes, Herr General. Or are being held at Drancy Prison," Wil said tactlessly.

Charlotte gasped. "Surely not! What have they done?" Charlotte looked suspiciously at the men in the office. "I am very hopeful that my parents have been repatriated back to Sweden and are not in Drancy Prison. I am here because I do not have papers and I love this house – it has been my home for most of my life. I am willing to work here to the best of my ability for however long it takes for my papers to be found or replaced." This was becoming some kind of ultimatum. "I will be loyal to you, General, to the staff of the house and to Germany."

"Thank you, Freya, we are—"

"I have not finished!" Both men looked in shock. "If I am subjected to any further … handling from that Gestapo man, I will have to review not only my loyalties, but also my elegancies."

"What exactly does that mean, Miss Jorgensen?" the general asked, plainly reeling from Charlotte's little speech, much to Charlotte's satisfaction.

"I know every nook and cranny in this house. I know Paris very well. I have many friends both in the house and in Paris who will be willing to help me if I get into trouble. I do not think you want me as an enemy. And General," she implored, with a complete change of character, "I don't want to be an enemy. I love it here and the work I do with Theodora."

The general looked at Charlotte, bewildered.

"Miss Jorgensen … Freya …. here are five hundred Reichsmarks." He reached for a drawer and pulled out a wad of notes, from which he peeled off twenty-five notes. "And here" – the general signed a piece of paper and a card – "is a temporary work permit and identity document. Go with Captain Wil and buy whatever clothes you need."

"Oh!" Charlotte took the notes. "Thank you, General. I don't know what to say." She had no idea how much five hundred Reichsmarks was. A dress from an ordinary dressmaker was about two thousand francs; from a reputable haute couturier, such as Lucien, it would be about one hundred thousand francs.

"Freya?" The general looked pensive. He removed his monocle and polished it with a handkerchief from his pocket, giving himself time to think. He replaced the monocle, wiped his small moustache and swiped his hand over his bald head.

"Yes, General?" prompted Charlotte gently.

"Freya, I cannot ever guarantee that a similar experience such as you had with Hueber will never happen again. It is out of our … control. However, I will try to find the underlying cause of your missing papers and organise your repatriation – if you want it. You are, however, extremely popular here with our visitors." He looked at her with kind eyes. He polished his monocle again, and while buffing the small round lens, he said, "You are one of the most valuable members of this household." He stood up and turned to look out of the large window. There was not much of a view, just a large wall covered with

Virginia creeper which ran alongside the driveway. "That will be all now. Good morning, Freya, Captain Wil."

Charlotte and Wil left the study. The sergeant, now back at his post, snapped to attention.

"I am sorry, sir. I went to warn you of the arrival of the Gestapo, but you had got to the office before I could find you. I hope—"

"Don't worry, Sergeant."

26

That was Charlotte's first encounter with the uglier side of her war. Even being slapped by Sergeant Becker five months earlier was nothing compared to what she felt when being "interviewed" by Hueber. She was confused why Hueber considered himself so important. Perhaps he was important. That nasty little man thought he could treat General von Ardle like an insignificant old fogey.

Theodora looked terribly worried when Charlotte told her of the morning's activities with Hueber. They sat in the little sitting room Theodora and Charlotte had created on the top floor. With the help of the now fully cooperative Sergeant Hildegard Becker, the bedroom that used to be the housekeeper's apartment, at the end of the corridor on the top floor, had been furnished with a sofa and two armchairs, a cupboard for drinks and a few coffee tables. There were curtains on the two windows on either end of the long room and it had a fireplace for the winter.

"The Gestapo," Theodora said quietly, "are a law unto themselves. They are the secret police, after all. Some of them, however, are nothing but cruel brutes. I am always very nice to them. I never get on their wrong side." Theodora bit her bottom lip and looked at Charlotte anxiously. "Karl Hueber is one of the more dangerous members of the Gestapo, and he is now second in command of the Gestapo in Paris. Göring himself appointed him."

"Christ!" Charlotte rolled her eyes to the sky and paced the room with her hand on her forehead. "Well," she said brightly, "I can't worry about that now. I've got five hundred Reichsmarks for a dress or two and some underwear, and" – Charlotte whipped two pieces of paper out of her handbag – "I have an identity card and a work document. Shall we go to Rue de Rivoli and see what is still open?"

"You will be surprised how much of Paris is still working," said Theodora. "Let's get Captain Wil to take us. It's safer and we don't have to walk so far."

*

The women cajoled Captain Wil into taking them to central Paris in his large Mercedes Benz. Armed with her five hundred Reichmarks, Charlotte and Theodora set out to find some clothes, with Captain Wil in attendance. He was delighted by the envious glances from other German army officers in the unusually quiet Rue de Rivoli.

The streets of Paris were empty. Groups of German soldiers swaggered and chatted, arrogantly strutting around as though they had always been there, laughing and smoking while the Parisians scuttled about trying to avoid being stopped by patrolling German soldiers. It was a cold Friday afternoon in late November. The shops were gradually opening after the shopkeepers had had their lunch. Theodora and Charlotte were having a wonderful time out of the confines of the house, ambling around, shopping. They stopped to have some drinks in a little café that Charlotte used to enjoy going to with Christina, as a treat before the war, in the Rue Sainte Anne, just off Avenue de l'Opéra.

Captain Wil sat with the women at a prominent table by the window. The staff in the café looked cautiously at Captain Wil's black SS uniform. The women ordered hot chocolate and some pastries but could only get chicory coffee – no chocolate had been served at the café for three years. As they talked and ate their pastries, the few French people who were in the café gradually left.

Charlotte was dismayed to think she could possibly be such a hated figure in Paris because she was sat at a table with an enemy officer and regarded as a hated German.

She sat and drank her unpleasant coffee in silence, looking out of the window. She spotted an art gallery on the other side of the street. It was closed, which was a shame as she would have loved to have had a look at the paintings. The windows on either side of the courtyard entrance displayed a single picture in each, a huge landscape in one window and a single portrait in the other. Charlotte could just make out that the portrait was of a lady. She looked familiar. Charlotte excused herself from the table and left the café, and walked over to the gallery.

The portrait was in oils. The subject, a woman, sprawled and relaxed in a steamer chair, was looking slightly to one side at something just over the viewer's left shoulder. She had auburn shoulder-length hair pulled back on either side of her head by ivory combs. Her face was striking, with a slightly large, angular nose and a thrusting chin. Her eyes were large, framed by sweeping lashes. Her expression looked demure and thoughtful.

Charlotte was looking at a beautiful portrait of her mother, Alice Barrett.

The gallery was firmly closed, the archway door to the courtyard and the rest of the gallery secured with a metal gate. There was no sign or anything to say what the gallery was called; it had been painted out. Charlotte could hear some building work going on inside. It was very frustrating.

"I finished your pastries," Captain Wil said behind her.

"What a lovely portrait," Theodora said, squinting through the window. "It looks just like someone I—"

"Captain Wil, I hope you have all my bags," Charlotte said loudly and walked hurriedly towards the Mercedes Benz.

"Wait for us." Captain Wil followed her.

Theodora looked at the portrait again and suddenly understood why Charlotte had jumped away. It was the same woman as in the photograph in Charlotte's room. She had an element of Charlotte about her. Theodora looked to see where Charlotte and Captain Wil had gone. As she took a last look at the portrait, she thought she saw a figure out of the corner of her eye ducking into a doorway beside the gallery. It could be someone who had seen Captain Wil and wanted to make sure Wil did not see them. Captain Wil was walking the other way up the road. She stood and waited for a time to see if he or she appeared again.

The man saw Theodora had spotted him. He stepped out onto the pavement, guiltily, from the doorway he had hidden in, and gave Theodora a nervous wave before going back into the gallery. He was slim, athletic and dressed in a black roll-top sweater, a scarf around his chin. He was youthful and handsome.

*

"Why is there a portrait of my mother in a gallery in the middle of Paris? No signature that I could see. No name of the gallery." Charlotte was unpacking her new clothes without enthusiasm. She should have been a little more excited about her new wardrobe but she felt no sense of glee. She thought Theodora seemed preoccupied too.

"Freya, did you see a man outside the gallery when you went out?"

"No, why?"

"Just thought I did."

"There is always a Gestapo man following us; it might be him."

"I don't know what that man you got tangled up with looked like ....
Hueber, wasn't it?"

Charlotte whirled around. "Small, dark, skinny ... ugly?"

"No, he was just ... oh, I don't know ... a man! Quite handsome, elegantly
dressed, dark ... he didn't look like he was in the Gestapo. He waved at me as
if he knew me."

"No, not Hueber."

"Are you sure that the portrait is of your mother?"

Charlotte picked up the photograph of her mother and scrutinised it. She
showed it to Theodora.

"Look" – she pointed at the combs in her mother's hair – "same combs,
same nose, nearly the same angle of her head."

Charlotte continued to unpack her new wardrobe. Not Hueber, thank
God. She wanted to stop thinking of Hueber and the portrait of her mother.
She wanted to try and think of happier things. Jost Krupp was returning after
a few months away. He was working for *SS-Sturmbannführer* Josef Kieffer, who
was in charge of the SS in Paris, and was also to visit La Palais that evening.

*

The impending arrival of Lieutenant Krupp filled Charlotte with excitement
and was what had prompted her to ask for new clothes. She intended to get a
little closer to him and dazzle him before he went off again.

That evening, Theodora and Charlotte were joined by two ladies from
Berlin: Agatha and Juliet. Agatha was mousy, small and not particularly
beautiful, but she was terribly witty. She played the piano, sang, and was,
apparently, according to Hans Wil, very popular with the Gestapo. Juliet could
not have been much older than Charlotte. She had long, wispy, white-blonde
hair and was slim with very pale skin. She had wonderfully sharp sky-blue
eyes and constantly wore a frightened expression, even when she was smiling.
Theodora stood close to her when the guests arrived.

27

Sir Sussex Tremayne's expansive walnut desk sat at the end of a large, dark and stuffy conference room. The single window at one end of the long room looked over Whitehall Gardens and the River Thames beyond. He had refused to move to an underground office as he said he was not a rabbit. He also preferred to be in a spacious room, not a poky rabbit warren.

There was a knock on the door. Lieutenant Commander Martin Stanley, in Royal Navy uniform, entered and stood to attention. "Baron Ferdinand Saumures, Commodore," he announced.

"Thank you, Stanley." Sir Sussex rose from his chair as Ferdi came in, dressed in a thick black overcoat. "Ferdinand, you made it! Was it a terrible journey, my boy?"

"Not really, sir. It just took rather a long time." Ferdi unslung a haversack and removed his overcoat to reveal a heavy dark-blue fisherman's jumper and dark-blue trousers.

"You look well, if not a little scruffy." Sir Sussex was also in naval uniform. "I doubt you have seen me in my full regalia, Ferdinand."

"No, sir."

"Don't worry, my boy, we are going to the dungeons this afternoon, Stanley and I ... you remember Stanley, don't you? You met in 1925 in Paris when ..." Sir Sussex saw that Ferdi was not really interested. "Ferdinand is my godson, you know, Stanley."

"Yes, sir, I remember," Stanley said.

"Well, anyway, we are to brief the Prime Minister later. Just Stanley and I, you understand."

"The dungeons?"

"The war rooms, very secret stuff. Can't say much more, really. I'm sorry I brought it up." Sir Sussex indicated a chair for Ferdi to sit on and went back to his own chair. He took out a cigarette case and flipped open the lid. He offered Ferdi a cigarette. Ferdi accepted and proceeded to insert his cigarette into a short ivory holder. Sir Sussex viewed this with some surprise and distaste. They both lit their cigarettes. Stanley produced a large ashtray and placed it on the desk between Ferdi and his godfather, and sat at a small table just behind Sir Sussex.

"Sir," Ferdi started. Sir Sussex put on his half-moon glasses and looked over the tops at Ferdi. "It has taken me over a week to get here, by boat, via Sweden. I hope what you want me for is important." Sir Sussex was slightly taken aback but realised he had not actually told Ferdi what the meeting was for.

"I am sorry, Ferdinand, I had forgotten you have struggled over from behind the lines, as it were." He looked up at Stanley. "Stanley, the file, please." Stanley presented a buff file marked TOP SECRET in red. "This file is for a new operation that we need you to run. It is called 'Wasp Trap' and is a minor extension to your current role in MI6." Sir Sussex could see Ferdi shifting a little in his seat, looking uncomfortably at the file. "Basically, using your contacts, and four new agents who are already *in situ*, as it were" – Sir Sussex took a long draw on his cigarette and blew out the smoke as if announcing a great event – "you will collect as much information as you can about the Nazis in and around Paris."

Ferdi opened the file. Inside were four sheets of paper, each with a photo of a man in SS uniform: three lieutenants and one captain.

"These men were placed in the Hotel Majestic – the German headquarters – when the hotel was taken over by the German High Command. They have all successfully infiltrated into the administration. They will work alongside your people …"

"Well, person at the moment, Sir Sussex, maybe a second, I am not sure."

"Why, what happened?"

"I have lost Franz-Joseph Deller. I lost contact with him last year. He sent me a letter, which I will have to tell you about."

"And the woman in Berlin?"

"She is now in Paris, I believe."

"Well, that is superb, Ferdinand. Where is she based?"

"I'm not sure, but Fuhrman says—"

"Ulrich Fuhrman, your SS officer?" Stanley asked.

Ferdi looked at Stanley apprehensively. "Yes, my SS officer. He thinks she is working in a house in Paris. I believe I saw her fleetingly outside my gallery three weeks ago. Unfortunately, I have only one photo of her, so I'm not sure if it was her. Fuhrman, who does know her, thinks it was. She was with a girl, a young girl, who I believe may be Charlotte de Tournet." Sir Sussex looked at Stanley with his eyebrows raised in question.

"The girl who disappeared, Sir Sussex, in June this year, during the occupation of Paris," said Stanley.

"Why do you think it could be this young lass, Ferdinand?"

"She spent a long time looking at a portrait of Alice Barrett – her mother – in my gallery window."

"One of yours?"

"Yes, sir."

"Well, there is nothing you can do about her now. Didn't the de Tournets have a house in Avenue Foch?" Sir Sussex asked Stanley, aware that the Gestapo headquarters were also in Avenue Foch.

"Yes, sir." Ferdi beat Stanley to it. "Nineteen Avenue Foch. The Gestapo headquarters are at number eighty-four." Ferdi put up his finger as Sir Sussex was about to say something. "Nineteen Avenue Foch is also where Sir Jason Barrett's mother lived, which brings me to a rather delicate point." Ferdi looked across at Stanley. "Is there a way we could discuss this just between us, sir?"

"Sorry, Ferdinand, but Stanley needs to be here." Sir Sussex was abrupt.

Ferdi sighed and carried on.

"I refer you to Franz-Joseph Deller's last letter, dated October last year." Ferdi took out a sheet of paper from his haversack. He unfolded it and looked at it thoughtfully. Sir Sussex had his hand out, waiting to see the letter's contents. Ferdi passed it over. Sir Sussex sat back in his chair and started reading, stroking his white beard from time to time. The more he read, the more apprehensive he looked.

"It says here that in September last year he bumped into Sir Jason Barrett at Hitler's headquarters in Adlerhorst." Sir Sussex lowered the letter. "I find this unlikely, Ferdinand. Does he even know what Sir Jason looks like?"

"He was their gardener," Ferdi said.

"Ah, of course," Sir Sussex remembered. "This bit about Sir Jason making Deller work for WASP ... I mean ..." Anger welled up inside him. "That

220

implies Sir Jason is a member of WASP!" Sir Sussex was stunned. "This is absurd, Ferdinand, it's made up."

Sir Sussex waved the letter at Stanley to read. Stanley read it, shaking his head with an expression of derision.

"That is impossible," Stanley said. "Sir Jason is a highly respected member of the War Office and part of MI6. That is a ridiculous assertion. We are going to have to ask him about this."

"Hang on, Stanley." Sir Sussex took a long draw of his cigarette and then stubbed it out. "We keep this to ourselves for now, do you understand? If Barrett is playing double dealings, we are going to have to find out another way. We don't want to put Deller at risk. Also, Sir Jason may have been in Adlerhorst on official business. We had only just declared war in September 1939. Deller may have seen him earlier. The really interesting thing is him being a member of WASP." Sir Sussex sat back and looked up to the ceiling in thought. He remembered Ferdinand saying Deller was a bit of a loose cannon, drank a bit. What if Deller was just muddying the waters for Barrett? "And you have no contact with Deller?"

"No, afraid not."

"I would be very surprised if he saw Sir Jason there – he must have got his dates wrong." Sir Sussex was concerned.

"How would he know about WASP?" Ferdi asked.

"Well, I don't know, Ferdinand." Sir Sussex grew angry again. "It sounds like your friend Deller has turned. Have you mentioned WASP to him?"

"No, sir."

"Bugger!" Sir Sussex slapped the desk. "Do we know if we can rely on this intelligence? How reliable is this letter – Deller's report, Ferdinand? Is he likely to make this all up? Isn't he a bit of a sensationalist?" Ferdi looked down at the carpet. Sir Sussex could not see his face to gauge what he was thinking.

"I believe Joseph could not make it up. He does not have that kind of imagination. If I catch up with him—"

"If you catch up with him, you somehow send him to us, Ferdinand. Is he still an SS major?"

"Lieutenant colonel, actually, according to that letter." Sir Sussex detected some pride in his godson.

"Good God," Stanley gasped. "You do not become a colonel in the SS because they like the cut of your jib. He is basically the same rank as you, sir!"

"Not quite," Sir Sussex said, slightly annoyed at Stanley's presumption.

There was a long pause. Sir Sussex stood up and walked towards the window at the other end of the long room. He lit a cigarette. He was in a quandary. How could Sir Jason Barrett, a respected diplomat, now part of MI6 with his knowledge of French politics, and a friend of Winston Churchill, possibly be a traitor? Sir Sussex shook his head in disbelief. All this information was most unreliable – and from an Austrian.

"Where are you staying, Ferdinand?"

"I don't know, sir."

"I will take you down to your house in Petworth. London is bloody noisy at the moment. You can then go on to Tangmere, the day after tomorrow."

"Tangmere?"

"Yes," said Stanley. "We thought it quicker if we flew you back and dropped you off just north—"

"Drop me off? Parachute, you mean?"

"It's quicker, Ferdinand. You have parachute training."

"Yes, six years ago!"

"You will be fine, my boy. Just keep your knees bent, that sort of thing, isn't it, Stanley?"

"But I have only just got here after travelling for over a week," Ferdi exclaimed. "Can't I stay for a few more days?"

"We don't want you to be missed. And in any case, we need this information pronto!"

"Where exactly do you propose to drop me, sir?" Ferdi asked.

"Just north of Paris. There is a field we use – well, three fields, actually. Different each drop. You will be met. Your code name, Baron, will be called out to you. You must then cry out '*Crêpe*' quickly or you will be shot at."

"Pancake?" Ferdi, for the first time that morning, smiled at his godfather. "Really?"

"No. *Crêpe*, Baron Saumures," said Stanley.

Sir Sussex gave him an exasperated look. "Belt up, Stanley." Sir Sussex sat at the desk again. "We will tell you all this again just before you leave. Listen, Ferdinand, this is an important assignment. We need this information. These agents," Sir Sussex said, tapping the file in front of him, "will help you get information" – he held up a sheet of foolscap paper – "on these Nazis." He placed the list into the file and patted it gently. "Do not allow this information to be seen by anyone else but you; not even your man Fuhrman should see this."

"What will you do about Barrett, sir?"

"I am not sure what to do about Sir Jason. I am reluctant to do anything. I am sure Deller has it wrong or has his own agenda to smear Sir Jason's name."

"That may be the case, sir," Ferdi said quietly. "He had a relationship with the younger sister, Alice, and she became pregnant."

"Why have we not heard this before, Ferdinand?" Sir Sussex stood. He felt anger welling up once more, astonished at his godson's evasiveness. "I am very worried about all this." He tried to temper his anger. "I don't think we can rely on whatever Deller says any more!" He slapped the desk again. Ferdi sat still, eyes cast down. Sir Sussex understood it was difficult being an agent in MI6 serving out in the field, worse if alone behind enemy lines. But holding back that kind of information was an indication that Ferdi may have been compromised in some way. He would have to have a heart-to-heart with him in Petworth.

"Was he the one responsible for the girl's death? Alice Barrett?" Stanley asked.

"Yes, I think he was. But he claims it was an awful accident," Ferdi said. Sir Sussex stood again and strolled back to the window at the other end of the room, stroking his beard in thought. He looked at his watch.

"Christ, we are meant to be at the War Office in thirty minutes, Stanley."

"Yes, we are, sir." Stanley stood, packed up his notes and took up the file on the desk with the list of names of Nazi officers and the four agents in Paris. "We will keep this report from Deller, Baron Saumures. Here is the Operation Wasp Trap brief. You must destroy it if you are captured, or about to be captured."

"Thank you, Commander Stanley," Ferdi said stiffly.

Sir Sussex waited for Stanley to leave the office. "Ferdinand, go and wait at my club. Use my card to get in. You will have to go through the back – you will never get in at the front dressed like that. There is a special room, with a bar for me and my staff."

"Thank you, sir," – Ferdi stood – "but I would prefer to go to a gallery—"

"We are not going to let you out of our sight. You will go with Ensign Murry to the All Services Club and have some lunch and a drink. We will then travel down to Petworth and remain there until you fly out tomorrow night. Do I make myself clear?" He eyed Ferdi, wondering if he could fully trust his godson. He would have to make a decision before he sent him off to Paris. Ferdi was his godson; he had watched him grow up. He didn't want to send him back to Paris, but he was too valuable a contact.

"Where exactly is this place I am being dropped off?" Ferdi asked.

"You will know when you land, Ferdinand." Sir Sussex picked up his cap, the peak heavily braided in gold, and stuffed an attaché case under his arm. "I will pick you up at the club in two and a half hours, Ferdinand." With that, he stormed out of the office.

Ferdi was concerned that his vagaries about Franz-Joseph, given his connection with Sir Jason and Alice, may have put a dent in his own trustworthiness. He had plainly upset Sir Sussex. Ferdi cast his eyes up and said, "Bugger!"

"I'm sorry, sir," a young ensign said as he came through the door of the office. "Did you say something?"

28

Albert Jaffery expertly brought his old thirty-two-foot, diesel-powered boat to the quay next to *Stützpunkt Hafenschloss*, or Castle Cornet as the fort was locally known. The vast grey fort jutted out to sea and guarded the entrance to St Peter Port, Guernsey. It was a frosty, windless late morning with a hazy sun trying to push its way through a veil of thin cloud.

"What time is it, Jaffery?"

"Twenty past midday, Sir Jason."

"My God, it has taken ages to get here." Sir Jason Barrett stretched his back after being huddled up in the cabin of the boat for seven hours.

"But we were not spotted by anybody, sir, which surprises me. We really must travel at night." Jaffery tied up the boat to the jetty and raised a small Nazi flag up the short staff on the stern of the boat. The name and port of origin had been painted over – the hull was just a plain dark royal blue.

"I can't see anyone here to greet us." Sir Jason pulled up the collar of his overcoat and put on his gloves and tweed hat. "It's too bloody cold to stick around here."

"Yes, sir. I'll go and find the dock guard." Jaffery stepped off the boat onto the jetty. "Someone is coming now, Sir Jason."

"You need to talk in German, Jaffery, or you will get us both shot at!"

Jaffery placed a hand over his unshaven chubby jowls, remembering he was in German-occupied Guernsey.

An SS captain headed a troop of five Waffen-SS soldiers, all with rifles slung over their shoulders. They were expecting their British visitors.

"Sir Jason Barrett, we expected you yesterday."

"What is your name, Captain?" Sir Jason looked the captain up and down, from his peaked cap all the way down his long black leather coat to his high black boots. He was rather taken aback by the abrupt greeting.

"Captain Gerhard Schultz, sir." He clicked his heels. "Is it just you, Sir Jason?" he said, glancing down the jetty at the scruffy, portly man in a dirty oilcloth coat.

"Just me, Captain Schultz. The weather hampered our progress from the English coast and we waited for these calmer conditions. None of my colleagues wanted to risk a crossing." Jason handed Jaffery his dispatch case while he jumped the short six inches to the jetty. "Can we get into shelter, Captain? I am chilled to the bone." He jerked his thumb at Jaffery. "What happens to my man here?"

"He can go into the harbour office canteen." Captain Schultz pointed to a building at the end of the jetty. "Are you all right with the stairs to the castle, Sir Jason?" The captain pointed to a zigzag run of steps that went up to the fortress rising high above them.

"Let's get on with it, then." Sir Jason started at a pace towards the steps. "I will get someone to call you at the canteen, Jaffery, when I am done."

"Yes, Sir Jason." Jaffery cast his eyes up to the sky.

*

As Jason made his way up to the castle steps, Jaffery wandered slowly along to the harbour canteen. He past two S-boats – high-speed torpedo boats, just slightly longer than his own. Both boats were badly damaged. One of them had had most of the superstructure destroyed – only part of the capstan remained and part of the cover that protected the helmsman. The hull appeared undamaged. The other boat had two huge holes in the hull and most of the transom at the stern was in tatters. A naval officer stood on what was left of the deck of the first S-boat.

"Do you like my boat, *mein herr?*" the German naval officer asked with a grin, an unlit cigar clamped between his teeth. Jaffery could see one of his arms was in a sling under his short, padded jacket.

"What happened to it?" Jaffery asked. The German stopped dead.

"You English?"

"South African. I have come here with a politician." Jaffery carried on looking at the boat. "Does it run?"

"Like a dream, but there are no guns or torpedo shoots, so it is useless. Why?"

"I need a boat to smuggle German agents into England. That" – he pointed to his ten-metre cruiser, looking nearly as shabby as the S-boat – "takes me most of a day to get here. But that" – he pointed to the slightly bigger, sleeker and more powerful S-boat – "would take only minutes. And I could travel at night." The naval officer looked at Jaffery as though he was mad. "Will the engines start?"

"You a spy?" asked the naval officer.

"Kind of. I work for the German Reich. Look." Jaffery brought out his orders to bring Sir Jason to the German-occupied Channel Islands. "I used to be on minesweepers in the German Navy before the war." The naval officer looked Jaffery up and down incredulously.

"Will you swap your heap of junk here for my nice thirty-two-footer?" Jaffery asked.

"Why would you want my heap of junk?"

"It goes a lot faster than anything else, and I can make it look like something else."

"You know it runs on diesel? There are no guns, no tubes," the naval man said.

"Doesn't matter, I don't need guns or tubes. It will go even faster. That runs on diesel too." Jaffery pointed at his boat. He was aching to see if the boat would run and steer. If the keel was not bent and the two tillers went fully to port and starboard, he could get it back to Newhaven quite easily while the sea was still calm. There were two obvious hurdles, however: convincing Sir Jason to buy the boat in the first place, and then getting him to agree to be taken back to England in a boat with hardly any cabin. But Sir Jason would be back in England in a quarter of the time it took to get over here.

*

Five men gathered in a meeting room that could easily be mistaken for a large prison cell, with one small window, whitewashed walls and a heavy metal door. Standing with his back to the room at the window was a man with grey hair in a black suit, gazing out over the harbour. The room was warm and well lit. It had thick carpet on the floor and a long mahogany table covered in green baize, surrounded by eight chairs. A Waffen-SS guard stood at the door.

"Thank you for coming, Sir Jason," Rudolf Hess said. "It must be difficult for you to arrange transport to get here."

"My pleasure, Herr Hess," Sir Jason said.

"Sir Jason, may I introduce you to the rest of the men at this table, before we go any further? I am here representing the Führer and the Reich. Gentlemen, this is Sir Jason Barrett, head of WASP, as most of you are aware. He was of great help in our rapid conquest into France and Paris. We thank him for his invaluable intelligence work for the Reich." Hess smiled at Sir Jason. "He has even given us his lovely house in Avenue Foch for us to use as we please."

"My pleasure, Deputy Führer." Jason offered a forced smile. He was feeling uncomfortable. The four men at the table nodded their heads and tapped the table in appreciation.

"General Alexander von Falkenhauser represents the army and is Military Governor of Belgium and France." Hess gestured towards a stately looking middle-aged *Wehrmacht* general. He then indicated the three remaining men at the meeting. "These two gentlemen are both part of the *Abwehr*: *Korvettenkapitän* Tristan Langer and Major Michel von Tüßling, and that is Admiral Wilhelm Canaris, head of the *Abwehr*." The man at the window turned and joined the table.

"How do you do, Sir Jason," Canaris said in English.

"It is an honour and a privilege to meet you at last, Admiral," Sir Jason said, an expression of concern on his face. "However, this is a meeting between WASP and the Reich and has been called by you, Herr Hess, as you require our help. WASP is a highly secretive organisation that very few people know about."

Admiral Canaris wore a stern expression and looked like he did not want to be part of the meeting.

"I called this meeting, Sir Jason, not Herr Hess." Canaris leant forward, his forearms on the table. He looked directly into Jason's eyes. "I wanted to meet the person who has provided all this valuable information. I just wonder, Sir Jason, why are you – WASP – working in the interests of your enemy?"

"I think you know, Admiral, we have the same aims as the German Reich: to purge our country of communists and Jews. To build a stronger Europe."

"And you are prepared to act against your country and government to achieve these aims?"

"Admiral, I have been through this with Herr Hitler himself. If you have any reservations about WASP, or me, I suggest you ask the Führer or Herr Himmler. I am a proud member of the Nazi Party. Great British politics have rejected protectionism and fascism. We in Europe have allowed communism to flourish in Russia, France and, to some extent, Great Britain. WASP is the intelligence arm of the British Union of Fascists and the *Parti populaire français* – the French fascist party." Sir Jason sighed. He was annoyed that Canaris appeared to be questioning his loyalty. "I am sure, Admiral, you know all this already."

Canaris still looked stern. This only served to irritate Jason, who was by now prepared to walk out of the meeting.

Hess stood again, looking nervously at Canaris.

"Gentlemen, we have one subject to discuss at this meeting. Your views and intelligence of the proposed Vichy Government. Sir Jason, I gather from your informants they are forming a more socialist, left-wing attitude, and they do not want to get rid of their Jews, and—"

"Herr Hess, if I may." Sir Jason raised his hand. Hess sat down. "I must tell you, gentlemen, this so-called Treaty of Vichy is a communist set-up, with communist Pierre Laval becoming a liability. However, my concern today is *not* the Treaty of Vichy; we can deal with that at a later date. My chief concern is that you still have a non-aggression pact with the Soviet Union, after the Führer assured me himself that the pact would last as long as the invasion into and occupation of Poland. The pact still stands even now. Why should WASP help the Reich any further?"

"You are right to be concerned, Sir Jason," said Canaris. He looked at the general who had not uttered a word so far. "Perhaps General Alexander von Falkenhauser can help with the answer."

The general cleared his throat.

"That is a question for the politicians, not the army."

"It was the army who wanted the pact," Hess said.

"Yes, so that we may take over the Eastern European territories without mobilising the USSR forces. If we offered Russia some of the territories, it would prevent them from taking any action against us."

"I understand that, General," said Sir Jason. "It is just that WASP gave valuable intelligence to the Reich. This meeting was to develop a plan, together with Great Britain, Germany and Italy, and aid from the USA, to invade Russia and to rout out communism. I am in discussion with Axis – which includes Japan – to squash any further escalation of the Communist Party in China. Why is there still a pact with the Soviet Union? Are you" – Sir Jason turned to Hess – "the Reich, expecting help from WASP to negotiate terms with Britain and Axis? I have had discussions with Churchill about a plan to talk terms; however, I cannot see this happening now."

"What is this nonsense?" Canaris said. "What plan to talk terms?"

"I know how you feel, Sir Jason," Hess said thoughtfully. "However, now that the British are back on their island, and with your help, Sir Jason, I plan to fly to Scotland or Ireland and negotiate peace." There was a stunned silence. All but the older *Abwehr* man and Jason gaped at the absurd suggestion.

"On what grounds, Herr Hess?" asked the general.

"According to Sir Jason, there is a possibility the British public would rather side with Germany against the Russians. Now we have France—"

"Some of France," Sir Jason interjected.

"Now we have most of France, with our allies in Italy and Spain, and with the help of Sir Jason and WASP, we should be able to broker a deal with Great Britain."

General von Falkenhauser leant over the table towards Sir Jason.

"What evidence have you that this is something the British are saying, Sir Jason?"

"I have recently been put in charge of liaising between the Pétain and the British governments. I am also working closely with MI6 and the British secret service," Sir Jason revealed. "I have intelligence that Churchill will be willing to meet with a senior representative of the Reich to negotiate a joint collaboration against Bolshevik and socialist Russia, drive communism out of France and Britain, and crush the Russian communist government."

"This is the first I have heard of this absurdity, Hess" – Canaris looked outraged at Hess – "and I am head of German Secret Service. I thought we were going to talk about a British invasion threat if the Americans join the Allies. Not this absurd idea of the Deputy Führer flying off to the enemy. Who is going to fly you to Scotland, Hess?"

"I will pilot myself, Admiral."

"Believe me, gentlemen," Sir Jason continued, "after the drubbing the Allies endured, the evacuation from Dunkirk and the bombing on London at the moment, the Allies have no appetite to invade German-occupied France anytime soon – if ever. The Americans are *firmly* staying out of the war, but my sources there tell me the Americans may come in with us and the Reich to hit against communist Russia. Herr Hess should be in a good position to have talks with Mr Churchill and the British Government."

*

After the meeting had concluded, Jason was approached by one of the secret servicemen.

"Sir Jason, could you accompany me to the Naval Signals headquarters? It's about two kilometres inland."

"For what purpose?"

"I have been asked by Wolfsschlucht, Hitler's headquarters, for you to contact them after the meeting." Jason was concerned.

"Why do you need me?"

"*Reichsleiter* Martin Bormann – my superior – would like a word."

"Very well. Do we go now? I will have to see my boatman first. Tides and such, you understand."

"Yes, of course. Thank you, sir." Both men collected their coats and strode off to a waiting Morris Oxford car with a Nazi flag tied incongruously over the bonnet. "My name is *Korvettenkapitän* Langer, by the way. I am head of the secret service in Northern France."

"I know who you are, Kapitän Langer. I was expecting you to make contact after this meeting. Do you know why Bormann needs to speak to me? Have the arrangements changed?"

"To some extent, yes. I believe the Führer has become more involved."

"I see," Jason grunted.

*

At the dockside, Jaffery convinced Sir Jason of the merits of acquiring the damaged S-boat. Jason was in a hurry and could not be bothered with Jaffery's fantasy.

"If you can get it fuelled and ready to go by the time I am back, in about an hour, I will be pleased to travel back to Shoreham in that craft."

Jason had no doubts Jaffery would have some difficulty in acquiring the damaged vessel but would not put it past him succeeding. He was also in favour of anything that would get him back faster than the journey over.

*

"Sir Jason, Heil Hitler, Martin Bormann here," said the scratchy voice of the head of the party chancellery and Hitler's personal secretary over the radio. "I am sorry about this communication, but it is vital we talk before you return to England."

"How can I help, Herr Bormann?"

"The Führer would be grateful if you could go ahead with your plan to help us get rid of Hess."

"One moment, please, Herr Bormann." Sir Jason removed his headphones. "I believe this should be a private conversation, *Kapitän* Langer."

"Yes, sir." Langer left the small radio room. Jason replaced the headphones.

"I trust this radio signal is secure, sir?"

"Better by radio than phone," said Bormann.

"Very well." Sir Jason licked his lips, paused and then said, "Yes, I have told Herr Hess that Churchill is willing to take part in provisional peace talks, which is not true, of course."

"Excellent. I believe from Langer that you have a new position with the British secret service, part of MI6, is that right?"

"Correct."

"And you are still prepared to share intelligence with the Reich."

"Correct. But only in the interests of WASP and the eradication of communism. I have some reservations, however, about your continued pact with Russia."

"You will be pleased to hear the non-aggression pact will wither away within the next few months." There was a slight pause. "Sir Jason, would you care to secure your position within the British secret service?"

Jason looked at the microphone with surprise. "Of course. How?"

"The Führer is very excited about the plan for the Deputy Führer's capture and to put an end to his ridiculous notion to try and broker a peace deal with England and her allies."

"I am glad it is working and the Führer is happy with our plan."

"He also wants to get rid of Hess without consequence. He would prefer that you kill him."

"The British secret service, or the British government? I doubt any would execute him. He may, however, not survive his landing."

"It is of no importance who executes him, as long as he never returns to the Reich. The Führer would enjoy as much publicity as possible of this reckless errand, and to humiliate Hess. He would like to stop any further foolhardy efforts of talks with the Allies about peace."

"Is that likely, Herr Bormann?"

"I regret we may have some other high-level ranks prepared to talk to the Allies about peace. Admiral Canaris and the *Abwehr* are a concern."

"Yes, the Admiral is here."

"You have not told him of the plan to rid us of Hess, have you?"

"Certainly not. But WASP and Canaris have worked successfully before. I presume he is still a trusted member of the Nazi Party elite?"

"Not any more. *Kapitän* Langer is now part of Himmler's new secret service, and your new liaison with us."

"I see." Sir Jason paused. He briefly wondered if this was some kind of trap but quickly dismissed it. "So – you would like me to get all the publicity for arresting Hess when he arrives on our shores?"

"You have grasped the situation admirably, Barrett. You can claim all the accolades for the arrest of the Deputy Führer."

"I am grateful, Bormann. I shall act on this when I return to Britain. However, this plainly delays any non-aggression pact towards Russia. Has the Führer any plans as to when we can expect talks of a joint venture into the USSR?"

"I regret we cannot say, Barrett. But don't worry yourself; we are on the brink of a spectacular victory." There was a long pause. Sir Jason was deep in thought. "Are you still there, Barrett?"

"Still here, Herr Bormann. We look forward to this victory." Sir Jason did not sound particularly enthusiastic. He suddenly thought of something. "One other thing, sir. Would you be so kind as to arrange that my boatman can take possession of a wrecked S-boat that is moored up here in Guernsey?"

"Well … yes" – Bormann hesitated – "of course. Put me on to *Kapitän* Langer."

*

Sir Jason returned to Newhaven from St Peter Port in Guernsey in three and a half hours. The sea was lit by a full, chilly moon and was flat. The S-boat sped along at an exhilarating pace of around thirty knots. Normally, Jaffery would drop his passengers off in Shoreham harbour in his fishing boat, but now he was in his S-boat, he thought it unwise to be seen. Jaffery steered into his secret, secluded boathouse on the Sussex coast, near Hastings, using the stars to guide him.

*

Deputy Führer Rudolf Hess, after misguided information provided by Sir Jason about Churchill being willing to talk terms with Germany, was pulled alive from the wreckage of his twin-engine Messerschmitt by members of the Home Guard of Eaglesham, just south of Glasgow, in May 1941. He had been guided in at night by pre-arranged landing lights placed at the end of a ploughed field by the British secret service following a tip-off. He crashlanded. The whole event was witnessed by members of the Scottish press and two members of the British secret service, Sir Jason Barrett and his colleague John Alderson of Special Branch.

Sir Jason Barrett was hailed as not only a valuable intelligence resource to MI6, but also a hero of the Third Reich. Hitler was rid of Hess and bestowed the Knight's Cross of the Iron Cross on Sir Jason Barrett *in absentia*.

As promised to Sir Jason by Martin Bormann, Operation Barbarossa – the code name for the German invasion of the Soviet Union – started on Sunday, 22 June 1941, thus removing the pact with Russia.

29

Major Kieffer arrived first at La Palais, with Jost Krupp. Charlotte's heart hopped with the excitement of seeing Krupp.

Kieffer was a sturdy man who had a square head and large dark eyebrows that met in the middle – a complete contrast to the elegant, chiselled features of Krupp, who exuded sophistication whereas Kieffer was cold and humourless.

Charlotte was delighted Krupp came straight to the sofa she was seated at when they entered the drawing room. He gave a little wave towards Theodora who was seated with Juliet on the other side of the drawing room. Walking intently towards Theodora was General von Ardle, who looked like he was about to lose his temper … again.

Krupp clicked his heels formally and bobbed his head at Charlotte, then took her hand, turned it over, and kissed gently on her wrist, a little too long for etiquette.

"Demoiselle Jorgensen, my heart has pined like a lonely hound these past months for the sight of your smile." He was rewarded with one of Charlotte's most dazzling smiles, accompanied by a flush in her cheeks.

"Thank you, Herr Krupp, you are so kind." She giggled as Krupp looked upon her with appreciation.

"That is, indeed, a superb dress, Fräulein," he said in a hushed voice, a mix of wonder and awe. Charlotte was dressed in shimmering gold brocade. The colour was not gaudy but a soft ivory gold, with an intricate and delicate floral pattern growing up from the hem of the dress, like a wild gold meadow. The dress was halter style, with thin gold ropes around her neck, revealing her shoulders and flawless skin. The dress pronounced her figure and complimented her Veronica Lake-style golden hair.

There was a cough behind Krupp, and he turned to find his commanding officer, Major Kieffer, waiting to be introduced. Krupp did not conceal his disappointment of having to share Freya with his superior.

"Ah … yes … *Sturmbannführer* Josef Kieffer – may I present Fräulein Freya Jorgensen," Krupp announced in German. The major hesitated for a split second, recognising the name. He clicked his heels and bobbed his head in a stiff bow.

"Your servant, mademoiselle. The talk of your beauty has not been exaggerated." The major spoke formally in fluent French, his face conveying no emotion and remaining stern and severe.

"Thank you, Major, how lovely of you to say." Charlotte was genuinely surprised that she had a "reputation". "Would you care to take a seat? I am sure the lieutenant will get us a drink." Krupp was lighting a cigarette and looked hurt.

"My dear," Kieffer said, pointing at the two pips on Krupp's shoulders, "Krupp is now a *Hauptsturmführer* – an SS captain!"

"Captain Krupp, I must apologise. Congratulations," Charlotte said coyly. "Would you get the major and me a drink, Captain?"

"Thank you, but not for the moment," said Kieffer, looking over towards General von Ardle. "Would you excuse me?" He walked off before Charlotte could react.

"Can I get you a drink, Freya?"

Charlotte was watching Kieffer walk briskly over to General von Ardle and was worried Kieffer was upset about something.

"Yes, Jost, whatever you are having." Charlotte smiled again. Krupp gave a brief indication to Helmut, who was hovering with a bottle of champagne and glasses, and sat down beside Charlotte. "How lovely. I have you to myself for the moment."

"Why did Major Kieffer not want to talk to me, I wonder?"

"There is no reasoning with the man, my dear. He must be mad." Krupp laughed. Charlotte turned to Krupp, leant towards him and clinked his glass of champagne.

"Where have you been these past few months, Captain?"

Jost Krupp was looking very dashing in his smart black SS uniform mess jacket, with equerry lanyards hanging from his right shoulder epaulette and black trousers with a sharp crease and light silver piping running down the side to his shiny black shoes.

"I have been only down the road at number eighty-four, actually," he said, slightly embarrassed. Charlotte was a little shocked.

"I met a rather horrid man from there," Charlotte said, her eyes cast down. "He was called Hueber."

"Really?" Krupp said in a flat way. "I can't really talk about the place, I'm afraid. Tell me about you. What have you been up to? You have changed, your hair, dress … everything."

She looked up and smiled again. Her attention was taken by a new medal on Krupp's uniform. She raised her hand and put it gently on his chest, her fingertips on an iron cross hanging just below his white bow tie on a black, white and red ribbon. Krupp took an intake of breath at her touch.

"You also have changed since last we met. What's this?"

"My Iron Cross. Presented to me by the Führer himself when I was in Berlin last week," he said with pride.

"What did you do to get it?"

"I led the attack on a group of prisoners who had taken over part of the Drancy Prison."

"Oh!" Charlotte was genuinely alarmed. "But you could have been killed!"

"Freya." Krupp was surprised at her distress. "It is war. We are fighting a devious enemy."

"Well, I think you are very brave." She stroked the Iron Cross again. "Where are you based now, Captain Krupp?" She looked up at him, fluttering her eyelashes.

"Well, between headquarters and the Drancy Prison, where I am in command," he said proudly.

Charlotte thought of Bo and Christina. Perhaps they were at Drancy and this could be a good opportunity to see if she could find them. She moved closer to Krupp and whispered in his ear.

"Jost, I would love to see you at your place of work." Krupp was startled. Tenderly, he took hold of Charlotte's bare shoulders and pushed her gently away to get her face into focus.

"What do you mean, to the prison? You certainly can't come to Eighty-Four."

"No, I wouldn't want to, I would be bound to bump into that horrid man."

"Why on earth would you want to see the prison?" he said and then smiled self-consciously. "Unless you want to see a lot more of me."

Charlotte giggled and looked up into Krupp's eyes. He was entranced.

Her power over him was getting stronger and she felt it. She took a deep breath for courage and said, "Well, I want to see you being busy and important. I am curious about the prison as well."

Krupp thought for a minute, looking into Charlotte's violet-blue eyes which were beseeching him.

"Well, of course you can," he said eventually. "It is not very ostentatious, except I have a pleasant office that overlooks the prison yard. You can see all the inmates milling around. You can watch the executions if you like." Charlotte used every ounce of control not to react. "Or we could just have a cup of coffee, have lunch and watch the—"

"Whatever you think I would be interested in. I would love to see the prisoners, see what they are like." She rested her head on Krupp's chest. He could not see her eyes were tightly shut. She was wondering if she had done the right thing.

*

The evening with her captain went on to be wonderful. He was charming, funny and gave her all his attention. They were interrupted every now and then with other men wanting to meet Charlotte. Theodora introduced Juliet to Captain Krupp, but he took hardly any notice of her. Juliet and Theodora had to entertain Major Kieffer, which was very difficult. He contributed nothing to any conversation; he would not talk about himself, his work or his family, and looked stern every time the subject turned to him. When Theodora or Juliet started talking about themselves, he looked decidedly bored.

Agatha was playing some Mozart and Richard Strauss on the highly decorated piano. Charlotte could not remember the piano ever being played before. She thought it was just there, in the corner of the room, for decoration and somewhere for her uncle Jason to put photographs of himself and important people. The photographs were no longer there. She loved hearing Agatha playing the piano. A group of men stood around her as she played, shouting out requests each time she finished a piece. Agatha was bright and bubbly; she laughed at all the men's jokes and her soprano voice soared above her admirers as they sung patriotic songs.

*

Theodora stood with Juliet, swaying to the music, when Kieffer appeared at her side.

"Tell me, Madame Theodora, why have you got Miss Jorgensen here?" Kieffer asked out of the blue.

"This was her home, Major Kieffer, she has nowhere to go. She has no papers here."

"But what does she do?"

"She has become a wonderful hostess here, Major, as I am sure you will agree."

"I am sure. But is she not a neutral … Swedish?"

"Yes, but she has spent little time in Sweden. This is where she has lived most of her life. She loves it here. She is willing to help me, and she is a huge asset." Theodora was beginning to worry. Kieffer had a reputation that was frightening. He was in charge of the interrogations at the headquarters of the Paris SS and Gestapo at Eighty-Four Avenue Foch, and she suspected he might have interrogated Bo and Christina Jorgensen.

"But Major, you are here to enjoy yourself," Theodora cooed, and took his arm and held it close to her body, knowing he would feel her breasts on his bicep. This was usually a great way to calm a stressed man down, and Kieffer looked constantly stressed.

Kieffer pulled away and looked at Theodora with a little contempt.

"Thank you, Madame Theodora, I am quite relaxed enough. I would like to talk to this lady if I may." He turned to Juliet who was now looking even more terrified. He smiled at her and took her hand, kissed it, and led her to a sofa, leaving Theodora utterly confused. She wondered if it was something to do with her dark Turkish skin or her long black glossy hair that may have offended him. Or even her thick Turkish accent. It had happened before, usually after a hot summer when she was even darker.

She watched as Kieffer sat with Juliet and chatted with her. She was the complete opposite of Theodora. Juliet gradually warmed to Kieffer and was chatting back, the frightened look on her face slowly melting away. Kieffer was a master of manipulating people's emotions, it seemed. He could reduce a person to a terrified wreck and then bring them up to thinking of him as a trusted father figure within minutes.

The room became quite busy. There were twelve guests, all but three of them dressed in SS officer uniforms. Two men were in evening suits and black ties – German businessmen, here to establish a German foothold in the French economy. One officer was in *Wehrmacht* army uniform.

*

Charlotte was having a lovely time with Jost Krupp who was giving her his undivided attention. They sat together at dinner, and afterwards in the drawing room they talked well past midnight.

Charlotte had only allowed herself two glasses of champagne; any more could have been dangerous. She nursed one glass before dinner and one glass during, and drank no wine with the food, just tipping the glass sufficiently to wet her lips. Jost Krupp managed to drink nearly two bottles, and with the cognac after dinner, he was steadily getting more than a little inebriated.

Over the past few months Charlotte had been putting together her life's story – the one of a Swedish girl who lived with a rich French family, daughter of the servants and companion to the spoilt daughter, Charlotte. She had used and developed the story, with slight embellishments, to entertain the guests who came to La Palais. And now she was using it to entertain Captain Krupp. The tale was of a girl who grew up with a French family, only visiting Sweden once when she was very young, and enjoying her life in Paris with Charlotte.

"Charlotte and I were split up when the de Tournets went off for a quick holiday to Biarritz. My parents went too, leaving me behind at school to sort out Charlotte's things." Charlotte stopped and moved closer to Krupp, her head on his shoulder. "My parents returned to pick me and the luggage up, leaving our papers behind. They returned at the same time you arrived, my captain." She looked up into his brown eyes.

"Will you excuse me?" Jost said, standing, swaying slightly, blinking as though trying to focus.

"Are you deserting me, my Captain?" Charlotte said seductively.

Krupp looked at Charlotte half draped on the cushions, looking like Ophelia in a stream, her hair splayed out over the floral cushion like a pre-Raphaelite painting.

"With the utmost regret, my love, I must talk to the major before he goes to bed. He may have some orders for me."

"Are you staying here, at La Palais?"

"Yes, I hope to," Krupp whispered.

"Come back to me soon. I will be here waiting," she said in a low voice.

"If you stay exactly how you are, I will be back even quicker." He walked off, looking at her all the way to the drawing room door.

Charlotte watched him, giggling at the spectacle he was making of himself. As he went out the door, she flopped back into the sofa, her eyes closed, remembering his face. She felt a warm feeling inside her, satisfaction at how well the evening was going. She had been looking forward to the evening for weeks, worried if Jost Krupp's passion for her had cooled over the months he had been away. Rewardingly, it was the opposite.

"May I join you?" a man said. Charlotte opened her eyes. An army captain in a grey-green unbuttoned jacket dropped down heavily onto the sofa, very close to her, uninvited. He was tall, big and scruffy, with thick, greasy black hair. He was sweating. He put a half-empty bottle of schnapps onto the coffee table. "I think we need to get to know each other." He leered at Charlotte, from her breasts – hardly covered by her revealing dress – down to her ankles.

Charlotte felt exposed, vulnerable for the first time in her life. Though inexperienced with such oafish behaviour, the encounters with her stepfather only a few years before came rushing back, and she was fearful.

"I am sorry, Captain, but I am waiting for—"

"Come on, girl, you're not waiting for anybody. That SS captain has left you to me." He smiled and leant in closer to Charlotte. "He said so." Charlotte flicked a glance over towards where she last saw Jost, momentarily believing what the lout had said, then just as instantly discounting it.

"I very much doubt it, monsieur."

He had gaps in his teeth and a scar that ran through one of his thick eyebrows. He was drunk, his eyes bloodshot and puffy like a boxer's. A wash of alcohol and body odour wafted over Charlotte. She put her hand to her chest, trying to cover herself up. She felt Theodora's cross and wondered if she should use it. She sat up. He came up to her face.

"Listen, you ..." he said through gritted teeth, "I need entertaining." One of his hands roughly grabbed the top of her bare arm and pulled her towards him. His other hand roamed up the outside of her thigh towards her left buttock. He drew her towards his face, his lips crashed into hers and he kissed her roughly.

"For Christ's sake!" She pushed him away with both hands, furious. He smiled and pulled her towards his mouth for another kiss. Charlotte had been angry when the man first appeared, but now she became increasingly alarmed. He was huge, and she felt helpless. Before he could kiss her, Charlotte pushed herself further away. She managed to release one of her hands and was able to slap him hard across his cheek. It was like slapping a plank of bristly wood; his manic smile did not change. He lowered his enormous body onto her. She turned her head away from his lips, so he started ravaging her neck and ear.

"Will you get off me?" She tried desperately to shout, hoping someone in the drawing room would hear her. But the room was virtually empty. Theodora was nowhere to be seen, and most of her shouting was drowned out by the cushions and the officer's vast carcass.

"Come on, girl, you'll love it," he protested at her persistent struggling. He sat up, releasing Charlotte. She stood and looked down at the captain. He still had hold of her wrist.

"I will not love it, you oaf." She realised then that as he was such a huge man, she would be powerless if he turned nasty. He stood, towering over her. He encircled her with his arms, and his hands reached down to her bottom. He squeezed her close to his groin. The smile on his face was replaced by ecstasy. "Please let me go, Captain," Charlotte said, slightly less stridently. She looked around the room. A few people were about, mostly around the piano at the other end of the long room. Captain Wil was busying around but did not see Charlotte and the large army captain.

The man then pushed Charlotte away from him, his hands still holding the tops of her arms. She felt manhandled, as though she was a rag doll.

"You are very pretty, Freya." He knew her name, she thought with disgust. "Let's see those lovely tits," he drooled.

He released his hold on one of her arms and gathered both her wrists into his giant right hand. She was powerless to stop his other hand that was going for the V of her dress. It was too easy for him, she thought. Was she too easy? She felt tears of anger gathering in her eyes. Fury was welling up inside her, as well as an element of fear. She was not going to allow this horrid man to molest her. She looked down for the cross Theodora had given her, but it had somehow fallen off. She then started to squirm, trying to release at least one of her hands, but she was helpless in his powerful grasp. She was about to scream when a hand grabbed the man's free arm just as it was about to rip the skimpy top of her dress and release Charlotte's right breast. Charlotte followed the arm up from the hand to see Jost's face, calm and purposeful, his eyes wide, his mouth set in a small, menacing grimace.

The big man let go of Charlotte's hands and with his fists bunched, fury over his face, he said, "Sod off, she's mine, boy. Go and find your own whore!" Charlotte tottered and fell back onto the sofa. The man went to grab Charlotte again, but Krupp's foot swung up between the big man's legs and crashed into his scrotum. The man gasped. As he tipped forward to cup his crushed testicles, Jost brought up his knee and rammed it into the man's face, shattering his nose. Armed with a fire iron in his left hand, Jost swung the poker down onto the back of big man's head. He crashed to the floor with a loud thud. The piano stopped playing at the other end of the room. All eyes were on Charlotte, who stood with her hands to her face, and the large army officer on the ground curled into a foetal position, his bloody face scrunched up with pain.

Jost took Charlotte in his arms protectively and sat her down onto a sofa on the other side of the room. The giant man stirred on the floor. Jost went back over to him and kicked him in the head. He then picked up the poker and laid into the man, pounding him over and over again about his ribs. The man groaned at each thrash of the poker.

"That's enough, Jost!" Charlotte screamed. Krupp stopped. He was unflushed, his face composed, as though he was thrashing a carpet on the line. He swiped back some of his hair that had gone astray and flung down the poker, hitting the man on his head. The big brute flinched. He gazed down at the man, only slightly out of breath, with a thin reptilian smile. Jost Krupp then strode over to Charlotte, concern over his face. "Are you all right, Freya? Did Moltke hurt you?" He looked Charlotte over as though she was an injured foal.

"You could have killed him, Jost," Charlotte said softly, in slight shock.

"I hope I have. I will make sure he will never molest another woman." The room suddenly filled with waiters and two of the guards from the front hall. "Take that army trash to Eighty-Four," Krupp instructed the guards. "I will deal with him tomorrow. He is a traitor to the Reich."

Captain Wil came from the door to the general's office and stopped at the crumpled large figure on the floor, looking nervously at the blood that covered the man's face.

"Who is that, Captain Krupp?" He sounded nervous and kept pushing his glasses back up his nose.

"He is a treacherous, moronic *Wehrmacht* shithead called Moltke. He must have bluffed his way in here somehow. He is one of the guard commanders at headquarters," Krupp said airily.

"Well, we will have to inform his commanding officer that his officer is—"

"Don't worry about him, Wil." The guards were having problems picking the injured captain up off the floor. "You'd better find a stretcher. I think I may have broken most of his ribs," Krupp said with a chortle.

Theodora appeared and went over to a shaken Charlotte.

"What happened, Freya?" Theodora sounded worried. Charlotte could not take her eyes off the large army officer, blood pouring from mouth, his broken nose and one of his ears. His whole face had purple blotches as the bruises formed. Between the guards and the waiters, they carted him off on a stretcher. He was unconscious.

"That bastard tried to molest Freya," Krupp said.

"Did he hurt you, darling?"

"No – it was just a bit of a shock." Charlotte began to shiver slightly.

"Come on," Theodora said. She found the cross, which had swung round onto Charlotte's back. "Let us get you off to bed."

"No, I'm fine, Theodora." She saw the disappointment on Jost's face. "I want to be with Jost. It's still early."

"I will look after her, Theodora," Krupp said tenderly. He took Charlotte's hand. She stepped closer to him and put her other hand onto his chest.

"Hmm. Well, if you're sure, Freya." Theodora looked sceptically at Charlotte. She didn't seem to share her enthusiasm.

*

"Freya, can I kiss you?" Krupp croaked in a lazy, deep voice. They had been sitting together, looking out onto the garden for hours, Charlotte with her head on Jost's chest, his jacket over her shoulders. She had slipped out of her shoes and curled her feet up onto the cushions, tranquil as Jost stroked her hair. Everybody else had gone to bed. The servants were clearing up; it was two o'clock in the morning and the room was getting colder as the fire died away. She rose up off his chest and looked into his hazel-brown eyes. They were half-closed with tired bliss. He sat up and stroked her cheek with the backs of his fingers. She pushed him onto his back and leant over, almost lying on top of him.

"Why do you want to kiss me, Jost?" she said, smiling, and she placed her forehead on Krupp's, looking deep into his eyes. She was slightly light-headed from the champagne.

"I think I must love you, Freya."

Charlotte took a swift inward breath of delight and smiled, biting her bottom lip.

"Only *think*? Come, come, you must be decisive." She chuckled. His arms went lightly around her waist. She gently lowered her lips onto his. They were warm, soft and exciting. Her golden hair fell across his face. Krupp sat up from the sofa as they kissed. Charlotte slipped back and he swung her legs onto his lap. She still had her arms around his neck as if trying not to break the kiss. She felt his hand rest on the inside of her thigh, gently stroking. A sensation like a light electric shock went up the inside of her leg.

"Oh Captain, are you being decisive?"

"Yes," he said huskily. He placed both arms around her waist and pulled her towards him, and kissed her with more intensity and vigour. She encircled his head in her arms and emitted a slight moan as they kissed. They parted long enough for her to see a look of wonder on his face. She was excited. Still sat on his lap, she put her hands behind his head and pulled him towards her, her lips slightly parted. She increased the pressure and caressed the back of his head and neck. She loved it – the embrace, the tenderness, the smell of him, his arms around her waist. She broke away from his embrace, and with a determined expression on her face, she slid off his knees. He sat up, looking confused. She fell back onto the cushions at the other end of the sofa while grabbing hold of the front of his shirt. With an excited smile, she beckoned him to come closer. He gently lowered himself against her body. Her arms folded around his shoulders. He slowly lowered his lips onto hers. She experimented with flicking the end of her tongue over his tongue. He tasted of brandy and cigarettes.

She broke away to look at him, her hair fanned over the cushions, a mischievous smile on her lips.

"My God, but you are so beautiful," he breathed, hardly able to control his desires. He rolled over to her side and looked at her breasts under the shimmering dress. His hand cupped, touched and explored. As Charlotte closed her eyes, a warm feeling ran through her. She inhaled deeply at his touch. She loved the feeling of his hand gently caressing her and the ecstatic sensations as he fondled her.

She pulled him on top of her again, his ear close to her lips.

"Jost … this is quite new to me, believe it or not. I am not an experienced lovemaker."

"Aren't you? I suppose not. You are not one of Theodora's girls."

"No, I am not!" Charlotte chided in his ear, adding more quietly, and a little sadly, "I am certainly not a whore." He pushed himself up off her to look at her, curious as to what she was trying to say. She looked sternly into Krupp's eyes. "Do I look like a whore, Jost?"

"You do not look like a whore. Not that I have any experience with whores."

"Will you sleep with me, Jost?" Charlotte asked after a long pause.

"Kiss me again while I think about it." With an expression of mock shock, Charlotte drew Jost towards her and kissed him passionately.

She had never been this excited, elated. She was even a little nervous. She had never experienced this pleasurable ache in her stomach. She thought a man entering her would be threatening after what she had suffered with her uncle. However, if she controlled things ...

"Yes?" She whispered in his ear. She did not have to wait for an answer.

*

Charlotte felt incredibly warm and secure in Jost's arms as they lay in bed, naked. She was smiling, looking up at the ceiling. She wanted Jost to make love to her again, but his soft, regular breathing indicated he had fallen asleep. She was content, in love, and did not want the morning to arrive. She knew Theodora would be unhappy about her sleeping with Jost.

She looked at her sleeping man, his long eyelashes, his strong chin, the shadow of his whiskers, the Adam's apple in the centre of his thick, muscular neck barely moving. She stroked his chest and the line of downy hair that grew between his nipples. He was an Adonis.

She was in her old room. She felt her journey from girl heiress to Swedish servant, to womanhood and lover, had been very quick.

But how she had changed. Her girlish whims seemed absurd now. She felt different, she looked different; she had learnt grace and deportment and enjoyed the attention of men, especially her lovely SS captain.

Her thoughts turned to her concerns for the future. What was going to happen to her and Jost? The war was not going to go on for ever. Theodora said Jost was not a man who gets married, that he was dangerous and, like most of the men that came into La Palais, not at all trustworthy.

Charlotte slipped out of the bed, took a blanket from the ottoman to cover her naked body and wandered over to the window. It was dark outside. Avenue Foch was barely visible.

She was worried if she had made a mistake. Is she doing the right thing? Plainly not or this would have been their wedding night! But look at him. She glanced back at Jost, his breathing steady, his mouth slightly open and on the verge of snoring. Perhaps she could change him, guide him into better ways.

She went over, knelt down and lay her head level to his, and watched him sleep. She smiled at him. Her heart ached with love for him. Her worries about their future evaporated.

30

Something woke Jost early the next morning. Freya's head was just inches away from his, her hair almost covering her face. She was half sitting on the floor, half laying on the bed, a blanket around her shoulders and clasped about her neck. To Jost's amusement, she was snoring, lightly, through her mouth. He gazed upon her with a satisfied smile. He got dressed, went to the bathroom and shaved, humming to himself, thinking about the wonderful night he had with Freya. She would certainly be among the most memorable of the women he had been with.

As he descended the grand staircase to the hallway, he was aware of a mild commotion outside the open front door. Cold air was blowing in, making the hall chilly. It was still quite early; the sun had only just risen, casting long amber shadows, and the damp cobbles outside glistened in dew. Jost heard loud whispers and a motor running. As he walked out the door, he saw a military truck with a canvas cover stationary at the end of the building. Three guards were pulling a *Wehrmacht* soldier from the cab and berating him with hoarse whispers. As Captain Jost Krupp strode up, all went quiet. The driver of the truck was let go as the three guards stood to attention and saluted.

"What is going on here?" Jost asked in a low voice. "There are important people asleep here." He jerked his thumb at the windows above.

The driver, relieved to see a superior officer, staggered to his feet and proffered a sheet of paper.

"My orders, sir."

"Who from?"

"Colonel Deller, sir."

"Really?" Surprised, Jost swiped the piece of paper out of the driver's hand and read the order.

"You may go back to your duties, gentlemen," Jost said.

One of the guardsmen stepped forward and saluted again. "But sir," he protested, "he says he is to drive this truck to the back of the house ... to the garden. We can't allow—"

"It is perfectly in order," Jost said. "Have you seen Colonel Deller this morning?"

"Yes, sir. He came out this morning and took the sergeant and the fourth guard with him into the house. He didn't say anything about this," he said, pointing at the truck.

"I will take full responsibility. You get on with your duties."

"Yes, sir. Thank you, sir."

Jost answered his salute and turned to the driver.

"In you get, lad." He ushered the driver back inside and closed the door. Jost stood on the running board. "Follow the drive down beside the house. You will see a pathway that runs along the fence; follow that to the large shed at the end of the garden. Don't brush me off in the hedges." The driver, still unsure what was going on, put the truck into gear and raced the motor before letting out the clutch. Jost winced at the noise. "Keep it quiet, man!"

As the truck slowly approached the barn-like garden shed, which was lit up, Jost could see the skinny form of Franz-Joseph Deller standing in the open double doors, excitedly bouncing on his toes. He had a huge grin on his face until he saw Jost drop off the running board of the truck.

"What can I do for you, Captain Krupp?"

"I have come to help, Colonel." Jost felt mischievous. He could hear hammering in the shed.

"We do not need help. Go back to the house. This is strictly confidential." Deller followed Jost into the shed, plucking at his sleeve in a lame attempt to turn him around. As Jost entered, the hammering stopped. The soldiers, all in their shirtsleeves, stood to attention. On the floor stood three large wooden crates sealed with Nazi markings and a stencilled destination address of Friedrichshafen, Bodensee.

On the ground was a fourth crate that was in the process of being packed. Inside, Jost saw there were five paintings of various sizes. Deller quickly stood in between Jost and the exposed crate.

"This is strictly secret, Captain. You have no authority to—"

248

"Oh, but I have, Colonel Deller. I am adjutant to the head of security in Paris. What are all these paintings?"

"They are destined to go to the Führermuseum," Deller sighed.

"As far as I know, the Führermuseum is in Munich, not Friedrichshafen. Where is Friedrichshafen?"

"Captain, I have my orders direct from the Reich."

Deller was trying to look superior, Jost thought, but it seemed to make him even more ridiculous. "May I see these orders, Colonel?"

Deller stalled.

"No, you may not!"

"Then I will have to report this to *Sturmbannführer* Kieffer."

Deller put his hands on his hips. A look of frustration came over his face. He turned around to see all his men standing there watching the two SS officers arguing.

"Get on with your work," Deller shouted. He grabbed Jost by the arm and guided him towards the old stable area, stopping at the threshold.

Jost had an amused smile on his face. "Shall we go into your office, Colonel?" He was enjoying watching the colonel squirm.

"No!" Deller hissed. "My papers are on the workbench." Deller walked over to the far end of the workbench on the other side of the shed. He picked up a clipboard and said, quite calmly, "What can I do to get rid of you, Captain? For you to keep your mouth shut?"

Jost thought. What would be the most preposterous, unimaginable thing he could think of?

"The painting of the girl in that crate would do." Deller staggered back, his mouth gaping in astonishment. "That is a Caravaggio, *Portrait of a Courtesan*. It is worth a fortune. You'll never be able to sell it."

"It will hang in Burg Krupp, in pride of place. I will pick it up after the war. It won't be long now." Deller was about to protest but hesitated. He looked at Krupp with a squint.

"All right, Krupp, I will put it by. I will remove it from the catalogue." Deller prodded Jost angrily in the chest. "If I hear any mention of what you have seen here, I will ensure that you will be arrested for treason. Do I make myself clear?"

Jost was amused by the lame threat and tried to hide his smirk. "Absolutely clear, Colonel."

"Then I need you to sign a document before you leave this barn." Jost was slightly less amused; Deller would now have evidence against him.

"I also would be grateful for a signed document from you, Colonel Deller, confirming our arrangement."

"Of course, Captain. But you must not say anything to the Freya girl. She seems to have an interest in her employer's art collection."

"Does she? I find that hard to believe."

"She used to live here, Krupp, or had you not gathered that? Anyway, she knows quite a lot about the collection, and you and she seem to be quite …" Deller did not finish the sentence. Jost picked up a hint of jealousy, which pleased him even more.

Jost signed a document stating the Caravaggio portrait would be his at the end of the war. Deller signed a document stating that he would hand over the painting and presented it to Krupp. Still holding onto the piece of paper, he said, as menacingly as possible, "Remember, Krupp, this is highly confidential. If this gets out, it will be you who gets it, not me. In the meantime, the painting will be stored at Schloss Friedrichshafen, in southern Germany, along with all the other art being relocated from Paris for the Reich."

Jost wondered if he would ever see the Caravaggio again. He decided to keep close tabs on Colonel Deller.

*

After the collection was packed away into the truck and the men had been paid off, Joseph wandered into the stable area. He looked at the sofa, now covered in dust. A corner had been eaten away by something. His heart felt heavy as he stroked the arm of the sofa. He bent down to smell the fabric, hoping there would be a residue of Alice's scent left, but all he could smell was damp dust. He pulled out a hip flask, twisted off the stopper and sat down. He took a long drink of schnapps, stretched himself out and closed his eyes. He tried to play back the wonderful experiences he had had on that sofa with Alice, but it was hazy. It was, after all, years ago. A tear rolled down his cheek as his vision of Alice's happy face looking down on him as they made love turned into a deathly chalk-white face with a tortured grimace. He could not erase the image of her grotesquely disjointed face at the bottom of the cliff, where she died.

Joseph stood up and wiped his cheeks. He reluctantly thought of Krupp. He was not at all pleased that he had lost one of the most valuable assets of the Barrett Collection, and decided that he would not, after all, store the collection at Sir Jason's castle in Germany, as arranged. He would find an alternative place to hide the collection, somewhere where he would have control of it. Somewhere he would be able to sit and look at it and think of Alice.

The End

Author's Notes

You may be interested to know, I have slightly changed events in the book referring to the 'Night of the Long Knives'. The SA (Sturmabteilung– storm detachment), was the initial paramilitary wing of the Nazi party, lead by Ernst Röhm. He and other SA leaders were arrested personally by Adolph Hitler at the Hanselbauer Hotel in Bad Wiessee, near Munich, (not at a Munich beer hall as in the book). Röhm was executed on Hitler's orders, along with other SA leaders. However, they were executed in their cells after being offered the opportunity to commit suicide, which they refused to do.

Gregor Strasser was shot and mortally wounded in his cell by the SS. It took him an hour to die, left to a slow death by orders of SS general Reinhard Heydrich, later to become the notorious architect to the Jewish genocide and the 'final solution'.

General Kurt von Schleicher was assassinated at his house along with his wife Elizabeth. They were gunned down by a group of SS men – for the book, I used Jost Krupp as the assassin. The last words and the shots that killed Kurt von Schleicher and his wife, were heard over the phone by the friend he was talking to when he opened the door to his assassins.

I am fascinated by the events in the run-up to the second world war. Over a hundred people were murdered during the Night of the Long Knives 'Purge' between 30 June and 2 July 1934. One or two people were even killed by mistake. It has never been established how many were executed, all because these people were a threat to Hitler and the Nazi Party. Röhm, his deputy, Edmund Heines, and many other SA leaders were well known to Hitler's inner circle for being homosexual. Goebbels utilized their homosexual activities, the use of limousines, hedonistic parties, and the fraudulent use of state funds by the SA leadership to justify the executions of Röhm and his colleagues.

Lightning Source UK Ltd.
Milton Keynes UK
UKHW041027071122
411782UK00004B/12